SO-AZC-962

Praise for *Changó's Beads and Two-Tone Shoes*
by William Kennedy

"His most musical work of fiction: a polyrhythmic contemplation of time and its effects on passion set in three different eras . . . This is not a book a young man would or could write. There is the sense here of somebody who has seen and considered much, without letting his inner fire cool. . . . The ambition and the ability to pull wildly diverse worlds together in a single story is rare. Kennedy, master of the Irish American lament in works like *Billy Phelan's Greatest Game* and *Ironweed*, proves here he can play with both hands and improvise on a theme without losing the beat."
—John Sayles, *The New York Times Book Review* (front page)

"Written with such brio and encompassing humanity that it may well deserve to be called the best of the bunch . . . In Mr. Kennedy's Albany, as in William Faulkner's Yoknapatawpha County, the past is never past. *Changó's Beads and Two-Tone Shoes* is invigorated by this same blending of new and old, of progress and recurrence. . . . There's more shot and incidence in *Changó* than in any novel of Mr. Kennedy's since *Legs*. . . . The style here has the sleekness and strength of good crime noir." —Sam Sacks, *The Wall Street Journal*

"Vivid and charming . . . Kennedy, now in his eighties, is in the embrace of nostalgia as he looks back on the adventures of his youth, and this gives the novel much of its not inconsiderable appeal. . . . He is a fluid, engaging prose stylist, and frequently a witty one. . . . Kennedy has maintained a high level of achievement throughout [his Albany Cycle], deftly blending comedy and drama as, over the years, he has painted a portrait of a single city perhaps unique in American fiction." —Jonathan Yardley, *The Washington Post*

"This great crescendo of a novel is worth the ten-year wait. Kennedy has woven all his visions, all his orphans and widows, all his demons, all his politics, lust and bloodlust, fears and hopes for America and mankind, hero worship, father figures, disappointments, and action figures into it. . . . The power of Kennedy's prose lies in his contrapuntal rhythm—dizzying dialogue followed by understatement so lean it feels like sarcasm, followed by speed, exaggeration, magic, Santeria. He writes a wild death dance to which every mythical figure is invited—they parade across the pages."
—Susan Salter-Reynolds, *The Daily Beast*

"Vibrant . . . Kennedy explores memory, confliction, and redemption. Love, loss, and betrayal. Small lives caught up with the big ones. The tastes and tones of neighborhoods, and the human stories that do a much better job of defining place than any map ever could. . . . With *Changó's Beads*, he's added a few welcome branches to some familiar family trees."
—Scott Martell, *Los Angeles Times*

"Kennedy's humor is sly and wonderful. . . . There's an almost deliriously rich cast of lowlifes here: gun runners, politicians on the make, street-corner agitators, prostitutes, winos. . . . [Kennedy's] description of Hemingway . . . is well-nigh perfect."   —Kate Tuttle, *The Boston Globe*

"Any list of important American novelists must include William Kennedy for his pure, though never puritanical, delights. . . . His prose is a revelation of lucid music in the American vernacular. His dialogue exults in delicious variability. . . . A furious cyclone of story within story spins tall and small tales, history and mystery. The ugliness is tempered, as always with Kennedy, by a generous perception of humans as inclined to decency whenever it's not inconvenient, and by a whiskey marinade of humor that flavors even grief."
—Katherine Dunn, *The Portland Oregonian*

"[*Changó*] is a commentary on machine politics, as many of Kennedy's books are. . . . In both its Havana and its Albany episodes, it illustrates what happens when the unstoppable force of individual conscience meets the seemingly immovable object of political power. As a treatise on race relations, it offers paradoxes that the nation would do well to contemplate. . . . The Albany machine, with its cruel, careless trampling of human wishes, has always been the perfect foil for Kennedy's real subject—the other machine, whose cogs are love and loyalty, friendship and community."   —Stefan Beck, *The New Republic*

"A rich, rewarding novel that reads like a three-act play, spanning the years from 1936 to 1968, with several forms of revolution serving as narrative threads . . . The novel is as intricate as it is brilliant."
—Betsy Willeford, *The Miami Herald*

"Kennedy's prose hangs on every deft noir-ish turn, never succumbing to lazy pastiche. Best of all is his Castro, an impressively human rendering of the Commandante who falls halfway between Brando and Marcus Aurelius."   —J. W. McCormack, *Bookforum*

"A virtuoso improvisation upon music and memory, revolution and race and romance, terrible loss and enduring love . . . The intricately structured second part of the book takes place on [a] single day. . . . It's a little like Leopold Bloom's walkabout of Dublin, if James Joyce had set it during the Easter Rising of 1916: a city's history compressed into a single explosive day."   —Colette Bancroft, *St. Petersburg Times*

"The dependably fine novelist William Kennedy goes far south in the latest installment of his Albany cycle, gluing an imaginative take on the early days of the Cuban revolution to a complex yarn about his longtime inspiration, the politics of the New York state capital, his hometown. . . . [Kennedy's] language, by turns terse as Hemingway's and wild as Joyce's, startles and pleases." —Carlo Wolff, *Pittsburgh Post-Gazette*

"Action packed . . . full of colorful characters . . . Perhaps the most surprising and salient character whom Kennedy has chronicled here is George Quinn, Daniel's father, who is slipping into dementia. Kennedy's depiction of George's confused but soulful point of view is both stunning and poignant." —Cherie Parker, *Minneapolis Star Tribune*

"Deeply explores the Cuban Revolution and the Civil Rights movement—but it also canters along at a sprightly pace, propelled by rapid-fire dialogue suitable for a Howard Hawks Golden Age romantic comedy." —Chauncey Mabe, *Sun Sentinel* (Ft. Lauderdale)

"A gorgeous and rewarding read, but also a profoundly humane one . . . [*Changó's*] masterful web connects sympathetic and singular characters, action and introspection, all across seemingly impermeable borders of time and place, class and race. . . . Kennedy weaves in [Quinn and Renata's] tragic but never doomed love so delicately as to appear as a given fact, a continuous cycle that cannot but parallel the larger revolutions that are as much a part of their history as history proper." —Zach Weir, *The Post and Courier* (Charleston, South Carolina)

"Travels far beyond the city limits of Kennedy's beloved, corrupt, and corrupting Albany, all the way to Cuba in the early days of a revolution . . . The story then returns to Albany a decade later for a flaming finale that showcases Kennedy's abundant gifts. . . . The storytelling has the irresistible pull of a riptide." —Bill Morris, *The Millions*

"Kennedy's journalistic training is manifest in a clear, sure voice that swiftly guides the reader though a rich, multilayered, refreshingly old-school narrative. Thick with backroom deal making and sharp commentary on corruption, Kennedy's novel describes a world he clearly knows, and through plenty of action, careful historical detail, and larger-than-life characters, he brilliantly brings it to life." —*Publishers Weekly*

"A jazzy, seductive, historically anchored novel of politics and romance, race and revolution . . . Music, rapid-fire dialogue, lyrical outrage, epic malfeasance, trampled idealism, and a bit of autobiography drive Kennedy's incandescent and enrapturing tale of the heroic and bloody quest for justice and equality and the gamble of love." —*Booklist*

William Kennedy's Albany cycle of novels reflect what he once described as the fusion of his imagination with a single place. A native and longtime resident of Albany, New York, his work moves from the mid-nineteenth to the mid-twentieth century, chronicling family life, the city's netherworld, and its spheres of power—financial, ethnic, political—often among the Irish Americans who dominated the city in this period.

The novels in his cycle include *Legs*, which evokes the flamboyant career of the legendary gangster Jack "Legs" Diamond; *Billy Phelan's Greatest Game*, about a pool hustler and small-time bookie who gets involved in the kidnapping of a political boss's son; *Ironweed*, winner of the Pulitzer Prize and the National Book Critics Circle Award for Fiction, which tells the story of Francis Phelan, ex-big leaguer and full-time bum on an odyssey of redemption through the lower depths; *Quinn's Book*, a boy's adventure-filled journey through the tumult of nineteenth-century America; *Very Old Bones*, a revelation of ancestral influence on a later generation of Phelans; *The Flaming Corsage*, about the charged relationship between an Albany playwright and his complex, seductively beautiful wife; and, most recently, *Roscoe*, the story of a suave, brilliant, unscrupulous lawyer, for twenty-six years the chief braintruster of Albany's notorious political machine.

Kennedy has also published an impressionistic history of his city, *O Albany!*, and a non-fiction collection, *Riding the Yellow Trolley Car*, which gathers literary essays, profiles, and book reviews that Kennedy has penned over the years. With his son, Brendan, he co-authored two children's books: *Charlie Malarkey and the Bellybutton Machine* and *Charlie Malarkey and the Singing Moose*. Kennedy's first novel was *The Ink Truck*. His work has been translated into two dozen languages. He is a member of the American Academy of Arts and Letters.

To access Penguin Readers Guides online,
visit our Web site at www.penguin.com.

CHANGÓ'S BEADS AND TWO-TONE SHOES

WILLIAM KENNEDY

PENGUIN BOOKS

This book is for
Natalia Bolívar Aróstegui, Norberto Fuentes,
Peter O'Brien, Leon Van Dyke, *and*
William Joseph Kennedy, Sr.

PENGUIN BOOKS
Published by the Penguin Group
Penguin Group (USA) Inc., 375 Hudson Street, New York, New York 10014, U.S.A. • Penguin Group (Canada), 90 Eglinton Avenue East, Suite 700, Toronto, Ontario, Canada M4P 2Y3 (a division of Pearson Penguin Canada Inc.) • Penguin Books Ltd, 80 Strand, London WC2R 0RL, England • Penguin Ireland, 25 St. Stephen's Green, Dublin 2, Ireland (a division of Penguin Books Ltd) • Penguin Books Australia Ltd, 250 Camberwell Road, Camberwell, Victoria 3124, Australia (a division of Pearson Australia Group Pty Ltd) • Penguin Books India Pvt Ltd, 11 Community Centre, Panchsheel Park, New Delhi – 110 017, India • Penguin Group (NZ), 67 Apollo Drive, Rosedale, Auckland 0632, New Zealand (a division of Pearson New Zealand Ltd) • Penguin Books (South Africa) (Pty) Ltd, 24 Sturdee Avenue, Rosebank, Johannesburg 2196, South Africa

Penguin Books Ltd, Registered Offices: 80 Strand, London WC2R 0RL, England

First published in the United States of America by Viking Penguin,
a member of Penguin Group (USA) Inc. 2011
Published in Penguin Books 2012

10 9 8 7 6 5 4 3 2 1

Copyright © William Kennedy, 2011
All rights reserved

Publisher's Note
This is a work of fiction. Names, characters, places, and incidents either are the product of the author's imagination or are used fictitiously.

THE LIBRARY OF CONGRESS HAS CATALOGED THE HARDCOVER EDITION AS FOLLOWS:
Kennedy, William.
    Changó's beads and two-tone shoes / William Kennedy.
      p. cm.
    ISBN 978-0-670-02297-7 (hc.)
    ISBN 978-0-14-312204-3 (pbk.)
    1. Journalists—Fiction. 2. Americans—Cuba—Fiction. 3. Cuba—History—1933–1959—Fiction. 4. Albany (N.Y.) Fiction. 5. Nineteen fifties—Fiction. 6. Nineteen sixties—Fiction. I. Title.
    PS3561.E428C47 2011
    813'.54—dc22   2011019764

Printed in the United States of America
Designed by Carla Bolte

Except in the United States of America, this book is sold subject to the condition that it shall not, by way of trade or otherwise, be lent, resold, hired out, or otherwise circulated without the publisher's prior consent in any form of binding or cover other than that in which it is published and without a similar condition including this condition being imposed on the subsequent purchaser.

The scanning, uploading, and distribution of this book via the Internet or via any other means without the permission of the publisher is illegal and punishable by law. Please purchase only authorized electronic editions and do not participate in or encourage electronic piracy of copyrightable materials. Your support of the author's rights is appreciated.

ALBANY, AUGUST 1936

❖❖❖

Just because my hair is curly . . . No. My hair's not curly, is what occurred to Quinn. The words must have come up and over the hall banister and eased their way into his sleep. Somebody is singing is what it is. *Just because I always wear a smile* . . . Quinn knew the voice. He opened his eyes to no daylight and he listened: *'Cause, I'm glad I'm livin'* . . .

Quinn threw back the sheet that covered him and stood up into the musical darkness. He was still dressed but no shoes. He found them and walked to the hallway and down to the first landing of the stairs where he could look through the uprights of the banister at whoever was singing in the parlor below. It wasn't the radio, not a Victrola. Somebody in the house was singing. *Just because my color's shady* . . .

"Bingo, you want the same?" somebody asked.

"Never change horses in a six-furlong race, Alex." Was it Bingo who answered? Bingo was the singer. There were other men in the parlor: Alex, this was his house, a Negro man Quinn didn't know, the one Alex calls Bingo, and one who was a stranger to Quinn. The front door opened and Quinn moved two steps down to see his father coming in with two more Negro men who were lifting a small piano over the threshold and onto the marble floor of the foyer.

"One upright piano comin' at you, Alex," George Quinn said.

"Into the parlor and behind the large sofa," Alex said. He pulled a roll of money from his pants pocket and gave it to George, who divided it between the two Negroes. They went out.

"Nice going, George," Alex said. "You did it."

"Jimmy was glad to let us borrow it," George said. "For that kind of money he can buy a new piano."

Alex went to the bar and poured from a bottle, was it whiskey? He put

1

it in five glasses and passed them out to the others. "To fast horses and beautiful women," Alex said, raising his glass.

"Or beautiful horses and fast women," Bingo said.

"Or fast horses and faster women," the stranger said.

"You're a speedy citizen, Max," Bingo said.

"Should I find some beautiful women to join us?" Max asked.

"Patience, Max, patience," Bingo said.

"This is one hell of a mansion you got here, Alex," the Negro said.

"The pharaohs didn't have it this good," Bingo said.

"Where do we sleep?" the Negro asked.

"You're in the guest house, Cody," Alex said. "I'll give you the tour."

"I didn't bring a toothbrush."

"We've got extras."

"You been here before, Bing?" Cody asked.

"Been to Albany but not in this manse."

"Bing and I go back a couple of years in Saratoga," Alex said. "My father bred thoroughbreds and Bing bought one of them."

Bing, not Bingo.

"A nice horse," Bing said, "not swift."

Quinn knew Bing from the radio. Bing Crosby is really singing right here. A party.

"You were with Paul Whiteman," George Quinn said.

"My traveling days," Bing said.

"Whiteman got my brother-in-law fired from Riley's," George said. "Billy Phelan. Billy was dealing at the crap table and Whiteman asked him for five hundred cash for an IOU. He called Billy 'sonny.' 'Give me five hundred, sonny.' Billy wouldn't give it to him and Whiteman said, 'Do you know who I am?' And Billy said, 'Yeah, you're the guy with that hillbilly band playing over at Piping Rock.'"

"Big Paul loved that," Bing said.

"They fired Billy."

"Too bad," Bing said. "He had a good ear for hillbillies."

"Music, Cody, we need music," Alex said.

Cody carried a chair to the piano and sat down. He hit a chord and Bing sang a note and held it. He sang some words:

"Just because my hair is curly,
Just because my teeth are pearly . . ."

Quinn looked at the five men, trying to understand this gathering. He jounced down a few steps. Bing sang:

"Just because my color's shady,"

Then Cody sang:

"You's a shady baby,"

Then Cody and Bing sang together:

"That's the reason, maybe,
Why they call me shine."

Cody saw Quinn at the foot of the stairs and stopped playing. "Hey, whose little man are you?"

"That's Danny, my little man," George said. "He's had to follow me around all day and all night. Peg had some work in Atlantic City."

"Come on, join the party, Dan," Cody said.

Quinn walked to his father, who put his arm around the boy's head and squeezed.

"Howdy, Dan," Bing said. He offered Danny a handshake.

Quinn shook hands and looked at all the men he only half knew. What were they doing? "You're Bing," he said.

"Hey, you been followin' me? You been tappin' my telephone?"

"I heard you on the radio."

"Can't deny it. I've been on the radio."

"He stays up till your show is over," George said.

"The boy will go far," Bing said.

Quinn looked at Cody and thought he should also shake hands with him. "You're going to stay in the guest house," Quinn said.

"You got a lot of information on people," Cody said.

"I like that song," Quinn said. "Shine—what's that?"

Nobody answered him.

"Shine," Alex said, "like a shine on your shoes."

"Or 'Shine On, Harvest Moon,'" Bing said.

"Like the thing at the end of our kitchen light string," George said. "It shines in the dark."

"'Shine' 's a song," Cody said. "Bing recorded it with the Mills Brothers. You ever heard of the Mills Brothers?"

"No," Quinn said.

"Well, you should," Cody said. "Get your daddy to buy you their records."

"Very great singers," Bing said.

"'Shine' isn't just a song," Cody said.

"No," said Bing. "It's an insult. A bad word but a great song. The song turns the insult inside out."

"What insult?" Quinn asked.

"I'll tell you later," George said.

"I got a boy like you," Cody said. "He's three. How old are you, Danny boy?"

"Eight."

"My boy's got five years to catch you."

"Is he coming here tonight?" Quinn asked.

"No. He's with his mama."

"What's his name?" Quinn asked.

"Roy. He's a shine. Like me."

"You're a shine?" Quinn asked.

"Oh, yeah."

"I'll tell you about it in the morning," George said.

"Can you sing the song again?" Quinn asked.

"Sure can," Bing said.

Cody turned back to the piano and he and Bing sang one chorus, then Cody played alone, his right hand roaming half the keyboard, his left hand showing how it could ramble, both hands flying at a furious speed that electrified Quinn, made him move his head and his hands and feet in ways he maybe never moved them before, seeing Cody's racing fingers and hearing, even feeling, the humming sound Cody was making with his mouth.

And then Cody sang:

"Bop bop a deep deep deep-a-deep dee . . ."

Then Bing sang:

"Deet deet du duderidda bombom . . .
Doosaday sosadah spokety spone . . .
Bahnzay dreeeem doodlediddle diddle diddle diddle diddle . . .
Dayddle-dayddle-deedle-dahddle seneday's beem . . .
Dah day tour-it's-in-his-dream . . .
Dig dig the deep peninsulate deem . . ."

Bing was funny and he sang fast, very, very fast, baby talk, crazy talk. Quinn couldn't repeat a single word, except diddle, but Bing's words must mean something. Quinn would have to find out. What good was there in secret language like that? Quinn couldn't say. But it was a wonderful song and he loved its beat and its mystery and he loved Bing's voice and Cody's voice and his piano. He loved everything about what he was seeing and hearing. Loved it.

Max came out of a second parlor with a camera and took pictures of Cody and Bing. Then Cody played alone, breathing out loud, humming in time with his own tempos—a boogie-woogie beat, a plunge into a left-handed bass solo, a rushing, double-handed domination of the entire keyboard, no phrase unfinished, every note on the money, no such thing as a wrong note from the magical hands of a maestro who hummed and he hummed and then he hummed very hard and then he slowed, and Cody sang:

"Just because my color's shady,"

And Bing sang:

"You's a shady baby,"

Then they both sang:

"That's the reason, maybe,
Why they call me shine."

Slam, bang.

The end.

Cody turned to look at Quinn. "Shine," he said.

"Shine," Quinn said, nodding and wanting to say what he didn't know how to say, no words about those words, that music. "That was good."

"Not too bad," Cody said.

"It was great," George said. "Great, great music. You may never hear anything like that again as long as you live, Danny."

"Unless he hangs out with Cody and Bing," Max said.

"Somebody's got to record you, Cody," Bing said.

"Oh, yeah, lotta people gonna record me," said Cody, and he stood up. "Great playin' for you, little man," he said to Quinn. "You hear the music. You're gonna be all right."

HAVANA, MARCH 12, 1957

◈◈◈◈

Quinn met Renata the same night he summoned the courage to talk to Hemingway. She too had come to El Floridita to see the great writer, in part because Alejo Carpentier, who was beginning to fall in love with her, spoke well of the man from their days in Paris and thought *The Sun Also Rises* was masterful. Renata had read much literature and believed she might one day write a novel and would feel stupid if she could have talked to a major living novelist but had not. She had seen Hemingway looking at paintings in the Palacio de Bellas Artes where she worked with artists, studied art, and served as a tour guide, a volunteer. She had no need for salaried work; her family owned two sugar mills on her father's side and tobacco on her mother's. Renata was twenty-three and for more than a year had been living a dual life: as an haute bourgeoise in the heady Cuban social swirl, and, clandestinely, as an associate of revolutionaries who were working to overthrow the government of Fulgencio Batista. One of her revolutionary friends had fought with the Republicans in Spain and later with the American army in World War Two; and he admired Hemingway for being unafraid to dodge bombs in the streets of Madrid. Her brother-in-law, Max, knew Hemingway and Max told her yes, if you approach him at the Floridita in the right way he may talk seriously to you, but it would be better if he was a few daiquiris in before you approached, for the rum brings out his friendly side; he has other sides and it's better to wait for the rum to do its work so you can avoid those.

Quinn had been in the Floridita almost two hours. He'd been in Havana a week and had come to the Floridita three nights in a row to wait for Hemingway, who never turned up. Then tonight here came the man, alone. He sat on a barstool in his corner, a bronze bust of himself on a high shelf over the end of the bar, and he chatted with the bartender. But he also turned his back on two people who approached him. Quinn waited, and when he saw him smile and wave at someone across the room he decided this was the moment. He stood up and made eye contact and by the time he was standing in front of Hemingway he was saying, "I'm Daniel Quinn. I just quit the *Miami Herald* to write a novel and you're responsible for me being out of a job. Does it bother you how many reporters you've led into poverty?"

"Did you eat today?" Hemingway asked, frowning with his eyes.

"I had breakfast."

"You had breakfast and you're drinking rum at the best bar in Havana and you're crying poverty?"

"I was exaggerating to make a point."

"Keep it up and soon you'll have a novel," Hemingway said.

His beard was white and so was what was left of his hair, and he wore a white guayabera with long sleeves. He still had his stomach but he was thinner than his photos and no longer the robust fisherman with the great chest and big shoulders.

"I may overcome my poverty," Quinn said. "The *Time* correspondent here may use me as a stringer. You think I can get an interview with Batista?"

"El Presidente *hijo de la gran puta*," said Hemingway.

"You know him?"

"No thank you."

"Will you write about him?"

"Not in this lifetime. What are *you* writing?"

"Grim stories about political exiles in Miami buying guns to send to Cuba," Quinn said. "The grimness is redeemed by my simple declarative sentences."

"Remove the colon and semicolon keys from your typewriter," said Hemingway. "Shun adverbs, strenuously. What do you think of the woman who's sitting at that far table?"

Quinn looked at the young brunette sitting at one of the square wooden tables, sharp nose, large black eyes, full lips in a curvaceous smile that was radiant, her black hair falling just below her shoulders and with a natural wildness in its curl. She was slender, in a white blouse, tan skirt, and sandals.

"She is spectacularly beautiful," Quinn said. "I could fall in love with her right now. I might marry her."

"The young man was last seen charging into the unknown at full speed," Hemingway said, "a valiant but rash course of action. If you marry a woman like that, when do you write your novel?"

"After the honeymoon," Quinn said.

"Who do you think she looks like?"

"Your daughter Ava Gardner."

"You are clearly a born novelist," Hemingway said.

The beautiful brunette had come in with a man maybe twenty years her senior and they were talking head to head. He was tall and thin, well-tailored in a tan cord suit that his shoulders filled out, white shoes, and yellow tie, a handsome figure who seemed overdressed for the very warm and humid night. He was giving close attention to the young beauty, and it was these two who had drawn the wave from Hemingway.

"What is her relationship to the man?" Hemingway asked.

"Close, but he wants it closer."

"You are closing in on chapter six."

"You know her? I saw you wave to her."

"I waved at the man, Max Osborne," Hemingway said. "He works in your abandoned profession—an editor at the *Havana Post*, very smart and also an American spy who talks about his spying to everybody. Some consider him a political buffoon but that seems to be his cover. I know a great deal about spying. I was a spy for several years and they called me a buffoon. They didn't know twiddle about the Nazis I hunted. Soon Max will come over to talk to us."

"Will he bring the girl?"

"Yes."

"Then I won't have to contrive how to meet her."

"A lucky day for Mr. Quinn. While we wait we'll continue our analysis elsewhere. Tell me, who is the biggest jerk in this place?"

Quinn scanned the room and focused on three noisy American men standing at the bar, which was filling up, all tables already occupied. "The man in the sailor straw hat and the orange shirt," he said.

"We'll drink a daiquiri and then test out your intuition," Hemingway said. He ordered the drinks and told the bartender to ask the man in the sailor straw to come over. The three Americans stared at Hemingway and then the man in the orange shirt came down the bar with a two-day growth of beard and a panatela between his teeth.

"How ya doin', bub?" he said through the cigar. "You wanna talk to me?"

"Just admiring your hat and wondering why you're in Cuba," Hemingway said.

"My wife thinks I'm at a sales convention in Miami. But we came down here on an airplane to gamble and check out the women."

"You're a sly devil. But this isn't the best place in Havana to gamble or to find women either."

"We already found them. Who are you?"

"I'm Dr. Hemingstein and this is my son Daniel. And you?"

"Joe Cooney from Baltimore. What kind of a sawbones are you, Dr. Hemingstein?"

"I'm a doctor of writing. I also actually write stuff."

"A writer. Hey, I'm a writer too. I write new lyrics for old songs."

"Could you write a new lyric for Daniel and myself?"

"Sure. Any particular song you like?"

"You know 'Sliding Down Your Cellar Door'? I learned it as a boy."

"Sure, I know it. You want me to do new lyrics for it?"

"You think you can?"

"Give me a few minutes I'll sing 'em for you."

Joe Cooney went away and everybody smiled.

"So far your intuition is getting high marks," Hemingway said to Quinn.

The man and the beautiful brunette got up from their table.

"Here comes the bride," Hemingway said.

Max made his hello and introduced his sister-in-law, Renata Suárez Otero. Hemingway introduced Quinn as his nephew. Quinn stared at Renata to engrave her beauty in his memory. He felt the impulse to take her face in his hand and kiss her before he spoke one word to her. He restrained himself and said only, "*Hola.*"

"Is she a real sister-in-law, Max, or just cover for your spying on us here?" Hemingway asked.

"I retired from spying last year," Max said. "You can't trust anybody anymore."

"We are related," Renata said. "Max married my sister, Esme."

"Esme Suárez. I know Esme," Hemingway said. "She sang for the troops in Europe during the war."

"That's where she met Max."

"I've heard her sing. She has a large talent. Isn't she in New York?"

"She was working on Broadway," Renata said, "but she's back here now."

"Are you married yourself?"

"I am wondering about it," she said.

"My nephew Daniel here is also wondering. In fact he was wondering as he looked over at you a few minutes ago. In between his wonderments he's writing a novel about Cuban gunrunners. He quit the *Miami Herald* to write his novel and a splendid work it is, with twelve chapters so far."

"Did you meet the gunrunners, Daniel?" Renata asked.

"I've met a few."

"Are they brave?"

"They seem fearless, sometimes mindless."

"Do you think they believe in something?" she asked.

"Yes. They believe in death. Do you know any gunrunners?"

"I read about them in the newspapers."

"Are you an actress? You are so beautiful."

"I'm learning to be a painter," she said.

"I would buy several tickets to see your paintings. Where would I do that?"

"I work at Bellas Artes."

"I'll come and see you," Quinn said. "I would like your reaction to my stories on the gunrunners."

"All right," said Hemingway, "that's settled."

"I have a friend who knew you in Spain," Renata said to Hemingway. "Carlos Sosa Prieto."

"The last I saw Carlos government troops were chasing the fascists out of Teruel. A good man. Where is he now?"

"In Havana."

"I would be glad to see him. Send him *mis saludos*."

Joe Cooney came back with a song in his heart. "Are you ready for my lyrics, Dr. Hemingstein?"

"Let me introduce you all to Joseph Cooney, the Baltimore thrush," Hemingway said. "He's going to sing an old song with new lyrics he just created for us. Fire away, Maestro."

Cooney sang enthusiastically and with bounce:

"Sliding down your cellar door,
What a thrill I had in store,
Sliding down into the grass,
Twenty slivers in my ass.
Thinking of those days gone by
Brings a teardrop to my eye,
Wond'ring if I'll ever see
Cellar door that beckons me.
Beckons me forever more,
Slivers from your dear old door."

Quinn watched Renata, who did not smile at the lyrics. She sees dementia in the man, he decided. Max was amused.

Hemingway leaned over to Quinn and whispered, "You're right about gooney-Cooney. We're going to put him away."

"How so?"

"We'll have him sing it again and at the finish I'll throw him a right and cross with a left."

"You're a harsh critic," Quinn said. "Maybe we should just temper our applause."

Hemingway smiled and spoke to Cooney. "You write lyrics like a poet, like T. S. Eliot. But do it once more with emphasis. It needs emphasis."

Cooney sang it again and on *"Slivers from your dear old door"* he took off his hat, raised both arms upward in an embrace of public lyricism, and finished on an emphatic note that turned all heads in the bar. Hemingway hit him according to plan, a right and then a looping left, launching him backward until his head hit the wall near the door, and he slid to the floor. As Hemingway was throwing the left Max saw it rising, ducked sideways, and lost his balance.

"Jesus, Ernest," Max said, "what was that?"

"Sorry, Max," Hemingway said, helping him to his feet. "Didn't have you in mind. That's two knockdowns with one left."

Renata's face registered confusion. *"¿Qué es esto? ¿Estás bien?"* she said to Max, and took his arm.

"Bien, bien," Max said, brushing dust off his coat and trousers. "He never laid a glove on me."

Renata stared at Hemingway. "So brutal," she said. *"¿Serás estúpido?"* and she left at a brisk pace. Max followed her.

Joe Cooney had not moved. His head was cocked against the wall. His two friends went to him and eased him down to lie flat, and a waiter put a towel under his head to blot his blood.

"Get that man to the *casa de socorros*," Hemingway said to the bartender. *"Está herido.* And bring me a filet mignon."

"¿Crudo?" asked the bartender.

"Raw."

The waiter went to the street to hail a passing car that would take Cooney to a first aid center. Cooney's friends were standing over him, staring at Hemingway.

The bartender put a white plate with a raw steak in front of Hemingway, who wrapped it around his right hand. He lifted up the steak and showed his bleeding knuckles to Quinn.

"See this? I've been out fishing, and the skin is dry from the salt and the sun. *Otro doble,*" he said to the bartender.

"I thought you were joking," Quinn said to Hemingway.

"Jerks are no joke," he said. "Jerks should not be given houseroom. He said he was a writer. What kind of a jerk says that to a writer and he doesn't even know who he's talking to? Jerks and fools are a form of death when they turn up in your face. Singing that song in public is like writing a suicide note. I spent my life looking death in the eye and fighting it." He paused. "I didn't tell you what I was writing, did I?"

"No, you didn't," Quinn said.

"It's not a suicide note. I'm reinventing my past in Paris, and I'm coming back with my trilogy," and he emptied his new double daiquiri with one uptip of the glass. "The land, the sea and the air, and most of it's been written for years. But there's a future to think about, and if I put it out all at once we could die of taxation from publication. They'll get it in time and it'll knock them all on their ass. You'll be very proud of me, Mr. Quinn."

"Didn't you do the sea in the *Old Man*?"

"Only part of it. I did that for a woman. There's more to come, kid. Let's have two more *dobles* here. *Dos más.*"

When Quinn began publishing his own novels in later years he looked at the notes he had made about Hemingway and about himself after this improbable night, and he understood there were important things he had left out, just as Hemingway had left things out when they talked. But as Hemingway had said, you can't leave out what you don't know, and in these years he had three novels in progress and could not stop writing them, or make them come together with meaning the way he could in the old days; because now everything had unendingly equal meaning, equal value. And he had left that out when he talked about it. Yet one must persevere. One must defy the forces that try to kill the spirit. One must not only persevere, one must prevail. And so Hemingway kept writing about what it was that was trying to ruin him, and the work became a love song to that. His one-two punches were part of it, just as Joe Cooney's cellar door was the Cooney love song to his own lack of talent. Witness my absent gift. See how well I apply it.

Failure can also be a creative act, Quinn decided. One must look straight ahead as one makes the forced march backward into used history. The death of ambition, gentlemen, is a great impetus for grasping this, and soon you will thrill to how urgently you are moving, how truly exciting this quest for failure can be. What you do not know at this point is that your quest for failure may also fail.

The waiter came in from the street and said he had found a car to take Cooney. One of the friends pointed to Hemingway as he talked to the waiter, and the waiter nodded. A brawny young black man came in and Hemingway introduced him to Quinn as his driver, Juan. Juan was alert to hostile possibility and stood by Hemingway, monitoring the crowd. Cooney was conscious and talking with his friends, who helped him stand, then walked him to the street.

The crowd in the restaurant stopped watching Hemingway and the tableau he had created, and went back to drinking. A trio of black street singers with guitars came into the bar but a waiter said they weren't welcome. One of them said they knew Hemingway was here and had written a song for him, "Soy Como Soy" (I am what I am), about a whore who can't be the woman Hemingway wants her to be. The waiter asked Hemingway if he wanted to hear the song and he said he did. Quinn listened and drank his daiquiri. When the singers finished, Quinn asked them, *"Conoce la canción,* 'Sliding Down My Cellar Door'?"

"No, señor," one singer said.

"Just as well," Quinn said. "It's a very sad song."

Hemingway gave the trio a five-dollar bill.

El Palacio de Bellas Artes was in old Havana, across Parque Zayas from the Presidential Palace, and at late morning Quinn asked for Renata at the information desk. They directed him to a second-floor gallery where he found her with forty high school children, explaining a new exhibit to them—a triptych of paintings inspired by one of the myths of Santeria, the religious cult of the African slaves the Spaniards had brought to Cuba. Quinn only partly understood Renata's rapid Spanish, but the paintings impressed him, and in days to come he would learn about the long-haired woman and the warrior who were their focus. The woman was Obba, and in the first painting her face was obscured by a white mask with only eyeholes. In the second painting her hair and a scarf covered the left side of her head, because, Renata explained, Obba had cut off her ear to make a meal for her husband—Changó, the warrior king of kings. When Changó realized what Obba had done he rejected her, for he could not live with a mutilated woman. Obba cried for so long and so hard at losing him that her tears created a river, which coursed through the third painting. This Changó was one exalted son of a bitch, Quinn concluded, but Renata made no such judgment. Tragedy was inherent in power, she tried to tell the students, whom she wanted to charm, shock, and instruct in the cruelty of these peculiar-looking gods.

Renata saw Quinn arrive and she smiled at him, not a large smile, and kept talking. She wore a white blouse and black skirt, pedestrian uniform of the museum guides; but she enhanced the uniform, and Quinn decided there was no garment she would not enhance if she wrapped herself in it. The student tour moved on through Spanish, French and Dutch paintings, and at its end Quinn said to her, "Art is long but life is short. Have lunch with me," and she took him to the American Café near the museum where, she said, she went often. She wanted only coffee.

"I don't like your friend Hemingway," she said.

"I can't blame you for that. He didn't behave well last night."

"He hit that man for nothing. The man was singing."

"That's why he hit him."

"You shoot a bird when it sings?"

"He felt insulted by the man's stupidity."

"I am insulted by *his* stupidity."

"I can't blame you, but he's not well, and he thrives on aggression. I don't want to talk about Hemingway. I want to talk about you. I want to go out with you. Take you to the beach, or dinner, go dancing at some nightclub, anything."

"I hate to dance."

"Why?"

"I do it badly. What I do badly I do not do. My mother loves to dance. She won prizes for her dancing."

"My father was a great dancer. He won prizes for his waltzing."

"My mother won a prize for waltzing."

"This is fate. We are children of prize waltzers. We are meant to dance together."

"I don't dance."

"I'll teach you. I'm a pretty fair dancer."

"I don't want to learn dancing. I am learning other things."

"What things?"

"I'm learning to be in love."

"I'm sorry to hear that. I wish I could say it was with me."

"It is others."

"Others? More than one others?"

"Two others. One is a diplomat in the Argentine embassy. The other teaches anthropology at the university. He is very fine, the finest man I can imagine."

"You love the fine one."

"I love them both."

"You have a busy love life."

"It is a curse. They have discovered that I love them both and they are crazy jealous. They are both mad to marry me. The diplomat wants to take me to Europe, but I can't do that. My mother would kill me."

"You love the anthropologist more than the diplomat."

"He needs me more. He's married."

"What do you do for him?"

"I drive him and his friends. He has a car but sometimes doesn't want to drive. I listen when he talks. People call him 'El Rey,' the king, because he owns the world wherever he is. He excites me like nobody ever has. But because he is jealous we have a big fight. I don't know where he is."

"Why are you sitting here talking to me when you could be with your diplomat or out looking for your fine and powerful king to patch things up?"

"I am fond of you. Instantly. *Anoche.* You have a manner. You seem to be different."

"From your lovers?"

"Yes. I think so. You have a way. How you look at a woman. It is possible I could marry you some day, but it is too soon to know."

"Your mother would kill you. Besides, you don't want to get married, especially to three men. Or do you?"

"Marriage is exactly what I want."

"I wouldn't have guessed it."

"I think you can be angry. You look angry with me. You looked at Hemingway in anger."

"Mostly I'm angry with myself. Would you really like to have three lovers at the same time?"

"It is possible. Many women do it. Men have many women, some women have many men."

"I only need one woman."

"You are a rare man."

"You are a rare woman to think I'm rare for needing only one."

"Men are liars."

"Women are greater liars and they are better at it than men. Do you want some more coffee?"

"I have to go back to work."

"I'll meet you later. We can go to dinner."

"Maybe another night."

"Am I on the way to being your third lover?"

"*Quizás.* But not today. It is too confusing today."

"I'm going to see your brother-in-law Max and ask if I can write for his newspaper."

"He is very much in love with me but I don't read his newspaper, which is for the tourists who do not need much news. But he is very intelligent and he seems to know everybody in Cuba. He talks literature with my friend Alejo Carpentier, he plays golf with Bing Crosby, and he has lunch with the gangster Trafficante."

"Will you ask him to hire me?"

"He will hire you without my asking. He always needs writers. They come and go like gypsies."

"Will you reconsider dinner with me tonight?"

"I think it's not the best night."

"Maybe it will turn out to be the best."

"You are persistent, but I must go back."

Quinn walked her into the museum and to an office where the guides gathered between tours. He was about to say he would come back to see her later in the day, but she saw something behind him and her face registered dark surprise. She walked away from Quinn and toward a man entering the museum. She stopped and talked into the man's face, intimate talk. Then she shook her head. The man talked while she listened and she nodded yes. She looked around the museum to see if they were being watched, and they were. He put his arms around her and kissed her, held her, then went out the way he came. Renata saw that people had seen the kiss. How could they not? She came back to Quinn and said, "I cannot talk any more."

"That was the lover who is the king?" Quinn said.

"Yes," she said. Tears came to her eyes and she went into the office.

Quinn had been reading the *Havana Post* for a week, thinking its twelve pages did not leave much room for him, but maybe he'd make room. It was a brisk, pop sheet with Earl Wilson and Winchell, Blondie and Alley Oop, ship arrivals, an Anglo-American social calendar, headline stories from the AP, and whatever local, sports, and social news the rest of the space could handle. When Quinn entered the city room only four people were at work: a barrel-chested old man with white hair and brown skin reading galley proofs at a long table; a fine-featured brunette in her forties, alone on the rim of the copy desk editing wire copy; a tall black man who with two-fingered typing seemed to be translating a story from a Spanish-language newspaper; and Max Osborne, with open-collared shirt and tie, reading that same newspaper at his desk in a glass cubicle. Quinn crossed the room, tapped on Max's glass and stood in his doorway.

"I asked Renata to urge you to hire me," Quinn said, "but she said you'd hire me without her. Is that true?"

"Hemingway likes your writing, is *that* true?"

"He's never seen a word of it. His praise of my novel was fiction."

"We don't publish fiction here."

"I brought you some clips." Quinn put an envelope on Max's desk.

"Are you any good?"

"I'm uniquely talented. Read me."

Max opened the envelope of clips, a few feature pieces Quinn had written for the Albany *Times Union,* and a dozen articles about Cubans for the *Miami Herald,* one on the two pro-Castro factions, one faction without money, one flush and probably CIA; also an interview with Carlos Prío, the president ousted by Batista's 1952 coup. Prío fled to Miami with millions in public money, but denied to Quinn that he was spending it on guns for rebels to bring down Batista.

"Do you speak Spanish?"

"*Suficiente*. I can get along."

"You talked to Prío."

"I saw him handing out cash in his hotel suite. People were lined up in the hallway waiting to beg money to feed the family, or get out of debt, or bring a relative off the island, or hire on for the next invasion. His assistant had a stack of cash on a table and if Prío liked what he heard he'd say, 'Give him an inch,' and the assistant with his six-inch ruler would measure off a bit of the pile and send the beggar away with a smile."

"I like your sentences," Max said after skimming the clips. "I'll hire you if you write something valuable."

"About what?"

"That's your problem."

"I can do maybe two pieces a week. I've got a novel to write."

"Two pieces will do if they're good."

"What about my press credentials?"

"You move fast."

"Get your story in the first paragraph."

"You'll get a press card if I buy your story."

"I may need a card to get the story."

"I'll give you a note." And Max typed on a *Post* letterhead: "The bearer is a reporter on a three-day news assignment for this newspaper. Please grant him all normal courtesies." He dated it and typed his name and signed it illegibly.

"Why are you in Havana?"

"It's closer than Paris," Quinn said. "I followed my nose, and it led here. I thought Miami would be exotic, but it's pointless. Havana has a point. In Albany they merely steal elections. Here they put a pistol in the president's ear while they show him the door."

"I know Albany. It had very entertaining corruption, and it was wide open, like Havana. I went there on weekends with a classmate."

"Albany's corruption is still in bloom and its sin is eternal."

"That's comforting. You know Alex Fitzgibbon?"

"Everybody knows the Mayor."

"We were at New Haven together. He comes here now and then."

"Wait a minute. Were you at Alex's house when Bing Crosby was there? Nineteen thirty-six?"

"I was."

"So was I. I was a kid."

"Sure. And your father got Bing a piano and he and Cody Mason sang 'Shine.'"

"Right. My father now works for Alex in the court system."

"And here *you* are, trying to work for *me*. Yale runs in your family."

"I don't work for you yet."

"But you're trying. My daughter, Gloria, goes to convent school in Albany."

"If we talk long enough it'll turn out we're first cousins."

"Coincidence isn't all that coincidental. How do you know Hemingway?"

"I introduced myself last night. He ever behave like that before?"

"Not quite like that, but yes. That fellow he punched out called this morning and wants us to tell his story. But Hemingway's not news when he punches somebody. If they arrest him, maybe, but now it's a dogbite story."

"Renata didn't think so."

"Renata. I saw how she got to you. Everybody goes ga-ga. She's easy to love, but she's not easy. She's tough."

"I told her I was ready to marry her. She's thinking it over."

"You do get your story in the first paragraph."

"That fellow who sang for us, Papa's punching bag, where's he staying?"

"Cooney? He's at the Regis."

"Maybe I'll go apologize to him for Papa."

"He's not a story either."

"I could interview him as a composer."

"Dog bites composer. It's still not a story."

Renata could not find Diego, her fine and dangerous lover, for good reason: he had been *acuartelado* in an apartment house in the Vedado with fifty-two other men for four days, waiting for the signal to attack the Presidential Palace and kill the dictator. Simultaneously fifteen other attackers led by José Antonio Echevarría, the leader of the Directorio Revolucionario Estudiantil, would leave from another apartment to take over Radio Reloj and announce to all Cuba that Batista was dead. Days and nights passed, the cool moon yielding to new morning and the return of smothering heat in the apartment, for no windows could be opened. Whispers, no other sounds, were permitted, for the young men's presence here was secret. Read, don't talk. Sleep, don't snore. Only five at a time can smoke, and only by the window in the back room. Nobody goes out except Carlos, the leader of the attack, and Diego, who will drive the streets of Old Havana in Carlos' car to estimate the presence of soldiers.

The attack had been set for the twelfth until Diego and Carlos, on the morning of the eleventh, found Calle Colón blocked to all traffic. Only the Colón entrance to the south wing of the Palace offered a door to be breached. That south wing faced Bellas Artes across Zayas Park. On the early morning of the thirteenth the street was still blocked, but an inside informant said the dictator had stayed the night in the Palace, and was there now. At eleven o'clock the barriers were gone, traffic was again moving, and Carlos and Diego drove onto Colón. A soldier with a machine gun was monitoring a car as it entered the south wing's driveway; so yes, access was possible. That soldier could be the first to die.

"We should go to Bellas Artes now," Diego said to Carlos as they moved. They saw Military Intelligence cars parked nearby. Diego went into the museum and found no troops, no SIM agents. Renata was talking to an Americano. She saw Diego and came to him.

"Where have you been?" she said.

"Don't talk. Today you must work here all day."

"I'm supposed to finish at two," she said.

"Work till six. We may need you to drive someone."

"What are you talking about? What is happening?"

"Don't go out of the museum. Stay inside and work all day, do you hear me?"

"I hear."

"Do you have your mother's car?"

"No."

"My car is on Agramonte. The key is in the ashtray. If you don't see me later drive it someplace safe and leave it. Someone will call you about where you put it."

"Why won't you drive it? Won't I see you later?"

"Who can say?"

He kissed her with a fierce mouth and squeezed the life in her body. Then he said good-bye my love, and went back to Carlos in the car.

At two that afternoon the fifty-three Palace attackers who had been *acuartelados* wrapped their Thompsons and Garands into the bedding they had slept on, came down the stairs silently in pairs, and climbed into the Fast Delivery panel truck parked by the side door. Four men, including the leaders, would ride in each of two cars. As the vehicles were being loaded two men turned coward. Carlos said he couldn't shoot them now because of the noise, but they would be held in the apartment at gunpoint by a comrade wounded in an earlier shooting. Maybe he would shoot them later. They knew this was a suicidal mission. We can kill Batista or they can kill us all.

The attack proceeded: Carlos driving the lead car, with Diego and two others, and the Fast Delivery truck following with forty-two men. The truck was unbearably hot, without light, and so overloaded that its six tires were nearly flat. The second car, driven by Aurelio, second in command, with three others, followed the truck. The plan was that once the three vehicles had breached the entrance, another hundred fighters in trucks and cars would arrive shooting heavy weapons, certain to demoralize Palace guards into flight. If the first wave found Palace access impossible, the attack would move against a secondary target—the Cuartel Maestre, the armory of the police—where they would seize its arms, then move to another police station for more arms. There would be no going back. The vehicles moved at inchworm pace through dense traffic. Menelao Mora, at fifty-three the oldest man in the truck, and an ex-legislator in the Cámara and former ally of Prío, told his young comrades what to expect, how to move and never stop. Machadito, holding the rope that kept the rear door from flapping open, saw his girlfriend crossing Aguila and said, *"Mi amor, allí está,"* and his comrades stared at him.

The truck turned onto Ánimas, the driver's mistake, and separated from the two cars. Carlos and Aurelio both waited for it to catch up at the Prado, and when the three vehicles were again in tandem they moved onto Colón, and there it was. Carlos very suddenly careened into the Palace driveway, hit the brakes and bolted from the car firing his M-1, running under the arcade of the Palace's gate, his surprise so perfect that the guards did not slam the gate shut or realize it was time to do that, or even see who was firing the machine gun that was killing them. Diego was behind Carlos, and Aurelio, leaping from the second car, took out the two guards shooting at Carlos' back. Then others jumped out of the truck—Machadito and Carbó and Menelao setting the pace, the rest in twos and threes shooting, remembering Menelao's advice—don't crouch, don't stop—run to the Palace wall out of the line of high fire from the upper terraces. But those machine guns roared, riddling the truck and pavement with such a hail of bullets that clouds of stone dust rose around the men who instinctively sought cover or stasis in the face of the impenetrable and died throwing a grenade or shooting at the sky. Carlos opened the gate and yelled, *"Arriba, muchachos,* it's ours!" Diego moved through the gate after him and the Palace was breached according to plan.

On the third floor of Bellas Artes, Renata was explaining to seventy American and English tourists that the young woman in the painting was named Sikan and she had met the sacred fish, Tanze, quite by accident. But for both it was a fateful meeting, for young Sikan would be kidnapped and dismembered as a sacrifice in order to recover the lost voice of the gods which was the voice of the fish. Why it was also fateful for the fish Renata did not have time to explain for the bullets came in through the front windows and then the screaming and warning yells— they're shooting! Renata now realized Diego would die.

She yelled to the tourists, Get down, somebody's shooting. Who's shooting? What does it matter who's shooting if they shoot you, get down you fool get down, and the fool got down. Renata knew Diego was now shooting at somebody and somebody was shooting at him. He was saying, We will kill the devil, we will butcher the butcher, as he entered the Palace with his M-1. That young man of such culture and knowledge and courage and beauty would be a sacrifice today. Renata listened as he whispered to her: Be careful, they will know I love you and will remember I kissed you, I shouldn't have, but now they will question you about me and you must tell them we only talked about painting and Santeria and of course they will believe you, for you look so innocent. He was shooting now and he will kill before he is killed. The *guardia* at the Palace will also deliver sacrifices today. She could see Diego shooting on the Palace stairs, so agile, so alert to the living instant, and she crawled to the museum's stairs to see everybody below, all crouching or flattened by the guns, which stopped, began, stopped, began. Why are they firing at Bellas Artes? We have no guns.

Diego saw Aurelio hit and lifted backward into the air and saw his pistol and grenades fly out from his belt. He saw Hernández, a year away from being a doctor, run toward the gate and die in a sprawl. Castellanos came yelling, *"Lo logramos,"* we got it, and shot a guard who had left his machine gun and was running back into the Palace.

The Fast Delivery was full of holes and Gómez sat behind it, waving his arms, already dead, the cement dust billowing around him. Diego saw Aurelio shake himself and stand up, without a weapon. The ground floor was empty of guards but bullets kept raining down across the open patio. Diego moved upstairs onto the left wing of the Palace's second floor with four others—Carlos, Almeida, Goicoechea, and Castellanos.

Five others had made their way up and along the second floor's right wing and from there Machadito lit the fuse of a seven-stick dynamite bomb and threw it to the soldiers on the third floor—who thought it was artillery, and their firing stopped, momentarily.

The five on the left moved along corridors and when the phone rang in an empty room Diego answered it. The caller asked was it true as José Antonio announced on Radio Reloj that Batista was dead? And Diego answered, "Yes it is true, we have seized the Palace and killed Batista. *Viva el Directorio!*" Then he followed Carlos across a corridor toward Batista's office. But the map from Prío showed an opening where now there was a locked door.

Carlos shot the door, which opened into a dining room—dirty dishes on a table and three servants crouching in a corner. Goicoechea wanted to martyr them, but Carlos said no. He asked where was Batista? They said he'd just had lunch but they didn't know where he went.

"*A singar,*" Diego said, fuck!—and he ran toward the Hall of Mirrors and to the glass door into Batista's antechamber. Diego heard voices beyond the door and called to them to surrender and a gunshot shattered the glass door in reply. Carlos tossed a grenade through the broken glass but it did not explode; he threw another, then a third, duds all. Diego dropped in a grenade that blew off the door and they entered the Batista sanctum shooting at two corpses.

The butcher has fled.

They looked on Prío's map for the secret passage to the third floor but found nothing. From the Hall of Mirrors balustrade they looked down at a dozen patrol cars on the Avenida de las Misiones where police, shielded by trees, fired up at them. They found their way across to the right wing to meet the five who were now four: Menelao shot, unable to get up, Machadito, Carbó and Prieto all firing upward, and Brinas dead in front of them.

Carlos tested the stairs going up but fell back from the shooting and said we need our backup men, I'll get them, and before Carbó could stop him he went toward the down stairway where Brinas had been shot and ran under the fusillade that was the last thing to touch his life.

Diego was hit but running. "I'll cover your retreat," said Machadito, and his machine gun silenced the troops above while Carbó and Prieto and Goicoechea made their way down, and then the last five were out of the Palace, all bleeding and running from the guns on the Palace roof.

Carbó was running with Diego toward Bellas Artes, but the gunners on the roof hit both—Carbó's arm, yet he kept running, and Diego, his shirt covered with the blood of others, who went facedown into the water of the Zayas fountain. The others kept on toward Montserrate, shooting at anything coming after them, anything ahead of them that impeded their way to someplace else.

◈

Quinn sat in a fifth-floor mini-suite at the Hotel Regis, studying the shape of Cooney's head bandage, which looked like a turban wrapped by a one-handed Arab, absurd enough to match the cause of the injury, large enough to match the reputation of the man who caused it. Cooney wasn't clear on Quinn's purpose in coming here, nor was Quinn. Cooney doubtless paired Quinn with Hemingway as the enemy, but Quinn had apologized in his call from the house phone, asking for a meeting to explain what he was not sure he could explain. He would not claim illness or pathological aggression for Hemingway; but the subject needed examination. It still might turn into an article for Max, but Quinn didn't need that either. He was out to affix reality onto experience for himself, maybe also for Cooney, and rescue the event from drift into fistic barroom legend that would otherwise end with a whimper as the stretcher exits the Floridita and another right cross and a left hook from Hemingway become a footnote in the archive. There was more to it than that.

One of Cooney's pals from Jersey sat beside him with narrow eyes and a pushed-out lip, keeping watch on this visitor who might be bringing new trouble. Quinn remembered the man from the bar. He didn't speak and Cooney didn't introduce him.

"How's your head?" Quinn asked.

"They say the skull's not cracked, just cut and swelled up," Cooney said. "But that son of a pup ain't heard the last of Joe Cooney, I kid you not."

"Are you a vengeful man, Mr. Cooney?"

"Revenge? I'm sure as hell gonna get me some."

"You've got a right. But I should warn you—he's got money and power down here. And he's very famous, and well-loved."

"They love him? Don't he punch out any Cubans?"

"Wouldn't surprise me. He's no stranger to fights. But he's king of the Floridita. That's his domain."

"King of a barroom."

"And of everybody who walks into it."

"How'd he get to be such a big shot?"

"He wrote some great books."

"That don't seem enough."

"He also fights in all the wars."

"I fought in the Pacific. Got a Silver Star."

"If he knew that he wouldn't have hit you."

"Why'd he hit me?"

"He had a problem with your song. He also likes power and thinks you get it with your fists or your gun. He's a serious hunter."

"So am I."

"You and he have a lot in common."

"He send you here to see what I'm gonna do?"

"No. I only met him for the first time myself last night."

"Hit me a sucker punch, for what?"

"I agree it was barbaric."

"Whatever the hell that means."

"It means savage, uncivilized. The primitive arrogance of force. Crude exercise of the ego. Everybody's an enemy who isn't himself. Nothing personal, now, but he sees you as a cipher, a zero, a cliché, a mark. Fair game for lofty thinkers."

"Shit," said Cooney's friend, and he stood up from his chair.

Quinn heard the fireworks outside, then explosions. Cooney's friend opened the louvered screen doors and went onto the balcony overlooking the street and Zayas Park.

"They're shootin' down there," the friend said. "Cops or soldiers looks like."

Quinn and Cooney stood up to look out. Uniformed men were shooting at people near the Palace. The street was chaotic, people running, crouching behind cars, in doorways, traffic stopped, police firing at civilians who were shooting machine guns. Machine-gun fire strafed a bus and shattered its windshield, and the bus driver climbed the sidewalk. A soldier in the turret of a *tanqueta*, an armored truck, looked up at the front of the Regis, then turned his machine gun and raised it. Quinn said, "Look out!" and instinctively backed inside and hit the floor as the soldier fired. Cooney's friend fell backward across the threshold with bullets in his chest. Cooney, splattered with blood, stood staring at his friend but Quinn grabbed his wrist and said, "Down, Cooney, down," and pulled him to the floor. Quinn crawled toward the door as more bullets came through the louvered doors and hit the wall, and plaster showered onto Quinn and Cooney.

"What is this Cuba for chrissake?" Cooney said. "They hit you for nothin' and they shoot you for standin' outside, even inside, and you didn't do a goddamn thing to them, this is fucking rotten hell if I ever saw it."

"Good reason to keep your head down," Quinn said. "Maybe they think you're a sniper. They don't know you're a tourist. Crawl to the hallway, head down. What's your friend's name who was shot?"

"Chet Looby."

"Where's he from?"

"Baltimore, same as me. Why you askin' me questions?"

"I keep track of stuff," Quinn said.

He crawled past a room where loud music was playing, a Cuban song he recognized, one of the few he could name, a *son*, "Lágrimas Negras." He equated it with old death in Cuba as announced on the *Miami Herald's* newswire, or rebels dead in the street trying to get rid of Machado, or the distant slaughter in the Mambí revolution his grandfather had written about—slaves and rebels on horseback, hacking out a mythic path with their machetes, a prelude to today's diorama of corpses baking on sidewalks in the park, a newly blooming garden of rebel death. In his historical memory these warriors fell without bleeding but now the gore was personal for Quinn, its splatter visible on his trousers, and he could hear its music. On the streets below, the attack wave of the new sacrificial generation was becoming aware that bleeding to death was its destiny and that suicide-in-arms is a noble choice of exit from a righteous war. And Black Tears from on high fell onto these very necessary corpses.

The hundred young rebels in the second wave, now sitting in cars, trucks or houses, waiting, could hear no music. Some heard on Radio Reloj that the attack had begun, some could hear the calamity of the Palace machine guns, but their leader, struck with indecision, could give no signal to attack those guns. And so the first wave was massacred and the president preserved.

The force of survival is as unconsciously fierce as the charge toward fatal heroism is willful. In the land of perpetual revolution, one never knows toward what one moves.

◈

As Quinn and Cooney came down the stairs into the lobby a woman in hysterics ran in from the street, a bellman moved to lock the doors, but another half dozen squeezed through after her; and then the doors were sealed against further sanctuary. People pounded the door in vain. Quinn saw two dozen people already sheltered in corridors off the lobby, away from windows and stray or not-so-stray bullets. Quinn and Cooney walked down the hallway past the refugees, and behind a half-open door found a man of managerial air venting anguish into the telephone. Quinn pushed Cooney toward the man and said, "An American tourist, name of Chet Looby from Baltimore, was just shot dead by street fire in five-oh-three, and this man is his friend and saw it happen." The manager's face registered panic as Quinn turned toward the corridor and said, "See you later, Mr. Cooney." Cooney gave a don't-go gesture, but Quinn was already gone.

When the police came to talk to Cooney they would advise him to say a random shot killed his friend; but Cooney would insist, "They pointed guns up at us, two soldiers did, and then they machine-gunned us. Wasn't nothin' random about it." The American embassy and the Cuban government both vowed to investigate Cooney's view of events. The day's early death count would be forty-seven rebels, six soldiers, and maybe a half a dozen civilians: the Chinese bus driver, who would die while his head wound was being treated at a military hospital, two of his twelve wounded passengers, both children, also Chet Looby, and who knows who else? Joe Cooney would find his blue seersucker sports coat riddled in his closet by machine gun fire. A painting in Bellas Artes, *A Faun and a Young Girl* by Rubens, would be cut in half by a blast from a fifty-caliber gun on the *tanqueta,* and the façade of the museum would be so ravaged by gunfire it would close for fifteen days.

Rebels and Palace guards would shoot each other for forty-five minutes. Firing from rooftops and streets, echoing from sites remote from the Palace, would go on for three hours, and Renata would keep her tourist visitors on the floor of the museum for more than two hours. One man in her charge would suffer a heart attack, four others would be cut by flying glass, and two women would faint and be slapped awake by Renata. After the third hour's final silence the museum's director would tell Renata that Diego's corpse had been found in the fountain of Zayas Park, and that the Military Intelligence Service, SIM, had been asking if anyone in the museum knew Diego, and someone said that Renata did.

"I knew him only through painting and sculpture, as a man of the arts," Renata told the director.

"Of course," he said. "Now go home and stay there and don't talk about Diego."

Quinn called Max four times from a pay phone to update the attack, the street scene, the sprawl of corpses. He dictated a story on the sudden death of Cooney's friend and Max told him he was hired. When the shooting fell away to single sporadic shots in the distance, Quinn walked toward Bellas Artes to find Renata, but was stopped half a block away by soldiers. He explained his work and showed his letter from Max, which the soldier could not read. A woman came out of the museum and Quinn asked her if she'd carry a message to Renata, and she agreed. Two men from SIM came out and took Quinn into the museum and asked how he knew Renata, this woman who knows rebels. Did Quinn know any rebels? He showed them his passport and Max's letter, and one of the men telephoned Max, who vouched for Quinn.

Quinn's first-person story of death at the Palace and death on a hotel balcony would be carried internationally with his byline by the Associated Press, in the week ahead *Time* would hire him as a stringer, and Quinn the newcomer would suddenly be a Havana newsman with cachet.

"Diego was in the attack. He's dead," Renata said, her first words as they left the museum. "Now, because I know him, they don't trust me."

"They don't trust me because I know *you*. But they didn't arrest either of us. Here you are. Here I am."

"You came to see me. You are a thoughtful man."

"I thought I'd take you home. I know they've been shooting at you."

"My mother is in collapse. She thinks I'm dead. But I can't go home. I have to know if Diego is truly dead. I want to go to the *necrocomio*, where they take the bodies."

"Don't tempt the police to arrest you. They're very, very nervous. I saw them kill a friend of that guy who sang for Hemingway."

"Oh no, oh the poor man. So many innocents killed. I'm sure I know many, many of the dead. I'm sure of it."

"I wrote the story of that man, and of the whole attack, for Max. He hired me."

"I knew he would."

They walked toward Agramonte.

"Do you have a car?" she asked.

"No. But I'll find us a taxi," Quinn said.

"I have a car."

They walked, and when she saw Diego's car she opened the door and sat at the wheel. She took the key from the ashtray as Quinn got into the 1952 Oldsmobile four-door with stains on its carpet. It smelled of oil.

"Is this your car?" Quinn asked.

"It is sometimes my car." She put her head on the wheel and sobbed.

"I can drive," Quinn said.

"Better if a woman is driving." She raised her head and started the car. "This is Diego's car."

"Diego's? Jesus, Renata, are you crazy? They'll be looking for it. They're probably looking for it now."

"It really isn't his," she said. "It's a stolen car."

"Oh, then there's no problem. They never look for stolen cars."

"He said to park it someplace safe and wait for a call to tell someone where it is."

"You're in serious danger in this car."

"I've been in serious danger for many months. Get out if you like."

"I said I'd take you home. Let's go home. Your home."

"I can't take this car home."

"Then take it someplace and let's park it."

She pulled out into traffic, which was just beginning to move again.

Hundreds were coming out of stores and offices, slowly and with curiosity, street vendors were back selling peanuts and peeled oranges, and two overfull buses were moving. People were walking backward in the street hailing rides.

"I can't give anybody a ride," Renata said. "They might be killed if the police stop us."

"No point in getting anybody else killed," Quinn said.

She turned onto the Prado, still in tears. But the mood of her eyes was different from the rest of her face, less sad, more on edge, and he saw her capacity for dualities. Of course. Two lovers going on three, minus one.

"How were you in serious danger for many months?" Quinn asked.

"Riding with Diego. We would rent rooms for his friends to hide in, or to use for hiding guns. We said we were man and wife. I think we would have been."

"Then you're a genuine gunrunner," Quinn said.

"Yes, and so are you. There are guns in this car. I knew as soon as I saw it. The rear end is very low."

Her passion had dried her tears and her eyes were evaluating how this sudden complicity with guns would change Quinn's expression.

"Do you like being a gunrunner?" she asked.

"It's delightful. I didn't know how beautiful my fellow gunrunners could be."

"Are you afraid of dying if the police catch us?"

"Not at all. I'll explain I'm writing a story about gunrunning."

"They will kill you anyway. They kill anybody with guns, anybody."

Quinn the gunrunner had fallen in love before he'd said hello to this woman, who seemed as guileful as she was innocent, primal polarities. She had offhandedly exposed him to intimate elements of her love affair with living-and-dead rebels, and had speculated aloud that Quinn might be on a waiting list. Her legs and thighs were on exhibition, skirt riding high as she drove, that skirt soiled from her time on the museum floor with seventy tourists. How had she kept them horizontal and alive? A persuasive presence. Now she confesses her clandestine movement of arms and turns him into an accomplice. Was this sudden inadvertence, willful intent, an inevitable truth she feels they should share? Who is he to be her confessor? Forces are in play, Quinn, which you are only beginning to confront. No American women in your life like this one, who's taken up residence in your soul overnight: invasive onset by a creature who commandeers the imagination: exotic, perhaps deadly. What did you get yourself into?

"You are ready to die," he said to her. "Do you know why?"

"Because I believe in the people I've been with. And because it is a form of love. It is not death you love but the nearness of death to the people you love and to yourself. And because it thrills me."

"You know what would thrill me?"

"Tell me."

"If you parked this goddamn car."

"I know the perfect place," she said. "They will never look there for guns. A beautiful house and it is closed. The owner is a very rich American woman who comes here only in winter. My sister lives nearby and we can borrow one of her cars."

They rode out Fifth Avenue and past the Havana Yacht Club, where Renata was a star golfer. They moved through Country Club Park where the American, British and Cuban social elites for decades had built their homes on rolling acres and great lawns that were emulations of the fairways of the Country Club's golf course. Renata turned into a driveway bordering a fairway and toward an elegant white-stucco Spanish villa with a half-dozen adjoining buildings.

"They had many parties here," she said. "I came as a child and watched them at night on that hill, dancing the conga with torches."

"Who was this woman?"

"Rene Fellows. She painted and wrote things and had money from her husband who ran a shipping line. She was one of Hemingway's mistresses and she was beautiful. People say she had many men."

"That seems to be a popular pastime."

She drove to the rear of Rene Fellows' house and parked in the covered driveway of a secondary building. She faced the car outward so anyone picking it up would not have to waste time turning it around. They were out of the sight line of neighboring houses. She put the keys in the ashtray.

"Esme lives beyond those trees."

"I'd like to see the guns."

Renata retrieved the key and opened the trunk on one Browning automatic and tripod, six machine guns, several belts of cartridges, and six .45 caliber pistols.

"I remember the Browning and the .45s from the army," Quinn said, "but I never dealt with those machine guns."

"They are old Thompsons, and they fit under the front seat of this car. I'll tell you a story about that some day." She closed the trunk and put the key back in the ashtray.

"How much do you pay for this many guns?"

"Thousands. I never do that part of it."

She led Quinn through a stand of banyans and flamboyans, laurels and coconut palms and a heavy growth of manigua, and when they came out on the crest of a hill she pointed toward a spectacle: an Italian Renaissance mansion with stairs and terraces sculpted into a hillside that ran to the beach.

"My big sister's ugly palace," Renata said. "It is so big she had to put in an elevator. She married a rich Spaniard who died in a plane crash and left her a fortune. Her house has fourteen bedrooms. And Batista. She loves Batista because of his power. I think she would make sex with him if she could. I wonder if she has. I try very hard to love her the way I used to. Her second husband Moncho I love very much. They were only married six months and she left him because he was never home. He is a lawyer and a crazy person and is one of my favorite in-laws. He visits Esme all the time, and they get along better than when they were married."

"Where does Max come into this? I thought he was your brother-in-law."

"Max was her first husband but she divorced him in 1953. He moved back in when the Spaniard died. But they aren't married."

"Your sister thinks in multiples, like you. What will you tell her about how we got here?"

"I will think of a lie. I am a very good liar and I am smarter than she is. She is older and more beautiful, but she is so beautiful I think she is ugly like her house."

Renata rang the bell and Felix the gardener opened the great wooden gates and greeted them. He said he'd let Esme know they were here, and then Renata and Quinn went into the main salon, which was dominated by what Quinn assumed was a portrait of Esme, standing on a seven-foot easel. Quinn looked for the beautiful ugliness that Renata had suggested, but he found only beauty and a strong resemblance to Renata. Esme had been married only six months when she sat for the portrait by the Spanish painter Berenguer, who had come to Cuba and expressed fascination with her provocative beauty. He made many sketches of her and asked her to come to Spain for a sitting. The finished portrait placed Esme in a spectral mode, a regal, standing presence, wearing a vexed expression and with her left hand pointing to the center of herself in an ambiguously sensual gesture. Berenguer said she wears her persona like a weapon, aggressive behavior for a great beauty. It was the most popular work in the artist's subsequent exhibition and Berenguer did not want to sell it. Esme's husband offered twenty-five thousand but Berenguer refused to sell. After months of persuasion he finally yielded the painting to Esme as a gift. How did Esme persuade him?

That is my secret, Esme always says.

It is no secret, Renata always says.

Esme came into the room four steps ahead of Moncho. She kissed and embraced her sister, greeted Quinn with an odd gesture of elevated fingers and pursed lips, with her breasts rising from excited inbreathing, a gesture of concern.

"So, you're alive," Esme said. "Mother called me five times. All that shooting she thought you were dead."

"I called her from the museum," Renata said. "All afternoon you could not use a telephone. If you stood up you'd be shot."

Esme looked to Quinn, and Moncho offered him a handshake. "Ramón Quevedo," he said.

"Daniel Quinn," said Quinn. "A pleasure to meet you. I understand you don't live here."

"Only historically," Moncho said. "It is not possible to separate from Esme. No husband should be asked such a thing."

"Husbands seem to play a peculiar role in Cuba," Quinn said.

"Husbands are extinct," said Moncho. "Wives are eternal."

"I may refuse to become a Cuban husband," Quinn said. "I've already proposed to Renata, but maybe I'll postpone the wedding."

"You proposed?" said Esme. "When?"

"This morning."

"When did you meet?"

"Last night."

"What took you so long?" Moncho asked.

"Daniel rescued me after the attack," Renata said. "He found a taxi to bring us here when no one else could. He's a reporter and Max just hired him to write for the *Post*. He was near the Palace all during the attack."

"How intrepid," Esme said, and she sat in the Peacock cane chair in front of her portrait. "You really proposed?" she said to Quinn.

"He suggested the possibility," Renata said. "He wrote the story of the Palace attack for Max."

"A pity they did not kill the *puta*," Moncho said.

"Be quiet or they'll arrest you," Esme said. "Did you see the shooting, Daniel?"

"I did, but my luck seems to be running," Quinn said. "I didn't get shot and I found the gorgeous Renata when the shooting stopped."

"You can do two things at once," said Esme.

"I do covet beauty," Quinn said. "That portrait of you is very beautiful, and it does you justice."

"The artist said he made me too beautiful," Esme said.

"There is no such thing. An artist can only imitate the exquisite beauty that runs in your family."

"Such a charmer. Please sit down, Daniel. Would you like a drink?"

"As my uncle once said, the last time I refused a drink I didn't understand the question."

Moncho exploded with laughter. "I understand the question and I will make you a drink," he said, and he left the room.

"Very droll," Esme said. And she asked Renata, "Nena, what brings you here on such a day?"

"I need a car. After today I absolutely must go away, anyplace, Cárdenas, perhaps, but I can't take Mother's car from her. You don't know, Esme, you don't know."

"Of course I know, dear. Take the Buick. Those hateful people trying to kill the president, shooting all over the city, nobody is safe anywhere, what's wrong with them? They're all insane and lower class. As soon as I heard the news I tried to get a flight to New York, but they closed the airport. Americans will be afraid to come to Havana now."

"Soldiers killed an American tourist," Quinn said. "I was in his suite at the Regis Hotel when they shot him."

"You weren't."

"An armored truck and a foot soldier both fired at us. I saved another man by pulling him to the floor when the shooting started."

"You saved someone? You are a clever person. What are you doing in Cuba?"

"I'm trying to figure that out. My grandfather wrote a book about the Mambí revolution and he put Cuba into my head. Now you've got another revolution going and it pulled me in."

"Did you come to write about Castro?" Renata asked.

"He's a good subject, don't you think?"

"Batista says Castro is dead or gone away," Esme said. "Batista should know."

"Of course," Renata said. "Batista knows everything."

"He knows nothing, he knows less than nothing," Moncho said, reentering the room. Oliva, a housemaid, followed him in, wheeling a serving cart with a bottle of white rum, a bucket brimming with ice, a bowl of powdered sugar, a plate of cut limes, four cocktail glasses and a silver shaker. When Oliva left the room, Esme said, "If the servants repeat what you say you'll be shot."

"She is right," Renata said.

"Of course she's right. Tell the truth they shoot you." Moncho squeezed the limes. "Batista's planes bomb the Sierra and kill *guajiros* but they find no rebel corpses. Fidel is not gone."

"Where is he?" Quinn asked.

"In the Sierra."

"How do you get to see him?"

"By invitation," Moncho said. "Without invitation they will shoot you as a spy."

"How do you get an invitation?"

"No one knows."

Moncho poured a cascade of rum into the shaker, added sugar and the lime juice. "I was in law school at the University with Fidel. He was a wild schemer with the political gangs, never went to class. But he learned something. He's outthinking Batista's army."

"We will change the *subject*, Moncho," Esme said. "Daniel's grandfather wrote a book about Cuba."

"Ah," said Moncho, shaking the shaker.

"He came looking for Céspedes, the revolutionary, and he found him."

"Céspedes!" Moncho said. "In 1948 I went to Manzanillo with Fidel to get the Demajagua bell, the one Céspedes rang to start the revolution. Like your Liberty Bell, Señor Quinn, a three-hundred-pound symbol of our rebellion."

"I know the bell," Quinn said.

Moncho poured daiquiris from the shaker and passed them around.

"We brought it to Havana to confront Grau, the president," he said, "but the police stole it from us. Fidel made a speech at the University about the bell and about Grau betraying the revolution he promised the people, and thousands came. He repeated Céspedes' words the day he rang the bell to summon his slaves—Céspedes called them citizens and said they had been his slaves until today but now you are as free as I am. He was launching the revolution and said the slaves could join him in the fight or go wherever they wanted, but all were free. Fidel knew how to use these words. He was very powerful. He lit a fire in their minds."

"They will put us *all* in jail if you don't shut up," Esme said.

Moncho raised his daiquiri glass.

"I drink to Fidel."

"You will be a prisoner," Esme said.

Quinn drank and Renata crossed the room and turned on the radio to a news broadcast. The Palace was circled with tanks and a newsman was saying that scores were dead and Batista had survived the attack on the third floor of the Palace with his wife, their ten-year-old son, forty soldiers, and an army colonel with a Tommy gun. The president rode out the attack with a pistol in one hand and a telephone in the other. The attackers never reached the third floor. The camera showed shooting, then the corpses piled in the street and the park. Corpses, corpses. Renata tried to hide her weeping. Batista praised his courageous soldiers and blamed Prío for the attack. Not Castro? asked a newsman. No, said the president, Castro is nothing, of no significance.

The bell on the entrance gates rang. Oliva came into the room and whispered to Esme, who then went to the door. She came back to say that the police were asking about a car abandoned nearby. "They want to know if anyone here has seen strangers coming or going."

"What did you tell them?" Renata asked.

"I said I saw no strangers, today or yesterday. Did you see anyone when you came in your taxi?"

"There was a man hiding behind a tree," Renata said. "He looked like Fidel Castro."

"Don't joke about such a thing," Esme said. "They will arrest you."

Renata drove Esme's Buick in a way that Quinn decided was more dangerous than traveling with machine guns in the trunk, and more liable to get them arrested on this day of assassins on wheels.

"Let me drive," he said. "You're too distracted."

"I am not distracted."

"You're speeding."

"They're not arresting speeders today."

"Let me drive."

"Later."

"Later we'll be at your house."

"I can't park this car at my house."

"Are you saying we have another parking problem?"

"I cannot do anything strange that will attract the police."

"Everything you do is strange. I hope you don't mind me saying this, but I'm falling in love with you because of your bizarre turn of mind."

"Thank you, Daniel."

"Thank me? For falling in love?"

"I love it when men love me."

"You have so many. How many is enough?"

"I don't think of it that way."

"How do you think of it?"

"I can't think of it. I have Diego in my mind. I can't think of other people's love."

"I don't want to be considered other people."

"Diego was my love."

"He was one of them. You can lose two or three and still have loves to spare."

"I don't like your attitude."

"I'm sorry for Diego but I can't grieve as you do. He was a very, very brave man and I'm sad a warrior of the revolution was killed. Yours is another kind of sorrow from mine."

"You must stop talking or I'll start to hate you and I don't want to hate someone who is falling in love with me."

"What are you going to do with this car?"

"Esme will tell my mother I have it. But if I park at my house and the police come, Esme will be involved."

"She's already involved. The police came to see her. They may even think she parked Diego's car."

"Never. She is too close to Batista."

"I can park it someplace."

"Yes, you can, can't you."

"I can park it by my apartment."

"Where is your apartment?"

"In the Vedado. Near the Nacional. I could even leave the car in the hotel parking lot."

"Perfect," she said. "Take me home—Twenty-second Street." She stopped the car and changed seats with Quinn. They were on Fifth Avenue in Miramar.

"Did your parents know Diego?"

"They heard his name, but they can't keep track of my life. I tell so many lies I can't keep track myself."

"I would like to meet them without lies."

"They will like it that you're an Americano. They will assume you have money. Do you?"

"I can pay my rent and still have some left over for the laundry."

"*Pobrecito.*"

On Twenty-second Street Renata said her house was on the right. Two Oldsmobile sedans, nobody in either one, were parked in front and every light in the house seemed to be lit.

"Keep going," she said. "Those cars are the SIM. They're probably talking to my parents. God, how my father will hate this. He hates all politics since Machado. My mother will be dying of anxiety."

"Which way do we go?"

"I have to talk to somebody. I know nothing. I want to see Diego."

"Diego can't help you. What about Max? He'll know what's happening."

"Max knows nothing I want to know. But I can use his telephone, yes, good. I so want to go to Diego."

Renata wanted to love a dead man. The living man next to her would not do. She needed love that was no longer available and she needed it now. Maybe they could find a dead man somewhere. There were many in Havana today. It impressed him that she was broiling at organ central, a woman questing to love death. If I take her to the morgue she will fall on the corpse. Usually you don't need to die to get laid in Cuba, but tonight it would help. She's from another dimension, perhaps nature itself, equally ready for life or death.

◈

In the city room Max was in his cubicle, his shirt wilted. He looked weary, and bored with whoever was on the other end of the telephone. Quinn watched him stare at Renata who was sitting at a desk in a far corner, next to a tall black man he'd seen on his first visit and who now was making up pages for the next edition. Renata was on the phone. She's close to Max and he's red hot for her and she likes it. She likes it hot. Max would, beyond hotness, also be gallant and suave with women. Quinn didn't trust him.

"We came for the news," Quinn said when Max ended his call. "Renata can't live without the small detail of what's happening. She's obsessed with knowing who's dead. I think somebody from the museum may have been killed."

"How did you hook up with her today?"

"I saved her from solitude after the attack."

"You move as fast as a sex tourist."

"Havana accelerates the blood."

Max preened and said he'd had a ten-minute exclusive interview with Batista after the attack, a bit of a scoop.

"What's exclusive in it?" Quinn asked.

"Nothing except he said it in English."

Batista had whetted Max's appetite for an interview with Castro. "I don't think he's dead and I don't think Batista thinks so either. He's sure the army's going to deliver his corpse. You want to try for an interview? Matthews' story in the *Times* opened him up but there's a lot more to get."

"Why me?" Quinn asked.

"You're on a roll. You go someplace and things happen. Is it always like this with you?"

"I try to keep the status quo at arm's length."

"I have a Santiago contact who may or may not get you started. But he can pass the word and then it's all whether they trust you. Fidel will trust an American newsman before a Cuban. Some Cuban newspapers are with Batista and the rest are monitored by censors."

"Not this one?"

"We are sometimes independent. You're from the *Herald* and you're a *Time* stringer, no? Those are definite pluses."

"Assistant stringer."

"But you did make the connection to *Time*."

"They didn't pay me yet and I didn't write anything for them yet. Otherwise it's a deal."

Renata came weeping to Max's office, blotting her tears.

"My friend's entire family was arrested," she said. "Seven people."

"Everybody was arrested today," Max said. "Anybody who wasn't will be arrested tomorrow. They're leaving bodies all over Havana, one hanging from a tree. Anybody linked to the Directorio is a target. A dozen attackers were students and they found some of their guns in an apartment near the University."

"Did all the attackers die?" Renata asked.

"Two or three got away, so the army says. You know any?"

"I may, but I don't know who was killed."

"We have a few names," he said, and he pushed a paper with six names on it toward Renata. "They're compiling the full list. We'll get it. What can I do to help?"

"Nothing." She was almost weeping again.

"I can take you to dinner, with your friend here, if you like. We can even pick up your parents."

"I couldn't eat," she said.

"Eating goes with grief," Max said. "You always have lunch after a funeral, then think of the Last Supper."

Renata smiled a very small and silent thank you but no, and stood up.

"I'll call you tomorrow," Max said.

"I may go away," she said.

"I'm here whenever you need me."

◈

In the car she said, "My friend said to stay away from the *necrocomio.*"

"Good. You should," Quinn said.

"And he says I shouldn't go to Diego's funeral. Diego had two children. He never mentioned them. My friend doesn't want me connected to anybody in the attack. He thinks I should go away until things calm down. I want to go to a *babalawo.* Do you know about the *babalawo*?"

"No."

"A wise man who reads the language of the soul. Narciso Figueroa. He's over ninety. He will know how my soul is damaged and will help me."

"You believe this?"

"The *babalawo* has visions. Do you ever have visions?"

"Not since grammar school when I saw myself playing the banjo in heaven. When I got older I gave up on heaven, also the banjo. I don't trust religion anymore."

"Then you don't trust me."

"You're a mysterious being."

"I'm a simple woman. The world is complex and Narciso is brilliant. He talks with the dead and with the gods. He has saved people."

"You really think he talks to the gods?"

"I do."

"I'd like to see him do that."

"Come with me."

"Where is this Narciso?"

"El Rincón, a very poor place. We will go in the morning."

"The morning? Where are you going to spend the night?"

"At your apartment. Is that all right?"

"Let me think about it."

"Yes, you should."

"I'll lend you a shirt to wear to bed."

"That will add to your laundry bill."

"Some laundry is more important than other laundry."

"I will sleep with you but we will not do anything together."

"Of course not. Not on the first date in bed."

"Do you love me?"

"More than I love guns."

"Sex is not love."

"It's something like love. Having sex is often called making love. Will you wear my shirt?"

"Yes. But we will only sleep. I must think of Diego."

"Who?"

"And I should get my beads at my house."

"Tonight?"

"In the morning."

"What if the police are there?"

"I will go in the back way."

"The police sometimes know about back doors. If they arrest you I'll lose you for a string of beads. What beads are you talking about?"

"My Changó and my Oshun beads."

"Changó. Right. The guy whose wife had no food so she fed him her ear for dinner and he killed her for it."

"Changó is a warrior who helps people in trouble. I am in trouble."

"His wife was in trouble with only one ear."

"I am in more trouble than that."

"I suppose you are. I think I am too."

"You will be in trouble as long as you are with me."

"Then that's that. I'll always be in trouble."

In her family's eyes Renata still lived as she had been raised, a strict Catholic who went to mass and communion. But in childhood she was introduced to Santeria by Olguita, a mulata who was first the housemaid, later Renata's nana and, through enduring closeness, her spiritual god-mother. Renata listened when Olguita talked about Santeria. She gave the child Renata holy artifacts which Renata the young woman added to in abundance—statues, flowers, herbs, amulets that fended off maleficent forces, paintings of the Orishas, necklaces and bracelets with the colored beads of each Orisha—so many objects that they filled a dresser drawer and covered two walls of her bedroom.

When she began studying art she filled another wall with her own paintings of the Orishas, and came to prefer their mystical lives and mir-acles to Jesus and the assorted Holy Ghosts, and those ascetic virgins who keep finding the Blessed Mother in a French meadow. The Catholic saints and their divinely nebulous arguments toward redemption offered some mystery, but they bored her. The Orishas' mysteries arose from jealousy, disgust, pride, womanizing, love, hatred, inability to keep a secret, their powers were earthly and practical, and their miracles embraced life.

Renata called a close friend and asked her to tell Renata's mother in person that she was well but wouldn't be home tonight, that she would stay at a friend's house and they would talk tomorrow. Then Renata, clad only in *pantaletas* and Quinn's short-sleeved blue shirt, which she left unbuttoned, it was hot, came to Quinn's bed and let herself be held in his uninvasive embrace. She sobbed openly over Diego, retelling herself that he truly was dead and she would never again feel his arms around her as she now felt a stranger's arms, offering comfort and perhaps love. She closed her eyes against this uninvited truth and as she burrowed toward sleep she was invaded by a vision of the violent struggle between Changó's women: Obba, his wife, who cut off her ear because Oshun told her this would win Changó's heart, and Oshun, the duplicitous Venus who controls love, money, and the river.

Renata saw them dueling with thunderbolts and herself as both wife and mistress, traitor and betrayed—very fickle of you to admit this, Renata—but she sensed, perhaps for the first time, that this was the true way of the world. She understood it better in the morning when she awoke without tears, Quinn's head on the pillow, his eyes on her, his arm comfortably under her shoulder blades. His fingers were curled lightly on her upper arm and she thought, he is protecting me from my dreams. "It's a comfort the way you hold me," she said. "You know how to hold a woman. Have you had many loves?"

"Not when it was really love. Half a dozen? Make that two. Three. One felt like love but it was only narcissism. Serious love did arrive, but it went away."

"Where is she now?"

"We don't stay in touch."

"What happened?"

"She belongs to my cousin. He's a lunatic, but that's no excuse."

"You are guilty."

"Is that out of fashion?"

"Love is the fashion. Nothing else matters."

"Very reckless. You will do damage."

"Love damaged me. I never feel guilty. I believe love will save us. I learned that through San Lázaro. We will see him today."

They were half an hour out of Havana, Quinn driving, en route to the home of Narciso Figueroa. They had gone through Santiago de Las Vegas and were on a ragged road that Quinn feared would snag the Buick's low-slung undercarriage. He moved slowly past scattered clusters of wooden shacks and small concrete slab houses that seemed built in a swamp.

"I came here when I was fifteen," she said. "It was in December, tens of thousands of pilgrims walking to the church of San Lázaro. Olguita said San Lázaro will get rid of your trouble. I told her I didn't have any trouble. 'You will,' she said."

"You certainly learned how to acquire it."

San Lázaro, Renata said, the Catholic saint resurrected from his tomb by Jesus, is also the Orisha called Babalu Aye, brother of Changó. Babalu Aye was young and handsome and trying to make love to every woman in the world. Olodumare, the owner of Heaven, told him to slow down, but he kept it up, so Olodumare turned him into a leprous beggar with leg sores that put him on crutches. Two dogs followed him, licking his sores clean as they all walked the world.

"There he is," Renata said, interrupting herself to point out a shack with an altar displaying Lázaro-Babalu on crutches. They passed another shack, another Lázaro. "He is all over Havana, but this is his road."

"How did Lázaro convince you love would save you?" he asked.

"Olguita walked me three miles to the church with the pilgrims, some on crutches like Lázaro. One barefoot man carried a sack of rocks on his back, women crawled on hands and knees, a girl no more than six moved forward on the gravel road, on her bottom, her mother saying, '*Ven, mi hija, ven*,' and the child slid toward Mama, leaving blood on the gravel.

"'Why is she making her do that?' I asked. 'For the child's health, she is sick,' Olguita said. 'Won't she get sicker from her bleeding?' 'San Lázaro will heal her all over,' Olguita said.

"I saw a man without a shirt sliding toward the church on his back, gripping a holy rag, one ankle chained to a concrete block. When he slid backward his leg pulled the block a few inches, and he had miles to go. His back looked raw and very scarred from years of this and when I asked why he did it he looked at the sky and said, 'My wife is alive, San Lázaro, and you did it, twenty years ago. I promised you I would wound myself if you saved her, and you did. I love you, beggar man.' He cried terribly, and then shouted to the sky, 'San Lázaro will never die.'"

"And this is what you call love?" Quinn said.

"Cure my legs, Babalu. Don't let my child die, Lázaro. Give a brain to my idiot son. Bring my wife back from the grave. Let me see daylight again. Cure my pox, my pain, my sores, my terror, my cancer, my nightmares. Give me back my breath, Babalu. Let me walk the world like you, Lázaro. Love will save us and remake us. Love will do what parents and doctors and spouses cannot do. Love will do it all if you take it into your soul and caress it. I wonder if I had true love with Diego. I look at you and think maybe we will have love, but maybe we are liars and neither of us knows love. In the church I asked San Lázaro how love lived in the heart of that man pulling the concrete block and he told me."

"San Lázaro talked to you?"

"Yes. He said, your love can be the beggar on crutches with the dogs of love trying to heal your sickness, and still you will perish. Nobody can know what love means, or how it arrives or how it lasts, or even if it exists, because we are never free of doubt. Since I was fifteen I have practiced love and I am good at it. I create love by making it, by believing in it even when it doesn't exist. Love can make love exist, but love cannot make itself last. All I can do is try to make love exist, and sometimes I succeed. That's what I do."

Narciso lived in the smallest house Quinn had seen on this road. Renata entered without knocking and Quinn followed her into a room with paintings of godly abstractions, masks, necklaces made with the Orishas' colored beads, jars of kola nuts, cowrie shells, coconut fragments, icons dangling from the ceiling. Shelves were full of trinkets, cigar stubs and bits of paper that Quinn decided must be venerable trash. The room exuded ancient complexity, urging him to bow before its absurd mysteries.

Narciso, with an unlit cigar at the corner of his mouth, made an effort to rise from his wooden rocking chair and failed. He tried again, pulled himself into a standing crouch, shuffled with baby steps and trembling arms to greet Renata. His skin was a deep black, his hair tight to his head and totally white, most of his teeth absent, and he did indeed look ninety, or beyond. He glanced at Quinn and then said to Renata, "Who is this? He is carrying fire."

Then, with sudden agility unimaginable in that worn body, he straightened his back and lifted over his head one of six necklaces he was wearing. He waved it in front of Renata and dropped it onto a table. The necklace was four feet in circumference and strung with sixteen oval-shaped, tortoise-shell disks.

"The fire," he said, pointing to the disks.

"What are you saying?" Renata asked. "This is my friend, a writer. I wanted him to see San Lázaro."

"He is a carrier," Narciso said, and he spoke to Renata in a chant:

"He is carrying fire and fire does burn,
He is bearing fire and the ashes it makes,
The dead surround and claim him as their own,
He wears the dead like the beads of Changó."

Renata's face was blank and pale, but Quinn read her blankness as cogency, concealed under a mask of innocence. *She* was the carrier of the dead, all those dying rebels in the forefront of her memory. She was shamming for Narciso, passing her dead on to Quinn. He watched Narciso reading Renata, and he sensed the man really *might* be reading the thought of another, which Quinn did not want to believe. But it has been done, hasn't it? Telepathy isn't quite so disreputable anymore. Somebody might legitimize it any minute.

"What have you been doing?" Narciso asked Renata.

"Nothing at all," she said, "nothing."

Narciso threw the shells again and spoke in a language Quinn did not understand. Renata translated: "He says you are in danger and that you must avoid the murderers walking the streets."

"Convey my thanks and say I'll be cautious," Quinn said. "Does he know which streets?"

"I give you this necklace as a shield," Narciso said to Renata. He took from around his neck a silvery chain with miniature cast-iron tools and weapons—hammer, anvil, pick and shovel, bow and arrow, machete, two-bladed axe—and circled it around Renata's neck. "Show these tools of the Orishas to your enemy and tell him if he harms you Changó will plunge him into a long and painful death."

"Changó will help and we will fight," Renata said in the rhythm of Narciso's fire chant:

"Changó will protect me
And we will fire the days."

"Changó is listening," Narciso said.

"My friend needs Changó's help," Renata said. "I would give him my beads but I cannot get to where they are. Can you give Changó to my friend?"

Narciso stared at Quinn, who saw himself being scrutinized as a skeptic. Does Changó help skeptics? Why help you if you don't believe in him? Narciso took another necklace of small red and white beads from around his neck, put them on Quinn and said, "He wears the dead like the beads of Changó." Then with abrupt finality he waved them toward the door and shuffled back to his chair.

❖

So the theme for today will continue to be the dead, not enough of them yet. When Quinn decided to come to Cuba and write about revolution in two centuries he accepted the likelihood of corpses, but at a distance; not in the air around him, not as mental transients. Renata was flummoxed not by death but by the death of what she thought was love. Fair enough. Quinn would not face such loss unless the relationship he was creating with her melted into sorrowful time. She is driven to track what was lost, follow where it leads; and Quinn silently signed on for the ride.

"You're the one who wears the dead like Changó's beads," he said to her. "You sent me images of those corpses at the Palace and Narciso saw them, which I consider a boffo performance. I may have to start believing in something."

"He says to get rid of the dead. I can't."

"They'll leave when they're ready."

"I don't want them to go. They're with me for a reason."

At a *farmacia* she called her mother who told her everybody was in nervous collapse because of her, her father was furious and hoped it had nothing to do with politics, the police wanted her to call them, and someone called twice but left only a number. Renata took the number and said, I am all right, Mama, and I will be home soon and I do not want to see the police because Changó told me this was not a good week for seeing police.

She called the number and recognized Aurelio and he said they must find Felipe Holtz and he knew how close Renata and Felipe were. Holtz, son of sugar baron Julio Holtz, was involved in a gun deal for the Directorio but it was aborted the day of the Palace attack. Holtz is the only one who knows the gun dealer and Aurelio has no one else to send, for all who survived the Palace are known, and traitors are riding with police looking for us all. Could Renata track down Holtz? Renata said she would.

"Why are you telling me all this?" Quinn asked. "They might kill you for revealing so much, and kill me for knowing it."

"They will not kill you unless I tell them to."

"Well that's a comfort."

She called the Holtz home in Santiago and talked to Natalia, her cousin, who said Felipe was in Mexico or Caracas, expected home next week. Renata didn't believe her.

"If your friends are in such a hurry," Quinn said, "I know somebody who might help."

"You know somebody with guns?"

"I told you I was writing about that in Miami."

"Who is this person?"

"Alfie Rivero. You ever hear of him?"

"Never. Can he be American intelligence?"

"Anybody can be American intelligence. Alfie's Cuban from New York with a tie to the Trafficante mob in Tampa, which means he can get you any gun you can pay for. I dated his cousin and I met him with her. He's the real thing."

"Is he in Miami?"

"I saw him at the Nacional two days ago. He's staying there."

"He will talk to you about guns? He trusts you?"

"He won't trust me, but I can ask a question for you. I wouldn't do it for anyone else."

"Will he take a woman seriously?"

"You're an unlikely buyer, but you seem trustworthy. If you aren't then you're a brilliant actress and a serious liar. But don't even think about lying to Alfie."

Quinn drove to El Vedado where the Hotel Nacional had been standing in its eminence since it opened in 1930. It was one of the elite addresses in Havana and the walls of its bar were covered with photomontages of celebrated guests—Churchill, the Windsors, Spanish royalty, Chaplin, Garbo, Gable, John Wayne. Since 1946, when Batista returned to Havana from Florida with Meyer Lansky in tow, Havana and its major hotel had become mob-hospitable, and Lansky and his brother Jake now ran its casino, which was probably Alfie's reason for staying there.

Quinn and Renata crossed the marble lobby under lofty ceilings and chandeliers and Renata said, "My father was shot here in 1933 in the civil war—after Machado's exile. Many Americans in Havana took refuge here from anti-American mobs, and a thousand army officers retreated here to protest Batista taking over the army. Batista shelled the hotel all day and many officers died. When they surrendered many more were killed by mobs for being with Machado. My father was shot in the chest but did not die. Batista sent him to prison in the Castillo del Principe and for a week my mother thought he was dead."

"Revolution haunts your family. I see where you get it," Quinn said.

"My father would have a stroke if he knew what I was doing here."

They went to the patio garden with its sculpted shrubbery and its long and beautiful lawn that rolled down toward the water. They took a table and watched two peacocks move imperially under the palms near the bottom of the garden. Beyond that you looked out at the Malecón, and then the sea.

"Order me a rum on ice. I'll see if Alfie is around."

Quinn knew from Alfie's rap sheet that he'd been arrested twice on burglary charges that didn't stick and had done ten months for a botched dope robbery. He had no convictions after that and when Quinn met him he heard his name linked to an armed excursion by two dozen young Cuban rebels full of invasion bravado who one day disappeared from Miami and turned up on Havana's front pages, faces and chests caked with blood, eyes wide or shot away, lying alongside their rifles on a rocky beach like a fisherman's catch, Batista's catch.

Quinn found Alfie at the pool with a long-legged middle-aged blonde, *his* catch of the day, who was rubbing suntan oil on his deeply tanned back and shoulders. Quinn sent a note with a waiter and Alfie came over.

"A business matter, Alfie. You still selling avocados?"

"In season."

"I'm not the one talking here, I'm just a writer."

"You write about avocados."

"Don't trust me."

"When did I ever trust you?"

"I have somebody who wants to talk."

"I sometimes talk to people who talk."

"Do we go someplace?"

"We are someplace. Where's your man?"

"My man is a woman, out in the patio."

"Bring her in. Has she got money?"

"I think so. And she's in a hurry."

"I'll talk with her in the pool."

"She doesn't have a bathing suit."

"Buy her one."

Quinn went back to the patio but Renata was not at the table. Their drinks were there, untouched. She was not in the garden that the peacocks ruled. He found a waiter who had not seen her, took a swallow of his rum and left money for the drinks. She wasn't in the lobby or by the public phones. At the front desk he asked about messages. None. He saw her coming from the far end of the lobby carrying a paper bag. She had followed him out to the pool and had seen him with Alfie. She read their lips about the bathing suit so she bought one at the boutique.

"Narciso reads minds and you read lips," Quinn said. "There's no privacy in Cuba."

They went to the pool bar and Renata changed into her new suit, dove into the pool, and swam like a dolphin before pausing in neck-deep water. Alfie stepped into the shallow end and swam on his back until he bumped into her. They then discussed avocados.

❖

A panel truck with two young men pulled into the driveway of Garage Miami in Miramar and parked in front of one of the two bays. A few yards back from the two gas pumps Alfie's blonde from the swimming pool was sitting in a folding chair alongside a pile of tires, her elegant legs crossed, a streetside attraction. Quinn did not think she belonged in a garage. The garage sign advertised PLANTA DE ENGRASE, SE COGEN PONCHES, ABIERTO 24 HORAS. Esme's Buick was parked in one bay and a pickup truck full of toys, lamps, and pots was on the runners of the grease pit's lift. The two young men in suitcoats came through the open garage door and Renata introduced the older one to Alfie as her friend Pedrito.

"And who is *his* friend?" Alfie said.

"My name is Javier," the friend said. "I am buying your guns."

"Pedrito is buying them, no?"

"We are buying them together. We are friends," Javier said. "Who is this?" And he gestured with his head toward Quinn.

"He's the one who started this," Alfie said. "He came to me. You don't trust your own contact?"

"I am grateful for the contact but I don't know him."

"This is Quinn," Renata said. "He is my friend, and he helped me and I trust him. You don't worry about him."

"I worry," Javier said.

"I would like to see *las cosas*," Pedrito said.

"I would like to see the money," said Alfie.

Pedrito took a fold of cash from his pocket and fanned it.

"Where do you want to make the transfer?" Alfie asked.

"Are you making a joke?" Pedrito said. "Where are they?"

"We can unload wherever you want."

Javier walked outside and looked up and down the street.

"We can do it here," he said. "There is little traffic. Take these vehicles out, we will pull in, then you bring in the guns."

"I don't bring them in," Alfie said. He lowered the tailgate of the pickup revealing three wooden boxes with toys, pots, rugs. He lifted off a pot and a rug and guns were visible. "Open your truck's back doors, I'll load them in."

"You want to load guns on the street?" Pedrito said.

"Load guns on the street?" Alfie said. "Who would do such a thing? We are moving pots and toys."

"You are very smart or very stupid," Javier said.

"Yes. I never know which."

"He is crazy, but smart," Pedrito said. "Do it."

Pedrito counted out four thousand dollars for Alfie as Javier climbed into Alfie's truck. He picked up an automatic rifle, removed the magazine. "Thompson," he said, "nice," and he snapped the magazine back in place, removed it.

"If you want to check every weapon," Alfie said, "we can go down to the beach, fire them all to see if they work."

Javier smiled at the maniac, then picked up a .45 caliber Spanish machine pistol and snapped in a loaded clip and put it in his belt under his coat.

"Open your truck," Alfie said and he lifted the box with dolls from his pickup and carried it to the panel truck. He slid it into the back and came in and said to Quinn, "I need a hand with the big one."

Quinn lifted one end of the box that was topped with a large model airplane and carried it out with Alfie. Javier monitored the loading while Pedrito talked quietly to Renata. Alfie loaded the third box alone and closed the truck doors. A car pulled up to a gas pump and the driver spoke to the blonde, who pumped gas for him while Pedrito and Javier pulled away in their truck. The blonde came into the garage and put money in the register. Quinn saw a triangle and five numbers tattooed on her left forearm.

"That Pedrito," she said to Alfie. "He is Aurelio from the Directorio. He was with Holtz when Gustavo and I met them on the dock."

"Did he recognize you?"

"I doubt it. Gustavo and Holtz did the talking. I sat in the car."

Alfie looked at Renata. "You're with the Directorio," he said.

"I have nothing to do with it," she said.

"Your friend Pedrito-Aurelio doesn't know he just bought the guns I brought in for him. He and his friend Holtz made the deal with my partner but they never came to get them. You don't know Holtz either."

"I know nobody named Holtz. I know Pedrito from the university. I did this as a personal favor to him."

"Aurelio paid too much," Alfie said. "Our price to Holtz was thirty-five hundred, not four thousand." He took out his cash and held out five hundred to Renata. "Give this to Aurelio."

"Why should I take this?"

"Aurelio will be angry they overpaid. You can do him another favor."

Renata put the money in her brassiere. "I will see if Pedrito takes this. If he doesn't, I'll return it. He will be grateful if it is as you say."

"The Directorio people are mostly dead," the blonde said. "That Aurelio now has more guns than people to use them."

"I don't know anything about the Directorio," Renata said.

"You should listen to the radio," said the blonde. "They are mostly dead."

"We should go," Renata said to Quinn.

"I want to take you both to dinner," Alfie said. "This was a good day for business."

"I'm sorry," Renata said. "I have to go." She got into the Buick.

"Dinner is a fine idea," Quinn said to Alfie. "Where do you want to go?"

"The Montmartre. The owner is a friend of mine. Their steaks are as good as the floor show."

"I'll talk to her," Quinn said, and in the Buick he said to Renata, "We have to let him thank us, and I want to know more about him. He's unusual."

"He is a gangster."

"Some gangsters are unusual. It's the Montmartre. They have good steaks. I told you not to lie to him. He knows who Pedrito is and you even took the money. I thought you were a good liar. You're a terrible liar."

"He knows I'm lying. He also knows I did not betray the Directorio. Are you so stupid?"

Quinn considered this. "It's possible I'm stupid," he said.

57

"I think Inez is a whore," Renata said. "She has the whore's manner, the coldness."

"You can't know that about her."

"I don't like what she said about the Directorio."

"She may be conditioned to be cold. Did you see that tattoo on her arm?"

"Yes."

"The Nazis did that to Jews."

"I never saw one before."

He backed the car out. Alfie carried the tires inside and locked the garage and Inez padlocked the gas pumps. Then they got into the backseat.

"So we're on for the Montmartre, you're both my guests. And we'll take Inez, who works in the casino there."

"That's fine," Quinn said. "Isn't that fine, Renata?"

"Yes, it's fine."

"Inez used to be a dancer," Alfie said. "She danced all over Spain and France in the war years."

"And in Havana," Inez said.

"Where in Havana?" Renata asked.

"Many places. The Sevilla-Biltmore, the Savoy, the Sans Souci. I was very young."

"The Sans Souci—I went often when my sister sang there," Renata said. "The dancers in those places always became whores. Customers offered them so much money."

"Is that what happened to you?" Inez asked.

"I was not a dancer," Renata said, "I would never take money for that."

"You only do it for love," Inez said.

"Exactly. Do you know the owner, Trafficante?"

"I do."

"My sister is a good friend of his."

"He is a generous man."

"We're going to the Montmartre, not the Sans Souci," Alfie said. "Lansky owns the Montmartre casino."

"I cannot like him," Renata said. "I dislike his eyes."

"He's a sweetheart," Alfie said.

"Who do you think that Javier is?" Quinn asked. "I think he's with Fidel."

"You may be right," Alfie said.

"I would love to work with Fidel," Renata said.

"I'm going to try for an interview with him," Quinn said.

"*The New York Times* just did that," Alfie said.

"Fidel can't have too many interviews. Batista's army kills him every day in the papers. He has to keep proving he's still alive."

"Everybody wants Fidel," Inez said.

"He's got momentum," Quinn said.

"He's the only game in town," Alfie said.

"Maybe you should move your store to Santiago," Quinn said to Alfie.

"Why didn't I think of that?"

"I am going to Santiago," Renata said. "Definitely. I've said it before but now I'm going to do it. I am."

"I'll do the driving," Quinn said. "Can we keep this car?"

The Montmartre was at O and Twenty-fifth and they dropped Inez at the door on Twenty-fifth that led directly up to the second-floor casino. After she was out of the car Quinn said, "She has a Nazi tattoo."

"She was in a camp," Alfie said. "Worked with her father in French nightclubs until someone betrayed them as Jews. She weighed seventy pounds when I met her in Europe after the liberation. She wanted to go to New York but they wouldn't let her in—Commie Jew. Then Trafficante gave her a job down here."

"Why did he do that?"

"I asked him to," Alfie said.

"I owe her an apology," Renata said. "I thought she was a whore."

"She was a whore. Her father pimped for her. Then they used her that way in the camp. She was gorgeous. Her father died in the camp and when she got well she survived as a whore. She couldn't dance anymore. They ruined her knees."

"Is she still a whore?"

"Yes," Alfie said, "but only for me."

❖

When Renata said she would not go to dinner in the tour guide's blouse and skirt she'd been wearing for two days, Alfie went into the club to arrange for the table and Quinn dropped Renata at a fashion boutique on Twenty-first Street that specialized in Paris imports. He felt obligated to call Max at the newspaper and find out what part of Cuba was erupting in blood, and should he be covering the spatter?

"Cooney's looking for you," Max said. "He called twice and then came in person and left you a letter. And Hemingway called you. Big day for you and Hemingway. Cooney's challenging him to a duel and wants you to set it up."

"A duel? Really? Rapiers or flintlocks?"

"That's up to Hemingway."

"Did Hemingway mention the duel?"

"He didn't even mention his name. He just asked for you and hung up. I recognized his voice. Cooney's letter is short. 'Dear Mr. Quinn, you're a friend of that bum Hemingway. Tell him I think he's a bum and I challenge him to a duel, any kind of gun or whatever he likes, I ain't particular. I'm not kidding here. I'm taking this public. You can write the story but if you don't want to I'll get somebody else. He's a bum to hit me like he did and I want everybody to know what a cheap coward trick it was. He's a bum and a cheap coward. I hear he's a good shot but so am I. Tell him to wear his soldier medals. I'll be wearing mine. Yours truly, Joseph X. Cooney.'"

"Good letter," Quinn said. "We can sell tickets."

"You know how to reach Hemingway?"

"Hang around the Floridita."

"I'll draw you a map to his house. Out near San Francisco de Paula. You should tell him in person."

"You mean now he's a story?"

"Dog shoots man. I'll print that."

"Get me his phone number."

"Have you seen Renata?"

"We eloped last night."

"Have you been sucking on the rum bottle?"

"That's my next assignment."

"How is she?"

"She's shopping for the honeymoon."

Max drew a long breath. "Are you up for this story or are you piped?"

"Get me his phone."

"Dial oh-five and ask the operator for five-four-four. The phone is listed under José C. Alemán."

"I'll let you know what he says tomorrow."

"Call him tonight."

"Would you interrupt your honeymoon to talk to a writer?"

Another long breath. "How is she?"

"Erratic but it doesn't interfere with her sensuality."

"You better do right by that girl."

"You can't believe how hard I'm trying."

Renata emerged from the store transformed into a denizen of the beau monde, stunning in a white off-the-shoulder sheath, white high-heeled pumps, white earrings and white sunglasses, blond hair upswept, and the necklace of the Orishas stylishly pendant on her bosom. She also carried a new suitcase that promised additional transformations.

"*Guapísima*," Quinn said. "I don't recognize you. Gorgeous."

"I am never the same, even when I am not somebody else."

"I think I may have to memorize that. You're a blonde."

"It's a wig."

"It's a good one. I thought you had gotten it bleached."

"Now we must get you a necktie."

Newly garbed, they rode the elevator to the Montmartre's second floor and stepped into a foyer of full-length mirrors, the vitalizing rhythm of a mambo drifting in from the nightclub on the right, and the clicks and bells of slot machines on the left beckoning arrivals toward the roulette and blackjack tables in the casino beyond. Renata took Quinn's arm as they went into the nightclub, which shimmered in black and chrome, its mauve curtains billowing on the elevated stage, its tables filling up. When Quinn pointed to Alfie at a center table two tiers up from ringside, the maître d' led them to him. Before they were seated Alfie had a waiter filling their champagne glasses.

"Hey-soos Maria," Alfie said as the newly designed Renata sat down; and his eyes said the rest. Another scalp in her saddlebag.

"Good table," Quinn said, changing the subject.

"They know me. The place will be packed by eight and it stays that way till four a.m."

"I always liked this club," Renata said. "I'm sure I sat at this table when my sister sang here."

The lights and the piped-in mambo went down abruptly and a voice boomed through the speakers, *"Damas y caballeros,* ladies and gentlemen, *el club Montmartre presenta la Orquestra de Bebo Valdés!"* Billowing curtains receded, twenty musicians on stage erupted with a magnified mambo that was quickly joined by twenty mulata dancers moving to the feverish beat with their feathers, flounces, ruffles, spangles and vast expanses of flesh, and the pulse of nighttime Havana skipped a syncopated beat.

Quinn was still finding it difficult to realize that he was actually a player in this manic culture—across the table from him a woman of hyperventilating beauty with rebellion running in her veins, and a loner hoodlum who peddles tools of psychotic vengeance to suicidal rebels. Keeping with this improbable beat he told them about Cooney's challenge to Hemingway.

"Viva Cooney," Renata said. "I'm on his team."

"I've read Hemingway," Alfie said. "He knows guns. Cooney's in trouble."

"Would you really arrange it?" Renata asked.

"Why would Hemingway even consider this? And why involve me? He's got a brigade of acolytes. But if he really does ask me to arrange the duel of the century, I'll do it, and put you both on the weapons committee."

"You should set it up in Madison Square Garden," Alfie said.

"Cooney's not a contender," Quinn said.

The steaks arrived and at mid-meal the headwaiter came over to Alfie to whisper the buzz in the room—Colonel Fermín Quesada had arrived in the casino fifteen minutes ago. Quesada, the army commander in the city of Holguín, the latest of Batista's avengers, had become the most hated figure in Cuba to the rebels. Alfie passed the news of his presence to Renata and Quinn on the chance they would consider it a threat. Quinn and Alfie agreed they had done a bit of gun handling, but who knew that? Quinn looked at Renata in her new whites. Did she look like a quarry of the army or police? With that wig she didn't even look like she looked yesterday. Renata said she was fine; they all felt remote from official scrutiny.

"I don't have sides in this revolution," Alfie said, "but that puke of a man, I could empty a pistol into his face right here. Last Christmas Eve everybody in Cuba is with the family, right? *Noche Buena*. And he arrests twenty-five men, one with seven kids, Twenty-sixth of July people mostly. A union leader, one from Prío's party, young guys, couple of commies. The soldiers are friendly, just come with us for a few questions, and they take them out of the houses and on the road they break their ribs, strangle them, hang them, shoot them, dump them. Two sons of my cousin Arsenio, an old outlaw who helped Fidel from the beginning, the army wouldn't tell him anything. Then a taxi driver tells him they found two bodies. They'd cut half the face off one of his sons. The other son they machine-gunned his crotch. Somebody heard a lieutenant say, 'He won't fuck anymore.' I'm looking for that lieutenant."

Noche Buena stopped revolutionary activity in Holguín for weeks, and overnight Quesada was the army's exemplar of Cuban peace through death. The army promoted him to colonel, Batista gave him a dinner at the Palace, and suddenly he was a candidate to lead the battle against Fidel in the Sierra. Now here he is playing roulette with the commander of Cuban intelligence.

Quinn saw Inez coming along the aisle toward them, in heels and a dark blue dress, her hair in a tight coif, a new image, not glamorous, but smart and sleek, befitting a casino hostess. She smiled at them all and said through her teeth, "Get out of the club now. Right now. Something is happening. Go. Go."

And so the three stood and walked casually out of the nightclub and Quinn pressed the elevator button in the foyer where two men in suits and neckties, one of them Javier from the garage, were playing slot machines. Javier saw them and turned his back, dropped a coin into the slot, and pulled the handle. As the elevator door opened, the slot machine rang its bell and delivered a rattle of coins which Javier made no move to retrieve. He popped another coin. Then the elevator door closed on the trio.

Did five minutes pass? Ten?

They were in the Buick when Colonel Quesada and Lieutenant Colonel López from the SIM, with his aide Captain Godoy, and their three wives, the men in civilian clothes, the wives in dinner gowns, entered the foyer from the casino. As the captain summoned the elevator, Javier and his comrade took machine pistols from under their suit coats and shot Quesada first, then López, also hitting both women who, in terrorized flight, collided with their own mirror images and slumped. One bullet grazed the necktie of the captain, who snatched the pistol from López's shoulder holster and fired at the shooters. But by then they were out of sight, on the run toward the casino's rear exit onto Calle 25.

When they reached the Nacional Alfie called Inez to find out what Javier and his comrade had wrought. It was chaos: López and the women wounded, Colonel Quesada executed with such extreme suddenness that he did not yet know he was dead.

At the hotel bar Alfie toasted Javier with daiquiris and Renata recapitulated the killing—carried out by Javier of the 26th but with guns from the Directorio—a refreshed alliance of the groups that had been working for the same cause, warily independent of each other. If the Directorio had killed Batista, Fidel would now be irrelevant. At the garage Aurelio had said the guns he was buying would go mostly to Fidel, a gift from the Directorio in exile. Renata had asked him then, "What of all the guns Diego and I put in the Sixteenth Street apartment?"

"Still there, but we have nobody to get them."

Renata remembered how Alfie's mouth had tightened with functional hatred when he said he would shoot Quesada in the face. Alfie was a crazy one, and he might help us bring out the guns. She would find money somewhere to pay him. She would give the guns to Fidel as another gift. Yes, Alfie would do this and Quinn would help. They would all talk about it. There was a bond among the three of them. Quinn did not seem afraid. They left the hotel and she watched him as he drove, memorizing his face.

"You must find a place to stop, out of the light," she said.

"Are you all right? Are you ill?"

"No, just stop."

Quinn parked on a dark street and looked at her staring at him. She leaned toward him.

"Love me, Quinn," she said.

"I will," he said, "I do."

Then, with their first touch of love since they'd met, he embraced and kissed her, and she crawled inside him.

"Love me," she said.

"I will. I will love you. I love, I love Renata."

"Love me, *lléname,* fill me."

"Yes," he said, "I can do that."

Struck by the brilliant light of the enabling moon, Quinn spiraled everything he knew about love into the center of this divine woman. At this sudden onset of joy he heard Narciso chanting:

"The dead surround him and claim him as their own.
He wears the dead like the beads of Changó."

Quinn received the music and his pulse skipped a syncopated beat.

At Quinn's apartment they stopped making love at three in the morning, not because they were finished, they were only beginning; but it came to Quinn that if Renata really did want to go home for her own Changó beads and to see her parents, this was the time. Checking out the home of a museum guide who knew a dead rebel would be low priority on the night the police and the army were out in major numbers tracking the two killers of Fermín Quesada. Renata said Quinn's suggestion was perfect and they would not even have to park near her house. They could park on the next street and keep hidden by tall bougainvillea the whole length of her garden, and go in through the French doors to the house.

From the bougainvillea they saw no one, only the light in Renata's kitchen, and just before four o'clock they entered her home like burglars. She took Quinn to the living room and he sat alone with the light from a street lamp glinting on the crystal chandelier, the huge silver punch bowl, and large silver-framed photos he could barely see but presumed were her parents. As he gained power over the darkness he saw a painting that demanded his gaze—a full-length albino figure, faceless except for cutout eyes, embracing a black figure with a hidden face, the albino holding a fish that was grinning like a devil. The figures were overlain with strands of seaweed, and the image haunted Quinn. He remembered a similar painting in the Bellas Artes, obviously by the same artist, illuminating the grisly myth of Sikan, who was beheaded for revealing the secret of the god Tanze; and in days to come Renata would tell him the grislier tale of the painter herself, dead of suicide.

Renata had gone quietly upstairs to her mother's bed, knelt beside it and whispered "Mami," then shushed her mother and held her arm so she would not move it and wake her sleeping husband. She backed away, beckoning her mother, and they retreated to Renata's room where she delivered a capsule history of two days of death, terror, and fear of the police who wanted to interrogate her as the friend of a Palace attacker. I knew him only through his painting, Mamita, it is such a tragedy. I am all right, as you can see and I have Esme's car and I have a friend downstairs, an *americano* who helped me, and we're going to Cárdenas to stay with Tía Gabriela, but you must tell no one where I am or they will come and arrest me. I need clothes and money, Mamita, and don't tell Papa or he will be furious and think I'm in politics. But the politics are not mine; they belong to an artist I knew who is dead.

While her mother went to get money Renata pulled from under her bed the large cardboard box where she kept valuables and letters. She took out the red and white Changó beads and put them around her neck. She uncovered the three pistols she kept in the box, put two back and kept the Colt Cobra .38, which she wrapped in her underwear and put in the suitcase along with blouses, skirts, makeup, hairbrush, toiletries, and the bottle of perfume, Gardenia, that Alejo Carpentier gave her.

Her mother sat on the bed by the suitcase and handed Renata six hundred dollars in cash, all she had in the house. Renata said that's wonderful, tell Papa I love him and I will call, or maybe someone else will call and say the clock is fixed, which will mean I am all right.

"Natita," said her mother, "you are a problem child and you do not tell the truth. I won't ask what this is about for it will kill me if it is what I think it is, and kill your father before it kills me. You have a second life. One life is not enough for you. You are the strangest child and I love you for that, but be careful with your precious life and do not be crazy. Now take me down to meet your American. Is he Catholic? Does he have money?"

Quinn instantly recognized Renata in her mother's beauty, obviously a genetic gift to this family. Even in her tightly clutched silk robe she had the elegant, lustrous look of a silent movie vamp—Dolores del Rio came to mind.

"My mother, Celia," Renata said. "Mama, this is Daniel."

Quinn took Celia's fingers in his hand and kissed them and said he was incredibly happy to meet the mother of Renata, whom he valued beyond words and whom he wanted to marry as soon as possible.

"Marry?" said Celia.

"The first time he saw me he told Hemingway he would marry me," Renata said.

"Hemingway? What does he have to do with you?"

"It is a long story, no, a short story, Mamita, but I have grown fond of Daniel very quickly. He is from New York."

"And that makes everything all right?"

"I knew you would like him."

"I don't even know his full name."

"Quinn," said Quinn. "Daniel Quinn. And I really believe it's fated that I'm in Cuba and fated that I met Renata. I'm tracking my grandfather who came here in the last century to write a book about your national hero Céspedes. I read that book in high school and dreamed of coming to a place like Cuba and writing about battles and heroes and villains in a war like your Ten Years War. Now there's a war in the streets of Havana, and in the mountains of Oriente, and I'm here and I've started writing about it."

"Why do you want to write about war?"

"To tell something to myself, and to keep myself from boredom."

"Do not get my daughter into this."

"It's the last thing on my mind. I want to save her from everything."

"You are impetuous, asking to marry her so soon."

"It's the sanest judgment I've ever made."

"Daniel is a new friend but a great friend," Renata said, taking Quinn's hand. "I don't know how it happened so fast but it is very real."

"All her life she was an incredibly loving child," Celia said. "Everyone loves her."

"I'm finding that out," said Quinn.

"We have to go," Renata said. "The police may return."

"I'm sorry to leave," Quinn said. "I wanted to talk about your dancing. Renata said you won prizes."

"You want to talk about my dancing?"

"My father won prizes for his dancing. He was a prize waltzer. You were too, no?"

"I was."

"You see? Another stroke of fate—Renata and I, children of prize waltzers."

"You are as strange as my daughter. Another time we will talk about dancing. Protect this child of mine."

"With my life," said Quinn.

He remembered that his grandfather wrote about Céspedes' child—his son Oscar. The Spaniards captured Oscar in battle and threatened to kill him if Céspedes and his followers did not surrender. Céspedes told the Spaniards Oscar was not his only son, that he was the father of all Cubans who died for their country. A firing squad then executed his son.

They went to the Ali Bar, where Renata called her contact number and spoke with a voice she recognized, and said have Pedrito call me here. They drank mojitos because she always drank them here for breakfast after all-nighters.

"Beny Moré sang to me here one night," she said. "He comes all the time. Everybody comes here. Gary Cooper sat right there."

"Do you see anyone who knows you?" Quinn asked.

"Nobody would know me with my blond wig."

"I'd recognize your mouth no matter what color hair you had."

They drank their mojitos and in twenty minutes Aurelio called. Renata told him Alfie could bring out *las cosas* from the Vedado apartment because he is shrewd and fearless and she trusts him and will pay him herself to do it. Aurelio said he'd call Alfie.

"I will go see Alfie now," she said, "but you must do the rest because I'm going to Santiago."

It was dawn when they left the Ali Bar and Quinn considered calling Hemingway about the Cooney challenge. He would be up and writing. He gets up with the birds. But does he answer the phone during bird-song? So they woke up Alfie and he met them on the Nacional's patio, which was empty of people. They walked down the garden path and stood under a royal palm with their backs to the hotel and Renata told him of the guns. He said he'd think about it after he talked to Pedrito, who, she admitted, was really Aurelio. But if the police were watching that apartment it would be dangerous.

"I will give you five hundred dollars now and another five hundred when I get back from Santiago. Is that enough? We are not buying these weapons, just reclaiming them," she said.

"These are Directorio guns?"

"Yes, but they will go to Fidel now."

"Is this Fidel's money?"

"No, it is mine."

"You're the new Directorio, all by yourself?"

"I worry the police will take the guns I put there. Fidel needs them badly."

"How will you get them to Fidel?"

"Maybe by yacht, or truck, maybe airplane. A car is impossible, there are too many guns. Aurelio will figure a way. Maybe you can help him. I won't be here." She handed him five of the six hundred dollars her mother had given her.

"Keep your money," he said. "Wait till I get the guns."

"You don't behave like a gangster. Gangsters like money."

"You don't behave like a debutante. Debutantes don't know anything about money."

"Fidel will be pleased if you get him these guns."

"I think I knew that."

"We'll be staying at the Casa Granda hotel in Santiago," Quinn said. "I'm covering an army press conference about Fidel."

"Are you going into the Sierra?"

"If I'm invited."

"If you see my cousin, drop my name."

"Who's your cousin?"

"Arsenio Zamora. Quesada murdered two of his boys. He is close to Fidel."

❖

What Quinn said when he telephoned Hemingway was, "Max took a call from somebody asking for me and he thought he recognized your voice."

"Max's ear is working," Hemingway said. "There may be hope for him as a spy. I read your story about the killing of Cooney's friend."

"Cooney just missed getting it and so did I. Pretty hairy."

"I'll pick up Cooney's doctor bills. Maybe you could work that out. But don't connect me to it."

"It'll go into the archive of lost history. Actually Cooney wants to reach you. He wrote me a letter. You know about this?"

"No."

"I should give you his letter in person."

"Sounds like top secret."

"I'll meet you if you come to Havana. Or I can bring it to you."

"Does this go into your novel?"

"Chapter seven."

"I'm here, but right now I've got a funeral to go to."

"Who died?"

"My dog."

❖

Hemingway's home, Finca Vigía, was twenty minutes southeast of the Floridita, a long, formidably handsome one-story white limestone Spanish Colonial built in 1882, uphill from the town of San Francisco de Paula.

From an adjacent four-story white tower where Hemingway famously wrote and kept his cats, there is a distant view of the sea he made famous. Since he moved into the Finca in 1939 it had become a place where the grand and the great among writers, generals, movie stars, journalists, baseball players, sailors, drinkers, and women queued on the front steps to talk, swim, party, flirt with, or just shimmer in the waves of mythic glow that emanated from this maestro of the word, the hunt, the deep sea, the saloon, the bull-ring, the wars, the self. The crowd pilgrimaged to this American hero in the way Lázaro's throng of beseechers crawl on their backs to him. Renata said she'd rather stay in the Buick.

"Nonsense," Quinn said. "He'll be good to talk to. He's already sorry about Cooney. There's a whole lot more to him than you saw at the bar."

"I dislike him."

"You said that. Try again."

"I have no reason to try."

"How about his link to Santeria? He gave his Nobel medal to the Virgen del Cobre—in Santiago."

"He gave the medal to *la Virgen*? Why?"

"He didn't trust Batista and his thieves, so he gave it to the Cuban people through their patron saint."

A great and ancient ceiba tree spreading itself magnificently at the front entrance welcomed Quinn and Renata to the Finca, and a middle-aged Cuban woman opened the door and said *el señor* was on the porch. She walked them toward Hemingway, who was sitting in a wooden Adirondack chair, wearing a long sport shirt, shorts, sandals, and making notes on a pad. He stood up.

"Mr. Quinn. Señorita Suárez. I'm sorry I frightened you the other night."

"You didn't frighten me," Renata said.

"I upset you."

"You were cruel to Mr. Cooney."

"I wasn't in my best form. I apologize."

"You should apologize to Mr. Cooney."

"Did you go to your dog's funeral?" Quinn asked.

"I was the funeral," Hemingway said.

"An old dog?"

"Not so old, still full of hell. Black Dog. One of Batista's goons bashed in his head with a rifle butt. They were chasing a rebel they thought had guns hidden near my pool. Black Dog didn't like the soldiers and bit one on the thigh, going for the money. Smartest damn dog in the western hemisphere and he's dead, a casualty of the revolution. Let's go inside."

He led them to the living room and gestured them to the sofa, then sat in an overstuffed armchair. The room had full bookcases on every wall and two hunting trophies, the mounted heads of a black-horned gazelle and a seven-point red deer. Rum, gin, bourbon and scotch bottles clustered on a table by his chair. "Too early to drink," he said, "and my doctor won't let me have a goddamn thing."

"I thought I detected you drinking daiquiris the other night."

"I was on shore leave."

"Did the soldiers find those guns by your pool?" Renata asked.

"I hope not."

"Do you know the rebels?"

"I fish with them."

"Are they with the Twenty-sixth?"

"I wouldn't ask them that question."

"I ask because I had friends killed in the Palace attack," Renata said.

"So did I," said Hemingway.

"We were at the Montmartre last night," Quinn said. "Ten minutes after we left they killed an army colonel at the casino, Fermín Quesada."

"You people know where the action is."

"We're heading for Oriente," Quinn said. "Climb the hills and see Fidel. I know your friend Matthews just did that, but Fidel is worth another interview, don't you think? Batista's people kill him every day in the papers."

"Batista's finished. Those Directorio kids at the Palace proved that. When fifty or sixty of the best young people in the country give up their lives to kill you, you're all done. Can you get to Fidel?"

"I'm working on it."

"You have to get past the army and their barricades. They're mean sonsabitches."

"There's an army press conference tomorrow in La Plata. I'm going."

"You ever cover a war?"

"The cold war in Germany, Fourth Division, your old outfit."

"Did they teach you how to climb mountains in a tropical rain forest when you're dodging hostile fire?"

"I missed that lecture. I'll have to wing it. I was writing sports for the Division weekly. But my grandfather came down here to find Céspedes during the Mambí war and wrote a book about it. He called it *Going to Meet the Hero*. Ever hear of it?"

"I read hundreds of books for a war anthology I edited, and I remember some Americans wrote well about Cuba back then. What was his name?"

"Daniel Quinn."

"Ah. Recycling family history."

"Why not? He covered the Civil War for the *Herald*, and rode with the Fenians when they invaded Canada. He got around. But his book on going to see Céspedes got to me. He walked the swamps, the jungle, and the mountains in Oriente, and he got to his man. The Spaniards starved him in jail and he damn near died, but he got out and wrote the story and then wrote the book."

"Now *you're* looking for jail time."

"I was in a saloon in Greenwich Village with a friend of mine who thinks his fame is just around the corner, either as a writer or an artist. He pointed to a Lindbergh poster behind the bar and said, 'Quinn, when are you making your solo to Paris?' I told him, 'I've got a train ticket to Albany.' Actually I took a job in Miami, and then Havana was just a short hop."

"Is your friend famous yet?"

"He's still in the saloon, monitoring Lindbergh."

Hemingway smiled, but somberly. He breathed deeply, then again, and his torso seemed to deflate. That exuberance and assurance, so in evidence at the Floridita, was missing.

"Were you writing your Paris book when we barged in?"

"Twenty-six words today," he said. "Twenty-six."

"It's only noon," Quinn said.

"I got up at six. I should be fishing by now, but I can't do that either."

"Here's something that'll cheer you up," Quinn said, and he handed him Cooney's letter.

Hemingway put on his glasses and Quinn and Renata watched him read. He finished, took off the glasses and squinted at Quinn.

"The Baltimore thrush is a throwback, and I'm a bum. It's a publicity stunt. What's this stuff about medals?"

"He was a Marine. He got a Silver Star in the Pacific."

"Silver Star. We should never underestimate thrushes."

"Cooney blames you for his friend's death. He said his head injury from that left hook was why they were still in their hotel room when the soldiers shot at them."

"Screw that, every inch of it," Hemingway said, and his exuberance was back. He sat upright and his face tightened. "Am I supposed to get weepy over these tourists who don't know when to duck? A duel? How about five rounds bareknuckle?"

"Bareknuckle. Are you serious?"

"How do you get serious about the Cooneys of this world?"

"I'm not sure, but he says he's going public with this."

"And you're writing about it."

"Only if you take him up on it."

"I couldn't win a duel with him, even if I killed him."

"You've been challenged to a duel before?"

"Half my life. Cooney says I'm a coward. I spent years facing that one down. But the question is, Doctor Hemingstein, are you afraid to face down a Marine war hero? It's the cliché of the western. 'Hey, Wild Bill, they say you're a fast draw. Go for your gun.' If I back out I was always yellow and I only shoot guns to get it up. I'm very brave when I shoot unarmed ducks. But the truth is everybody's yellow till they get over it. They're going to shoot you or shell you or bomb you, so you organize your coward maneuvers and you go AWOL the night before battle, or you run the other way when they start shooting, or you shoot yourself in the foot and they send you on sick call. You know how to get rid of a yellow streak? Stop thinking about what's next. Think about right now and that you aren't dead and probably won't be. You got your weapon. They're not shooting at you this minute and if they start they may not hit you. If they hit you you're dead. But who gives a goddamn at that point? Not you. You're dead. Fuck it. Fuck death. It's just another goddamn thing you can't do anything about. Have a drink, climb a tree, shoot a duck, fuck somebody. Don't worry about it. You're dead or you're not, and either way it's not up to you. Stroke your weapon."

"Will you duel with Mr. Cooney?" Renata asked him.

"What do *you* think I should do?"

"I think you shouldn't."

"Why not?"

"It's beneath you."

"Thank you. What about you, Mr. Quinn?"

"I like five rounds of bareknuckle. I think you'd take him in three."

"Two."

"Then again, maybe one. He does have a glass jaw."

"Challenge him with a song," Renata said.

"I'd lose. He'd sing the Marine Hymn."

"What shall I tell him?" Quinn asked.

"Tell him I'll pay his doctor bills and buy him a round-trip ticket to Paris. Tell him to stay out of the Floridita. Tell him to watch out for slivers in his ass. Tell him to fuck off, and that I really liked his song."

"Never apologize, never explain," Quinn said.

"John Wayne said that, a hell of a writer."

"What if Cooney won't go away?"

"Tell him if I wanted to die I wouldn't let *him* do it, I'd do it myself. This is a suicidal country, does he know that?"

"I'll try to send your message."

"Tell him I don't want to kill anybody. Tell him my dog died."

❖

Quinn wanted to see Demajagua, where Céspedes rang the bell and freed his slaves, but there was no time. He had to get to Santiago, settle Renata in at the Casa Granda where she'd stay until she made contact with Felipe

Holtz, and then he'd board an army plane ferrying newsmen to the press conference at El Macho, a temporary army base on the south coast. Some forty reporters and photographers would be converging there for this theatrical army venture that had been in the works for weeks, its focus La Plata—the army outpost that Fidel, risen from the dead, had attacked in January. Fidel's death was old news. His look-alike corpse, which the army took credit for, had been on front pages in December after the disastrous landing of his boat *Granma*—less a landing than a shipwreck—in a swamp at Playa de Las Coloradas near Niquero. The eighty-two seasick invaders made their way to Alegría de Pío, where the army cornered and killed two-thirds of them, even after surrender, and the survivors fled in chaos into the Sierra Maestra. Silence followed.

Then came dead Fidel and other photogenic corpses.

Then came La Plata, a new army outpost on the Magdalena River near the sea. Two new barracks were being built on a vast estate owned by the Domech family (bordering the Holtz family estate). The barracks were built next to the living quarters of three Mayorales—overseers who as a cadre policed most of the major estates in Oriente (not the Holtz estate), and whose main job was to drive off the Precarista peasants who perennially squatted on the estates. War was perpetual between the Mayorales and Precaristas.

Fifteen soldiers had been assigned to La Plata to track the ragtag Castro rebels, wherever they might be in the Sierra. But the rebels moved first, proving to the world and Batista that they were not dead, attacking the barracks January 16. The army said two soldiers and eight rebels were killed. Six weeks later the army said well, actually, forty rebels died, twenty were taken prisoner, and twelve of our soldiers died.

Now at El Macho Quinn listened as Colonel Pedro Barreras, the commander in Oriente, told reporters that the seriously final count at La Plata was five soldiers killed with knives while they slept, three wounded and left for dead, and three who escaped the rebel knifing. No rebels died. Castro led the attack, so he obviously didn't die in December, and we think after Niquero he joined a gang of Precaristas in the Sierra, the murderous outlaws who have lived up there for decades, a law unto themselves. They even keep harems, five to ten women for each man.

The army, the Colonel said, now has 566 troops in the Sierra plus 250 intelligence agents in disguise among the peasants. There is no doubt whatever that Castro is no longer in these mountains. Our patrols and planes are covering an area eighteen by nine by nine miles, from Las Mercedes to Manacal to Aji de Guani, "the critical triangle" where Castro has been operating. We have seen no movement and are certain he's not there. His famous interview with Matthews of *The New York Times* may have taken place in Cuba but not in the Sierra. And the photo of him holding a rifle with a telescopic sight while Matthews takes notes is obviously a fake.

Quinn asked the Colonel: Who are those outlaws with harems?

Julio Guerrero, said Barreras. Chichi Mendoza, Sergio and Manuel Acuna, and Arsenio Zamora.

Arsenio.

Barreras announced that the army would fly reporters over the critical triangle to prove how serene and rebel-free it was. They would also drive everybody to La Plata. Quinn, with triple credentials—*The Havana Post*, *Time* magazine, and *The Miami Herald*—rode in the second jeep with a Lieutenant Cordero, behind the jeep of Colonel Barreras, who guided the tour over steep and narrow mountain roads. The forest was so dense with an overgrowth of leaves, hanging flora, and a waist-high undergrowth of plants and vines, that sunlight could never reach the ground; so what pilot could see a nest of dug-in rebels through such natural cover?

"Do you find anybody trying to join Castro's force?" someone asked.

"Nobody is that stupid," Barreras said. "The army has cut off all traffic to the mountains."

The Barreras convoy of jeeps and chain-driven lumber trucks, the only vehicles that could navigate these wretched roads, stopped at tiny settlements, none with electricity, to let the press hear peasants talk about their loyalty to Batista (not Castro, as the myth of the day had it), these grateful souls all but genuflecting before the Colonel in praise of the food, medicine, money, and new houses the army had given them.

At the tiny village of La Marea del Portillo Quinn fell back from the press cluster and studied the forest, looking for his grandfather who, in

1870, also set out from Santiago on his journey into rebel domain. A Spanish colonel had told him he could go anywhere in Cuba within Spanish lines; but added with a smile that the army will shoot you with great pleasure as a spy if you cross into Céspedes territory. The officers staging this La Plata playlet today will do the same for anybody trying to see Fidel. But like his grandfather, who made it to Céspedes without getting shot, Quinn was obligated to be here, convinced by a capricious education that he should track what was fundamental; and the fundamentality that was Fidel was now at large in these mountains. That Herbert Matthews of the *Times* had just been here did not diminish what Quinn was doing. Hemingway might think of it as the left hook after the right cross to prove twice that the hero is alive. Quinn felt exhilarated doing what was in his blood to do. He saw his grandfather—the Cubans called him El Quin—on horseback moving through a plain of high guinea grasses and climbing into these hills.

He was following a trail written out in detail in an anonymous letter to him at his hotel saying, we heard you want to enter Cuba Libre. Was the letter a trap by the Spanish army, or by thieves who knew he traveled with gold? Perhaps, but he was driven to find Céspedes, talk to him and prove his existence, give the lie to the Spaniards who said he was dead, and confront personally this singular fellow who anointed himself as the Cuban messiah and who courted death, avenged it, surrounded himself with the dead, created the dead.

Quinn's grandfather wore tall boots, a palm-leaf hat, and carried two revolvers and a machete to fend off the marauding robbers the Spaniards warned him about. The warnings were an effort to discourage his daily expeditions toward Cuba Libre; runaway niggers the Spaniards called them, brutal savages, little more than cannibals. He rode four hours to the destination given in the letter, a ceiba tree so large it might have been part of primordial Cuba, and he waited near it till darkness, ready to fight highwaymen with his machete, ready to be shot and found with his pockets inside out. He dismounted and sat in the desolate darkness, nothing to do but trust that all his conversations had made his purpose known and his message had reached the Mambí leaders, who desperately craved the worldwide publicity for their movement that he represented. He could give the lie to the Spaniards' claim that they had killed most of the rebels and there was no serious war.

Quinn heard a whisper and movement and saw, indistinctly, a man on foot, then, as clouds moved beyond the moon, saw he was brown-skinned, with a straw hat, shirtless, a fragment of tattered linen on his loins. He wore a machete on his side, a cartouche, and a rifle was slung on his back. Quinn spoke the code word mentioned in the letter and then they moved together toward Quinn knew not what—the beginning of something that had taken shape in him long before he ever heard of Céspedes.

◈

Colonel Barreras was telling the news people at La Marea del Portillo about the Batista government's generosity toward a family of six, and reporters followed him into a rebuilt shack. Quinn walked toward a peasant in tattered clothes who was sitting crosslegged in front of his house, a *bohío* with thatched roof, earthen floor and two chickens visible inside; and Quinn read in the man's face something other than gratitude to the army. This house had not been rebuilt. Behind the man sat a near-toothless crone holding a child with what Quinn took to be rickets. The child was drinking water out of a tin can.

"*Hola, amigos,*" Quinn said to the peasant and his woman. "What did the army do for you?" He spoke in Spanish.

"They gave me beans and rice."

"What work do you do up here?"

"There is no work."

"How do you earn money?"

"There is no money."

"How do you live, how do you eat?"

"I eat what grows. I cut cane last year and I drove a cane truck, worked in the coffee harvest last year, but not this year."

"I have a relative who drives a truck up here," Quinn said. "Arsenio Zamora. Do you know him?"

The man cocked an eye with surprise in it, but said nothing.

"Arsenio Zamora is my wife's cousin. Renata Rivero from Holguín. Her brother is Alfie Rivero. Renata has not seen Arsenio in two years. She very much wants to see him. They are cousins."

"Arsenio Zamora has five thousand cousins."

"My wife would stand out among ten thousand. She is called Renata. She is beautiful and Arsenio will remember her. He has an eye for women. If anybody sees Arsenio please tell him Renata, the sister of Alfie Rivero, wants to see him."

"I do not know people who see Arsenio."

"If you do, tell them Renata married a reporter from the *Miami Herald*."

"What is reporter?"

"Newpaper man. A writer. Miami newspaper."

"Newspaper?"

"Okay, *olvídalo*. My wife is a cousin of Alfie Rivera. *Se llama Renata. Prima de Arsenio. ¿Entiende?*"

"*Prima.* She want to see Arsenio?"

"*Exactamente.* Renata. Cousin of Arsenio."

Lieutenant Cordero came over to them and asked the man, "What are you telling him?"

"He's telling me," Quinn said, "how he cuts sugar cane and harvests coffee for a living, but he didn't work this month because the army helped him and gave him free food. *Él está muy feliz,* very happy, *verdad, señor?*"

The man shrugged an ambiguous yes.

"He is very grateful to the army," Quinn said.

"We're moving on," the lieutenant said to Quinn.

Quinn saluted the cross-legged man and went with the lieutenant.

❖

In the forest El Quin and the brown rebel, both on foot, chopped vines and briars with their machetes as they moved, the horse moving with them. They rested in a dry streambed, faces bloody with scratches from trees and thorny overgrowth, and ate berries they had picked. El Quin sipped from his canteen and asked the rebel why he had joined Céspedes as a Mambí warrior. He said if he had not become a warrior he would still be a slave. Whether warrior or slave he would die, but it was better to die as a killer of Spaniards than to let the slave drivers kill you. Quinn wanted to tell the man he had lunch with three slave drivers in a sugar mill at Villa Clara, pretending to seek work as one of them. But then he decided that the warrior might misunderstand his ruse and would only hear this stranger saying he wanted to be a slave driver. He would then swing his machete and slice off Quinn's head.

❖

Renata heard the drum in a dream, a Santeria drum, and was moved by it. She opened her eyes and the drum was not a dream. She opened the window of her hotel room and as she listened she moved to its beat without willing the movement. It entered her, took charge, and reminded her of her mother dancing at the Biltmore Yacht Club, moving in a way that she herself had never moved, nor wanted to; but the beat was as old as Cuba. She had heard the Santeria drum so often, but this seemed new, and she was dancing. She looked out to find the source of the drum but saw only a few army cars parked on the empty edges of Céspedes Park. Then she saw women in black dresses, dozens of them streaming out of the cathedral in what was clearly a planned demonstration. They immediately raised placards, CESEN LOS ASESINATOS DE NUESTROS HIJOS—MADRES CUBANAS—Stop killing our children—and walked from the cathedral to the park; but a dozen soldiers with rifles blocked their way and more soldiers moved across the park as backup. The women took a new direction and the troops followed them in a moving blockade. A military car stopped on the edge of the park near San Pedro and an army lieutenant colonel stepped out to watch what was unfolding.

Renata was dressed for driving, flared gray skirt, powder blue blouse with buttons. She put on her blond wig and pinned it, pushed into her shoes. She found a black scarf and put it in her skirt pocket. She went down the stairs to the lobby, crossed the park to where the women, three dozen at least, had been halted. She spoke to a heavy woman at mid-throng, but with only partial knowledge of the reason for this protest. She had heard on the radio that two bloodied bodies of young men who had disappeared from their homes or cars in recent nights had been found on the beach horribly abused; but she was not yet aware of the official madness of the past three nights, a terror unleashed against the people of Santiago, none of it reported on the radio.

"Did you lose someone?" she asked the heavy woman.

"The son of my sister."

"I lost my greatest friend."

"Here?"

"In Havana."

"Everybody is losing," the woman said. "The disease. I am old enough to remember Machado when I lost two uncles, and my mother remembers the war with Spain when the beast Weyler killed whole villages."

"My father was shot in Machado's time," Renata said.

"The soldiers will come after us now," the woman said. "They will beat and rape us."

"Do you want to kill them?"

"I don't kill things," the woman said. "I would make them disappear back up into the cursed stomachs of their mothers."

"What are you doing here?"

"The new American ambassador, he is in the Ayuntamiento just there," and she pointed toward City Hall where three cars and a limousine were parked. The lead women moved down Calle San Pedro but they did not get far. The troops held them back with rifles. *Libertad*," one woman yelled and many echoed her.

Renata wondered: Why am I talking with strangers under siege? Is it true I'm in love with death? Diego was in love with death and killed himself out of love. Am I a child of suicide? If I die the revolution loses a soldier. She tied the black scarf around her arm in solidarity with the women. She could still hear the drum but faintly, moving away, and she did not understand its source. But she felt the beat and still felt the impulse not only to dance but to dance well. This was strange and now she had the thought that all this came with Quinn, who is new and rare and a bit mad.

The women in front were arguing with the soldiers. Why can't we go down San Pedro? A lieutenant said, nobody goes, an answer as arbitrary as the new military violence that had been terrorizing the city in recent nights—reprisal for work stoppages, for the growing public support of the Santiago underground and for Castro's rebels. Three rebel bombs had gone off this week, one on the patio of navy headquarters. Military jeeps now patrolled the streets and the central highway, and the roads to Ciudamar, El Caney, El Morro, and the airport were all barricaded, with checkpoint guards stopping every car. Most businesses were closed, and pedestrians few.

Three nights earlier packs of army, navy, and police raiders invaded public plazas and parks, clubbed pedestrians with gun butts, slashed them with whips, overturned tables in cantinas, yanked people out of cars or off porches of their homes in random attacks against all classes of the population who might or might not be guilty of rebellion, or thinking about rebellion. The raiders picked up one youth who had grown a beard, which was the black flag of the revolutionaries, for Fidel wore a black beard. The raiders crucified the youth, spreadeagled him on top of a police car and drove him through the city with eight other police cars blowing their horns to show the town what happens to rebels who let their hair grow. People locked their doors and windows and stayed home. The count of men who had disappeared rose to seven, then to eighteen, but no one thought that was the end of it. Of these very new events Renata knew almost nothing when she started talking to the woman protester.

Renata felt a hand on her shoulder and turned to see Felipe Holtz with a great new shock of black hair, he had let it grow, and a substantial new mustache, well shaped and deep black, more handsome than ever. He wore a tan linen sport coat and she thought him very attractive; but she was not in love with him. She knew that immediately. She had loved many things about him for years. She did not think he would ever become involved with the rebel cause. He was smart and serious but he did not seem drawn to this danger like Diego. He seemed a man for whom danger was déclassé.

He said to her in English, "We'll go now, my dear," and squeezing her arm firmly he pulled her away from the woman and toward Calle Heredia that bordered the Hotel Casa Granda. He put his arm on Renata's shoulder as they walked and with deft fingers untied the knot in her black scarf, pulled it off her arm and palmed it. Renata stopped to look back and saw the women yelling at the soldiers as two fire trucks and four police vans arrived. A lieutenant colonel was shouting orders to the fire trucks and troops. The women broke ranks and moved singly into the park and stood on sidewalks, watching City Hall. The troops separated to widen their blockade of the dispersed women.

Holtz led Renata into the open entrance walkway to an apartment building and said, "That is a wig you're wearing, isn't it?"

"It is."

"Give it to me," and he stuffed the wig flat under his shirt and buttoned his sport coat. He rolled her scarf into a ball and pushed it into a crevice in the brick wall of the walkway. Then he led her back to the street and made her walk ahead of him.

She had not expected to see him. She had left him messages and knew if he got them he would call and invite her to his home. She tried to tell him this but he said don't talk, just walk, you must be a crazy person to stand in the middle of a protest with soldiers about to pounce.

"You are correct," she said. "I am a crazy person."

"That's no excuse. Do you think you will get up to see Fidel by being arrested?"

"Why do you say I want to see Fidel?"

"Because everybody wants to see Fidel. I also talked to Moncho who talked to Max who talks to everybody. You'll come to my house."

"Of course I'll come to your house. That's why I'm here. Where is Moncho? I saw him at Esme's house after the Palace attack."

"He's in Palma Soriano. You'll see him. He thinks the SIM may be after him and it's possible, but he also may be bragging."

"Moncho is very beautiful when he is angry. His words are beautiful."

"And you are more beautiful than ever," Holtz said.

"Are you still in love with me?"

"No. I've known you too long and you live in Havana. Also you are too beautiful to love."

"I'm traveling with an American who loves me."

"I know. In spite of that we will bring him along."

"Why are those soldiers surrounding the women?"

"The women are very important today. They have a message for the ambassador."

"Am I in trouble for being with the women?"

"It's possible. The military has big eyes. They trust no one. But at least you're no longer a blonde."

A woman screamed and as Renata turned she saw a soldier striking the screaming woman with the butt of his rifle. Other women broke through the ranks of soldiers and yelled things Renata could not understand as they ran toward the men coming out of City Hall. Firemen opened their hoses and the force of the water knocked down many of the women, drove them against buildings. Still they came running, and soldiers clubbed a few. Two women, both drenched, reached the limousine and were yelling to the man Renata took to be the ambassador, and they shook their flyers at him. The man took one flyer and waved his hands to the troops to stop the water cannons. He spoke inaudibly. Soldiers were dragging and pushing most of the women into vans. Renata counted two dozen arrested and saw the lieutenant colonel approaching the ambassador.

She and Holtz were now past her hotel and out of sight of the women and soldiers.

"Those brave women," she said.

"They are ready to die for their anger. We have to get you away from Santiago and out to my house," Holtz said. "We don't want you dead."

"I must go to the hotel."

"Not now. They have *chivatos* spying on people like you, and they monitor the phones. One of them may have seen you at the protest. You're out, so stay out."

"I have no clothes."

"You can wear Natalia's. You're the same size. Later we'll find a way to get your clothes."

"I have a gun in my suitcase."

"What kind of gun?"

"A Colt .38. A Cobra."

"What do you want with a gun?"

"I want to give it to Fidel."

"Then we must get it. Give me your key. They're not looking for me yet."

"Bring my chartreuse blouse and black skirt. The pistol is wrapped in my underwear. Bring my underwear. And the bottle of Gardenia perfume. And my Changó and Oshun beads. You know the Changó and Oshun beads, don't you? Of course you do."

"I will carry what I can hide on my body. I can't come out bulging in unusual places."

"Then just the blouse, the gun, and the underwear. You can wear the beads. I do."

"Don't tell me how to behave, Renata. You are insane and insane people do not give good counsel. Go sit in that café and have a coffee. I'll come by on the other side of the street and then you follow me at a distance."

"Where will we meet Quinn?"

"Moncho will contact him at the hotel or he'll find where he is from Max. Don't worry about Quinn."

"I do worry. I met him two days ago and he wants to marry me."

"Smart *americano.* I'm glad to see you, Renata."

"I am very happy to be rescued by you, Felipe. You are a dear man."

"I'm trying to get over that. We also rescued your guns from the apartment on Sixteenth Street, your friend Alfie and I."

"You got them? *Maravilloso.* Where are they?"

"On the way to Fidel."

"How did you do it?"

"Alfie was superb, I'll tell you all about it. He's quite clever, and fearless."

"He seems to be a first-class criminal."

"It's nice to meet one who isn't in politics."

❖

The army flew the press back to Santiago airport from El Macho's landing field, and Quinn took a taxi to the Casa Granda to call in his story. It was mid-afternoon when he got to the room and he found Renata gone. His phone message that he'd be here in an hour had been delivered but lay unopened on the floor. Her purse and all her clothes were here, no note. He called Max with his story and told him Hemingway wasn't interested in the duel, so it was back to Cooney—go public if that's what you want.

"If he does go public Hemingway will have to come up with some sort of reply."

"No, he won't. He's Hemingway."

"He'll look like he's afraid."

"He's in mourning for his dog. And his writing isn't going well. He said if he wanted to die he'd do it himself."

"Is that his statement?"

"Not really. But he said it, and a lot more. But no."

"I'll tell Cooney."

Quinn dictated his army story to the desk man he had seen on his first visits to the *Post*, a black Americano named Julian Stewart, a New York actor and aspiring playwright with a Cuban wife, who edited copy and did layout. He laughed at Quinn's paragraph on the fluctuating army death tolls in the battle with Fidel and he told Quinn, "You should go to Fidel and get the real total." Quinn agreed that was a good idea. "Tell him I said hello," Julian said, "and I'm available if he needs help."

Quinn flopped on the bed, nothing to do till Renata connected to the Holtzes. He raised his memory of her at their first meeting in El Floridita with Hemingway. Amazing, stunning, incomparable. Quinn now decided he would marry her before they left Oriente province. He was absolutely firm on this, but he also decided he would not tell her. He would make his plan public only when necessary; yet it was real in his imagination and now he needed only to actualize it. The ceremony would require no priest to sanctify it, no judge to make it legal. A *babalawo* would do, even if the union was legitimate only in Yoruba; for Renata saw the *babalawo* as a comfort figure. Quinn believed she was not yet aware how ready she was to marry him. The intensity of what he felt for her was without precedent, and her reaction to him certainly seemed strong. Her grief at losing Diego was enormous, but in its freshest hours she slept alongside Quinn in his bed; and in the wake of the Quesada murder she took revenge on the caprice that killed her love and gave herself to Quinn, transforming them both. She is a creature of perpetual intensity and mystical need, a nymph who could betray you in a blink with a stranger, if that act lit the flame that lights her days. You have an aberration wrapped into your life, Quinn, a walking, loving astonishment. Marry her quickly. She will understand your perception and will accept. Twice in the brief time you've known her she has admitted the possibility of marrying you someday, and she will accept now because of your persuasively absurd insistence. She is love insatiable but she has never accepted long life with her other lovers, who have all had the life expectancy of mayflies, products of her youthful misjudgment, her proclivity for fractured dreams, and her co-conspiracy in creating wrenching separations. You are a gift from an Orisha that arrived during her craving for something beyond the sexual fadeaways of her commonplace book of love, and your impromptu marriage scheme looms as a gesture any Orisha would respect, bespeaking your fluency in the language of the soul.

But be aware, Quinn—Renata does not yet know she knows these things, and you certainly should not push her to premature awareness, for she may make a hasty mess and bend everything to her adorational needs of the moment. Let her discovery arrive during your next eureka moment together, which should be soon. Do not tell her that she wants to marry you above all her other lovers past or present. Do not spoil her surprise.

❖

Renata waiting for Felipe: another of the Holtz family taking in another of the Otero women. He would soon drive her to his mansion where her mother, Celia, had been taken in and raised, and where Renata visited as a child, never quite understanding back then why this had happened. But she had exotic memories of vacations here with her cousins, of games played in their vast house and in the stables and outbuildings, with secret hiding places and cuddling until they found you, early intimations of romance, which seemed to be what they called it. Whatever it was those visits were always too brief, always interrupted, and always with that hovering mystery no one talked about but everyone (except Renata) knew—the secret life of her grandmother.

She sat at the first table in the café, near the door, and ordered a coffee. The waiter had a large scar on his neck, a rope burn from being hanged?

Remnant of a murderous throat-slitting? But, Renata, might it not have been accidental? No. Something so egregious is rarely accidental in Cuba. She saw her Grandmother Margaret's hooded eyes, and her scarred eyelids, and don't try to tell Renata *that* was accidental. She conjured the face she knew from young photographs before the eyes were attacked. Such a wild creature, Margarita Lastra Pujol de Otero, who came to Cuba on a tidal wave of passion, unable to live without her husband of a few months, Jaime, who had left her in Spain in 1896 to join the war against Cuban rebels, also to elevate his military status, war can do that for a privileged young prince of a wealthy family.

Renata was now sitting a few blocks from where Margarita, with her year-old Celia, had first lived in this city while Jaime was making forays into rebel territory. Her townhouse belonged to Jaime's uncle, Sebastian Holtz Otero, who derived his wealth from one of the few sugar mills to survive three wars in Oriente Province. Jaime came there twice to be with her, brief visits but wild with conjugal frenzy and bliss and such emotional consummation that he composed a will against the day he might die in war, giving her all he owned or might inherit. What he asked in return was her eternal love and fidelity, which she granted with the first blink of her eye, her worship of his penstroke and sexual fury, his teardrop on the letter, his mouth on her own and on her body and on the spiritual lips of her love. You will kiss me everywhere and forever, she wrote him. In these days he sent her three letters, all he could manage, but they were very like the twenty-seven he'd written when courting her: passionate, even shocking. They burned her imagination; she thrived on their heat.

Renata wanted to receive letters like those. As she grew older she heard her parents talk of them, then found the key to the strongbox where Celia had hidden them, because such things were not fit for young eyes. Renata sat and read them all, her first schooling in the language of sex and the thrilling persiflage of love. She wanted to own the letters but her mother discovered her reading them and put them in a bank vault, telling her: When you are ready.

Renata was ready now. She wanted to read them again, see farther into those words that had shaped an obsession in her grandmother. She wanted to walk to the town house, which was still there, for it would put flesh on her memory. Here is where it all happened, here the point of tragedy of the solitary young mother who one day hears Uncle Sebastian say Jaime has died in battle, nobly. In fact his head had been split in half by a machete stroke. Renata imagined the fall of her grandmother's spirit, her instantly cracked heart, her life suddenly without meaning. Margarita did withdraw, her agony turning to delirious flights of conversation with the dead; and she seemed to have forgotten that the baby Celia existed. Jaime's uncle, whom she rarely saw and who lived on the Holtz estate in Palma Soriano, monitored her condition through daily briefings from the nana he sent to care for mother and child.

A modest fortune accrued to Margarita, sent as income to her from Spain by the executor of Jaime's estate, a friend of the Holtz-Otero family. The inheritance came with the proviso that Margarita not remarry, and if she did the inheritance would go to Jaime's daughter with her, Celia. Margarita was oblivious of such detail, victim of the single-minded disease of love. She dwelt in grief and took pleasure only in the historic passion and memorious fantasy the love letters aroused in her.

Jaime's uncle tried to reverse her withdrawal by sending his son Evelio, like Jaime a Spanish lieutenant, to comfort and restore her, a gesture so naive that his family thought him demented. Margarita was twenty-nine, Evelio thirty-four. Evelio visited her, offering comfort; returned the next day and the next with new comfort, which begat the word, the soft stroke, the fervor of immediacy. And there you have it.

They began in secret and were interrupted when Evelio was sent into unequal combat against the invading American forces. She welcomed the defeat of the Spanish military by the Americans for it meant the restoration of a lover to her life, a lover who banished all her guilt over the swift relegation of Jaime to memory, just as he banished her melancholy with his passion. Three months after Evelio's release from the army Evelio secretly married Margarita.

Renata, remembering this, wondered, am I my grandmother? She saw the parallel to Diego and Quinn just as she looked to the doorway and saw Quinn coming toward her.

"Let's go," he said. "I just met your cousin Felipe."

"My coffee," she said.

"I'll get you another one."

"I didn't pay for it."

Quinn put money on the table and led her out to the street.

❖

"Those guns of yours," Felipe told Renata as they moved out of Santiago in his car, "we loaded them into a truck with fake floorboards that made room for them all. There were six Thompsons. Alfie found the truck. He knows how to get things."

Holtz had been quietly supporting the Directorio with cash infusions until the previous week when two fourteen-year-olds he knew, neither with any connection to the rebels, were tortured and killed by police; and his outrage escalated. He flew to Havana and told his friend Aurelio he wanted to do more. Aurelio took him to a boat basin to meet a gun dealer, since Holtz had offered to buy guns. But neither money nor guns changed hands that day, the transaction aborted by a cruising police car. The transfer was to be the next day, but that afternoon the Palace attack was launched and Holtz went underground, surfacing only when he knew Aurelio had survived the attack; and by then Alfie, through Renata's and Quinn's intercession, had delivered the guns to Aurelio and Javier at the gas station.

When Renata mentioned yet more guns in the Sixteenth Street apartment that she and Diego had rented, Aurelio put Holtz together with Alfie to find a way to rescue them. Two nights later Fidel's people were poised to bomb a major electrical grid; and if it succeeded, much of Havana would go dark, a propitious time for burglary. The weapons' preliminary destination was an empty warehouse where they would be put on a commercial truck bound for Oriente. But then Holtz said to Aurelio and Alfie, if there are no guards at the Santa Fe landing field, and usually there are not, I could fly them to my father's airstrip in Palma Soriano and Fidel's people will unload them.

"So we put them on my plane and took off at dawn," Holtz said to

Quinn and Renata. "Four of Fidel's peasants met us and took them. Fifteen minutes after our landing the army showed up to search the plane, but there was no contraband to be found."

"Where is Alfie now?" Quinn asked.

"At the house," Holtz said. "He's waiting for us."

On the road to the Holtz estate, going north out of Santiago, they faced a major army checkpoint with a *tanqueta* at the ready, a dozen armed soldiers at the barricade, and four cars ready to pursue any vehicle that would try to crash the barrier. Holtz told the soldiers that Renata was his cousin and Quinn her fiancé, and they were visiting at his home. The lieutenant recognized Holtz's famous name and let them pass.

"These checkpoints are all over the Sierra Maestra," Holtz said. "If we do go to see Fidel we must have a reason or they'll turn us back." Holtz said he'd brought one *americano* up to meet the rebels, presenting him as a businessman buying land from a defunct sugar mill.

"Can we go as a family, having a reunion?" Renata asked.

"I'd like something more specific. We have an *americano* here."

"What if the reunion is a wedding?" Quinn asked.

"Whose?"

"Renata's and mine. You and Alfie can be cousins in the wedding party. Do you want to get married, Renata?"

"Is this a proposal or just a way to fool the army?"

"One reason is as good as another for marrying you."

"Do you mean a wedding in a church?" Holtz asked.

"That's too complicated. Just have a *babalawo* do it."

"You are crazy," Renata said.

"Do *babalawos* do weddings?" Holtz asked.

"I never heard of it," Renata said.

"*Babalawos* do everything," Quinn said. "If I marry you I want a *babalawo*. They read minds, they predict futures, they heal your soul."

"But they don't do weddings," she said.

"All right, we'll get a priest too," Quinn said.

"I like this," Holtz said. "It's oddball, which makes it real."

"It will be real. All we need is a *babalawo* and a priest."

"A crazy man wants to marry me," Renata said.

◈

Felipe's sister Natalia, who had grown plump since Renata last saw her, she is eating for her pleasure instead of having sex, met them in the foyer, the only family member in the house, her parents en route to Mexico. Holtz took Quinn to find Alfie, and Natalia gushed over Renata looking so lovely, and why haven't you called? Renata said I called three times for Felipe.

"Ah, but that is different," Natalia said. "Who is this man Quinn?"

"I just met him," Renata said. "He wants to marry me."

"Another one?"

"Yes, another. What year did Margarita die? I was thinking of her," Renata said.

"Of course you were," Natalia said, "another marriage maniac. I don't know the year but she lived too long—for her. I don't want to die like she did."

"You should worry about not living like she did," Renata said.

Natalia went to the kitchen to have the cook prepare late lunch for the visitors and Renata roamed the parlors and dining room, loving to feel again the grandness of this house with all its historical elegance, although she now sees decline. It isn't crumbling, just aging visibly, yet with grace and formidability—its baroque floor-to-ceiling mirrors, the Carrara marble on the floors, walls, and staircase; the chandelier with eighteen globes and uncountable strands of crystal beads, a creation of high elegance made in emulation of the one in the Captain-General's Palace in Havana; and, in the music room, the grand piano on a small, elegant stage where the music of civilization, written in the old world, was performed in the new.

The house was called a palace when they built it in the 1850s, the Holtz Palace, and how it must have dazzled the elite society of Oriente. Celia grew up amid it all, coming here as an infant when the maddened Margarita stopped functioning as a mother and became the pure *enamorada*— who lived only for love with her secret second husband, her god-sent lover who was wilder at sex than her first husband, and who lived for the bed the way Margarita did.

93

The marriage secret was short-lived, and when it became gossip in Santiago the word flew to Spain and into the ear of the estate's executor, who cut off Margarita's inheritance and the child Celia's as well. The catastrophe was compounded within weeks when Evelio, discovering that his wealthy new wife was penniless, left her and moved into a small house with a former housemaid from his father's estate. The executor wrote Margarita that under the terms of Jaime's will he could give her such support for residency as she might find in a convent, and if such a convent existed in Cuba, she would be free to seek it out. If not then she could return to Madrid and find residence in any of several convents. The child, in any case, will be cared for by the Holtz family in Santiago.

◈

Getting married in order to see Fidel—this may be Quinn's ultimate sacrifice. Fidel. What would Quinn ask him? Herbert Matthews had confirmed his survival, described him as a demigod, as an intellectual, nationalistic, anti-Yankee, anti-imperialistic, anti-communist revolutionary, a dedicated fanatic, a man of ideals, a tough, charismatic hero fighting for a socialistic, democratic Cuba, who has polarized the majority of Cuban youth against Batista and seems invincible.

Can't top that.

So talk to him about the how of what he did—how he made the La Plata attack and what it achieved. Or a longshot—the link between politics and gangsterism. Wasn't he a gangster in his university days? That's a new take on the revolutionary. And Arsenio, the rural gangster, collaborating with the connected Alfie to bring you these guns. Isn't gangsterism just low-level political pragmatism? Machado with his gangster police—the deadly Porra; Prío as president giving jobs to two thousand gangsters to curb crime; Batista making the Italian mob his partners—likewise partnering with goons, the homegrown Tigers of Rolando Masferrer, your University classmate and now your enemy, Señor Castro—gangster then, gangster now. It's all very tidy and of the moment, yes, and Fidel might be amused. But why would he talk about any of that? What would Hemingway ask him? Nothing about gangsters. He'd talk about Fidel's gun. He'd ask about logistics, methods, attitudes, what he thinks about war, what was your first revolutionary act and did anybody die from it? Hemingway wouldn't talk politics. He'd say if you put politics into the novel, and if the book lasts twenty years, you have to skip the politics when you read it.

Ah, so you are writing a novel about me, Mr. Quinn?

No, just tracking the hero the way my grandfather tracked Céspedes, and you qualify as heroic merely on the basis of your survival. How do you explain not dying in combat at the Moncada barracks? Or when they captured you there? Or when they had you in Batista's jail? Or when as an invader you shipwrecked in a swamp? Or now, when you're dodging aerial bombardment and being hunted by half the Cuban army? All this smacks of a scripted life for Fidel Castro—Achilles without the flawed heel.

Renata will love this idea: a new Orisha in control of the mountains, fated to defy death from every angle, too original to die. Originality is an ingenious form of defiance, don't you think? Or do you have a simpler vision and consider yourself lucky? Was Céspedes lucky? He said his children were beggars, or on the cusp of prostitution. The Spaniards executed his rebel son by firing squad the same year his infant son starved to death among the fugitive Mambí. They got to the man himself in '74 when his originality failed and he feared he was being eclipsed by his general, Máximo Gómez, and was deposed from the presidency in a leadership coup. He ran out of luck, or was it intuition, and he retreated alone to the mountains where the Spaniards caught up with him, and a Cuban volunteer with the Spaniards pulled the trigger.

But he is still the father of Cuba, El Padre de la Patria, is he not? Was he a chosen figure or did he imagine himself into existence? My grandfather came to Cuba on a bizarre and solitary quest to interview him for a New York newspaper and confirm he was alive—and he later wrote a book about it—*Going to See the Hero,* have you read it? I'll send you a copy.

◈

El Quin and the ex-slave, his name was Nicodemo, were moving toward a moun-tain they could not avoid climbing without exposure to a Spanish fort below. The horse would probably not make it but Nicodemo said they could try and he led the horse upward as they chopped brush to clear their way. Fifty yards up the horse fell twenty feet, rolling, snapping trees, ripping off its harness, rising up, falling and rolling again, you don't see that every day, scattering El Quin's belongings and his second pistol and ammunition. The horse righted itself, pushed downhill through the trees and ran onto the guinea-grass plain, gone forever, so long horse.

Nicodemo retrieved pistol and ammo and they rolled up the strewn clothing and carried it on their backs—slipping, falling, slashed by briars, crawling over boulders on all fours—emerging onto a mesa that was a relief from incline but opened them to the punishment of a scorching Cuban sun that could quickly crisp El Quin. He rolled down his shirtsleeves and put on his straw hat and they walked two more hours before seeing Mambí troops. The troops had halted next to a great brick tower, taller than any building Quinn had seen in Cuba outside of Havana and whose function he could not imagine; but he would learn that the tower was all that remained of a sugar mill burned by the rebels. It was topped off by the slaveholder's crow's nest where, from daybreak to nightfall, a lookout had watched 360 degrees of fields for trails being made in the high grass by runaway slaves who sometimes chanced death rather than live another day creating sugar for the Spanish swine.

Quinn and Nicodemo walked into the midst of twenty Mambí cavalry soldiers, horses tethered in a grove of trees. An officer with a full beard, wearing a hat, an open, high-collared linen jacket, leggings, and a pistol with belt and bandolier, greeted them.

"Capitán Díaz Rodón," he said, "I welcome you to Cuba Libre."

He released Nicodemo from duty and Quinn offered the ex-slave his gratitude, which he acknowledged with a brief nod. The Capitán said Quinn should rest, take water, eat something; my troops will protect you while we are in this territory where Spaniards have been seen. He would send a message to President Céspedes to say Quinn had arrived. Did the Capitán know a Lieutenant Castellón? He did. He is an aide to the president. Quinn had a message for him from his wife in New York who has raised much money for the Mambí cause. Capitán Díaz said they would not go directly to the presidential camp, near Contramestre, but would jog west to cut Spanish telegraph wires between Palma Soriano and Jiguaní. Later they would meet General Máximo Gómez's battalion and move toward a town with entrenched Spanish troops and try to lure them out from their barricades. President Céspedes thought it might be bracing for Señor Quinn, and good for what he was writing, to see our troops in combat. You can watch from well behind the lines and be safe, if you keep your head down, but not too far down or you will miss the battle.

❖

Natalia found her brother in the library with Quinn and Alfie, who had retreated there hours earlier to wait for Holtz to return. Alfie had been perusing topographical maps of Oriente Province, educating himself on the land, a modest preparation for flying guns into this territory, when Natalia said to her brother, you have a visitor in the *casa del ingenio*. And Holtz led the visiting pilgrims to the sugar mill where Arsenio Zamora, the charismatic bandit, was standing alone by the great gear of a grinder, a picture of anxiety in process, violating Fidel's first commandment that thou shalt not stay anywhere that can be surrounded. But the public enemy was here on a mission Fidel had sanctioned. And he stared at Holtz and his entourage of three as they entered the mill.

Arsenio, an essential figure in the revolution's strategic defense in the Sierra, had accumulated not five to ten wives but twenty, and at last count, seventy-five children. He was forty-one but from the rugged life in the Sierra he looked sixty to Quinn, a long, wrinkled face, a full head of hair whose blackness had survived climate and age, with eyebrows and mustache more gray than black, the tash not cultivated but under control, perhaps a vanity marker, or a less intrusive brush for his harem. He wore a battered black leather hat, not quite a fedora, and smoked a dark brown cigar.

He had been born on the seven-thousand-acre Holtz estate in a small village of Precarista squatters that two generations of Holtzes had never tried to remove. He began as a young cane-cutter and laborer for Holtz padre, became a cane truck driver, grew into a leader of his village by his late twenties. Smart and aggressive, revered and feared as he was, he evolved into an anti-poverty outlaw. Many of the Precaristas were illiterates who lived without electricity or running water, and their villages served as sanctuaries for outlaws. Quinn would hear the region compared to the wild west in America, which his grandfather had written about in the years after the Civil War.

Before Fidel arrived in Oriente with his eighty-two expeditionaries Arsenio was already an ally, and had hunkered down in Niquero for two days with a hundred men, and trucks loaded with guns and supplies for the invaders. But the fate of the invaders was not to land at Niquero but to sink into a swamp near Belic. Most of them were quickly shot on the run by Batista forces, but Fidel eluded the troops and made it to the Sierra with Che Guevara, then his brother Raúl, and in short order a dozen altogether, with Arsenio's banditry and leadership at his disposal. Arsenio knew every peasant who had food, knew where to find water, knew every road, and roads that were not roads, every impasse and cliff. He offered Fidel a hundred men but without arms, and Fidel was grateful, but who needs the gunless in battle? He accepted a few helpers from Arsenio; and the outlaw chief also put three of his sons to work with shotguns as *escopeteros*, robbing travelers to feed the rebels.

When Holtz called Moncho to have someone meet his plane with the guns, Arsenio was the man, and he and three others were alongside when the plane stopped on the grass runway. In ten minutes they had offloaded guns and ammo onto an old Dodge truck. Within twelve minutes they were rattling over a narrow road through a cane field into the dense brush of the forest's edge into a village where a dozen or, if necessary, two dozen human mules would backpack the weapons up to the lofty, new Cuba Libre.

In the sugar mill Holtz told the pilgrims to wait and he walked to Arsenio and asked did he want to talk to the visitors. Arsenio said no, who are they? I heard of a *periodista* who claimed to be married to my cousin but I have no such cousin.

Holtz, who knew nothing of what Quinn had set in motion in La Marea del Portillo, said no, she's *my* cousin, Renata Suárez Otero, very close to the family for years. From Havana, and she worked with the Directorio. Those guns we just flew here, she sent. She had also negotiated with Alfie for guns for the Directorio but now most of her Directorio friends are dead. She wants to join the revolution here. She is a brave woman.

"Women can do some things," Arsenio said, "but there are few here, very few. I will ask about this."

"Alfie Rivero is also here and he really is your cousin, no?"

"Yes," said Arsenio, "and sometimes I trust my cousins."

"He says he can get many guns for Fidel," said Holtz. "He's connected to Mafia people in Miami and he has airplanes. He knows guns and he will do anything."

"We will talk with him about the guns," Arsenio said.

"The *periodista* Quinn, all he wants is to interview Fidel."

"Is that all?" said Arsenio.

"Will Fidel see any of them?"

"I will know tomorrow."

"Is there a plan? Will we go toward the mountains?"

"If the answer is yes then Moncho will know the place. He will tell you."

"Should all four of us go? Are we too many?"

"It makes no difference. It is dangerous, no matter how many. Not all of this group will go to Fidel."

"How many army checkpoints where we're going?"

"Who knows? They keep moving them."

"I assume we should have a good reason for going."

"The army asks who you are and why you are here and where you are going."

"I can say I'm on business, buying land that was part of an old sugar mill."

"There are no mills where you are going."

"Then you know where we're going."

"I know where you might be going."

"What about a family gathering? Quinn has the idea of doing an actual wedding celebration to marry Renata and he wants a *babalawo* and a Catholic priest to perform the ceremony. Alfie and I would be the bride's relatives, and Moncho actually is a relative—he was married to Renata's sister. Marriage seems like a good reason for going someplace. I do like the idea."

"Is this a real marriage?"

"Quinn wants it to be. I don't know if Renata wants it."

"I like the marriage."

"I know. You do it often."

Arsenio dropped the stub of cigar he was chewing on and took a new one from his shirt. He put it in the corner of his mouth but did not light it. He stared at the pilgrims who all wanted to go to see the hero.

"Moncho will come here tomorrow," he said. "You follow him in your car. The mafioso will go with me. Your cousin *está muy buena.*"

"You have a fine eye, Don Arsenio."

Arsenio nodded at the pilgrims and walked out of the mill.

Quinn may or may not be about to meet with Fidel Castro and is now in the midst of the waiting game Fidel plays with visitors. He is in the main room of a house in Los Negros, a crossroads village near the northern foothills of the Sierra, where Moncho had led him and the other pilgrims from Palma Soriano. They passed two army checkpoints without trouble, Moncho explaining they were going to a wedding and the bride and groom are in the car behind me. The soldier inspected the Buick Quinn was driving and Renata said yes it's true, and showed him her grandmother's wedding ring that she would be wed with, and the soldier waved them on.

Quinn, waiting for Fidel—is now into his sixth hour in this house which belongs to one of Arsenio's fifteen or twenty *mujeres,* wives of a sort. This wife lives here with two of her four daughters—and Quinn is witnessing an impromptu prelude to his wedding, a Santeria dance ritual, organized for Renata, that will, he hopes, lead into a divination, the calling down of one, maybe two Orishas who might hint at the destiny of the bride and groom, or offer a prognosis of the marriage, or faux marriage, whichever it is. Quinn hasn't quite got a handle yet on the details of either the divination ritual or the marriage, but he's getting there.

The ritual is being enacted by two principals brought here by Moncho—Ezequiel, who is playing the tambor beta, or sacred drum, and Floreal, who belongs to Ezequiel and is a Santera, a priestess of lesser station than a *babalawo* but empowered to invoke the Orishas. Floreal is singing as she dances barefoot, a chanting singsong in Yoruban verse evoking one of the hundreds of mysteries of Ifa, which is a belief system, a method of divination, an all-encompassing myth of the history of the universe. Her song is melodious despite the limited range of the music. She is wearing a head wrap, something like a turban but also like a crown, and she is floating her great blue skirt, another blue skirt beneath it (blue because that is the color associated with Oshun, the Orisha with whom Renata wants to commune). Floreal dances with graceful twirls and revolutions, with arcs of her body and subtle rhythms of hips, arms, and shoulders akin to the moves of the mambo, but a subdued mambo, elegant in twist and thrust.

This is taking place in the main room of this modest wooden house that Arsenio built for his old wife long ago. Chairs have been pushed to one wall. A table, with a white cloth covering it, is serving as an altar and is set out with two coconuts and a hammer, two stones, a glass of water, several bowls, one with water, two with offerings to the Orishas being summoned. Changó's is the second bowl, which is wooden so it won't break. Changó can be rowdy. Both these bowls are full—with beads and sunflowers and small cups of honey, plus herbs and other elements Quinn cannot identify. Behind the table a large fabric, red and light blue, has been hung to transform the room, and there is a festive quality here.

Quinn is fixated on Renata, who is totally absorbed by it all; and she is scoring dance points with Quinn by her effective emulation of Floreal's moves, which isn't easy. Quinn is reveling in Renata's aesthetic control of her body. Grace and beauty prevail in all realms of her being, it seems to him. He is exploding with love for her; and immersed as he is in all this mumbo-jumbo, he would not be surprised to see his love materialize somewhere in this room in the shape of an idea, a corporeal rendering of his possibly insane desire. He would not go on record at the moment as to his own sanity.

Renata had told him she did not like to dance and would not dance with him. But she lied, or perhaps she just changed because of the impulse that started her dancing yesterday in her hotel room and took hold of her again here when Ezequiel's drum began singing to her and Floreal's chant and elegant movement brought her to her feet.

Quinn is also on his feet now, dancing with Renata at a distance, he too emulating Floreal's steps; and he feels the power of this dance. He is with its beat, which is a slow mambo, he has definitely decided—you go with what you know. Floreal gave Quinn a small smile because of the way he was swaying his hips, not bad was his reading of her glance. His only exotic dance specialties were the merengue and the rumba, but soon he'd really nail this mambo, and maybe even the salsa, what the hell, he was in Cuba.

Moncho knew all about the involvement of Ezequiel and Floreal in Santeria from his time in Los Negros, and he approached them at their home to do this rite for Quinn and Renata. Moncho first thought he should dissuade Renata from this hasty marriage, she being so young and tempted. But as a believer in irrational love he offered no objection. Also, he had taken a liking to Quinn who is a bit strange, but seems to know what he wants—that fixation of his on *babalawos* and he doesn't know anything about them. But there is no *babalawo*, for *babalawos* really can't legally do weddings. And there's no Catholic priest either. Moncho told Quinn and Renata, You don't need a priest, I'll do it.

All-purpose Moncho, a sometime criminal lawyer and public defender, is also a *notario público* appointed for life by Carlos Prío when he was president, with the power to draw real estate contracts and perform other legal functions, marriage among them. Moncho now sits in a corner and observes, across the room, in motion, the two daughters of the house. Holtz, who dances reasonably well, is focusing on the elder daughter. Arsenio's old wife, and Moncho's driver, Epifanio, who works with Arsenio, are all dancing, and the seated Moncho is moving his shoulders to the beat of the beta. Then he rises and gets into it. Is Moncho a believer like Renata? Who cares? Moncho dances, betraying ballroom talent and moving like a Cuban Fred Astaire—he could dance for a living—and he jangles toward those two daughters in long dresses, into a communion, perhaps, sanctified by Ifa, competing with Holtz for their attention.

This readiness of so many to dance, and dance well, astonishes Quinn at the moment, for it certainly isn't the reason these people are here. Dance has resurfaced in their lives and they are seizing the day. Ezequiel has been drumming nonstop for half an hour at least, and all in the room are dancing. Dance is the Cuban national contagion, as ubiquitous as rum and the cigar—keeping together in time, as somebody put it; and those who dance will bond and rise, will overshadow, maybe even overpower groups that do not dance. The military dance, the march, the goosestep,

the cheerleaders' kick step, the fox trot, the close order drill, the dance of shamans, the dance of sex (George Bernard Shaw said dance was the vertical expression of a horizontal desire), the dance of love, the wedding dance, the aboriginal war dance, the dance of death (Socrates took dancing lessons when he was seventy), the slave dance. Quinn's grandfather watched a slave dance eighty-five years ago in a Mambí encampment.

◈

"It is time for music," Céspedes said to El Quin after their dinner together— broiled steak, sweet potatoes, boiled corn and bread made from cassava roots—the second night after bloody Jiguaní, the dead buried, the wounded lying on their couches of twigs. Quinn had talked half a day with the president in his thatched-leaf hut, and the success at Jiguaní had produced ebullience in the leader.

"It is time for the people to dance," he said after they ended their talk. This was a man who wrote music in the years before he declared war on slavery and Spain, wrote as a youth the words for a love song, "La Bayamesa," which later gained new lyrics and evolved into a battle anthem of the Mambí rebels. He and Quinn walked from his hut to the broad patch of level ground where two Mambí drummers, plus six musicians with flutes, cornets, a bugle, and a guitar, all captured from Spanish troops, were just sitting down to begin their music, the danza, Céspedes called it. People sat at the edge of the dance turf, and officers and soldiers came forward with their women. They all danced on the same turf, but with wide separation between officers and troops. Most were mulatos (two-thirds of the Mambí army) among some whites, and all moved with vital pleasure in the accumulating darkness, lit by a few torches. The music was brassy but mellowing to Quinn, the drumming alluring, evoking chants and clapping from dancers and others who had come to watch and feel the beat: keeping together in time.

When this music paused, a black drummer staked out a patch of ground closer to the forest, and a dozen black men and women began not a danza but something wilder. Quinn went to watch with Céspedes, who said that only the black Africans danced this way and to this beat, which was mesmerizing to Quinn in its fury—bodies contorting with frenzied invitation but never touching, dancers grunting their communal joy in wild and guttural singing, repetitive and monotonous; but in monotony there is truth. Their joy was echoed by the wildly vocal spectators, all supremely aroused, the entire spectacle looking to Quinn like a warm-up for a hot evening to come.

Nicodemo, the strapping near-giant who had guided Quinn into Cuba Libre—wearing a clean uniform, but still of tatters, his bandaged left arm hanging limp—moved with great vigor and thrust toward two women dancers, first one, then the other, and he spoke to the drum and the women in a language Céspedes said he could not understand. Quinn said it sounded like the universal language of heat. The women received what Nicodemo was sending them and answered with body language of their own, an exotic dialogue in motion. Nicodemo's slave persona was nowhere in evidence, his movement now obeying memory of an instinctual order, his manic excitement transforming him from machete warrior to warrior of the erotic night.

❖

Quinn, waiting to see another hero of a latter-day revolution, moved in synch with Renata—no need to watch Floreal now, we know the moves—and, as he felt his and Renata's spirits seriously mingling, he decided this was the corroborating stage of the wedding ceremony.

"It's time to do the marriage," he said to Moncho.

"We are still in the dance," Moncho said.

"We're getting past it. It seems time. Are you ready to marry me, Renata?"

She broke her trance to throw back her head and laugh, not inclined to stop dancing to be wed. She was in collusion with the chant and the drum, generating the movement of love. "I am getting close," she said.

"Will you kiss me now?" Quinn said to her. And she danced toward him and took both his hands, then kissed him with a passion that seemed greater and more nervous than when they had last made love; and he decided this was yet another irreversible step toward the ceremony. Renata closed her eyes and danced away to the table. She picked up the red and white beads from Changó's bowl and put them around Quinn's neck.

The drumming and the singing stopped.

Floreal, with wide eyes, faced the table, picked up the coconut, and hit it with the hammer. She drained its milk into a dish, broke the coconut into pieces with her hands, and washed the four largest pieces in another dish of water. She threw the four pieces on the floor and stared at how they fell—the white of the meat or the brown of the outer shell facing upward. Ezequiel resumed his drumming, the same beat but slower. Floreal moved toward and then away from Renata and, circling the pieces of the coconut, began to talk to the room. "A woman alone in a room is knitting," she said, "always knitting, and she knits because she is trying to save you."

"It is my grandmother," Renata said. "She did that for years. Is she saving me from marriage?"

"Nothing can save you from marriage," Floreal said. Then she told Quinn that the Orisha wanted him to speak to Renata what he knows about love.

Quinn said there are fifty million definitions of love and its abortive and deadly and gorgeous and mystifying nature, and he knows quite a bit about it, but he never knew what it felt like before Renata, and *that* love for her is unbelievably great inside him, and growing, and intoxicating his soul. He said he believes its mystical power will conquer every doubt in Renata's heart about the speed of this leap into marriage, and he rambled on, full of what he remembered others saying of love— love, the itch, and a cough cannot be hid, love conquers all things, to fear love is to fear life, love lodged in a woman's breast is but a guest, will you love me in December as you do in May? And when he heard his own babble he stopped talking.

Then the drum resumed, and Floreal spoke of the handsome young Babalu Aye who had many women until he was struck with leprosy by Olodumare because of his disobedience—going with a woman on Holy Thursday, which was forbidden. The woman he went with awoke in his bed to see him covered with sores, and she fled. Babalu Aye went to the house of Olodumare and begged to be restored to what he had been, but Olodumare slammed the door and Babalu Aye died on the street. The women of the world wept and went to Oshun and asked her to help bring Babalu Aye back to life. Oshun was moved by their tears and went to Olodumare, who had been her lover years ago. She brought with her a gourd with the special honey Olodumare had loved to kiss off her lips.

She put it on his door and when he came home he recognized its aroma as Oshun's, but she had turned herself into a crone with running sores. When Olodumare saw her he wept. When you gave leprosy to Babalu Aye, she said, he gave it to me, for I was with him on Holy Thursday. Olodumare said he would restore her to health but she said not unless you resurrect Babalu Aye. He did this and Oshun also became her beautiful self and smeared honey on her face and parts of her body, which drove Olodumare wild, and he licked all the honey away. Babalu Aye stood up from the grave, but still with his leprosy and putrid odor, and he walked the world with his dogs licking his sores. People loathed him, and his brother Changó did not even recognize him at first, but Changó took pity and bathed Babalu Aye in the river and prayed to the powerful Olofi, and his prayer was so beautiful that Olofi told Babalu Aye that he would become the king of Arara. Babalu walked the world for a lifetime and then one night when the dry earth broke open and great torrents of rain fell, he believed he had reached the end of his journey, so he lay down to die. But the sky dawned bright and he was young again and people were on their knees worshipping his presence, for they knew he was the prophesied king who would arrive after the storm. And the land was called Arara.

"That's a sad and happy story," Quinn said to Renata. "Now you must marry me and my Changó beads. Did you just hear what Changó did for your favorite Orisha, Babalu Aye?"

"I heard," she said, "and will you always do that for me?"

"I will," he said. "And will you give me such love that the gods will be jealous?"

"I will try."

"Then it is time to marry," Quinn said, and he put her arm in his arm and he walked her to the table with the bowls of Oshun and Changó, and he looked to Moncho, who called Epifanio, his driver, and one of Arsenio's daughters, Encarnita, as witnesses, and then Moncho spoke from memory the civil ritual that made Quinn and Renata man and wife. Felipe Holtz gave the bride away.

Arsenio's old wife brought many plates of food to the table, and the wedding feast carried on until after midnight when a messenger arrived and talked to Moncho, and together they told Quinn that it was time for him to meet Arsenio in the forest. His bride would not be going with them. She should see a woman in Havana who would find a meaningful connection for her in the revolution, and Moncho would tell her that woman's name. Quinn passed this on to Renata who said if I go back to Havana they will arrest and kill me. I will go back with Felipe to his house and wait for you. Then she kissed Quinn, her new husband, and went alone to their marriage bed.

Quinn and two of Arsenio's people went out the back door of the house and walked through a black forest, mostly uphill, and after the first hour Quinn was short of breath, his knees aching, his arches ready to collapse, why the hell did you wear these shoes? Because they're the only tough shoes I own and what's more I'm hungry, I should've brought a sandwich. At his wedding Quinn had eaten a forkful of tortoise stew (Changó's favorite), a quarter of an *aguacate,* and the bread pudding he publicly designated as the wedding cake—one mouthful, with which he kissed Renata, and food then became irrelevant. But, listen, sometimes the only thing the Mambí troops had to eat was sour oranges and tree rats. Quinn blocked the hunger nag and focused on the light of the large, almost full moon (the same moon his grandfather saw—he was with the Mambises in March, and beyond). Its light filtered at times onto the path Arsenio's men were following through the dense foliage; but when the blackness resumed they still moved with great certainty, eyesight being only one of their navigational tools.

They walked without speaking, not a word. The burlier of the two men was the leader and carried on his back something like a bedroll wrapped in straw, which, Quinn would see when it was delivered to Fidel, was not a bedroll but a Thompson machine gun and cartons of ammunition, a gift to Fidel from Arsenio who got the Thompson and a Garand from two of Batista's soldiers, killed after they left a whorehouse in Bayamo.

The Garand was strapped over the shoulder of the second man, Omar, a son of Arsenio who was joining Fidel, and that was possible only if you brought your own weapon.

Omar had been driven off his land by the army, which was clearing out all villages where Fidel had gotten, or might get, help or supplies, creating a no-man's-land where friend or foe would be shot on sight, and which opened great areas to the bombing raids the air force was planning. This was a replay of 1896 and '97 when Capitán-General Valeriano Weyler, the Spanish commander of all Cuba, emptied villages to isolate rebels who lived in them invisibly. He herded 300,000 peasants, maybe more, no one kept count, into reconcentration camps where hundreds of thousands died of hunger and disease, earning Weyler his Cuban sobriquet, "The Butcher," and establishing his reputation as one of history's great villains.

In the seventh hour of their journey Quinn and Arsenio's son waited at a small creek while the burly man went ahead to confirm that they were near their destination. He returned and they walked thirty more minutes into the sunrise, feeling the onset of the intense morning heat, and found the Comandante at his headquarters of the moment, a primitive hut whose occupants had been evacuated by the army. He was sitting on a stool, two men with him and four more circulating around the hut watching for danger. Quinn would count another twenty-some men at rest among the trees.

"Mr. Quinn," said Fidel, standing up and confirming that he was six-feet-three, three inches closer to the moon than Quinn, "they tell me you interrupted your honeymoon to come here." There was that noted beard, black as the forest night, and an amiable smile. He wore fatigues and a cap he kept on throughout the interview.

"They are right," said Quinn, "but my pilgrimage here is part of the honeymoon. Without coming to talk to you about revolution I wouldn't be married."

"Then you are in my debt. You are wearing beads of Santeria. Are you a follower?"

"My bride is, but I am learning. A *babalawo* gave me these beads. They represent Changó."

"My mother was a Catholic but also followed the Santeria. When she was pregnant a *babalawo* told her I was the son of a warrior god. She initiated me with a ceremony when I was still in the womb and she said Changó put in an appearance."

"Wherever I go in Cuba I run into Changó. But the womb is new."

Fidel was thirty-one, a year and a half up on Quinn, and he looked fit, sanguine, and on edge, which Quinn thought was probably his permanent condition. He talked softly and told Quinn to do likewise, for the moisture of the morning carries words great distances and who knows who might be passing by out there? He spoke in Spanish, with one of his soldiers interpreting in English. Quinn identified himself as Daniel Quinn the Second, grandson of Daniel Quinn the First who came to Cuba to prove Carlos Manuel de Céspedes was not dead, as the Spaniards were claiming; and Herbert Matthews did the same for you. Now you're famous for not being dead; and Fidel agreed. Quinn said he would point out in his story that during an interview one month after Matthews, the Comandante still showed no symptoms of death.

Fidel thought he remembered the *americano* Quinn's book on Céspedes from his University days. Quinn said the Cubans called his grandfather El Quin. Fidel remembered an American called El Inglesito, fellow named Reeve, who had been a Union soldier in the Civil War and then came down and fought four hundred battles with the Mambises.

Quinn said he had found parallels between Fidel and Céspedes, who told El Quin, We survive off the enemy. We take their guns, their food, their clothes, their horses, even their guitars and bugles. "You did that at La Plata, no?"

"Yes, but only a few guns, some shoes," said Fidel. "We need many more guns."

"My wife sent you that batch of weapons Arsenio delivered yesterday," Quinn said.

"Your wife?"

"Renata Suárez Otero. She runs guns in her spare time. She was close to the Directorio but most of them are dead from the Palace attack."

"You must send her my deep, deep gratitude. That attack, it was useless bloodshed. We don't want to assassinate Batista. We want to abolish the system. We are fighting against reactionary ideas, not individuals."

"Spain sent six sets of assassins to kill Céspedes," said Quinn, "and all of them failed. He survived the war for five years."

"Assassination is at large on the streets of Cuba," Fidel said. "When Grau was president there were a hundred political assassination attempts in four years, and more than sixty of them succeeded. I was at the University and I survived one myself."

"Your survival," Quinn said. "How do you explain it? You didn't die in combat at the Moncada barracks, or in Batista's jail, or shipwrecked in the swamp, or being hunted up here by half the Cuban army? This smacks of a scripted life, Achilles without a fatal heel, your mother giving birth to a divinity. Do you think that's the reason you don't die? Or are you just lucky?"

"Luck reduces the merits of a man," Fidel said. "When I was captured at Moncada they were ready to cut me in pieces and fry me, but a lieutenant in Batista's army would not let his men shoot me. He even refused to give me to his superior, who was a famous killer. 'You can't kill ideas,' the lieutenant said, and he turned me over to the police for trial. Batista tried to poison me in jail but people handling the food sent me warning notes, so I went on a hunger strike. Later I got food from elsewhere.

"When Batista visited the prison, I sang the Twenty-sixth of July marching song to him, and he put me in solitary for forty days without light. He is not a music lover. I read books by the light of a liquid olive oil candle with a match for a wick and it lasted three hours. Then I had to get out from the mosquito net to make another candle, and the mosquitoes would follow me back under and torture me until I killed them all. People sent me books and I also asked the jailers for José Martí's writings, but they said he was too revolutionary. So I asked for Marx's *Das Kapital*. I told them I wanted to become a capitalist when I got out of prison, and they gave it to me. Until then I had read Marx only to page 380.

"Also, this wonderful peasant bandit, a Precarista who helped us survive when we first came up here, went home to see his mother and betrayed us to the army, taking ten thousand dollars to kill me. He rejoined us, and that day I decided we should move our camp. Why? Not because of luck, but because he had asked questions about where we posted our sentries. I still trusted him, but nevertheless we moved to a higher point that we could control and conceal. That night the traitor slept with his pistol under a blanket, right alongside me. He could have killed me but his *cojones* had shriveled. The next morning B-26 bombers and F-47 fighters bombed and strafed the area we had abandoned. We survived, but not by chance. My moving us was instinctive, not lucky."

"What happened to the traitor?"

"He died with lightning. We shot him during a thunderstorm."

Quinn made coded notes on all that was said, as brief as possible. He would rely on memory for reconstituting this talk, for if he was caught by the army, explicit notes could be a death warrant.

Fidel offered him a plate of *congri*—rice and beans cooked together— but Quinn said he could not take food out of the mouths of the rebel army. Fidel insisted and said there was plenty for today, that the men had eaten their fill; and so Quinn ate with great relish. He brought up Hemingway, a perennial soldier and man of the gun, and told of Cooney's song and Hemingway's one-two, and the challenge. Should Hemingway fight such a duel?

"Yes, of course," said Fidel. "He is too important to refuse a challenge. He loves war, and a duel is war on a scale of one to one. Cubans love duels. Prío, when he was president, passed a law making duels illegal, as if that would stop them. It's like passing a law against war. Tell Hemingway he must find a way not to lose. If he can wait until we defeat Batista I will organize the duel and see that he wins. He is too valuable to lose his life for such a thing. I like the way he writes, how he has conversations with himself. His novel on the Spanish civil war can teach you about battle."

So now Quinn would pass along the Comandante's advice to Papa: take ten paces, turn, and put a bullet in Cooney's heart, but shoot first and not into the air. Do not turn away as a gesture of contempt that invites him to shoot you in the back. Above all, don't allow him to shoot you just because of your acute sense of irony. Papa always went to war for the macho thing—drink and fuck and fish and hunt and fight and kill and put yourself in mortal danger and prove your courage and be a hero of the just cause. Quinn is going through a little of this in the here-and-now, and Hemingway is watching from the sidelines. But it isn't simple emulation by Quinn, who doesn't hunt or fish, but he drinks and fucks and here he is in danger in a war zone because he has come to see the hero. He's not doing it because he thinks he's a coward, or because of a personality disorder, or a love affair with war such as Hemingway has had. He's doing it because it's a continuation of an earlier life choice: to be a witness, a writer, something to do while he's dying that isn't boring; and he will write about that, which seems his primary motive. He has a strong impulse to salvage history, which is so fragile, so prismatic, so easily twisted, so often lost and forgotten. Right now a full moon is rising on the revolution, rising on a day like none other and, if Quinn doesn't report on it, who will? It will fade into the memory bank of those here, and if they survive they'll tell what they remember, fragments of the actuality which they'll skew with their prejudices (and so will you, Señor Quinn). Yet monitoring the whatness of the previous unknown, that seems to be Quinn's job: I was there and then he said this, then this happened, and then they went that way—following the path of the machete, you might say.

Why bother?

Well, Quinn is young and his motives may be more opaque than they seem, but he has no interest in gaining power for himself. He's fascinated by those who want to transform the day, the town, the nation for other than venal or megalomaniacal reasons. Is working for the just cause one of his motives? It seems to be on his agenda. He intuits that it's worth his time to bear witness to people living for something they think is worth dying for. He also has another reason: he wants to escalate himself in his grandfather's dead eyes.

"That peasant who helped you before he betrayed you, it seems bandits and gangsters become valuable players in a war," Quinn said.

"I knew a few who were trying to make a revolution when it was not possible," said Fidel, "and they were killed as gangsters. Today they would be heroes."

"What makes a man a revolutionary?"

Fidel sat down on a rock outcropping beside the hut. "What a question." He puffed his cigar and exhaled his answer.

"The passionate embrace of the vocation," he said. "The obsession with changing the order of existence. Reading Martí, my early hero, the poet who organized a war. Listening to the voices from the French and American revolutions. The insights of Milton, Calvin, Luther, Thomas Paine, Montesquieu. I read Marx and I studied Roosevelt's New Deal in prison. Also I was always awed and horrified by Cuba's wars, and by the parade of tyrants who oppressed us. And then there is the absolutism of belief."

"In what?"

"In the possibility of revolution."

"So much revolution in Cuba," Quinn said. "If it's not erupting it's being planned. It's like Trotsky's idea of permanent revolution."

"We are still fighting the wars of '68 and '95 that Céspedes and Agramonte and Gómez and Maceo and Martí waged," said Fidel. "But we have never in our history gotten near Trotsky's idea of taking the country from the bourgeoisie and putting it into the hands of the workers. We are always fighting another *hijo de la gran puta*—Spanish villains like Valeriano Weyler, or our own despots, Machado and Batista. And we are always weakened or betrayed by Cubans who fear they'll lose their wealth if there is a revolution. The cockroaches! *Coño!* They turned away from Céspedes because he had so many black Mambí leaders that they feared a black takeover. Many Cuban plantation owners would not give up their slaves. They had fought Spain in the past, not for independence but to annex Cuba to the U.S. as a slave state. *De pinga!*"

"But when the tyrant is impregnable," Quinn said, "the Cuban revolutionary seems to turn suicidal. Eduardo Chibás shooting himself during his own political radio speech. All those Directorio youths facing down Batista's machine guns. José Antonio Echevarría walking toward a police car firing his pistol. And Martí charging into battle on horseback as if his leadership skills in bringing an army together were nothing compared with the damage he'd do by galloping into the blasts of Spanish guns. He needed to die. They all needed to die."

"I would differentiate among them," said Fidel, "and also between suicide and challenging danger. There is a moment of transcendence, and when it rises up in you, then sudden death can be a mundane fate of no consequence. I am sure José Antonio was in that sort of moment when he walked toward the police car, shooting at it. I see him as totally unafraid to fail.

"With Martí it may have been the opposite—death becoming more important than life. Distance had come between him and the two major military leaders of his war. He had been given the rank of major general, and people were also calling him 'El Presidente' of Cuba Libre. But Máximo Gómez, who made him a general, said that as long as he himself lived, Martí would never be president. And Maceo, a negro general of great intelligence, told Martí to his face that he was not a fighter and not fit to be called a general.

"An unverified but enduring part of this legend is that Maceo pulled the general's epaulets off Martí's shoulders. If that was how it was for Martí—and we may never know the truth of this alienation—then his galloping into the Spanish guns very soon afterward can be read as a tactical stroke of recreating himself as a martyr. And revolutions need martyrs. Leaders plan the revolution, but the force grows from the tyrant's oppression, and then come the argument and the ideas, and when you are in the season of insurrection, the momentum will overcome very great resistance. The leader sometimes realizes how minuscule he is, another energetic figure, but just a small gust of wind moving with the hurricane."

"The palace attack," Quinn said, "if it had succeeded would that have started the hurricane?"

"Even if they had killed Batista," said Fidel, "it would only have been a beginning. Their backup force failed them. They did not have unity. They would have been easily defeated by the army."

The Comandante's tone was suddenly abrupt, edgy. He needed Batista alive for his revolution. He took two cigars from his shirt pocket.

"Do you smoke cigars, Señor Quinn?" He offered Quinn one. "A Punch Double Corona, a very old brand owned by a tobacco baron I knew in

Havana, an old reactionary who made great cigars. A box of them arrived yesterday, a gift from a Santiago lawyer who supports us. I view it as a gift from the gods, perhaps from Changó, although Changó hates cigars."

Quinn accepted the cigar and said, "I smoked my first at age eleven and spat for half an hour. In 1945 I was working a Christmas job in the post office and a mailman gave me a Headline, a sweet nickel cigar and I loved it. I graduated to ten-cent White Owls, but I know nothing of serious cigars. I'm ready to learn."

"Cuba will teach you, and about many other things also," Fidel said. "It has already taught you about women."

"I'm not quite sure what I've learned," said Quinn.

"You learned how to take a wife."

"That was a miracle."

"Yes, they sometimes happen in Cuba."

Fidel led Quinn outside and they walked from the hut to the edge of the woods and back with all the men watching them, the interpreter at Quinn's side speaking into his ear. Fidel lit Quinn's and his own Double Coronas with a Zippo and Quinn puffed his alive, savored it, and between puffs gestured his approval to the Comandante.

"They are truly great," said Fidel. "And the smoke also repels mosquitoes."

"To get back to revolution," said Quinn. "My grandfather quoted Maceo that you don't beg for liberty, you win it with the blow of a machete. He was awed by it. Do you know the battle of Jiguaní?"

"I know the machete. Battles were encounters in that war, not designed. Armies came upon each other and fought."

"That was Jiguaní," said Quinn. "Gómez had tried to lure the Spaniards out of their barracks, but failed, so he sent troops to burn Jiguaní's cattle farm and kill the Spanish herd, and sent hundreds of former slaves, *convoyeros*, to bring back the meat. The unarmed *convoyeros* were carrying great slabs of beef back toward Gómez when Spanish foot soldiers ambushed them. Gómez heard the firing and moved with his six hundred white-shirted troops—the charge of the whispering machetes—and the Spanish front disintegrated. Mambí horsemen cut off their arms, or split them in half, a great slaughter. The wounded crawled into the woods to hide, but the Mambí soldiers followed. Nicodemo, the slave who had guided my grandfather into Cuba Libre, was shot in the left arm, but with machete in hand listened for moans from the wounded and beheaded eighteen. He piled their heads at the forest's edge."

"First," said Fidel, "I want you to know that we do not execute enemy wounded. At La Plata we treated them with our medicine. And second, if the troops had formed their Spanish square, those charging machetes would have fallen from Spanish volleys. The machete was effective when the war began, for the surprised Spaniards could not match it with their single-shot rifles and bayonets. It was a weapon for close combat, not attack. The machete was still used in '95, but when Gómez ordered a machete charge in a battle at Cascorro the Spaniards had repeating rifles, Mausers, and they slaughtered the Cubans, dead horses everywhere. That legendary charge of the machete had come to an end."

Quinn and the Comandante had been sitting elbow-to-elbow on the outcropping, Quinn's cigar down to a stub. Fidel stood up and two of his men moved closer to him.

"I would like to explain in detail to you," he said, "just how we are waging our war on Batista's army, but that would give him the edge. He has three thousand troops in Oriente. We do not have so many. But I can tell you this, that the way into the Sierra Maestra is not easy. Every entrance is like the pass at Thermopylae, where fourteen hundred Greeks held off a hundred thousand Persians for seven days, slaughtering a multitude until a traitor showed the Persians a path where they were able to outflank the Greeks."

"The traitor is eternal."

"Yes, but sometimes he does not prevail."

With a smile and body language Fidel moved the interview toward closure. He extended his hand and Quinn shook it.

"Señor Quinn," he said, "I thank you for making the journey here. The interview has been a good one. You did not try to entrap me in political conundrums. We must continue another day. But now I have an appointment with President Batista's armed forces."

"Thank you for your words, and the *congri*, and the cigar," said Quinn.

"Hasta luego," said Fidel.

"Buena suerte," said Quinn. Good luck.

Quinn and Omar, heading back to meet Moncho at Arsenio's wife's house, were both on their stomachs in a sparse growth of young trees, small bushes, and tall grass, not moving, for Omar had seen four Cuban army soldiers below in a jeep and he waved Quinn to the ground and hissed *"Abajo,"* then dropped himself into the bushes. Lying on his side looking through the grass Quinn saw no soldiers. He saw a woman's painted face looming large before him, oval, pale-blue and off-white with very red lips, and she hovered, so vivid that he was about to ask who sent you when she vanished, and all he could see was the undergrowth he was lying in and wishing it were deeper.

Omar lay thirty yards ahead which, Quinn would come to know, was Fidel's method of moving troops—one by one, a hundred yards between them, not thirty. Omar kept Quinn closer than a hundred for he did not want to lose him; but Fidel's method was one man in the lead and if they take him down the second one is aware, and new directions are taken. One dead is a big loss but not as big as when one squad leader, ignoring Fidel's standing order, piled his men into a truck to get there faster and was blown to fragments by an army bazooka, ten gone. Batista's troops took home nothing from this about the liability of togetherness and they continued moving in a column on the principle of power and safety in numbers, and were shot in multiples by hidden rebels as they came into range. They could then either die returning fire at the invisible foe or survive in retreat.

Quinn and Omar were another hour getting to the rendezvous house, a seven-and-a-half-hour trek. Quinn was desperately tired, soaked in sweat, and all he wanted was sleep. The painted woman's face returned above him as he walked, her forehead and nose powder blue, eyes rimmed with the same blue, her cheeks, chin, and neck all off-white and her hair a bright yellow. What brings you here, lovely lady, creature from an exotic realm? Is your painted face an enticement to love? Your place or mine?

Where is your place? I'll need a nap first. She didn't answer, just stared over his head, an aloof one. Maybe she's the mime of Oshun, isn't blue her color? Or Renata's grandmother, desolate spirit, love clown in grief coming late to our wedding. Was she Sikan, about to be sacrificed for capturing the sacred fish, or was this what Renata would look like in ten years? She abandoned Quinn when the sun grew brighter and he was left with a sense of urgency to do something, but what? He could not say, and his urgency turned to anxiety.

He recapitulated his three hours of conversation with the Comandante, trying to fix on a lead for the story he would write. He liked the line about luck but that wasn't news. The Comandante's "appointment" with the president's armed forces was newsy, if it happened and Quinn could get it into print before or on the same day the appointment was kept. What would it be? A modest attack like La Plata? Fidel did not seem to have many men. Quinn had counted about thirty visible around the hut. Quinn you are thinking like a beat reporter. Forget news and profile the revolutionary who doesn't die. Yes, that was how to do it.

Quinn was as deceived as Matthews about the real number of the rebel force. Matthews guessed two hundred when they were twenty, Quinn counted thirty but they were sixty. Four hours after Quinn had wished him luck the Comandante moved his troops out, a ten-mile march to the army outpost at El Uvero, a wooden garrison on a lake with fifty-three soldiers. The rebels approached at a crawl for half an hour and took attack positions forty yards from the garrison. Fidel fired first at two o'clock under a genuinely full moon and army rifles flashed with return fire. The fight lasted three hours until the rebels had the garrison in crossfire from two .30 caliber machine guns on tripods, and the army raised the white flag. The rebels counted six dead, the army fourteen, and fourteen taken prisoner, the bloodiest encounter in this war. The rebels loaded an army truck with forty-six rifles, two machine guns, six thousand rounds of ammunition, medicine, clothes, food. The victory proved the value of Fidel's tactics and the vulnerability of army outposts. All were closed and the troops moved to Oriente's main military bases.

❖

Moncho and Alfie were waiting for Quinn at the house of Arsenio's old wife. Quinn briefed them on his interview and his cigar and said he needed to sleep before he could utter another word. They put him in the backseat of Moncho's car with a pillow and Moncho drove to Palma Soriano where Renata and Quinn would resume their honeymoon.

But Renata was not there.

Holtz said he had driven her back from Moncho's in the Buick an hour after Quinn's departure for Fidel. She said she did not want to sleep in that house, and when they got to Holtz's she immediately went to her room. Holtz woke at eight this morning to find that she and the Buick were gone, and no message left.

Quinn was baffled. She knew she was a target for the police or the SIM through her link to Diego, and maybe because she joined the protesting women in Céspedes Park. Was she angry at not seeing Fidel? She knew it was unlikely. Punishing Quinn for going without her? And how does vanishing compensate for being left out? Isolating herself to cool down? Going off alone to affirm her intrepidity, self-sufficiency, guts, and defiance—making a willful leap into rebel-fugitive status?

They checked airlines to see if she flew to Havana. Would she take a train? Drive? They checked hospitals for accidents. Would she go home? Unlikely. Her mother said the police had come to the house looking for her. Should we call the police in Santiago to see if she's in custody? No. Retrace her steps—follow the road back to Santiago to see if the car had a breakdown, or was abandoned. Check city streets, restaurants, the Yacht Club. Check the hotel—she's still registered and has clothes in the room. Have Holtz call anybody left in the Directorio to see if she made contact. Call Esme. Call her aunt in Cárdenas, the one she lied about going to see. Natalia would call Renata's friends in Oriente, but she only knew a few. Moncho called people in the 26th underground in Santiago. He sent a message to Fidel's people to be on the watch, also to Arsenio. Moncho had family contacts to call. Holtz and his sister got nowhere. Moncho turned up nothing. Quinn called Max who instantly blamed Quinn for letting her go off alone. He said the *Post* couldn't run his Fidel interview because of new censorship pressure. Max said he'd pass the word to his spies in high places, the Buro, the police. "If anything happens to that girl, Quinn . . ." and he hung up.

She would call. She would come back to Holtz's. She would get a message to Quinn, her husband. She was so wildly in love that she had married him before she got to know him. She was a resourceful woman. Savvy. A good driver. Didn't drink much. Knew how to protect herself. Wouldn't willfully put herself in jeopardy. Smart as they come. Brilliant. A survivor. Narciso said danger lay ahead for her and gave her that necklace, told her to show it to her enemy and tell him if he harms her Changó will kill him. She took that seriously. Narciso said Quinn was in danger from murderers. The police? The SIM? Batista's freelance gangsters? Alfie said he'd put his friends on the case. Alfie was worried. He really liked Renata. He'd look for her with Quinn, wherever, however long it took.

◈

Quinn entered the hall, his hair thick in a casual torsion to the right, and very black. He smiled at the group, mostly men, though he could not be sure whether women were among them. Their number seemed to diminish, which was of no matter. He was ready to speak, and did, text in hand which he did not look at or need, and what he said evoked laughter from all, and he knew the audience was ready for him and he grew confident. He spoke about faces and masks, how we need them to survive, which was a gaffe. He suddenly realized he knew several of the men and they were dead. To his left sat an old colleague, dead, but full of smiles that seemed earnest, which was unlikely, for there was bad history here. Perhaps it was a welcoming, glad to see you here among the dead.

The reason Quinn was speaking of surviving to dead men would become clear, he was sure. He talked on but the audience was now lost to him, vanishing rather quickly. The old colleague stood up and smiled, not speaking, but giving enthusiastic gestures for all Quinn was saying. Then he left and Quinn turned and spoke his next words to half a dozen listeners, his hair moving and then flung back in a manner that suggested a brilliant British film actor whose name he could not remember. He wondered if any in the audience would recognize the dramatic effect of the thrown hair, which was a bodily gesture of completion, confidence, singularity. It was a most dramatic effect for any actor. It did not matter that the audience was gone. Quinn knew how witty, how meaningful his remarks were.

"The arc of justice," he said to the empty room, "the arc of justice . . ."

ALBANY, WEDNESDAY, JUNE 5, 1968

◆◆◆◆

Daniel Quinn's day began with the tragedy of Bobby Kennedy comatose but wide-eyed on a hotel kitchen floor, vigils for him now unfolding across the nation, including one in Albany. Quinn's story in yesterday's paper on the silencing of Albany's radical Catholic priest had also infuriated blacks and college students, and a protest meeting set for tonight could inflame a city already quivering with racial tension.

Quinn's father, George Quinn, lived with Quinn and could not be left alone. Renata had gone to the clinic to bring home her niece, Gloria, and Ursula, the family housekeeper who doubled as keeper of the quixotic father, had totaled her car, broken her arm, and would do no keeping of any sort today. Quinn went upstairs and found his father dressed for dinner, wearing his gray Palm Beach suit, maroon paisley tie, and tying knots in one of his two hundred neckties. The ties hung on five wooden hangers in the room's closet, a dozen or more of them knotted and reknotted, one tie outstanding with four knots in it. Quinn moved his father away from the ties and began the daily unknotting.

"How you feeling?" Quinn asked.

"I'm several flavors of excellent. How's yourself?"

"I'm tip-top but Ursula isn't coming today. She totaled her car and broke her arm."

"Was she hurt?"

"She broke her arm."

"Ursula?"

"Yes."

"How did she do that?"

"She totaled her car."

"Was there much damage?"

"It was totaled."

"That doesn't sound good."

"No, and it means we should get you out of the house. Get a little recreation. What do you say?"

"Recreation is fine if you don't get too much of it."

"How about a few hours? That's not too much. Get you out on the town. Whataya say we go down to the Elks Club? How does that sound? I'll drop you when I go to the paper."

"There's people who come in and out and you don't know who the hell they are."

"You'll know some of them."

"It's neglect all the way along."

"What do you mean, neglect?"

"Right up to snuff."

"What do you mean, snuff?"

"The best. The griff. The spiff. The whole thing here is static."

"What do you mean, static?"

"Static has got to be good."

"All right. Get your hat and we'll go down to the Club."

"The Club?"

"The Elks Club."

"I joined the Elks when the bishop wouldn't let us have beer in the K. of C. alleys."

"I remember. You were a ringleader in the protest."

"Beer and bowling go together."

"You can get both of them at the Club."

"The Club."

"Get your hat."

Quinn called Pat Mahar, custodian of the Elks, and told him George was coming in and could he keep an eye on him for a couple of hours? Leave me a message at the paper if he needs anything, Pat. Just keep him busy, give him a beer or two, not too many, put him in the card room, he can still play blackjack, or in the TV room or at the pool table, just get him talking to his friends and he'll be all right. He does what he's told, most of the time. I know you're not a nursemaid, Pat, but try to keep him in the club. I'll owe you. Twenty bucks for your trouble, how's that? Even with the twenty Quinn didn't trust Pat to do any of this, but it was a start. He'd stop at the Club himself when he got a few minutes.

He called the city desk for any change in his assignment and Markson, the city editor, said Quinn should interview the Mayor on Bobby Kennedy and on the racial tension in town.

"Did you forget the Mayor leaves the room when I arrive?"

"He'll get over it. Tell him what a great job he's doing. We want your perspective on the machine's hostility to Bobby when he ran for senator. You know that inside out. And pump him on what he's doing to hold down any violence. You also got a message. Max Osborne wants to see you but he didn't leave a number."

Max. What the hell kind of message is that with no number? "I can't guarantee I'll get through to the Mayor," Quinn said as he hung up, and George Quinn came down the stairs wearing his coconut straw hat.

"Are we ready?" George asked.

"We are." But as Quinn reached for the knob on the vestibule door he saw Matt Daugherty coming up the porch steps, in shirtsleeves and with a grim smile.

"Matt. We're just leaving, but come on in."

"Only a few minutes," Matt said. "How are you, George?"

"I'm three flavors of excellent, how's yourself?"

"I'm trying to figure it out," Matt said.

"I'm taking him down to the Elks Club," Quinn said. "You want coffee?"

"How about a beer?"

Quinn opened him a bottle of Irish Cream Ale from the fridge and they sat at the kitchen table. George stood by the stove, hat on.

"We'll go in a few minutes, Pop," Quinn said.

"Whatever you say. I care not for riches."

The Reverend Matthew Daugherty, OFM, voluble, forty-four-year-old Franciscan professor of religion and theology at Siena College, built for football, hard-charging, soft-spoken rebel of the faith, self-anointed radical missionary in the slums who, in speeches, offhand remarks to the press, and letters to the editor, had repeatedly attacked the Mayor and the Albany Democratic machine for indifference to the poor and especially the black poor—a brazen stance in the holy shadow of the Albany Catholic diocese, and unheard of in this town in this or the previous century—had been silenced by his superior at the college, told to stay away from the inner city, teach your classes, shut your mouth. But the order had obviously come down from the hierarchy of the diocese; and what else could you expect from those lofty Democratic clerics except an edict to stop bothering our generous politicians who are all regular communicants?

Matt drank half his beer and said, "I just took a ride with Penny. She dropped me off up the block."

"Didn't you take a vow of chastity?"

"All we did was talk. You gotta hear this."

"Tell me."

"She says the machine is out to get one of their enemies, to set an example. She doesn't know who but it won't be pretty. Somebody told her."

"Who?"

"She wouldn't say but she swears it's true. She says it could be me."

"Didn't they already get you?"

"Then maybe it's you. Or one of the Brothers."

"You don't really trust Penny, do you?"

"Penny's all right, Dan. I know what you think, but she does good work with the neighborhood groups, for no pay. I respect that even if I don't always trust what she says."

"Why are you riding around with sexy women on the make? Aren't you restricted to campus?"

"I can walk. I walk the golf course. I wave at the golfers. She picked me up on the road that runs along the seventeenth hole. After we talked I thought I should come down and tell you."

"You called her?"

"She called me. We've talked before."

"You hear her confession?"

"Not as such."

"But she confides in you."

"She's got troubles like everybody."

"Does she cry into the shoulder of your robe?"

"She's got emotions."

"But you don't. Salty women with major tits don't disturb the serenity of your chastity."

Matt swallowed some beer.

"I'm guessing she put the moves on you," Quinn said.

"I guess you could call it that."

"What did she do?"

"You know how it goes."

"Actually I do. She did it with me."

"You did it with her?"

"No, she did it with me. The moves. Then she called Renata to say she was sorry for keeping me out late. I wasn't out late, but that's her method. She sandbags you, then rats on you for doing nothing. Disturb the equilibrium, that's her game."

"I can handle this stuff, Dan. I been handling it for years. I'm not that horny lowlife I used to be. I found other ways of getting in trouble."

"Shooting off your mouth."

"My specialty."

"Look, are you all right? I mean it's been a rough couple of days for you." Quinn stood up.

"I'm getting a grip. You gotta leave?"

"I do. Tremont Van Ort is bad off. He's flat out on his stoop on Dongan Avenue and won't move, or can't. Claudia called an ambulance but they don't pick up on Dongan Avenue. Claudia asked if I could get him to the hospital. I said I'd see what I could do."

"I'll go with you."

"The South End is off-limits for you. What if you're seen?"

"What else can they do, confiscate my socks? Gotta help Tremont."

"You want a beer for the road?"

"Why not?"

In the dining room George Quinn was sitting with his hat in his lap, facing the large wall mirror over the sideboard. He was waving to his own image, telling him to come on over, but when he saw Quinn he changed the gesture and blessed himself.

"Bless me father for I have sinned," he said.

"You haven't sinned today," Quinn said. "Let's go."

"So that's it," George said. "We're all set. I got my hat." He stood up and put his hat on and walked to the door.

"My father was asking for you, George," Matt said.

"Your father?"

"Martin Daugherty."

"Martin Daugherty. We were in France together."

"I know. He says you were the best-dressed soldier in the AEF."

"Martin Daugherty was a good fellow. You could always trust him. He wrote for the papers."

"He's out in the Ann Lee Home."

"I didn't know that," Quinn said.

"He's been there six months but I got a letter from the county that they're kicking him out."

"For what?"

"They don't say. I figure it's the politicians pressuring me."

"Those bastards."

"Martin Daugherty lived on Colonie Street," George said.

"He did indeed," Matt said.

"We should be going. I've got my hat."

"You're goin' out on the town," Matt said.

George answered in a song:

"Put your feet on the barroom shelf,
Open the bottle and help yourself."

"Look out, Albany," Matt said. "Here comes George Quinn."

What Danny said was, "There's the Club, right up those steps, okay?"

Of course it's okay.

"It's two forty-five. I'll meet you at the Club bar at six o'clock. You have your watch?"

Of course I have my watch. And George got out of the car and took two steps toward the Club, and when Danny pulled away George turned

127

around to watch him go. He looked up and down the block for the Club, crossed State Street and walked down the hill and crossed Pearl Street. Steps is what Danny said. Steps loomed. Five of them. Brown. Nobody outside. He pushed open the door and walked across the mottled marble. He stopped and stared at all the glass and brass.

"Can I help you, sir?"

"The Club."

"Which club might that be, sir?"

"It's right up to snuff."

"This is a bank, sir. Do you have an account with us?"

"I certainly do."

"Fine. Let me take you to a teller. Your name?"

"My name for what?"

"The name on your account."

"George Quinn."

"Welcome to the New York State Bank, Mr. Quinn. I'll check your account for you."

"It's right up to snuff."

"I'm sure it is."

George took his wallet from his back pocket and opened it to find two five-dollar bills. He poked a finger into a pocket of the wallet and pulled out a check. He opened it and read his name on the check.

"Right over here. You can write your check right here. Here's the pen. Is there anything else I can do for you?"

"What else is there?"

"How much would you like to write this check for, Mr. Quinn?"

"It's got to be enough."

"I hope it will be."

George poised the pen over the check and thought about numbers, then wrote "two hundred" on a blank line. He put down the pen and handed the check to the man at his elbow.

"You have to sign it, sir."

George looked at the check and picked up the pen. He signed "George," and gave the check to the man.

"Your full name, Mr. Quinn."

George wrote "Quinn" after "George."

"Now fill in the amount with numbers," said the man. "Two hundred, in numbers. Two-oh-oh."

George wrote "200" and handed the check to the man, who took it to a teller. He came back and handed the check to George.

"I'm sorry, Mr. Quinn. I can't cash this. This is one of our checks but your account here was closed last year. Perhaps you have an account in the Albany Savings Bank or the National Savings, or City and County? Mechanics and Farmers? Do any of those banks sound familiar to you?"

"My bank is close to the Club."

"I'm not sure which club you mean."

"Why the hell are you in business if you won't cash a check and don't know where the hell anything is?"

"Shall I call Albany Savings for you? I could have someone walk you over there."

"Don't bother," said George, and he went out. He looked up State Street at the Capitol, which he had watched burn in 1911 and he wondered if they ever finished rebuilding the damn thing. Yes, and maybe no. He had worked in the Document Room when Jimmy Walker was a senator and Al Smith ran the Assembly. Big Bill Sulzer wasn't around yet, was he? It was Al who was the big man. Get me the *World*, the *Sun*, the *Times* and the *Tribune*, Georgie, Al would say. Big smile on his kisser. Here's a dollar and you keep the change.

George crossed State and looked at Van Vechten Hall and thought of going to Beauman's to meet the ladies, but it's early, isn't it? He felt for his vest pocket watch, no vest, no pocket, no watch. Wrist? There it is and it's three o'clock, too early. Beauman's musicians don't set up until seven.

"Hello, George," a fellow said.

"Hellee, helloo Brzt, Bitts, Billdy," what the hell is his name?

"Where you off to?"

"The Club," George said.

"You got time for a cuppa coffee?"

"All right," said George. Bradz, Bonzi, Bunzy turned into the Waldorf Cafeteria and George followed him in, took a ticket. Crenzy ordered the coffee.

"I was talking to the sheriff yesterday," Renzi said when they sat down. Renzi. "He says you're not coming back to work. I told him, George'll come back when he's well. I don't think so, he said. I told him, you don't go through two cataract operations and get right back at it. George is recovering."

"That's how it is," George said. "I got these new glasses, and eye drops," and he showed Renzi his eye drops.

"Just passing on what he said. Just so you know, George. I don't think it's good news. Give him a call."

"I'll do that," George said.

"What'd you think about Bobby Kennedy?"

"I voted for him. Patsy passed the word to cut him, but I voted for him. I'd vote for anybody named Kennedy."

"They shot him."

"Who shot him?"

"Some guy, I don't know who. But they caught him right away. He's probably a communist."

"Kennedy's not a communist."

"Get the paper, Georgie. It's all in the paper. After midnight last night, out in L.A. He just won the primary and they shot him."

"Who won the primary?"

"Bobby."

"They shot him because he won the primary?"

"Probably."

"I voted for him."

"Call the sheriff and ask him when he expects you back to work," Renzi said. "I'll pay for the coffee," and he took George's ticket.

"They don't shoot you when you win a primary," George said to Renzi's back. But Renzi kept walking and George didn't like the coffee. He went back out onto State Street and stared up at the Capitol. I saw that burn in 1911, the State Library. Two or three days it burned, maybe a week. He walked toward the Capitol and looked over at The Tub, the hotel where Al Smith stayed. The sign is down. Al doesn't have to stay there anymore. Al didn't have much money then but he's got it now. When

Bobby Kennedy came to Albany, George was there. Wasn't I? I was there for Truman when he came in on the back end of a train. I was there when Adlai's train came in and he talked to the crowd from the station platform at Columbia Street. When did Bobby come? His old man owns the Standard Building. Bootlegging, that's how the Kennedys got their money. It was Jack they shot, not Bobby. I was there when Jack came to Albany to have lunch. His father asked Patsy for an endorsement, and Patsy backed him all the way. Patsy never liked FDR, but he backed Jack. That's how Jack got to be president. They didn't cut Jack. George crossed State at Eagle Street and walked toward City Hall and past it. Here comes somebody. Vih. Vivuh. Viv. Vivian. Nice Vivvie.

"Hello, Georgie," the woman said. She was wearing a yellow straw hat.

"Hello, Vivvie," George said, and he tipped his hat. "Going to Beauman's, are you?"

Vivian stopped. "Oh, I wish," she said. "Beauman's. Those were the days. No, Georgie, just going over to Cody's and meet a friend."

"Cody's."

"Cody's Havana, you know it well. No Beauman's. No more."

"Havana? I know it. Beauman's." Vivian walked on and George watched her go. She had legs like. Legs. Like. I'm tying the leaves so they won't fall down and Nellie won't go away. Pag. Pog. Legs like Peg. George turned and saw the Court House and he stopped. Can't go there. Why not? George turned back toward City Hall and saw the Chedge coming out. Chedge Epstein and somebody. Fitz. No. Fitzmayor. No. The Mayor. They saw him coming and waited at the corner. George crossed to meet them.

"Hello, Chudge, hello Maaa," George said.

"George, where've you been? We miss you."

"Been in and out, up and down," George said.

"Damn it all, George, let's get you up to the lake. Get a few fellows together and play a little golf."

"You said it, Judge. Golf. Haven't played golf in quite a while."

"You feeling all right, George?" the Mayor asked. "I heard they operated on you."

"New glasses, Mayor, new eyes."

"That'll improve your putting," the Mayor said.

"Putt-putt," George said. "Going over to Havana."

"Havana Cuba? I love it down there, but that's a long way to go to play golf," the Mayor said.

And George sang:

"Cuba, that's where I'm going,
Cuba, that's where I'll stay."

"Haven't heard that one in a while," the Mayor said.

"Stop in my chambers, George," the judge said. "We'll talk about you coming up for some golf."

"I will, Judge, I will. I'll say a prayer for you."

"A prayer? You think you can beat me?"

"Two Hail Marys," George said.

"That's the wrong religion," the Judge said and he and the Mayor both laughed and walked up the street.

Judge. Epstein. Morris. Always wants me to play golf. Mayor Fitz. Fitz what? George watched the Judge and the Mayor walk up Washington Avenue. Going to have a beer, that's what they do after work. Up to the Club. Fort Fitz. The Fort. Mayor Alex Fitz. George decided he wanted a beer, wanted it cold, the foam sliced off the top by the bartender and the glass with frost on it. He did not know where to go to get such a beer. Fort Fitzgibbon? Fort Orange? The Club has beer. Where is it? He walked down State Street past the Elks Club and turned onto Lodge Street, down past the old Christian Brothers Academy. Brother who, taught reading and writing, arithmetic, taught to the tune of the hickory stick. Brother . . . I never liked him . . . Knocko. Brother Bernardine was a good fella. Brother William Knocko. He walked past Jack Shaughnessy's old Towne Tavern, but it's not there, new place there, don't like the looks, a dump. He walked down Beaver Street past Rudnick's, Jack's old Oyster House, Apollo Billiards, that's where Billy won the candy store. We booked numbers in the back of the store and Billy dealt poker. George crossed to the other side of Beaver and walked back the way he came and up the hill to where Beaver met Eagle. He saw the second police precinct, stay out of there, and across from it he saw a word in the window that he liked, Stanwix. Patsy. He went in and stood at the bar. People on barstools were watching television. Bobby Kennedy is out of surgery. It's shocking. In critical condition. The nation is stunned. Big colored fella behind the bar looked at George.

"What can I get you?"

"What's in the window."

"What do you want?"

"The sign in the window."

"You want the sign?"

"I want that," and he pointed at the neon window sign with Stanwix spelled backward.

"You want a Stanwix beer, is that it?"

"Yes. What's the name of this place?"

"Cody's," the man said.

"This isn't the Club, I know that."

"It's Cody's Havana Club, if that's what you mean."

"Cody's Havana Club," George said. "I've been here before."

"I'll get your beer," the man said.

George took a swallow of the beer and he loved it. He looked at it, watched it sweat. He rubbed the sweat, then lifted the glass and sipped. He loved the taste, the coldness on his tongue, in his throat. I should drink more beer. He tipped up the glass and finished it. He licked the foam off his lips. The bartender looked at him.

"Do it again?" he asked George.

"Do what again?"

"Have another beer."

"Good idea. I'll have another beer and do it again."

The barman drew another beer. "Only costs you a dollar," he said.

"What does?"

"The beer."

"A dollar? That's way too much. Beer costs a nickel. Some places they charge a dime. A glass of Bordeaux wine costs ten cents in Paris."

"That's before I was born," the bartender said. "You want a beer today it's fifty cents a glass and you had two glasses. One dollar."

George took out his wallet and fished for one of his five-dollar bills. He gave it to the man and stared at him.

"Is your name Dick?" George asked.

"No."

"You look a lot like a friend of mine. I haven't seen him in a while. You know Van Woert Street?"

"I do," the bartender said.

"Dick. That was his name. Dick Hawkins. Did you know him?"

"Never heard of him."

"Nigger Dick Hawkins," George said. "He could go in and out of any-body's house on Van Woert Street, just like a white man."

"Nigger Dick on Van Woert Street, imagine that," the bartender said.

"Wonderful fella," George said. "He'd do anything for me. They'd come around and tell me this and that and Dick'd say to them, 'You leave this kid alone, he's a friend of mine,' and they'd never touch me. Looked a lot like you. Is your name Dick, by any chance?"

"No, my name is George. Nigger George. I live on Van Woert Street. You ever heard of me?"

"No, can't say that I have and I live on Van Woert Street. Nigger Dick I know. Wonderful fella. Looks just like you. He'd do anything for me."

"You know what I'll do for you?" the bartender asked.

"No."

"I'll get your change, you'll finish your beer and then I'll kick your ass the fuck out of this bar."

"Hey, what are you saying?"

"I'm saying I don't want your business, motherfucker."

"Are you crazy? You can't use that language in public. There's women in here."

Everybody in the bar was looking at George. Man wearing his shirt outside his pants, two women in straw hats. George tipped his hat to the women who were sitting at the bar, separated by one stool. That looks like Vivvie. George saw them all staring as if they expected something from him, so he picked up his beer and raised a toast: "I care not for riches or wealth of the best, I care not for finery grand. Just give me a lass who owns a good name and give me a willing hand." He smiled and took a mouthful of his second beer. The woman in the yellow straw hat raised her glass to George and took a sip.

"He's all right, Roy," she said to the bartender.

"Sure he is," Roy said.

"No," she said, "I know him a long time. He works in the court. He handles the grand juries."

George broke into song:

"Good-bye, gang, I'm through.
Old pals I can't forget.
I say good-bye to you, without the least regret."

"I know that song," the woman said, and she sang along with George:

"I'm through with all flirtations.
There'll be no more fascinations.
There is one to whom I'm true.
Good-bye boys, good-bye girls, good-bye gang, I'm through."

Behind the bar Roy turned up the volume on the news show. The woman came over to George at the bar.

"George Quinn," she said, "you're still a rascal."

"George Josephus Jeremiah Randolph Franklin Aloysius Quinn," he said. "A pleasure to see you, my dear. Will you kiss me now or will you wait?"

"You're a scream. The last time we were in a bar together was at Farnham's. Do you remember?"

"Farnham's is a wonderful place. Right up to snuff."

"Oh, I know. I love the atmosphere. That wonderful dark wood."

"The atmosphere is wonderful. The wood."

"You mustn't mind the bartender, George. He's a sensitive boy, he doesn't like that word you used."

"What word?"

"Nigger." She whispered it.

"Nigger Dick, I knew him well."

"Yes, but you shouldn't say his name like that anymore. Just call him Dick, and don't say nigger."

"That's his name. Nigger Dick. He was part of the Sheridan Avenue Gang. I knew every one of them. There was only one Nigger Dick."

"Just don't say it anymore, okay? You understand? Don't say it or he'll throw you out. Roy can get very excited."

"Roy, who's Roy?"

"The bartender. He said his name was George, but it isn't."

"Right. He's not George, I'm George."

"You certainly are. George Quinn."

"That's me. Will you be going dancing at Beauman's this evening?"

"You're still thinking about Beauman's."

"It's right up to snuff. King Jazz's orchestra. You can't beat it. I don't recall your name."

"Vivian, Vivian Sexton, George. You know me a hundred years."

George took off his hat and held it out to her. "It's venerable to know you so long, Vivian," he said.

"You are such a gentleman," she said.

"I would be privileged to buy you a drink, Vivian. We could sit at that table over there. I'm on my way to the Club and I have to cash a check. The clock of life is wound but once and no man has the power to tell just where the hands will stop."

"That certainly is true, George, and it's a very poetic thing to say. I'd be glad to have a drink with you."

George placed his hat over his heart and he asked her, "Will you kiss me now or will you wait?" And Vivian kissed him on the cheek.

Max Osborne, wearing a white guayabera, alone at the end of the bar, studied Roy and saw the father in the son, a much larger version, a laboring man's arms and chest, a heavyweight, but the undeniable child of Cody: that same rigid backbone, same barrel of a chest, hands with their long fingers, skin a shade lighter than Cody's, but no evidence in the son of Cody's quiet talent for avoiding public conflict. This fellow had a talent for chastising the world. But he's Cody's boy. Like Max's girl. Children of a new day.

Max compared Roy with the four photos on the wall above the baby grand, blowups of the man and his icons: Fats who took Cody on as a protégé, and Billie—ah Billie, so unbelievably young, with the young Cody playing while she hits a note with eyes closed. Also—with the open back of a piano, trombone on the floor, light on a cymbal—the Duke, hunched at the keys so you couldn't know it was him, but who else could it be? And then Bing, leaning on the piano and singing at Cody, telling him to shine. Bingety-bing-bing.

"That photo of Sonny and Bing Crosby," Max said to Roy. "You know anything about that picture?"

Roy squinted for a tighter look at Max, then turned down the TV.

"You know Sonny?"

"Since the late thirties. You're his boy."

"Boy. Do I know you?"

"My name is Max. *Do* you?"

"I heard of a Max. But the man's not Sonny anymore."

"I know all about it. I thought it'd get your attention."

"How come you know so much?"

"I could tell you a story about the night your father played and Bing sang. I was there. You run this place for your father?"

"Not my line. What do you do, Max?"

"That's a personal question and I don't usually answer personal questions on religious grounds, Roy, and I am a religious man. But I'll answer you because you're Sonny's boy, Cody's boy, and Cody is a genius, although who am I to say that? A musical moron, that's who I am. But I have been a golf star, an actor on TV, I ran a newspaper in Cuba, I'm a retired spy, I taught literature in college, I'm producing a movie about Bing Crosby, who's an old friend of mine, and that's not a complete list. What's your line?"

"Goin' to college and bustin' my ass to do it. Who'd you spy on?"

"The universe. You know who took that Bing photo?"

"Cody knows."

"He does indeed. I took it. And where is Cody? He coming here?"

"He'll come by, but he won't stay. He's got a concert."

"Where?"

"DeWitt ballroom. His Farewell Concert they're calling it."

"Farewell to what?"

"Cody's sick."

"No. How sick?"

"Walkin'-around sick. Lung cancer."

"Hey, no, no. Since when?"

"He's got some time, but not a whole lot. He can still play."

"Where do I get a ticket?"

Roy went to the cash register and took a pack of tickets off the back bar. He put a ticket in front of Max.

"Twenty bucks, dinner included. It'll help pay some medical bills."

"I'll take two," and Max put a hundred-dollar bill on the bar.

"Will you turn up that TV, Roy?" a woman at the bar said. "They're talking about Bobby." Roy raised the volume and a TV newsman said the vigil outside the Los Angeles hospital where Robert Kennedy lies, perhaps mortally wounded, is ongoing. Attorney General Ramsey Clark said today that there is no evidence of a conspiracy at this moment in the shooting.

Roy gave Max a second ticket plus sixty bucks change and served the beer drinkers down the bar. "I met him when he campaigned here for senator," Roy said. "He mighta made a good president."

"I knew him in L.A. when he was chasing Marilyn," Max said. "Bing played golf with Jack."

"Bing and Jack, Bing and Sonny, Bobby and Marilyn. You know everybody. Anybody you don't know?"

"There's these two guys in China."

"So who shot Bobby?"

"I'd bet on the mob. The Teamsters hated him, Hoffa especially. But somebody'll blame the Cubans. They always blame the Cubans. But they hated him too."

"I'll bet you know Fidel, right?"

"We're pals. You like Fidel?"

"I respect him. He beat the system, did the time, fought the fight. He's been good to blacks from this country. I like it that he rattles the cages of politicians in this country."

"You do any time lately, Roy?"

Roy stared at him.

"I know a few things about you. You're a political animal."

"I'm political. I'm no animal."

"Bad word choice. I apologize. Radical, that's closer to it, isn't it, you and the other Brothers? A maverick among mavericks, isn't that so?"

"The Brothers say what needs sayin'."

"Tell 'em what's on your mind. Admirable."

"What's on your mind, Max? What is this quiz you got goin'?"

"I hear things, Roy. I hear the Brothers got the Albany cops on their backs, and the Mayor too. That's a heavy load, the cops and the Mayor."

"Who the hell are you?"

"Max Osborne. Your father played piano for my ex-wife in Havana. Esme Suárez."

"Esme. She's Gloria's mother."

"Bingo. Gloria. My little girl."

Renata was squirming on a metal bench in a corner of the empty day room when the orderly arrived with Gloria. Renata embraced her niece.

"She's packed but she doesn't want to go," the orderly said.

"Is that true, *mi amorcita*?" Renata asked.

Gloria shook her head no, then nodded yes. She was dressed to leave, white blouse, black slacks, heels, her beautiful yellow hair brushed into a familiar, casual fall. She looked like herself except for her violet eyes, which were wide with alien bewilderment.

"You want to stay here?"

Gloria shook her head no.

"Everybody here thinks it's all right for you to leave. Will you come home with me?"

Gloria shook her head no.

"You are not talking?"

Gloria shook her head no.

"You are so afraid."

They sat on the bench and faced each other. Gloria hugged herself, keeping a grip, Renata decided, on the forces that had put her here. She had driven into the Quinn driveway but couldn't get out of her car for an hour. Renata found her and coaxed her into the house, but she wouldn't speak about what was wrong. She hid under the bed covers for a day and a half without eating, silent until she slapped and smashed a window in the bathroom, slashing her hand. She took George Quinn's straight razor out of a bureau drawer and sat on the floor. Daniel heard the crash and found her holding the open razor, trying to decide where to cut herself for more serious bloodletting. After eight days in the psychiatric ward she did not seem improved to Renata; but there was no money to keep her here even one more day. It was out of the question to call Esme, who would lose her mind with worry, so Renata called Max to ask for money for her three overdue mortgage payments and didn't mention Gloria.

"I'll be down the hall," the orderly said to Renata, and he went out.

A flat-nosed little man in a black sweatsuit came into the day room. He had been walking rapidly up and down the hallway when Renata arrived. He looked at both women, then spoke to Gloria. "I'm the leading Garden player on this planet. I'm the universal linchpin. All the scum played sex games so the plants would poison the dogs. Garden wants you to send your phone numbers right now."

Gloria reached out to the man and took his small, gnarled hand. He pulled his hand away and scurried out of the room.

"You don't belong here," Renata said. "Sometimes you can live next to death without dying, but you should get out of here."

Gloria said nothing.

"There is a reason to come home. Your father is in Albany."

Gloria sat upright.

"Perhaps he knows you are here," Renata said, "but I don't know how. We talked last week but he said nothing about coming to Albany. Will you see him?"

Gloria almost nodded yes.

"And tonight is Cody's concert, probably his last one. You must see him play, even one song. He'd love it. Have you been in touch with Roy?"

Gloria shook her head.

"Has Alex been here?"

Gloria shook her head violently, turned her face away.

"It is very silly to be upset because I mention him. People know about it, *mi amor*. Daniel's editor asked him what he knew about you and Alex and Roy. You are no longer a secret. Hiding in here changes nothing. You have to talk about what happened. Whatever it was, it isn't worth your death. You survived it. You will survive better if you tell me about it."

Gloria said nothing.

"Since you won't speak I will tell you a story. You know everybody in it—your mother, Max, Cody and me. I was in school in Havana with *las monjitas*. Your mother was not getting work on Broadway because they wanted her only as a Latina and there were no Latina parts. She was beautiful, her English was perfect, her singing voice still rich, and she wanted to keep on with her career. So she came back to where she began, the nightclubs of Havana. There were more clubs than ever and more customers, so many Americanos and she was Esme Suárez, the Broadway star. The hottest clubs wanted her, Tropicana, Sans Souci, Montmartre, you know all this. She would work some weeks, then stop working, but she would always go to the clubs for dinner. Max did not like clubs the way Esme liked them, so she took me as her chaperone and we would see Chevalier and Cugat and Beny Moré and Dietrich, so many. The managers would bring the stars to our table and everybody adored your mother. So spirited, *qué viva, qué alegre*! Now I am going to tell you something. Sometimes men would take my hand and ask me to dance, but your mother would say, 'Look but do not touch.' She was thirty-two and I was sixteen, a nightclub virgin. You were a virgin when you asked me for lessons in the sexual life. They were for Alex, no?"

Gloria closed her eyes on the question.

"Of course they were. But your virginity is of no importance, nor is mine. One night at the Club Montmartre Max came to our table with a black musician, Cody, the first time I met him. He was from New York but he wanted to leave it and Max got him work at Night and Day, an American piano bar in old Havana. Max and Cody were friends since Cody was with Billie Holiday. He was the first to play for Billie and the newspaper said they were going to marry, but it ended. Billie loved Cody but she was a crazy person who worked very hard to destroy herself. Cody would never hurt her and she seemed to go with men who did hurt her. Many women are like this. Not me. If they hurt me I will do everything to hurt them. But that is not what I'm telling you. This night we had dinner and Cody talked very much with me, a sweet man who would never hurt anybody, shy almost, handsome, and your mother's age. I liked him very much and I knew I could fall in love with him if I was older. I was almost in love with him while we talked but I did not know much about love yet. I felt it without knowing what it meant. But Max saw it in my face before my sister saw it. I was also in love with Max. I was in love with all men who liked me because I did not yet know about love. Max, and you know this, is a womanizer. Everybody knows this. He womanized with me when I was fourteen but he did not touch me. Never. We would laugh and he would talk about movie stars in love and tell me I would soon be a movie star and should know everything about love. Max loved many women. He had favorites, like your mother, but he went to the woman who was in front of his eyes. This night I am talking about he saw Cody touch my arm. Cody was telling me about his sad life, that his wife had left him and taken their son and he could not see the boy. It was years after this before he got his son back, and his son, of course, is Roy. He was telling me about Roy, that he was two years younger than I and that I would like him. I was listening very hard and I was sad for Cody. He touched my arm and when he did I touched his hand. Max was watching us and he said, 'Get your fucking nigger hands off her.' Cody could not believe it. I could not believe it. Cody said to him, 'Sure, boss, sure,' and got up and left the club. Max had never used such words in front of me. I went to the *baño* and cried for Cody and when I came out Max was gone. The next day your mother went to a lawyer to divorce him."

Gloria leaned close. "Because of what he said to Cody?"

"No, *mi amor*, because he was obsessed."

"With Cody?"

"With me."

◈

Gloria had known Alex Fitzgibbon since before she could remember. He had flown to Havana in the late 1940s to carouse in winter and see his old Yale buddy who was a resident expert in Cuban carousal, Max Osborne. Max brought Alex home to meet Esme and Gloria, and even when Esme and Max separated in 1953 for the first time, Alex kept the social connection.

Batista had made his coup against Prío in 1952 and he and the mob were thriving from the casinos, the brothels, the tourists. Castro was in jail for leading the assault on the Moncada barracks in Santiago in 1953, and Batista's repression of rebels was vast and deadly. Esme, working steadily in nightclubs, kept Gloria, now seven, in the care of a nana, but grew fearful of violent politics. Max was political, but who knew on which side? Death came easily to such men and their families from the madness abroad in Cuba, in which the vengeful punished the innocent as readily as they punished their enemies. And if Esme would not herself leave Havana (she believed she'd never leave it again) she could protect Gloria. And so Esme decided to put her in the hands of the same Catholic nuns who had educated Renata and herself in convent schools in Cuba and Manhattan.

The Manhattan convent school Esme had gone to no longer existed in 1953, but when Alex came to visit he told her of one in Albany where Latin Catholics for decades had sent their innocent daughters to be educated bilingually by an order of nuns that was as elite as the Jesuits. Esme flirted casually with Alex, without consequence, and though he owed her nothing, she knew he would godfather Gloria's every need. He was, after all, Max's close friend, the Mayor of a heavily Catholic city, he had political power, and he was an Episcopalian, which was almost Catholic.

"Those nuns are purity itself," Alex told Esme, "and they'll preserve her from excessive sophistication."

The words were magical to Esme, who wanted Gloria to have the adolescent purity that had eluded her. And so, at age seven, Gloria was enrolled in the convent school at Albany and, except for one year in Cuba with her mother after Castro's triumph, she spent her elementary and high school years in a cocoon of holiness, as that concept was understood by the holy women of Sagrado Corazón.

❖

When Gloria asked Renata for instructions on how to behave with a man—"What are the special secret things and how do you do them?"— Renata worried about wounding such innocence.

"Do you mean kissing and touching?"

"Yes, but more," Gloria said.

"You mean complete sex?"

"I don't know how to think about it complete."

"You know how it is done, *verdad*?"

"I may not," said Gloria.

"You know the sex parts of the body."

"I know my own, but I don't know much about them. About that."

"What don't you know?"

"I don't know what I don't know. In health class we saw a slide show on female anatomy but Sister Mary Kneeling Bench referred to those parts of the body in Latin, so we didn't understand the words. We were told never to wear open-toed sandals because our toes might look like the male organ, which most of us had never seen. Our chests had to be flat, our knees invisible, and we weren't allowed books, magazines, or movies that might be obscene."

"Did you ever see boys from other schools? At dances?"

"We were chaperoned. If we danced we had to be a foot apart, and if we ever sat on a boy's lap we were told to put a telephone book under us before we sat down."

"No sane person would tell you that."

"Some people say the nuns are insane, but they are only holy women."

"You know how to get a baby—tell me they let you know that much."

"I know it somewhat. When you menstruate you can have babies. I asked Mama if nuns menstruated and she said they did. Then why don't they have babies? And she said because God knows they're not married."

"Oh, my silly sister. Child, why do you come to me with these questions?"

"I have a friend, and I want to behave right. I know you know how to behave right with men."

"What is right? Sexually safe? Is that your fear?"

"What do you mean by safe? I want to know how to do things, or not do things, whatever those things are. Do you understand?"

"I am trying."

"I want to be with him."

"But that is the point. How do you mean, with?"

"What do you mean how do I mean with?"

"I mean do you really want to sleep with him? That way, with."

"I want him to like me."

"I'm sure he does already."

"When we're close I want to be sure how to do things."

"You don't want to disappoint him if you sleep with him all the way."

"What is all the way?"

"All the way is everything, giving him your body."

"Is that so easy to do? Exactly?"

"Very easy, even when it is not exact."

"I think I want to sleep with him even if I don't sleep with what you call everything."

"You don't sleep with everything, you do everything."

"Then no."

"No? What do you mean no?"

"It seems too soon for everything since I really know nothing."

"Oh, child—*ay ay ay ay ay.*" And she waited. "I don't recommend this, but perhaps, just perhaps to begin, you can tease him and then stop."

"Is it possible to stop?"

"Once you start, the body will want to continue. But you can teach yourself in your mind."

"How would I tease him?"

"You do not say no when he asks. You say yes, *un poquito.* But not all the way yes. Maybe later it will be yes. Then you push him away, but nicely, and kiss him while you do it. Has he asked about any of this?"

"No."

"What does he do?"

145

"He kisses me."

"That's all?"

"Yes. He's tall."

"Does he touch your body?"

"My face and arms, my hands. He doesn't do any of the with thing you mentioned."

The with thing. They educated this child to be a social idiot. So Renata spoke of seduction, how to talk to the man, how to be shy, how to grow bolder, when to laugh, because sometimes it really is funny, but you must not laugh at the wrong time or he will lose his mood. She spoke of clothing being loose here, tight there, the positioning of skirts, the crossing of legs, the ways of sitting. Renata put on a dress that shaped her figure but did not drape it, modeled a blouse and a skirt and demonstrated the visible arcs of the breasts, fleeting evidence of stockinged thigh, and the gradations of temptation through lingerie. She spoke of the control of one's eyes and mouth, the things a man or a woman may desire and which desires you must postpone till another day. She did not speak of coition in explicit language. She did not want to use those words yet, either in Spanish or English, but she spoke of specific places being touched and pushing his hand away from other places. When you decide not to push him away then you are more or less doing it, and you will probably do it all, and then you will be with him. She mentioned the condom, without which you do not do the with thing. She spoke of a favored way of being with and suggested one angular variation on that. There are many ways of being with, she said, but you do not have to do them all at the same time, although some day you may try. The essential attitude when you are finally deciding not to say no is to think deeply about what you are doing, to think of yes as an act of love. One should not, on this night, or this afternoon, be with him just to be with. That may come later. On this night, or perhaps it is an afternoon, one must be the vessel of love, and when that happens you will know everything forever and will need no more lessons.

"Do you know what love is, *amorcita*?"

"I think I do," Gloria said.

"Good. Then the nuns have not totally destroyed you."

Gloria's lesson in not going all the way came in March of 1964 when she

❖

was a second-semester freshman at Bard College and Alex, every other week, came for her in his Cadillac to take her to lunch. Renata and Quinn had wanted her to go to the State University where Renata was taking art history and literature courses to finish her degree, cut short when Batista closed Havana University as a revolutionary hotbed.

But Gloria chose Bard because it was out of the city and she would live apart from family, but still close to Albany, and Alex. She was a scholarly and intense youth, undistracted by the common teenage fixation on romance. The school offered a focus on her potential career: social work and political science, an outgrowth of the awe she felt for her Aunt Renata, the political rebel. Renata, soon after she and Quinn moved to Albany in 1963, took Gloria to the civil rights protest March on Washington, and being with the vast black throng as Martin Luther King delivered his Dream speech was Gloria's baptism in racial politics.

Alex's political life also seemed unorthodox but fascinating. His lunches with her in Rhinebeck turned into something beyond dining one day when he took her to a rural apartment for a rest, he said. But there was no rest, which was why she asked Renata for guidance into the unknown. She absorbed the counseling but continued wavering on the great yes that Alex was seeking. She finally abandoned her virginity when she walked in on two of her classmates doing it with their boyfriends, all in the same room. They laughed at her virginity, couldn't believe it. Her own "boyfriend," which was all she could think to call him even though he was fifty-four, talked her into staying in Albany for the summer instead of going to Cuba to be with her mother.

She lived with Renata and Quinn, and Alex found her a summer job at City Hall in the office of Public Housing, but she left it after a week, bristling at the city's official condescension toward tenants. Quinn found her more compatible work at Holy Cross Institution, a former Episcopal settlement house, now a nonsectarian social agency that was overseeing the Kennedy-Johnson war on poverty as waged in Albany's worst slum, The Gut. Quinn brought her to see Baron Roland, the wild-eyed, mercurial, black college professor who directed Holy Cross, and he put her to work with Better Streets and Homes, joining social workers, white volunteers from uptown, and street-savvy nuns unlike any she'd ever met, all these workers coaxing the have-nots of the neighborhood into coping publicly with the social ills that contaminated their lives.

Gloria was suddenly a friend of lumpen youths, of women who shoplifted by day and whored by night, of winos with nothing better to do once they woke up and found they were still alive, of matrons with children but no husbands, scraping a life together, battling their rotting houses, of widows and retirees looking for an alternative to solitude. Many of them came to Better Streets meetings at the Gethsemane Baptist Church on Franklin Street to voice their grievances to slum landlords and politicians—fix our leaky roofs, kill our rats, pick up our garbage, get us a health clinic, close the brothels, tear down those empty houses. Gloria heard Albany described as a social and political sewer, a city without a soul, ruled by plundering, racist titans. And public titan number one was always Mayor Alex Fitzgibbon, her wonderful lover.

Maybe twenty people came to the early meetings, mostly women, led by Claudia Johnson, a three-hundred-pound black mother of nine children with a gift for talk, candor, and telling other people how to behave. But when Claudia's words appeared in newspaper stories written by Quinn and others, Better Streets' attendance rose—forty, fifty—which is when the ward-level politicians started their threats: Support those commies and you're off welfare, out of a job, out of luck—and attendance plummeted. But some were immune to political threats and they were joined by uptown whites, and Protestant and Catholic clerics. The draw was Claudia—with her schemes of picketing City Hall on the garbage issue, or dumping garbage on the Mayor's front lawn to make her point. After two months the city decided to haul a hundred truckloads of garbage and junk out of South End backyards and tear down twelve tumbledown houses.

"Hey, people," Claudia preened, "the Mayor is listenin'!"

Feeling sassy, and with the 1967 election coming up, Claudia invited the state attorney general to come and tell Better Streets members about poll watching—how to check the voting machines, how to challenge any voter who signs the wrong name; and don't let absentee ballots be counted till the polls close, and watch for people spying on the voters to see how they vote, or telling them how to vote. Gloria passed out mimeographed flyers on the subject. Quinn counted thirty-two attendees, including Mary Van Ort, the black seamstress and her wino husband Tremont, who never missed a meeting, and Lester Sugar, another regular, a white man whose oversize suitcoat hung on him like a poncho and who was famous for collecting four thousand bottles and cans for the Girl Scouts, and Father Matt Daugherty from Siena, and college students, and two newcomers who looked like narks.

"We're talkin' about poll watchin'," Claudia said. "This gen'man don't say it but we know we need to catch them cheaters votin' dead people, and passin' out five-dollar bills to buy your vote. They been stealin' elections in this town since before this big mama was born. It's gotta stop and we can stop 'em."

"Whatayou mean we can stop 'em?" Tremont asked. He took off his hat and stood up. "And who is them?"

"Them is the politicians, honey. Them aldermen, them bosses, the Mayor and his scumsuckin' gang. We gonna stop 'em from stealin'."

"How we gonna do that?"

"We find us some volunteers who'll go into those pollin' places and check out who is exactly who. We see them passin' out those fives we say, 'Hey, mister, I seen that and it ain't legal.' And we call the attorney general and tell him."

"You think they gonna do that passin' out so's you can see it?"

"They got to get the money to the voter, so you just keep lookin' till you see 'em do it."

"They prob'ly go around the corner and do it," Tremont said.

"That's exactly what they do," said Lester Sugar. "I was there last year and I watched 'em go 'round the corner."

"You watched 'em givin' out five-dollar bills?" Tremont asked.

"I never saw the money, but I had a scrutiny on it."

"That's the problem," Claudia said. "My mama used to say, 'unless you in the bedroom standin' over 'em with a candle, they's no way you gonna know what they're up to.' This stuff might get nasty, so whoever signs up gotta be ready to stand up to those bozos. Now who's gonna do it?"

No one responded.

"I'd sign up," Mr. Sugar said, "but I did it last year."

"I'd sign up," said Mrs. Wilson, "but I broke my glasses and I can't see what they be doin'."

"Nobody in Better Streets ready to take a chance," Claudia said.

After a silence Tremont said, "All right, where do I sign?"

Gloria passed a basket for donations, and cookies and soda followed.

◈

After Quinn dropped his father at the Elks Club he headed into the South End with Matt Daugherty, destination Dongan Avenue, where Tremont Van Ort was lying ill on the stoop of the old three-story brick town house that had been his family home for thirty years. Quinn walked Dongan Avenue as a boy and had forgotten it until he began to write about Better Streets. Before Dongan Avenue became a street it was part of the Pastures, where the Dutch colonists grazed their livestock. Dutch, and then English homes rose on the Pastures greenery and so began the seething American panorama of occupation—swarms of Germans and Irish replacing the Dutch and English; and then Jews, Italians, and now southern blacks— who had The Gut largely to themselves these days—all replacing one another with serial hostility.

Quinn came to know The Gut with his father when its streets throbbed all day with commerce and all night with sin. George Quinn worked daylight hours out of a second-floor flat in an 1830s wooden house between Dongan and Green Street, the office of Joe Marcello, a numbers-game banker. The game was Policy, which Marcello called "nigger numbers" after the black Caribbean gamblers who brought it to America. White and pale pink Policy slips were published twice a day, six days a week, with twelve winning numbers. You could bet on combinations of numbers from 1 to 78, the odds ranging from 5-to-1 to 400-to-1. You could bet on a "flat" (two numbers) at 30-to-1 or a "gig" (three numbers) at 200-to-1 or a "horse" (four numbers) at 400-to-1.

George Quinn walked The Gut door-to-door, picking up the play, paying off winners; and when there was no school, Daniel made the rounds with him—the Turk's grocery store, with a one-arm bandit on the counter, the Double-Dutch Tavern where girls worked the bar day and night, the soap factory, the Albany Water Works, Big Jimmy's nightclub, the old *Times Union* where the journalism bug bit Daniel.

"Any candy for me?" George asked his customers, and they'd give him their numbers. If they couldn't read or write, George would write their play and their bet on a notepad, take their nickel, quarter, dollar, and put the notepad in his shirt pocket, the money in his coat. When the weight started ruining the coat's shape George would go to a grocery or a bar and change his coins for bills. Quinn helped count coins and could keep leftover pennies for candy, or the penny punchboard. He played the punchboard once and won fifty cents. Eight years old and already rich.

Now, thirty-two years later, Quinn, at the wheel of his '59 Mercedes 220S, with Matt Daugherty beside him, moved through the streets of the old Gut, houses crumbling and boarded up, pavements pocked with potholes, sidewalks buckled, no people, only the heavy, black dust of a slum in its terminal stage. He drove down South Pearl to Herkimer, this the old Jewish neighborhood and this the street where Isaac Mayer Wise founded Reform Jewry with a fistfight in the old Bethel synagogue, still there, also the street where Claudia lived. He crossed Green and went on to Dongan Avenue, passed St. John's, the oldest Catholic church in town, built by the Irish, and where Father Peter Young was now helping drunks dry out and get back in the game. Dongan, right there, was where Big Jimmy ran his nightclub, and three blocks south would be where Tremont was lying on his father's old stoop.

"You said you came here as a kid," Quinn said to Matt.

"I was seventeen," Matt said. "Before the war, bar hopping, tryin' to kick the habit."

"Coke?"

"Pussy. Didn't fit with the seminary. I figured I'd give it the big ride and then kiss it good-bye."

"Did you?"

"I gave it the ride."

"And kissed it good-bye?"

"Eventually."

"Understood. You remember Big Jimmy's club? That's his old building."

"I remember his name but I was never in the club."

"Famous guy, Jimmy Van Ort, maybe seven feet tall, wore a fedora and a vest with a gold pocket watch and chain, best known black man in Albany. One of his ancestors had been a servant to the Good Patroon. Jimmy bet fifty on a number one morning, around 1936, and hit it. In the afternoon he rolled over his payoff on another number and he hit that. He won like eleven thousand, a fortune in '36. My father wrote Jimmy's bet."

Quinn had heard the story eleven thousand times from George Quinn: how news of Jimmy's hit spread so quickly George insisted on a bodyguard to deliver the winnings. And there came George through the swinging screen doors of Big Jimmy's—small stage to the right of the doors with an upright piano and jazz till sunrise, where Cody first played when he came to Albany, and, to the left, a room where a card game went on and on. George carried a suitcase and had his cousin with him, Timmy Ryan, a uniformed cop from the Second Precinct. George put the suitcase on the bar.

"You want to count it, Jimmy?"

"What do you think, Georgie?"

"I think you want to count it."

"You count it."

"Where?"

"Here."

George opened the suitcase on the bar, and he sang:

"Put your feet on the barroom shelf,
Open the bottle and help yourself."

He dumped the cash and counted it for Jimmy just as he'd counted it for Joe Marcello before packing it. After the final dollar Jimmy said, "Take fifty for yourself, Georgie."

"Fifty?"

"Yowsah, man, fifty. You the fella brought the luck. You the fella bringin' the loot. Take a hundred."

"A hundred?"

"Take two hundred."

"Two hundred," George said. "A nice round figure. Like one of my old girlfriends."

"Biggest tip my father ever got," Quinn said. "With his commission for writing Jimmy's winning play, plus the tip, he made fourteen hundred bucks—all in one day in 1936, a lousy year for the world, but not for Jimmy or George. Jimmy told his bartender, 'Give Georgie and his friend a drink. The party starts right now. Free beer at Big Jimmy's for three days and three nights.' It was like Mardi Gras, a miracle in The Gut, Big Jimmy's as a shrine to that great corporal work of mercy—give strong drink to the thirsty. My father ordered a small beer."

Quinn paused.

"Tremont was around for all that, little kid, eight, nine years old. Big Jimmy was his father. Big dad. Big, big dad."

"Tremont had something to live up to," Matt said.

"And he put himself out there. Spiffy duds, like his old man. And gutsy, doing that poll watching."

"I get a kick out of Tremont," Matt said. "I first saw him sitting on a pile of timbers with a couple of guys, passing the wine. I had my collar on and he says, 'How you doin', Monsignor?' 'Hey, I'm a bishop,' I told him, and he said, 'Yeah, and I'm a senator.' 'Senator,' I say, 'you wanna go to a meeting? They're serving soda and cookies at Better Streets over at the church. Eat enough cookies you get to stay alive to drink another day.' Story short, he shows up with Mary. She's sober but just bones."

Tremont came to the meeting in a pink shirt, red tie, double-breasted tan suitcoat with baggy brown slacks, brown and white wingtips, and a brown, jauntily cocked fedora. The suitcoat had major wine stains and the shoes were all but gone, but Matt saw that Tremont was a dude with ambition. Even the limp that came from a badly healed shrapnel wound he'd turned into a strut.

He was living then in his father's old house with Mary and Peanut, their seven-year-old, whom Tremont had found naked in a vacant lot when he wasn't a year old, his mother propped against a wall. "Didn't even have no diaper," Tremont said. And the mother told him, "You want that little ol' thing you can have him." So Tremont took the infant home to Mary, and Peanut grew up as a mascot for the wino crowd, a wild boy who didn't function in school; but when Mary got the diarrhea Peanut found money somewhere for her Kaopectate.

Quinn and Matt saw Tremont horizontal on the stoop of the house, windows and doors boarded up. Tremont had gotten himself up to the top step but then, with neither the tools nor the strength to pull the boards off the door, he collapsed. He was wearing only his trousers, his shirt, socks and shoes beside him, his coat rolled into a pillow. His legs dangled through the wrought iron railing and a portable radio blared at his ear, Johnny Cash singing about Folsom prison. Rosie, the last whore on Dongan Avenue, wearing her uniform—short skirt and tight sweater—was in a folding chair on the stoop next door, her windows boarded but not her door.

"Back in business, Rosie?" Quinn asked.

"Can't do business here no more." She winked at him. "They cut off my water and took down the power line. Gonna knock all the houses down pretty soon." She winked again. "I just came to get somethin' and I see Tremont layin' there and I wonder, anybody gonna help this man? If nobody was I'd of found somebody, but Claudia said somebody's comin'.'"

"Very neighborly, Rosie."

"I know Tremont thirty years," she said. "I tended bar for his father. But he's so sore you can't even touch him. I tried. He can't keep his shoes on. I give him my radio and put that coat under his head, but he can't move. He is a most sorry man."

"Is that true, Tremont?" Quinn asked as he climbed the steps.

Tremont made a sound in his throat.

"You can't talk?" Quinn asked.

"Hurts."

"What happened, you get hit by a car? Somebody beat on you?"

"No . . ." he said slowly, "I got that new-ritis . . . and some of the old-ritis. Pain goes with them ritises. Got the pain all over."

Tremont's facial muscles were out of control and Quinn remembered him that way months ago. An emergency room doctor diagnosed it as peripheral neuritis, from acute alcoholism, pain so severe that clothing became a punishment. Tremont stopped drinking and found day work but then the County took away the welfare check for Peanut because of Tremont's link to Better Streets; and Mary began drinking toward the grave. Tremont told Quinn: "I saw her on the street once and she was kissin' a friend of mine and I swore I ain't never gonna talk to that man again." Then Peanut ran off forever and Mary came home to bleed on the mattress, rising only to drink the dregs.

"Woman," Tremont said to her, "you're in the bed."

"I know, Tremont."

"You know what that means?"

"I know."

Tremont kept sober for her wake and the long wait at the bus station for her relatives, who never came. He sat in the house until the caked blood and the odor of rotten food drove him out. He slept in the bus station until the weather changed, or so he told Claudia when he showed up at Better Streets for cookies. But they no longer did cookies.

"You look god-awful, Tremont," Claudia told him.

"Could be," he said. "I ain't seen myself lately."

"I'll call somebody, get you into that rehab."

"Sure," he said. He walked out of the meeting and the next Claudia heard he was on the stoop.

Matt came up the steps. "Hey, Tremont," he said. "It's the Bishop. We're taking you to the hospital."

Tremont almost smiled. "Okay, Bish," he said. "Got the 'ritis. Bottle of wine'd cut the pain. They say I'll die from the wine, but the pain won't even let me go get the wine to kill myself."

"Lift him," Quinn said.

"He gonna scream," Rosie said.

"Gotta do it," Quinn said, and they lifted Tremont by the legs and armpits and Rosie was right, he screamed, and as they carried him down the steps he cried. Rosie opened the car door and they stretched him out on the backseat. Rosie went for his clothes and put the rolled coat under his head.

"So long, Tree honey," she said.

Tremont writhed as the car moved, and with every jolt came a yelp, a moan. "Where we goin'?"

"Memorial Hospital," Quinn said. "Do somethin' for your pain."

"I can't stay there."

"Yes you can."

"You don't know," Tremont said. "I got a guy after me."

"What guy?"

"Bad mother."

"Are you talking drugs?"

"No, man. We go to the hospital you gotta stay with me. He finds out I'm there he'll be comin' for me."

"Who will?"

"Zuki. He was talkin' guns, shootin' people."

"What people?"

"Took me out shootin'. Wanted to see how I do. He heard the army give me those sharpshooter badges. Wanted me to shoot somebody."

"Shoot who?"

Tremont didn't answer.

"Who is this Zuki? He have another name?"

"No."

"Is he black?"

"Brown."

"Who'd he want you to shoot?"

"Talked about a landlord owns bad houses."

"Shoot a landlord for his bad houses?"

"That's what he say. Then he say the landlord's gonna kill Claudia 'cause she makes trouble for everybody."

"He name this landlord?"

"Never said no names. But killin' Claudia, that wasn't real."

"Who was real?"

"Can't say."

"You gotta say, Tremont."

"He'll come after me. He say this is important, and if I goof out he'll find me, and I won't like what happens."

"We'll get you protection."

"From who, the cops? Cops'll put me in jail forever. All Zuki's gotta say is I was gonna shoot a politician."

"You were?"

"That's what he was talkin'. I told him I needed money to eat and he give me a few and said he'd see me in the mornin'. But I drank two days on that money and I ain't seen Zuki since. When I got the pain I went to the house to lay down but I couldn't get inside."

"Who was the politician?"

"Can't say."

"This is crazy, Tremont. You can't keep this secret if you want protection. Who was it?"

Tremont said nothing.

"Was it Bobby Kennedy? He was coming to Albany next week but they shot him last night in Los Angeles."

"They shot Bobby? Who did?"

"Some guy nobody knows."

"I wouldn't shoot Bobby Kennedy."

"Who would you shoot?"

"Wouldn't shoot nobody."

"Tremont, who was it?"

Tremont said nothing.

"Tremont."

"Zuki talkin' about the Mayor."

"The Mayor? Alex Fitzgibbon?"

"Yeah." Tremont was moaning.

"Where did you meet this Zuki?"

"He came into the Brothers and talked to Roy. I was there. He say 'Let's go have a drink,' and I said why not and we went down to Dorsey's."

"Who is he? What does he do?"

"He say he's in college."

"Which college?"

"Didn't say."

"Does Roy know about shooting the Mayor?"

"Roy don't know none of it."

157

"How do you know that?"

"Zuki said nobody knows. Nobody. Him and me the only ones know. And now you-all."

"Zuki say why he wanted to shoot the Mayor?"

"Called him a fascist fuckhead dictator. Said he's no good."

"You think the Mayor's no good?"

"He ain't done much for me, but that ain't a reason to shoot him."

"How'd you leave it when he gave you the money?"

"I said I'd eat somethin' and meet him in the mornin' at Chloe's Diner. But I drank two days, maybe three, and then you come and got me."

"How come Zuki didn't go to the house to see you?"

"Zuki don't know nothin' about me and that house."

"Who do you think Zuki's working for?"

"I dunno, but he's a bad ass."

"What kind of gun was it?"

"AR-15 What they had in Vietnam. I never shot one of those."

"Zuki say where you'd be when you shot the Mayor?"

"On a hill out in the mountains. Every day the Mayor goes out to see the old political boss, Patsy McCall. Sit up on that hill you got a clear shot when he gets outa the car."

"Zuki would take you out there?"

"He talked about it."

"What about the getaway?

"A car waitin'. Go down the other side of the mountain before anybody know where the shot came from."

"Did you buy that?"

"You get down to the bottom of that mountain they be waitin' for you with the Third Army."

"But you didn't say that to Zuki."

"Just took the gun and said I'd see him tomorrow."

"Where's the gun now?"

"In a locker down at the bus station, in a black bag."

"A black bag."

"Yeah. Ain't that how it goes?"

"That's how it goes."

"Where's the key to the locker?"

"In my pocket."

❖

Tremont heard about Roy through Quinn's story in 1965 of his one-man picket line. Roy had come to the Laborers Union every morning for six weeks but never got a day's work from Carmine Fiore, who ran the shapeup. On the morning that a white stranger showed up and was hired, Roy painted his sign: CARMINE FIORE IS A RACIST, and walked with it.

Quinn interviewed Roy as he picketed and when the *Times Union* story came out the next day four black men joined Roy's picket line and Tremont was the first of the four. Twenty more joined the day after that, including Baron Roland, who taught the history course Roy was taking at Albany City College. The unofficial title of Roland's course was "Social Justice, an Oxymoron." Roy and his fellow picketers were all so full of fire and grievance that Roland suggested they organize to face down racism. The strength to do this, he assured them, would grow out of their collective anger, and more would join them, for black power was in the air. Within two months the Brothers existed three-dozen strong, picketing unions and city hall, speaking at churches, joining peace marches, giving slum tours to the press and the clergy, and, in the spirit of Claudia Johnson, dumping cockroaches on the desks of slumlords.

The Brothers took on the aura of the Black Panthers, America's badass militants. They disavowed Panther talk of killing white cops, but they loved Malcolm more than Martin, and when Malcolm came to town they sat with him in the gallery of the Senate chamber. When Stokely came he visited the Brothers' storefront and said riots in Newark and Detroit were an unavoidable movement toward urban guerrilla war. Roy Mason, who spoke cogently and without rant as coordinator of the Brothers, clarified the group's position. "No, we're not Stokely, and we don't advocate violence. But we don't advocate nonviolence either."

Tremont spent less time with the Brothers and more time going with his wife to meetings of Better Streets. As Election Day 1967 approached, the Brothers accumulated enough signatures to put one of their own, Ben Jones, on the Liberal Party ticket for alderman of the Third Ward. They announced plans to picket polling places to urge blacks not to sell their vote. Roy tried to register as a poll watcher in the Third Ward but it had already been assigned to Tremont Van Ort of Better Streets. "I'll help him out," said Roy.

Roy was alone on the corner of Westerlo and Green streets at 5:45 on the clear, twenty-four-degree morning of Election Day when Quinn and Matt Daugherty arrived in Quinn's car. Cardboard signs with POLLING PLACE had been nailed to telephone poles on the block, and one was pasted onto the window of Tony Romildo's storefront clubroom, where old-timers who couldn't speak English gathered to drink coffee and grappa. Store lights were on and men were moving a table. One man saw the group outside and came out. He was a white-haired pudge with a facial flush and razor nicks.

"You people here to vote?"

"We're waiting for a friend," Matt said.

"Tremont Van Ort," Roy said. "He's your poll watcher today."

"You're all waiting for a poll watcher?"

"I'm from the *Times Union*," Quinn said. "I'm doing an all-day story on the election."

"We don't need any poll watchers. What are you gonna watch, people pullin' the lever?"

"That's it," Roy said. "See it's done the way it's supposed to be."

Another man came to the door.

"They're poll watchers," the first said.

"Listen," said the second, "I'm a Republican and I been livin' in this ward forty years and I never saw anything down here that wasn't legit."

"I run this district," the first said. "Anything funny I'd hear of it. Nothing at all. Nothing."

"Then it'll probably be a nice, quiet day," Roy said.

"Here comes Tremont," Matt said.

The two politicians watched Tremont approach with his game-legged strut. Gloria was with him, carrying two paper bags, and Tremont wore the new white shirt and blue tie Claudia bought for his big day at the polls.

"You're the poll watcher?" the first man asked Tremont.

"Yes, sir," Tremont said.

"Go home. There's nothing to watch."

"I got credentials to give to the man in charge."

"That's me," the man said. "Fred Malloy, president of this ward."

"Can we go inside?" Gloria asked. She pulled open the clubroom door and set the bags on an empty table. Quinn followed and asked her, "Aren't you supposed to be in school?"

"School? You think I'd miss this for school? Show him your credentials, Tremont." Tremont handed his accreditation to Malloy and Gloria said, "Here's his list of duties from the attorney general. Check that the voting machine counter is set at zero, check the voting machine curtains. There's more." She offered the paper to Malloy, who didn't take it.

"Curtains?" he said. "Whataya don't like the color?"

"Make sure they're not transparent, and that they close properly," Gloria said. "And the counter."

"You wanna see the counter, see it," he said, gesturing to the machine.

Tremont closed and opened the curtains, then looked at the voting levers with the candidates' names and parties. "I don't see no zero," he said.

"In the back," Malloy said.

Tremont went to the back of the machine. "I still don't see it."

Malloy opened the counter's cover. "Zeros. See that? All zeros."

"Zeros," Tremont said.

Gloria passed out coffee and donuts.

"Whata we got here, a coffee klatch?" Malloy asked.

"This isn't done," the Republican said.

Malloy handed the credentials back to Tremont. "You can stay," he said, "but that don't mean the rest of you. You're lookin' for somebody gonna pay five dollars a vote, is that what you wanna see? I been here all my life and never saw any of that stuff."

"Anybody gonna do that," the Republican said, "common sense they'd have done it last week."

"Nobody said anything about any five-dollar vote," Matt said.

For the first time Malloy saw Matt's collar.

"You're a priest?"

"A Franciscan, at Siena College. Matthew Daugherty, OFM."

"What's the Catholic Church doing in politics?"

"Hey, Pope Paul went to the U.N."

"For peace," Malloy said.

"And justice," said Matt.

"You oughta be ashamed chasin' politics, a priest."

"God made us all sinners, and he included politicians," Matt said.

"Shame."

"I ain't ashamed," Tremont said. "It's all legal. We got our rights to be here. You seen those papers."

"Coffee klatchers outside," Malloy said. "This guy wants to stay the chair's right there. The rest of you get lost." He motioned to the Republican and together they moved the metal fence behind which voters would line up to vote. The move pushed Tremont's chair into a corner, as far from the registration desk as it was possible to be.

"I also got credentials," Roy said.

"Is that so?" Malloy said. "What're they doin', passin' 'em out with bubble gum?"

Roy offered his AG papers to Malloy who glanced at them but didn't touch them. "One at a time is how it goes," Malloy said.

"I'll wait outside," said Roy. "If Tremont has to leave I'm here."

"You people got a regular army. Big stuff. But you ain't gonna find squat. This is all on the up and up."

The front door opened and a man walked in waving two letter-sized pages. "I got the dead list," he said to Malloy.

Malloy snatched the pages from him and pushed him back out the door. "You fucking moron," he said in a failed whisper. He turned to the others, holding the door open. "Everybody out."

Tremont's cheering section moved out onto the sidewalk into the frigid morning. Tremont sat in the corner with his coffee and donut and at 6:03 two voters came in and voted. They looked legal to Tremont.

◈

At 6:40 Roy was on the corner alone, two policemen in a patrol car idling across the street. Quinn and Matt had gone to another polling place, and

Gloria had left to drive Claudia to vote. She told Roy she'd be back. At 6:50 Tremont came out and told Roy a man had identified himself as Mortimer Monroe to the woman registering Democratic voters.

"He ain't Morty Monroe," Tremont said. "He's white and Morty's black. Not only that, Morty was shot in a card game. Morty's dead."

Roy went in and confronted the voter and Malloy.

"We're challenging this man's identification," Roy said.

"On what authority?" Malloy asked.

"The attorney general, I'm a poll watcher. You know it. I showed you my credentials."

"I never saw 'em," Malloy said.

"Yes you did."

Roy took his credentials out of his pocket and flashed them at Malloy, then moved toward the white Morty Monroe who was backing toward the door without having voted.

"Wait a minute, Morty," Roy said. "You got a driver's license?"

"You ain't Morty," Tremont told the man. "Morty's dead."

A uniformed policeman came in and he and Malloy converged on Roy, who countered with an elbow that put Malloy on his back atop the voting ledger in which Morty had almost registered from the grave.

One month later Roy was a public example of swift electoral justice in Albany: fourteen months for disorderly conduct and third degree assault. He served three months and, when his conviction was thrown out for insufficient evidence, Baron Roland welcomed him back to Holy Cross as a civil rights hero and put him to work with the Community Action group Better Streets. He shared a desk with Gloria.

After the election Alex found Gloria an apartment in an upscale Pine Hills housing development, in the same building where his seventy-three-year-old mother, Veronica Fitzgibbon, lived with an on-call chauffeur and a live-in maid. Alex visited Veronica almost daily, a dutiful son; and so any proximity to Gloria was unremarkable. He luxuriated in the frequency of love with Gloria. My gorgeous virgin, he would whisper.

"Don't say that," she said one day. "I was a virgin too long."

"All your life you were a virgin waiting for me."

"Somebody will catch us."

"There's nothing wrong with you being my mother's neighbor. And it's perfectly normal for your godfather to visit you."

"What if they catch my godfather in my bed?" she said, thinking of Alex catching Roy in her bed, where he had been only twice, but twice is dangerous. The first was the afternoon she drove home to change for a fund-raising dinner at Holy Cross. Roy was with her, and leaving him in the car would have been rude, even racist. She should have dropped him someplace and come home alone, but there he was, so she said, "Come in."

Whenever they were alone in the office Roy would touch her arm, or rub the ends of her long blond hair between finger and thumb, or run a fingernail lightly up her spine through her white cotton shirt, always backing off with a smile and an upraised hand, testing the wind, which proved to be fair. Now, as they went into Gloria's apartment he ran a finger up her back. She turned to face him and found him unbelievably attractive. And there was the bed.

"I worry about your wife," she said to Alex. "Doesn't what we do affect her, even if she doesn't know?"

"Don't ever talk about my wife," he said.

So she did not. But through the society pages she tracked her—Marnie Herzog Fitzgibbon, ash blonde from Boston whose grandfather had made a fortune in coal, who had gone to Smith, no nuns in *her* life, owned and rode show horses, golfed at Schuyler Meadows Country Club, handicap 15, raised funds for children of an African famine, and traveled often, unlike her husband who was moored to City Hall. Gloria clipped photos of Marnie in her lush gowns at balls, galas, and the famed parties she gave at Tivoli, the Fitzgibbon family estate. In early May Marnie came to visit Veronica and glimpsed Alex going into a first-floor apartment. She found that the apartment was rented to Gloria Osborne, about whom Alex sometimes spoke; something about Cuba. Marnie hired a private detective who discovered Alex's repetitive, hour-or-more-long visits to Gloria. Also, when Alex took a week off to go trout fishing in Maine with his army buddies, the detective noted a visit to Gloria by a black man who arrived by taxi at mid-evening and stayed till dawn.

Gloria was naked in her shower when the doorbell rang. Roy, without calling? No. Alex? Never at this hour; he likes the afternoon, and afterward a whiskey before he goes back to City Hall. She called out, Just a minute, stepped out of the tub and wrapped herself in her terrycloth robe. Rubbing her hair with a small towel she opened the door to the face from the newspapers, Marnie Herzog Fitzgibbon, always three names.

"I'm the wife of your godfather," she said. "May I come in?"

"Of course," and Marnie entered the living room, bouncing slightly on her toes, feisty, her half-smile as aggressive as Mother Superior. Gloria followed, tension in her chest. MHF looked younger than forty-eight, tenaciously Junior League in a simple off-white summer dress, bodice stylish over those tiny breasts, but the short skirt doesn't cover her knees and they're not quality. Her hair was freshly coiffed—for this visit?— those waves much too tight, scold your hairdresser. MHF raised her hand toward the bedroom door, which was ajar.

"That's the cozy corner, is it? I really don't want to see it." She touched the arm of the sofa. "I'll bet anything you do it here too. It's where he first did it in college."

"I have no idea what you're talking about," Gloria said.

"Of course not. You *are* cute. So young, and a lovely figure."

Gloria pulled her robe tight, accenting her formidable breasts. "This conversation is over," she said.

"What a perfect thing to say. Lovely poise. I see what attracted him. I could give you the days and times he arrived and left, I could give you photos and tapes of your talks. I didn't listen very long, but you do seem well educated for a little convent cunt."

"I won't listen to this tripe. Get out of my apartment." Gloria, amazed with herself, opened the apartment door and raised her voice: "Out."

"No, no," Marnie said softly, and she did not move. "You're the one who's out. Didn't you ever anticipate this? Probably not, innocent little puss."

Vindictive bitch. Would she cut me? Hire somebody to do it? Disfigure. If Alex knew about this he'd have called. Gloria closed the door.

"Did you think you could just carry on and on without consequence?" Marnie said. "You're finished at Holy Cross. The board of directors does not abide sluts. Was it those sweet little nuns who taught you how to succeed as a slut? You are quite achieved. I never did it with a Negro. I suppose I should have. Is your Negro larger than Alex? Alex would hate that. Oh, and he's finished at Holy Cross, too, your Negro. No sluts, no pimps."

Gloria screamed. Did anybody hear?

"Very strong voice," Marnie said. "Are you in pain? I hope so."

"Getoutgetoutgetoutgetoutgetouuuuuuuut!" And she screamed again.

"Excellent," Marnie said. "I suppose it is time. Be smart. Take that sexy little ass of yours back to Cuba where it came from."

Her impulse was to call Alex, scream at him, do you know what just happened, my godfather, my love? No, he probably doesn't know. She would save it till later, relish retelling the pain. Call him anyway, am I his? And she picked up the phone, but it's tapped, and she put it back in its cradle. She searched the room with the frantic eyes of the trapped fox. Take what?—the good jewelry, the Oshun necklace Renata gave her, the letters from Mama and Max, clothes, makeup, no, leave them, leave them. She couldn't find the necklace. She put the letters in her purse and abandoned the rest. Alas Oshun. She drove to an outdoor pay phone on Madison Avenue and called him, can they tap City Hall? She got his secretary, tell him Gloria, and he said, Yes? And she said I'm coming to see you now, a disaster, your wife, I'll be in front of City Hall. No, he said, yes, she said and hung up and double-parked on the corner near his office window. He came down the City Hall steps and bent to her window and she said your wife knows everything and has photos and tapes. He looked over at Academy Park, up toward the Capitol, looked both ways on Eagle Street, anybody could be on a bench, in a car filming this. I can't talk here, he said, and she said I can't talk anywhere, where do I go, what do I do? They're firing me from Holy Cross. How long have you been seeing the nigger, he asked. Is that all you can say? And he said nothing. She stared at his mouth. Handsome mouth, betrayed, betraying, no reverence for what was and which now is without meaning. Sex is death and God is angry with Gloria. In hell you run in the putrid swamp, devils scourge you when you fall, and your blood colors the slime. She smiled at Alex, put the car in gear and turned on the radio. Aretha Franklin. My hero, she said to him, and drove off.

❖

Traffic at the bar in the Havana Club had picked up and Roy was busy. Max was avoiding conversation with newcomers at the end of the bar, and George Quinn and his old friend and newfound blonde, Vivvie, were on their second beer when Cody Mason came through the door. He looked the place over and then walked directly to Max and shook a finger at him, "Hey, Mighty Max, where'd you come from?"

"Roy tells me you're sick," Max said. "You don't look it. Sick—it's your con, right? Tell 'em you're sick and it's a sold-out concert."

"Yeah, man, and I get to stay in bed all day. Where you been?"

"Florida. Just passing through, but I had to see your club. People keep telling me about it down there, all the big dogs coming to see you—Lips and Trummy and Satch, and you got a new record coming, so I say, 'Max, go say hello to Cody while he's red hot.'"

"He says he knew you in Cuba," Roy said to Cody.

"Right," Cody said. "Max got me a job in Havana when I needed one and I stayed two years."

"He packed 'em in, a jazz club in the Vedado called Night and Day. The Cubans loved him."

George had come over from his table and was standing a few feet off, staring at Cody.

"Get lost," Roy said to him.

Cody turned and saw George. "Georgie Quinn," he said. "Damn, how you doin', Georgie?"

"Don't tell me you know this dickey-bird," Roy said.

"More than thirty years. Since I came to this town."

"Cody," George said with a large smile, "what're you gonna do when the shine wears off?"

"Son of a bitch mouth on this guy," Roy said.

"Shine," Cody said. "You remember, Georgie." And then he said to Roy, "Shine's a song, Roy, you know the song. Mills Brothers and Bing. Lotta people recorded it."

"Shine's a song," Roy said. "Yeah, I did hear it. Shuffle stuff. Coon song."

"Better than that," Cody said.

Max pulled over an empty barstool for Cody.

"The piano," George said. "I got Big Jimmy to lend us his little one. Ben whatsisname Bongo gave me three hundred to rent it for the night. Jimmy says to me, 'Three hundred? Keep it two nights, keep it all week.'"

"Not Bongo," Cody said. "Bingo. That was Bing Crosby. Bing."

"Bing," George said, nodding.

"That's the piano he's talking about," Max said to Roy, pointing at the wall photo of Cody and Bing.

"Dickey-bird was in on the Crosby night?" Roy said.

"He got the piano and people to haul it," Max said. "He knew Jimmy, who owned the bar where Cody was playing."

"My first job up here," Cody said.

George was looking at Max, trying to bring him back.

"I'm Max Osborne, George. It was nineteen thirty-six. I brought Bing down to Big Jimmy's with Alex Fitzgibbon. You remember Alex?"

"Alex Fitz. The Mayor," George said.

"You mean the Mayor was there too?" Roy said.

"He wasn't Mayor yet," Max said. "He was still in the legislature. He took us all out to his place that night, Tivoli."

"Tivoli," George said. "Greatest house in Albany."

"I met Alex at Yale," Max said. "I put him and Bing together on the golf course in Saratoga. They both had horses at the track that year."

"Mayor Fitzgibbon is a fascist motherfucker," Roy said.

"Sure he is," Max said, "but what a nice guy. I told Bing how great Cody played and that he was a protégé of Fats, and Billie's first accompanist. So Bing said if he's that good let's take a ride, and we all came down from Saratoga and found Jimmy closing the place."

It was one o'clock when they got there, never a late hour in Albany, but Jimmy had been open fifty-six straight hours, serving free beer to all comers, snarling traffic and quintupling the drunk quotient on Green Street. The night squad finally said, okay Jim, enough's enough. Jimmy had been sharing the wealth after winning eleven thousand in Policy by parlaying his morning hit on an afternoon number and hitting that too. George always thought it was fixed. Nobody hits Policy twice in a day for that kind of money in Albany unless the boys in charge want it to happen. They must've been thanking Jimmy for a favor he did them, but what kind of favor is worth eleven thou?

"Last call, people," Big Jimmy said to the bar. "Party's over. They're closin' me down and nothin' I can do about it."

"We just got here," Bing said to Jimmy. "We came from Saratoga to hear Cody."

"You got ten minutes, if he's still up to it. He been playin' three days and I never see the man sleep."

"I sleep during the slow tunes," Cody said.

So Cody played a few minutes for Bing, "Nobody's Sweetheart," his good luck theme, and Bing hummed a little. Cody would've played all week for Bing, but Jimmy hit the lights and two patrol cars were sitting out front and that was that. Alex the thinker then said, Cody, why don't you join us out at Tivoli and play awhile. Stay overnight and we'll get you anywhere you want to go tomorrow. But we need a piano. Cody was wrecked, but this was Bing, so he said okay, I ain't really dead. George said Jimmy's got a piano in the back room, and so it began: the coda to Jim's open house: jazz all night and Cody playing himself into a lucky new day, with a promise at dawn from Bing that he'd try to work Cody into his next movie. Bing had just gotten Satchmo star billing in *Pennies from Heaven*, a first for a Negro in Hollywood.

Cody rising: He'd never tell it on himself but Max knew Cody when he was still Sonny, when somebody told him to go up to Pod's and Jerry's in Harlem where Willie the Lion was playing, but not for long, and see Jerry and tell him you want the gig. Sonny beelined it up and that night the club was thick with main men: James P. Johnson, Benny Goodman, Tommy Dorsey, Bunny Berigan, and Sonny squirmed. But he sat there like Jerry told him to, watching Willie bust that piano. Did they love Willie? Oh, yeah. Then Willie stood up and he knew Sonny wanted his chair. So you play a little? he asked. A little, Sonny said, and so he did "Nobody's Sweetheart," which they liked all right, and then he did "Twelfth Street Rag," eight choruses, eight variations, no repeats, and they loved it so much he did four more—no repeats—and they couldn't goddamn stand it. He met all the main men and he felt bigger than he used to and along the way he really got to know Fats. Jerry said to him, all right, fourteen bucks a week five nights and you also play when the girls dance (you know those girls), five of them moving among the tables (you know how they move) and share their tips. So Sonny kept suspense in the tune; and when somebody put folding money on the table and a girl picked it up with her between and kept it, Sonny gave her achievement a little arpeggio. Then the other girls used their betweens, and Sonny's arpeggios earned him eighty-four dollars, seventy-four more than he'd ever made in a whole week playing piano. Sonny bought a new suit. Great lookin' devil, one of the girls said.

It was 1935 and Max was a junior at Yale, immersed in the fusion of economic, political, and cultural history, and coming to New York on weekends for some history making of his own, which is when he discovered Sonny. He, and sometimes Alex, hung out, drank, talked music, watched Sonny hold his own (relatively) with Fats and James P. until one night Sonny wasn't playing anymore and Max couldn't find out why. He heard some record company had set up a recording date but Sonny didn't show. You gotta be dead not to show for a record date. But Sonny wasn't dead. He wasn't even Sonny. Years later he told Max he missed his train, but everybody knows you don't miss trains. He turned up in Albany after his no-show calling himself Cody Mason and with a gig at Big Jimmy's—two shows Friday and Saturday, singers, unfunny comics, and sexy rumba dancers who would drift in from the rooming house next door; and when Cody played for them after hours he found out they had never used their betweens to pick up tips. So he told them how it was done (one girl could do a split to swoop the money off the floor) and he played their mood music. His income went up but that was only money. Cody played alone on weeknights, played like a wild man, you don't get that kind of talent in Albany, and you never ever got it before at Big Jimmy's. Within six weeks the bar was buzzing; in three months Cody was a main man and Jimmy's was jazz central.

Max rediscovered Cody when he came to Albany with Alex in the summer of 1936, and Alex knew every saloon in The Gut. Sonny! Max! Alex! Whataya know! This was the summer Max met Bing through Alex in Saratoga and they all played serious golf (Alex's 18 handicap was not serious) at the MacGregor links in the morning, and serious horses in the afternoon at the track. Max warned Bing that he played for Yale's golf team and could give fellows who shot in the 70s a run. You're pretty sure of yourself for a young fella, Bing said, and Max said, well, maybe, if you think twenty-one is young, but it's all in the short game and the long putt. Bing said if I was a betting man I'd put five on the table says you won't break 80. Max said you're on and he shot 75 to Bing's 79. Bing pressed a fiver into his hand but Max said, no, no, I knew I could beat you. Bing also came to know this, losing six more matches that week to Max the wunderkind, who took to advising Bing on his short game.

Then came the long night at Tivoli with Max, Alex, George, Bing, Cody, and "Shine," a hell of a night. When Danny Quinn grew older he kept saying he was going to write about it. Doosaday sosadah spokety spone. It happened two weeks after Max had been arrested for cheating a horse breeder out of nine thousand on the golf course. Hustling is all it was, but the Saratoga Keystone Kops (who turned a blind eye to mobsters fleecing the summer population at crooked upscale casinos) called it grand theft by a con man. The victim was a Kentucky aristocrat who wouldn't miss the nine but was furious that a Pontiac dealer's son had conned him. Max's hustle was strictly to raise his Yale tuition, for his father's car dealership tanked in '35 and the old man died of grief; but after the arrest Max was expelled from Yale and never went back to school. Bing posted his bail, Max gave the nine back to the horseman, and charges were dropped. Max did not let all this interfere with his social life, and in late August he brought Bing down to Big Jim's to hear Cody play.

George, standing at the bar next to Cody, looked at Max, and he remembered that night at Big Jim's with Bongo. Bingo. He remembered Cody playing "Shine" that night and he said, "Are you going to play us a tune, Cody?"

"Not now, Georgie, but I got a concert tonight."

"You don't say. Concert."

"Over at the DeWitt."

"Will there be dancing?"

"Gotta be. Mike Flanagan's band's playing with me."

"It's a fund-raiser, twenty bucks a pop," Roy said. "Includes food."

"Twenty bucks?" George said. "That's out of my league."

"Five bucks if you don't eat dinner," Roy said.

"That's good," said George. "Five bucks for no dinner."

The bar phone rang and Roy answered and handed it to Max. "The call you been waitin' for."

Max took the phone as far from the bar as the cord allowed, and hung up after a few muffled words. "I need a cab," he said.

Roy picked up the direct taxi line. "Five minutes," he told Max.

Max put a ten-dollar bill on the bar. "Gotta move, Cody. I'll try to catch some of the concert." His tickets were still on the bar. He pushed them toward George.

"See the concert on me, George," Max said. "Dinner included."

George picked up the tickets. "These are for me?"

"All yours," Max said. Then he shook Cody's hand, the same hand that had stroked Renata's arm at a Havana nightclub and loosened Max's scurrilous tongue. Max had done penance for fifteen years, and Cody said forget it half a dozen times, and then finally told Max, "Don't bring it up again. It's history. Some of my best friends are racist fuckheads."

Roy looked across the bar at George. "You got yourself a night on the town Dickey-bird."

"Dickey-bird," George said. "Is your name Dick? You look like a friend of mine."

"Don't start," Roy said and he moved down the bar.

George went back to Vivian and put the tickets on the table in front of her. He took off his hat, put it over his heart. "Vivian, may I call you Vivian?"

"You certainly may."

"Vivian, there's a concert this evening at the DeWitt, and it would be wonderful if you could join me. They're serving food and I relish the hope that you'll have dinner with me."

"That is so lovely, George. I'd be very happy to join you."

"The man said there would be dancing."

"Oh, good. Then we won't need Beauman's, will we? When is the concert?" she asked.

George read the ticket. "Seven-thirty is dinner," he said.

"Then we should be going," Vivian said.

They stood up and George gestured her toward the door where Cody was talking with Max.

"Thank you for those tickets, sir," George said to Max.

"Max, George. Call me Max."

"Max. Thank you. Cody, will you be at the concert?"

"I sure will, George," Cody said.

"Then I'll see you there," and George offered his arm to Vivian and they walked out onto Eagle Street. George stopped outside the bar and looked in both directions, torn. But Vivian stepped out toward the DeWitt Clinton.

"I'd like to go to the bank and cash a check," George said.

"Banks are all closed now, George," Vivian said.

"Are they? Then let's stop at Big Jimmy's. He'll cash a check for me any time. He owes me."

"I've got money, George, don't worry about it. You won't need money for the dinner, you've got the tickets. And I'd like to stop at the house before we go anywhere."

"The house?"

"My house. It's just a couple of blocks over, on Columbia Street. We still have time."

"Columbia Street? I lived on Columbia Street."

"You did? I thought you lived on Van Woert Street."

"I lived on Van Woert after my parents died."

"They died together, didn't they?"

"I think they did."

"What happened?"

"It was a big accident."

"A train wreck?"

"That sounds right. A train wreck."

"What did your father do?"

"He was in the Civil War. He knew very big people. Grant, Lincoln. And Clover. Adam Blake. Sheridan. He wrote for newspapers. Grover. Wrote a book, in fact. Two books. Commodore Cleveland. Cuba. Maybe three books. I'll have to look it up."

"He knew Lincoln?"

"He shook his hand at the Delavan House."

"And he knew General Grant?"

"He was invited to his funeral."

"Your father was an important man," Vivian said.

They could see the Capitol now from Eagle Street, 1913 it was when George was close to power. "Martin H. Glynn was an important fella. He made the speech when they put General Sheridan's statue in over there. He was Bill Sulzer's lieutenant governor, Chew-o'-tabacca Bill. They kicked Bill out of being governor." George had often been in Sulzer's office, and then in Glynn's after they impeached Sulzer and Glynn took over as governor. "I came home from the glove factory to vote for Glynn in 1914."

"And you knew Mr. Glynn?"

"He ran the *Times Union* after he lost. Killed himself over his back pain. If he had money he could've been one of my closest friends."

Vivian smiled and tightened her grip on George's arm. "Mr. George Quinn-who-knows-everybody, we'll have a good time tonight."

Arm in arm, George Quinn arm in arm with. He looked at Vivian. With Vivian, a friend, old friend. Beauman's we knew, other places, on the water? Al-Tro Park on the Hudson? He looked at her again. He liked her hat. Who had a hat like that? Pagger? Pag? Peg. But Peg's hat was white straw. I'm tying the leaves. He patted her arm, bare arm. Whose?

"Vivian," he said, and she smiled. And then he sang:

"Al-Tro Park on the Hudson, that's the place for me,
There's singing and dancing when you're out on a lark,
Take a trip with your sweetheart to Al-Tro Park."

"All right," said Vivian. "Here we go."

◈

Vivian lived in a second-floor flat on Columbia Street, just up from North Pearl. She opened the door and held it for George, and he went into the front room and took it all in: nice furniture, clean; doilies on the arms of the chairs; Persian rug, shiny table, walnut, polished, pictures on the wall, W. E. Drislane Choice Family Grocers. Biggest grocer in Albany. Vivian Drislane?

"Drislane's," George said, looking at the old photo. "On Pearl Street. I was in it many a time. Wonderful store. They bottled their own beer."

"One of my uncles was a Drislane," Vivian said.

"Very neat room," George said. "Not a pin out of place."

"I suppose I'm neat," Vivian said. "But I don't have anybody to mess the place up. Can I get you a beer? Or a highball?"

"Friend highball," said George.

"Highball it is." And Vivian went to the kitchen.

Her bay window looked up the street to the back entrance of the Court House where George worked for so long, Supreme Court of the State of New York to be held in and for the County of Albany Honorable Justice Morris Epstein presiding hear ye!

"I was born on this street," George said, but Vivian didn't hear him.

Directly across the street from Vivian was the Kenmore Hotel's side entrance, Adam Blake's hotel. George's father stayed there sometimes and he knew Adam Blake, didn't he? He was a bearer at Blake's funeral. Important fella, and rich, Blake was, and colored. George never saw him but that was his memory. Colored and rich. You don't meet a whole lot of *them*. If George's father stayed at the Kenmore why didn't George? I'd have to go to the book for that one.

In the kitchen Vivian opened the half-full bottle of White Horse and poured ample shots into two cut glass tumblers. She ran water to loosen an ice tray and added a bit of tap water to the mix, then came into the parlor and handed a tumbler to George.

"Friend highball," she said. And she clinked glasses with him. "Sit down, George, relax while I change my dress and spruce up."

George sipped the highball and did not sit. He watched her.

"Okay, don't sit down. I'll be back." She went to the bedroom with her highball.

Her moves were familiar. Peg? Vivian was it? Arms and legs, the way she carried herself on the high heels, very erect, very similar, and that front on her too, a nice size. Her dress looks fine the way it is.

"You don't need to change your dress," he said. "That's a very nice dress you're wearing."

"But I've had it on all day, and I'm going out dancing," she said from the bedroom. "Is your highball all right?"

"Friend highball," George said. He looked at it and then sang to it:

"Friend highball, friend highball,
You've been a dear pal to me."

He kept singing as he walked to the bedroom door, which was ajar.

"Years may come, years may go,
But forever my comrade you'll be."

Vivian, in her slip, was taking a robe from the closet. You don't often see them like that.

"Friend highball, friend highball,
What memories you recall . . ."

"Georgie, you're peeking at me."

"When trouble draws near me,
The first one to cheer me,
Is my dear old friend, highball."

"You know all the songs," Vivian said. She pushed her arms into the robe then opened the door wide. "Come on in, if you like. I don't mind." She put her dress on a hanger and hung it on a door hook.

"Very katish, this room," George said. He looked at a picture of Pierrot and Columbine that hung above her bed next to a crucifix. "I don't see the hoi polloi." He stared at her.

"You want to look at me, do you?"

"Looking at you is one of the pleasures of what they call a sight for sorry eyes. A proviso, a takeup for the fair and fancy."

"So I don't look too bad for an old lady."

"I don't see any old ladies on this block."

"You're a dear, but age is age." She picked up her highball from the dresser. "Shall we sit in the parlor?"

She pulled her robe together at the front but as she sat in the platform rocker the robe again fell open.

"That is a lovely color," George said, pointing at her slip as he sat across from her in the armchair.

"They all wear pink, but I like the pale yellow because it goes with my hair. Some of my hair."

"Peg likes black slips. And white."

"Peg had the most beautiful black hair. Peg was a beautiful girl. I knew her since we were in school. Was it a big shock to you, about her?"

"Shock?"

"That picture in the *Daily News* of her and her boss on the Atlantic City boardwalk."

"I was in Atlantic City when Czolgosz shot McKinley. I never saw any newspaper."

"I understand. You don't want to talk about it." She crossed her legs.

"Those stockings remind me," he said. "Wonderful legs. I always like the stockings. Sheer they call them, if I'm not mistaken. Some legs are thick at the ankles, beef to the hoof, we used to say. But not Peg. And no beef there," and he pointed at Vivian's ankles. "Those legs there are always just right. They slope in and out. Straight legs don't have the makings—those women look like six o'clock, straight up and down. But not these slopes." He moved his hands in a churning motion at Vivian's legs. "When they slope up and down and in and out like these here they're a great glim. Great glimmer. The thing about legs. A great glimpse. You couldn't predicate a leg like that right there without saying to yourself, George, what hills will those legs climb? They are prize-winning. Those legs can waltz, and I've seen them do it." Invite her to waltz, that's the main thing. Always invite her to waltz.

Vivian uncrossed her legs and extended her right leg, pointing the toe of her right shoe at George. "That's my prize winner," she said.

"That's a honey of an outlook. Beautiful is what I say." He could see her thigh above the garter. He raised his glass. "Here's to it and from it," he said.

"You like to see me this way?"

"I haven't seen this kind of contention."

"Oh, sure you have. Peg had great legs. She was a beauty. She got a little heavy at the end but she didn't lose it in her legs. Didn't Peg sit like this for you?" Vivian brought her foot back to the floor and her slip rode upward, putting both thighs on display.

"Peg let you know where you stood," George said, "where you could pile up her questions. How's it going? What kind of pork chops do you like? Pinochle or poker? Peg knew all the detours on the way to anyplace you wanted to swim, or shoot the chute, or rent a boat."

"I like the pork chops," Vivian said.

"Some things are miraculous before you know where they are." He gestured at her with open palm.

"Ed loved to sit where you're sitting and I'd do these things for him." She pushed her robe off the right shoulder, then off the left. "I went with Ed twenty-two years. He gave me an engagement ring when Eisenhower was elected. We weren't like married people. I wasn't cut out to be the little wifey. I don't know what I was cut out to be, Georgie. Ed and I were together four or five nights a week, we'd go to the movies, have dinner, then we'd come back here. He'd get me to take off this, then that. He liked me to make the first move and he loved me to talk. 'Say it, Viv, talk about it,' he'd say. And I'd say to him, 'You mean my vadge?' 'Yes,' he'd say, 'your vadge.' And I'd tell him about my vadge and how it felt and he'd tell me what it looked like to him and how he loved it. We could go on for quite a while until the words did what they were supposed to do and then we'd do it."

"Vadge," George said.

"That's my word," Vivian said. "I invented it for Eddie. I never say it anymore. I haven't said it in eight years. I guess that means I want you to look at me the way Eddie used to."

George stood and took off his coat and loosened his tie. He raised his highball in a toast: "Here's to it and from it and to it again. When you get to it do it for you may never get the chance to get to it to do it again." He drained the highball and set it on a table. He sat down and stared at Vivian's center.

"That's what Ed used to do," she said.

George hummed a few notes. Let me.

"Forty years in the post office and then he died. I never figured it out. Still haven't. I should've grabbed *you* when I had a chance."

"Why would you grab me?"

"We went out twice. I met you down at Kinderhook Lake, Electric Park by the Ferris wheel. We danced a few dances at the pavilion and then we came back to Albany on the trolley. A week later you took me dancing out to Snyder's Lake in your convertible. You were with a bunch of sassy fellows, with mouths on them. You weren't that way but I thought you might be, so I didn't encourage you. And then Peg took you out of circulation."

"Electric Park only kept the lights on till ten, and then the hicks went to sleep. The last trolley was at ten-fifteen. Thirty-five minutes to Albany, a grand ride, even in the dark."

"Sometimes romance went on in the back of the trolley." She shifted her body forward, closer to George. "You're a lovely man, Georgie."

He put his hand on her stocking so that his forefinger touched the flesh of her thigh. "Let me call you sweetheart," he said.

"You can call me that."

And he sang:

"Let me hear you whisper that you love me too."

"Love," whispered Vivian. "Where do they keep it?"

"Will you dance with me, Vivian is it?"

"I surely will, Georgie." She stood and tossed her robe onto a chair.

"Keep the love-light glowing in your eyes so true."

George put his right arm around her waist as he sang. He put one finger under the straps of her slip and her bra and moved them downward until her left breast was free. He kissed it.

"Oh, George, it's so nice to have you here tonight."

"Let me call you sweetheart . . ."

As he sang he tried to move her to the waltz tempo, but the crowded room allowed for no pivoting and so he waltzed her in place, his feet moving one-two-three, with hers doing the same, but he held her so they did not move forward, just one-two-three, and again, in place, right here is just fine, and it's getting better, and he ended the song:

"I'm in love with you."

He stopped moving and kissed Vivian, a long kiss. There's something about a kiss that you can't get anyplace else.

"Vadge, is that it?"

"That's it, Georgie. You got it."

◈

Quinn the Samaritan parked by the Emergency entrance to Memorial Hospital and went inside for a stretcher. An orderly wheeled one to the door and with Matt's help lifted Tremont out of Quinn's backseat onto it. Medical expertise would now banish all 'ritises from the peripheries of Tremont, the assassin-in-progress. Drug that man. Be kind and send him back into the world painless.

"You're back," the orderly said to Tremont.

"You know Tremont?"

"He's a regular," the orderly said.

"He's sick as hell," Quinn said.

The orderly nodded and wheeled Tremont inside. Matt followed.

"You ain't leavin'," Tremont said.

"I'll be back. Matt'll be with you." Matt would stay with Tremont until he was safe in a room. Keep in touch through the city desk, Quinn told Matt. We'll reconnect after my interview.

"Who you interviewing?" Matt asked.

"The Mayor."

"Very timely. Tell him not to accept rides from strangers."

❖

Markson, the city editor, had cigarettes going in two ashtrays at the city desk where he was whittling away at a pile of copy with his pencil. In shirtsleeves, tie loose, loafers, no socks, pot belly gaining on him, Markson looked up as Quinn crossed the city room. Ten reporters were typing their stories, the copy desk editing them in full frenzy as the *Times Union* moved toward deadline for the first edition.

"The Mayor," Markson said, "did you nail him?"

"I didn't call him yet. Frankly I don't think he'll talk to me. I'm a public enemy, but that's not the point." Inhaling Markson's twin columns of smoke Quinn reached over to stub out one cigarette but Markson slapped his hand.

"I need all the smoke I can get," he said. "I called the Mayor myself. He *will* see you. If he's not in his office he'll be at the Fort Orange Club. He'll interrupt his cocktail hour for you. I told him what a great job he and the police were doing to keep down tension in the city and that we wanted to help and that you're doing the story. I didn't ask him about Bobby. You do that. You interpret what he says, even if it's no comment. He'll probably praise the hell out of him."

"Patsy McCall once said Bobby was a stiff and a louse. Alex didn't contradict him."

"No need to resurrect that one. Let's not make Alex sound like an assassin, all right?"

"How about an assassin's target?"

And as Quinn sketched the assassination scheme Markson dropped his pencil and pushed his chair away from the desk. Quinn motioned him toward the teletype cubicle where the clacking covered their voices, and told him Tremont's tale of Zuki, using no names, not Tremont, not

Zuki, no mention of the Brothers, which was Markson's first question: Are they in on it?

Quinn said, "I have no idea and I'm making no accusations and I won't name a name till I find out what's real. I'll keep you posted. I don't want my source jailed as a conspirator, or maybe killed. He did nothing illegal. He backed off this scheme."

"He went to target practice."

"He did, and that was a mistake. He backed off when he heard Alex's name."

"We couldn't run the story even if you verified it, which you can't. Everybody will lie. Your shooter's a patsy and your man giving him the gun is either nuts or a provocateur. It's conspiracy horseshit—let's get the lefties. We got beaucoup stories tonight. We don't need speculation."

"Unless somebody does shoot Alex. If not my man, somebody else."

"Goddamn it, Quinn, you're a shit-stirrer."

Markson walked out of the cubicle, heading for the hierarchy on the second floor. No way he can handle this alone; no way Quinn can handle it alone either. Quinn checked the wire for the latest on Bobby: Condition critical, probably brain dead; police searching for a woman in a black and white polka dot dress who ran down the hotel stairs after the shooting and yelled in exultation, "We got Bobby Kennedy." At his desk Quinn called Pat Mahar at the Elks. George never arrived. You sure? Positive. Beautiful, another goddamn calamity. Where the hell did he go? Where *would* he go? Quinn wanted to call Roy to find out what he knew about Zuki but first he called Doc Fahey at the detective office and asked him to have the night squad keep an eye out for George on the street, he may be lost, and he's wearing a gray Palm Beach suit and a tan coconut straw hat. The cops know him for years, maybe not the young ones. He knows the city better than me, Doc said, but I'll spread the word. Doc was right. George couldn't get lost for very long in this town. Quinn called home and Renata told him Gloria was sleeping and Max was on his way there, she'd reached him at Cody's. He's very mysterious about coming to Albany, she said. He had lunch with Alex today at the Fort Orange Club. Maybe that has something to do with him coming here. Quinn told her George was roaming loose in town.

He called Jake Hess, the newspaper's lawyer and a personal friend for years, and asked, "Can I come over right now, Jake? Something dangerous is going on."

"You sound desperate."

"I'm too confused to be desperate."

"Come on over."

A copy boy dropped a note on Quinn's desk. Quinn read "Max," and a number. He dialed it and a voice said, "Cody's Havana Club," and Quinn said, "Is that you, Roy?"

"That's me."

"It's Quinn. This is weird. My next move is to call you but I get a message to call Max Osborne and you answer. Max—is he still there?"

"He's Gloria's father."

"He certainly is."

"I hear she's sick."

"She's all right. She's with my wife."

"Tell her I said to get better."

"Listen. Tremont Van Ort's the sick one. I just dropped him at Memorial Hospital and he's in fantastic pain, probably from booze, but he's also in serious trouble. You talk to him lately?"

"Two weeks ago, maybe. He was juiced. What trouble?"

"I'll tell you when I see you. This is important."

"To who?"

"You, me, Tremont, the whole town. What's your schedule?"

"Half an hour I'm done here. Then I'm at the Brothers."

"Will you be there long?"

"We'll probably be on the street trying to head off trouble before it starts. I'll be in and out."

"You know anybody named Zuki?"

"Zuki? Why?"

"I need to find him."

"Why?"

"You win the Twenty Questions prize. Let me talk to Max."

"He left. A woman called and he went out. I know Zuki. He works with Baron Roland at Holy Cross, I don't know what he does. He's a student at the university. He showed up at the Brothers two weeks ago, wanted to talk but I didn't have time."

"Do you trust him?"

"Who am I to trust anybody?"

Markson came back and said he'd told the story to Wheeler, the managing editor, who turned blue-green and took him down to Craig Penn, the publisher. "They want to call the FBI. I said it wasn't real and might never be, but they want the FBI in on it and a report from you with names."

"You write it," Quinn said. "You know as much as I do. Tell them I went to Troy to buy a shirt." And Quinn picked up his notes and went out.

Quinn referred to Tremont as Tex and Zuki as Roxy when he told the story to Jake Hess. Roxy, a young black in college, writing a book on Black Power, and Tex, a penniless, powerless, malleable, dying, grieving black man at the bottom of the world, in and out of jail half a dozen times as drunk and vagrant, also a veteran, Purple Heart, full of anger that can't be mobilized against all the white bosses who stunted him, crippled him, his wife a drunk and now dead, his child a slum creature run off forever. And solitary Tex broods on fate, his gorge rising as he listens to Claudia the matriarch, the heroine of Better Streets, as she spews venom against the politicians who ignore us and our streets and treat us like the garbage they don't even collect, like we live in a dump, she says, yeah, yeah, yeah a dump, says Tex, and the drink makes dump-life easier, calms him enough to let him imagine how the same people who killed Martin Luther King also killed Mary, poisoned her wine and gave him wine with the 'ritises in it, but Tex says I'm stronger than she was, little bird of a thing couldn't cut it, they killed my Mary 'cause they can't handle us, so they guttin' us one by one. And Roxy says to him, that's the truth and we gotta get even. And Tex says you right, we gotta do that, and he reads a mimeographed letter signed by Black John that Roxy happened to find on the bar where they had gone to share their grief, and Black John says in his letter that black men gotta get up and move, stop hanging on the apron strings of the old mammies, those sweet old gals who want to run the town, let 'em try, ain't doin' no harm, but nobody in power's gonna pay 'em no mind, you gotta go out on your own, black man, do what Black John is doin', stand up to the white man, be a damn man, black man, be a man, don't let the fat women talk for you, talk for yourself and let 'em all know you're livin', show 'em what a black man can do. And Tex says to Roxy, who is this Black John? Damn if I know, Roxy says, he just writes these letters and sends 'em around. Well, says Tex, he's right, but what we gonna do and how we gonna do it? And Roxy says, we got to think this out, and that's just what I been doing, writing this book about it, about the black man getting power, we had power in Korea, didn't we? You were in Korea? Tex asks, and Roxy says, you know the battle of Chipyong-ni? I know it, Tex says. Hell of a show, says Roxy, and I got me some gooks. Tex says I got me a few, and Roxy says I heard you did, I heard you were a good shot and that you got the medals to prove it. I am a hell of a shot, Tex says. You can make money bein' a hell of a shot, Roxy says. How you do that, Tex asks, hold up banks? Take out some of these no-good motherfucks, Roxy says. Take 'em out? And Roxy says, Get somebody nobody gonna miss or mourn and they don't even ask who did it. He's gone, he's all done, that's fine, thank you kindly, mister. Like Bobby Kennedy, that no-good, just because he's a Kennedy, fuck him, you could shoot him. Shoot Bobby Kennedy? Who could? What the hell you talkin' about? And Roxy says I'm talkin' money. And he takes Tex out to practice his shooting.

Jake Hess cocked his head and said, "Bobby Kennedy?"

If Jake knew that Quinn was talking about Tremont thinking about shooting Alex Fitzgibbon and not Bobby, who was already shot, he'd pick up the phone and call Alex; for Jake, though now counsel for the newspaper, had for forty years been part of the legal brain trust of the Democratic political machine that ran this town—Patsy McCall and Roscoe Conway and Elisha Fitzgibbon, and now Elisha's son, Alex Fitzgibbon. And Jake knew where all the bodies were buried. Yet Quinn never trusted anybody in politics more than he trusted Jake Hess, a principled man who would be the first person Quinn called if he went to jail, which was why he was now talking to Jake, who would know which way to move through this conundrum. Jake's parents were Russian Jews who had fled the pogroms, a cultured man with ashen hair, gold-rimmed spectacles, gold watch chain looped across his vest, never without his suitcoat, soft-spoken, a 24-karat smile, and a conscience that, against the odds, had survived the political wars.

"You're saying Tex is the one who shot Bobby?" Jake asked.

"No, Tex was here in town, too drunk even to shoot himself. Bobby's just my for-instance," Quinn said.

"Some for-instance."

"Roxy had somebody else in mind, but I can't get specific yet."

"What's your question?"

"Can they arrest Tex just for being ready to shoot somebody like Bobby Kennedy?"

"He would have to commit an overt act before anybody could prosecute him," Jake said.

"What about being part of a conspiracy?"

"You need the overt act."

"Is giving Tex an AR-15 and taking him for target practice and giving him money to do a shooting—is that an overt act?"

"Any witnesses?"

"I don't know, but Tex says he's still got the AR-15."

"An overt act isn't necessarily a criminal act."

"What about trying to talk somebody into a crime?"

"Criminal solicitation. But you need something that puts it into play."

"What if somebody like me finds out about a conspiracy or a criminal solicitation? If I don't tell anybody is that a crime?"

Jake's phone rang and he mostly listened to whoever it was, not looking at Quinn. When he hung up he said, "That was your publisher."

"Penn?"

"Penn. He mentioned your assassin and said the Mayor is his target."

"He talks too much," Quinn said. "See why I can't use names? He probably already called the Mayor."

"He hasn't but he wonders if he should."

"Did he call the FBI?"

"He wants to."

"You didn't tell him to go ahead, did you?"

"I said I'd call him back."

"What about when I go out that door, will you call the Mayor and give him my news?"

"I think he'd rather hear it from you."

"I tell the Mayor somebody's planning to shoot him, that's your legal advice?"

"He's had threats before. I'm sure he'd appreciate the tip."

"How do I protect Tex?"

"He's safe. He hasn't done anything wrong."

"What if I don't tell the Mayor and somebody actually shoots him?"

"You might have a problem, but not a legal one."

"Guilt?"

"Guilt is an elective. Reprisal, perhaps?"

"If I'm arrested will you represent me?"

"Only if you feel guilty."

"You think this will make a good book?"

"Your friend Tex, you mean?"

"Everything that's happening, the whole megillah. Who'd believe what's going on right this minute? Tex, Roxy, Claudia, Roy Mason, Matt Daugherty, Bobby, riots, vigils, my wino friends, and maybe you and me thrown in for the hell of it. There's a lot of mystery and they're all telling me to pay attention to them."

"Sounds like a panoramic newsreel."

"That's not worth writing. If I can't find a focus the hell with everybody. People like the title—The Slum Book—but they don't like the subject. Another protest book? The woods are full of them. I see heroes but editors see winos and bums. Who wants to read about bums, especially bums in Albany?"

"They don't know our bums."

"I also want to put Cuba in it."

"Quite a place, Cuba. I went to Havana in '27 when Mayor Goddard was thrown out of an open car. Do they have any bums in Cuba nowadays?"

"No bums allowed. They're all communists."

"Society isn't complete without bums."

"Tell that to Fidel. You know my grandfather wrote about Cuba. You ever read his books?"

"I remember he was quite an achieved figure. What was his name?"

"Daniel Quinn."

"Unforgettable name."

"He wrote about Grant at Vicksburg, Sheridan at Cedar Creek, what a story that is, and he did a book on the Cubans' Ten Years War against the Spaniards and their slave empire. He went down there in 1870 to find the Mambí rebel leader nobody could get to, and he got to him. He rode with the Mambí troops in a battle with the Spanish, he wrote later on Irish genocide that started in Cromwell's era, and he turned up stories of Irishmen in Albany who'd been sold as slaves in the West Indies. He also rode with the American Fenians when they invaded Canada after the Civil War to take Ireland back from England, and he tracked the famine Irish, which he came from."

"He consorted with death and darkness," Jake said.

"Exactly, and it fed his argument on the children of desolation, dead millions destroyed by true believers who waged the holy and then the unholy wars. He concluded that the great losers never lose, and revolutions never fail; they evolve heroically, with the memory of martyred multitudes and the survivors' imagination perpetually breeding a counterforce, and new heroes to drive it.

"He wrote of a runaway slave in Cuba, Nicodemo, wounded in the war with the Spanish, left arm useless, doing a furious dance of sexual abandon to the beat of a Mambí drum and galvanizing the black men and women watching his every twitch. He equated Nicodemo with an illiterate slave of sixteen, Sooky, who yearned to be a poet and sang her poems at the Albany Pinksterfest, a wonderchild to all who heard her. The Pinksterfest, held when the azaleas bloomed, was a week-long Mardi Gras where the slaves of Albany vented their misfortune through music, dance, and carousing.

"Nicodemo died in battle a week after his dance, beheaded by the Spanish. Sooky carried live coals in her shoes to burn her slavemaster's barn to ashes and was hanged as an incendiary on Pinkster Hill, where she'd sung her poetry. Albany cancelled the Pinksterfest forever, believing so many blacks drinking and dancing held the potential for revolution."

"Your grandfather wasn't old enough to see a Pinksterfest, was he?"

"No, but he knew the old Adam Blake, who was always master of the revels. Body servant of the Patroon, an unlikely revolutionary. But my grandfather imagined such people having ecstatic dreams that rose up from a dimension of the spirit where revolution against the invincible is perpetual—no matter how many billions are massacred or destroyed. Nicodemo and Sooky were such warriors. We insist, therefore we continue. Call me dead, call me phoenix."

"Your grandfather sounds like Candide," Jake said.

"But Candide wound up tending his garden. My grandfather never quit throwing himself into losing causes and war all his life, not as a warrior but as a witness who needs to know how it turns out. It became his political necessity. I heard his weird music in high school when I read his books and scrapbooks, and it eventually sent me down to Cuba, which was lush with death, spurious gods, and pernicious doctrine, but also with that century-old Mambí warrior spirit that had never died. It drew me into compacts with gunrunners and I went up in the hills to see Fidel. I even married a gunrunner in a ceremony presided over by ancient African spirits."

"I'm deeply sorry I missed that. Is this what animates your book on the slums?"

"Ethereal slumgullion, a mythically nutritious new literary form. Are you aware my first novel comes out in September?"

"The story of the political kidnapping?"

"That's the one. It's about my uncle, the pool hustler."

"Am I in it?"

"Under another name."

"Any true believers in it?"

"Under another name."

"Will I recognize them?"

"I call them politicians."

◈

Renata put Gloria to bed and monitored her until she was asleep. Then she called Max at the number he'd left and told him to get a cab and come up here. Twenty minutes later he walked in with suitcase and briefcase in hand, wearing a white guayabera and tan shoes, a bit of leftover Cuba in his style, the first Renata had seen him in a year. He put down the bags and kissed her on the mouth, tried to linger, but she backed away and sat in an armchair. She pulled her skirt over her knees and he smiled. He thinks I'm on guard. She did not want to be alone with him, but it was necessary.

"Those bags," she said. "You don't have a hotel room?"

"I'm not staying. In transit, you might say?"

"Where are you coming from, and where are you going?"

"Miami, and I'm not sure what's next."

"You flew in?"

"I did. A charter."

"How flamboyant. Do you want to stay here?"

"A tempting offer but I don't think it's in the cards."

"You're mysterious, Max. What is going on?"

"Everybody's dying and I'm sick of it. First Inez Salazar, and then an actor I knew, both in Miami on the same day, now Bobby Kennedy shot, and an hour ago I hear Cody Mason's on the way out with cancer—all this in two days."

"I know about Cody. I told Gloria we'd go to his concert tonight. That great talent disappearing. How did you hear about him?"

"I was at the Havana Club and he came in. He's thinner, but he looks pretty good. His son says he's out of time."

"You talked to Roy?"

"He tends bar. Smart and radical, like you."

"Why are you talking about these deaths?"

"They seem connected."

"Is death following you? Is that why you left Miami?"

"Problems came up. I saw Alfie in Miami the day before yesterday. He always speaks well of you. He's done ridiculously well since Havana."

"Is he as wild as he used to be?"

"People don't change."

"Was he with Inez when she died?"

"He took care of her, paid her rent and medical bills, but after she developed cirrhosis he wouldn't go near her. He took it as an omen. Is liver disease an omen?"

"We create our own omens."

"I saw her in the hospital, bloated and almost comatose. Her eyes followed me and I'm sure she was cursing me for being alive."

"Poor Inez. Life was so unfair to her. She probably saved my life in Cuba the night they shot Quesada, and then what she did for me at the embassy."

"I remember the embassy," Max said. He picked up a small statue from an end table: bearded man on crutches, his bandaged head bleeding, a cloth around his loins, two dogs at his heels. "Lazarus in Albany. Babalu Aye, a bit of Havana."

"I've tried to keep Cuba in this house. That, for instance," and she pointed to a painting of an arresting figure, Sikan, a woman in black and white net body wrap holding a fish that embodies the god Tanze, a discovery that threatens Sikan's life. "It was the one painting I took when we left Havana," Renata said.

"You miss the old life. The country clubs, partying till dawn, all that shooting."

"I did love it. Not the shooting."

"I think you loved the shooting."

"I loved what was sensuous and unpredictable in how we lived."

"You don't have that?"

"Sometimes. I went to North Carolina for two weeks with a group from the university to register black voters. And I went to Selma for the march, the second one, after the blacks were gassed and run down by men on horses and beaten."

"You're still fighting the revolution."

"Of a different kind."

"Were you hurt?"

"No. No battle scars."

"What about your social life? No nightclubs."

"None like Havana. I never go. I'm too old for children's games."

"You were no child when we played our game."

"Shhhh," she said, shaking her head and pointing to the ceiling.

"Would you go back to Havana?"

"It is not possible."

"It's possible if you want to do it," he said, and when he smiled she saw a gauntness that was new: his cheeks, his neck slimmer than ever, his guayabera loose on his frame. The thin man. Was he sick? He seemed younger than his true years, hadn't lost his hair, something of that old magnetism still there.

"I didn't expect you to come to Albany," she said. "I thought you'd wire the money through a bank."

"Was your bank really going to foreclose?"

"They threatened, which is why I called you."

"Don't you have money coming in?"

"Daniel tells everyone his annual salary is below the federal poverty level, and I could make more begging on the street. The museum doesn't pay serious money to my kind. They use wealthy women who take no salary, the same as in Havana. But we'll be fine if we get through the summer."

"And after that?"

"Daniel's book will be published. That will bring a check."

"How big a check?"

"Not big. We do not do anything that makes money."

Max pulled a two-inch fold of cash from his trouser pocket and took off the rubber band that bound it. He counted out ten one-hundred-dollar bills and pushed them aside, counted another ten. "Two thousand," he said, and began a third pile.

"Two thousand is all I asked you for."

"I'm giving you six. You want ten? Have ten."

"Six? Ten? My god, *hombre,* no. We could never pay it back."

"No need. Tell me a number." He counted out six piles, then made them into a single pile.

"Six thousand?" she said. *"Un milagro!"*

Max handed her the money, then pocketed the still hefty wad. She put the six thousand in her purse.

"Do you always travel with so much cash?"

"It's very spiritual to carry large sums, a holy form of danger. I once carried eight hundred thousand in two suitcases."

"*Madre de Dios.* Eight hundred thousand. Why?"

"I was delivering it."

"Political money?"

"I took it to an embassy."

"Ah."

"You think my money is evil. I see it in your eyes."

"I don't know you anymore, Max. It's been a long time."

He leaned toward her and went down on one knee.

"It stuns me to see you, Natita. After all these years I'm still tortured in your presence. It's an obsession. I've never been able to love anyone else, not even your sister."

"Max, get up. This is bizarre."

"You should've married me," he said. "Leave your poverty and marry me now." He put his hand on her knee.

"Max Osborne marries whichever woman is next to him." She lifted his hand off her knee.

"Don't scold me. I'm your fool. Love me. Love Max the fool."

"Get up. Fools don't kneel for anybody."

He stood and he leaned over to kiss her. She did not turn away.

"Sit down, fool. You haven't asked about Gloria."

"No. Tell me," and he sat. "What's the matter with her? Why is she sleeping when her father is here?"

"Father? *Sinvergüenza.* You haven't seen your daughter in a year."

"I came to take you away from your husband."

"Nonsense. You have another motive."

"You read minds, like your *babalawos.*"

"So do not lie to me. Why did you come?"

"I want to go to Cuba. It's unlikely they'll let me in, given my agency connection, but what I know may interest Fidel."

"He'll think you're still a double agent. Why do you want Cuba?"

"Cuba doesn't extradite you to the U.S.—hijackers know this. So do black rebels who've gone down there. So do fugitives on the run—like me."

"You're a fugitive? From what?"

"I've been working with Alfie. They raided his operation and he left town. And so did I. I haven't seen the papers but I assume they've gone public with my name."

"Those suitcases were Alfie's?"

"Yes."

"Drug money."

"I deal in money, not drugs. I'm just a courier."

"This is a *tragedia*, Max, a man of your intelligence doing crime."

"You think intelligence serves only law and order? What about all your intelligent Directorio friends who died trying to murder Batista? The lust for adventure can arrive at a late hour."

"A late hour. Are you ill? Dying? What is it, Max?"

"Let's say I'm aging rapidly."

"Why are you telling me all this?"

"I need help in getting to Fidel. He's the only one who can make it happen. I want you to take me in. We can go through Mexico, or Canada. You have the connections and I have the money to buy our way in. You can't imagine how much money I have."

"You think I have connections? You are *loco*. I am out of favor in Cuba."

"You were important in the struggle, even after you left Cuba, and Fidel knows it. Also, Moncho has risen very high. He's close to the inner circle. He can get Fidel's ear."

"I am an outsider to the revolution. I live in Albany."

"People talk of you. Renata Suárez is still a heroine for the torture she suffered and never giving them any names. For getting guns from Miami to Fidel with Alfie."

"You are an appealing liar."

"And you were a lover of Fidel."

"I was not Fidel's lover."

"You were one of them."

"They say that of hundreds of women."

"And it's true of hundreds of women, maybe thousands. And of you."

"Believe what you like."

"It's valuable that you slept with the Comandante."

"Valuable to whom?"

"To anybody who needs the ear of the mighty, and right now that's Max Osborne. I rescued you from death, now it's your turn to rescue me."

Max unbuttoned his guayabera to reveal a thin, brown leather shoulder holster belted across his chest. He lifted out a .32 automatic and set it on the coffee table. Renata clapped her hands and laughed.

"A gangster, Max. *¡Qué mono!* How cute you are. And your pistol is cute, maybe too cute to do what you ask it to do. Do you remember I carried a Cobra in my purse when I drove with Diego?"

"I'm not as serious a shooter as you, my dear. I only want to protect myself."

"You will shoot the police when they come for you?" Gloria said as she came down the stairs.

"Gloria, *mi amor*, how are you?" Max said, and he walked to the bottom of the stairs, kissed his daughter, held her, stared at her. "You are a magnificent child, my Gloriosa, are you all right?"

"She's been working and studying too much. Life is overwhelming her," Renata said.

"Who are you going to shoot, Papa?"

"I have enemies."

"Who is Alfie? What kind of criminal is he?"

"He's a Cuban we knew in Havana who ran guns. Never mind Alfie, tell me how you are."

"I just came home from a psychiatric ward. I'm not the Gloria you knew, Papa. I'm a crazy person and I can't live here anymore. If you go to Cuba I want to go with you. Will you go with us, Aunt Ren?"

"Do not make such plans," Renata said. "That is not possible."

"Wait a minute," Max said, "what happened to you?"

"They locked me up, Papa. I tried to kill myself. I smashed a window to cut my wrist and I tried to bleed myself with a straight razor."

"But why?"

"I'm worthless, useless. I foul what I touch."

"You are priceless," Renata said. "You are a perfect woman."

"They fired me from Holy Cross. They called me a slut."

"Who did?"

"A woman on the board at Holy Cross."

"Why would she say that?"

"I had sex with two men. One of them is her husband."

"Two men doesn't qualify you as a slut."

"Don't mock me, Papa."

"She has discovered the liberality of love," Renata said.

"Everybody knows what I did."

"How do they know?" Max asked.

"The woman told them."

"Who is she, who is her husband?"

"Alex Fitzgibbon."

"The son of a bitch."

"Yes, that's him," said Gloria.

"Who is the second one?"

"Roy Mason. We work together. You don't know him."

"I spent this afternoon with him."

"No. Why, where?"

"I went to Cody's club. He tends bar there."

Max groped for a way to respond. Distant father suddenly privy to his daughter's crisis, wise counsel now expected from him to manage her imagined disaster. Counsel her to change her ways? Absurd advice from Max the libertine. Point out she's neither a slut nor crazy, that some women think one love, one man, is never enough, your Aunt Renata always needed a crowd. For years Max had imagined Alex turning his cultivated eye to the beautiful virgin on his doorstep. Women always stood in line for him. No doubt he gave her a graceful introduction to love, but the bastard shouldn't be anywhere near her. Doting godfather, father substitute for the absent Max. During their lunch he said she was working well with a social agency that dealt mostly with inner-city blacks. He was voluble on Roy, who worked for the same agency and who also fronted for the Brothers, a Panther-like bunch that sees the Mayor as their enemy, and he says they're ready to fan the race riot that could erupt any minute in this town.

"You're not crazy and it's certainly not a tragedy," he said. "Tragedy would have been that straight razor."

"Alex will punish Roy," Gloria said. "He already sent him to jail once."

"For the poll watching."

"How do you know that?"

"I had lunch with Alex today. He talked about Roy. He knows Cody and I are friends."

"Did he mention me?"

"He said you were working with a social agency but that he hadn't seen you lately."

Gloria now knew she was stupid, knew nothing, was wrong whatever she did or thought. She has learned to be a freak, failing even to die properly, and an imbecile with sex. Who thinks as mindlessly as she? Parents, nuns, priests, teachers all instructed her in ignorance. Why didn't she discover anything on her own? The only wisdom came from Renata, who was with Fidel and Quinn and my father and who knows how many others, but is not a slut. Tell me how this is so.

"Were you really Fidel's lover?" she asked Renata.

"No one should ask or answer such a question."

"Will you open the door to Havana?" said Max. "Will you try?"

"I don't think so."

"I don't have much time. I can't stay in one place."

"I bet you can do it," Gloria said.

"I will think about it," Renata said.

Actually the world might improve if we all went to Cuba. They say Fidel has a romantic memory. But that was nine years ago. He looked at her and asked, And what about you? And Renata answered, Only after you take a bath.

Quinn called Renata on his way to interview the Mayor and she told him that Alfie and Max were fugitives from a major drug bust, and that Max wanted her to get him into Cuba.

"How does he think you'll do that?"

"Through Moncho."

"Isn't that far-fetched?"

"Moncho has connections and Max is ready to buy his way in."

"Max has money?"

"He gave me six thousand cash. He wanted to give me ten," Renata said.

"For what?"

"I asked him for two thousand last week to pay Gloria's hospital bill. I said it was for our mortgage."

"You ask for two and he gives you six."

"He's a generous man, he always was."

"Did you find a way to reward his generosity?"

"Not yet. Gloria heard Max talking about Cuba and now she wants to go down there with him."

"She wants to be anywhere but here. How is she?"

"Max perked her up. I think she likes criminals."

"Of course. That's why she took up with Alex. I'm seeing him at seven at the Fort Orange Club."

"Tell him I spit on the tits of his mother."

"I'll try to work that in," Quinn said.

"Can you find out if the police are really looking for Max?"

"Where was the bust?"

"Miami, Alfie's house and loft. They found a few ounces of marijuana but Alfie wasn't there."

"Did it get into the papers?"

"In a big way."

"How does Max come into it?"

"Somebody saw him in Julian Stewart's movie last month and recognized him as the man who delivered money for Alfie. Max now carries a gun."

"Why does a fugitive with a gun spend a public afternoon at Cody's bar?"

"Max is not logical. Maybe he decided not to behave like a fugitive."

"Then he won't be a fugitive long. Are you and Gloria going to Cody's concert?"

"I hope so. I put Gloria back to bed so she'll be rested," Renata said.

"And will Max go?"

"We haven't discussed it. I think Max is sick. Maybe seriously sick."

"From what?"

"I don't know. He's very thin, and he seems obsessed with death."

"Crime doesn't agree with him."

"I'll try to meet you there. Pop is going too, with a woman he met someplace."

"Pop with a woman?"

"Vivian something, she knew my parents years ago. She's fine."

"George has never gone with another woman."

"We don't know that. Sometimes people start over."

"You really think so?"

"You couldn't prove it by me."

Renata had been leaving Quinn for years, but not yet, and not for anyone; though there were two or three in waiting, not including Max. The Santeria marriage warning lingered, Floreal saying a knitting woman was trying to save me from I never knew what, and the *babalawo*'s advice last month that this wasn't a good time for separation. And Gloria: no way I can leave her alone. I am my grandmother, who knows, who knows how to lead her away from disaster, how to sort out her chaotic sex. But Renata, how do you do that? Become her therapist? Love, oh yes, love. She and Quinn had begun well with love. It had been instant, true as blood, and it lasted, but it evolved into love-in-waiting, starved for joy. Renata found joy elsewhere, furtive alliances with *guapos y jóvenes* who kept her from boredom, filled her cup, addictive. She might break the addiction if she replaced Quinn, or if Quinn replaced himself. But how? He's forty. Can an old dog teach himself old tricks? Well, he does find his way, perfume on the coat collar, out till three exploring the night, Giselle always here for their family reunions.

"I'll be at the concert," Renata said. "I don't know who I'll be with."

"You never do," Quinn said.

❖

George and Vivian were walking on North Pearl, taking the long way to the DeWitt Clinton Hotel and Cody's concert. They were under the Kenmore Hotel's marquee and George stopped and looked in through the glass door toward the old lobby. It was a mess. A welfare hotel now.

"My father lived here," he said. "He was friends with the rich colored man who owned it. His name, what's his name? My father thought the world of him, I think he wrote about him. What was his name, Eb, Ebble, there was a slave in there somewhere. Blee, Blay. He built the hotel, high class."

A flung rock smashed the storefront window of what used to be the Kenmore bar, and flying glass cut George's head. He and Vivian turned to see six young negroes across the street, all with rocks in their hands.

"Hey you," George yelled, "what the hell are you throwing rocks for?" One of them threw another rock and broke the window of the Federal Bakery and the six then moved up Pearl Street. Vivian saw George's head was bleeding and she took his pocket handkerchief and blotted the cut. She walked him four steps to a parked car so he could lean against it and she gave him the handkerchief to press on the wound to stanch the blood. She picked up his hat from the sidewalk and saw George staring again into the old Kenmore lobby.

"Adam Blake owned this hotel," he said, "and his father was Adam before him, a slave born in 1770 who died at ninety-four up on Third Street in Arbor Hill, and my father wrote about him because the old man, the old Adam, was king of the Pinksters, the big holiday when the slaves sang and danced all week on State Street hill. When my father went to Cuba he saw somebody dancing just like Adam danced in the Pinkster-fest, only he was in the jungle. Young Adam was a prince of a fella, everybody loved him, you couldn't ask for better, he had money and style and he made the Kenmore the best hotel in Albany."

George seemed to have sudden and total recall of those old times, with more control of specifics than Vivian had heard from him all day. A siren wailed, coming this way, and they saw the six young negroes running toward Clinton Avenue, breaking windows in a liquor store and the Grand Cash meat market as they went.

"This is like Petey Hawkins," George said. "His barber shop was right around the next corner, on Sheridan, and he gave me many a haircut, because he was my only colored customer when I cut hair myself. I was in his place the week of the Jeffries-Johnson fight and I told Petey I'd take Jeffries and he says, George, don't bet against Jack, he can't lose, he wants it too much, his daddy was a slave and he wants to be as big as President Arthur, he tells his mama that. Jack's been to Albany and I shaved him when he wasn't the champion and he's gonna come here again and I'm gonna shave him as the world champion. He's gonna be a great man and he sure gonna win this fight, George, and I don't wanna take your money. I got ten bucks says it's Jeffries, I said. Georgie, Georgie, tell you what, don't give me no money, and I'll pay you ten if you win but if you lose you ride me down Pearl Street in a wheelbarrow, down to State Street and back to the barbershop, and I said, Petey, you'll never take that ride, but you're on.

"He was taking a ton of bets, odds were ten to seven against Jack, and Petey bet every nickel he had and was holdin' money in his safe for dozens of other bets, most honest man in Albany and everybody knew it. Jeffries was this huge, hairy Irishman, world champ, retired undefeated in nineteen-five after twenty fights when he run out of challengers. Johnson lost two fights out of sixty-four and took the world heavyweight title from Tommy Burns in Australia with a TKO. But all this country'd give him was the colored world title. Yet he beat every white man that come along and he kept saying, I want the champ, I want Jeffries, but Jeffries wouldn't fight him. Jack kept up the nag and then five years after he quit the ring Jeffries says, all right I'll come back and beat your black ass, and every Irishman in Albany was for him. The fight was in Reno in front of fifteen thousand and the big-time champs were there— Corbett, Fitzsimmons, John L., Tommy Burns, all with Jeffries. But Stanley Ketchel said different. Ketchel knocked Johnson down in nineteen-nine but Johnson got up and hit him an uppercut and got two of Ketchel's teeth in his glove. Ketchel knew the man and he said Johnson's gonna send Big Jim out of this town with a broken heart. Petey and I went down to Beaver Street, front of the *Times Union*, to get the teletype bulletins round-by-round. They'd read 'em out loud with a megaphone and then post 'em on a big board. First three rounds Johnson's playin' with Jeffries and by six everybody knows Jeffries is outclassed and after eleven he's hopeless. Petey says to me, You own a wheelbarrow, Georgie? Johnson knocked Jeffries down twice in the fifteenth and then stood over him with fists up. Back before the first round Jim Corbett was saying, He's gonna kill you, Jack, and Jack says, That's what they all say, but now Jeffries is down and Corbett's yelling, Don't, Jack, don't hit him. Then Jeffries gets up and Jack throws a right cross and two left hooks and down he goes forever, bloody and senseless, his mother wouldn't recognize that face. His doctor jumps in the ring and says, Stop it, don't put the old fellow out. They sit him in the corner and Jeffries says, I was too old, I couldn't come back. Only mark on Johnson was an old lip cut Jeffries reopened with one of the few he put in Jack's mush. Jack beat him fair and square, no yellow streak in the man. He's the champ. Nobody'll beat the Big Black.

"So there we were, me pushing Petey Hawkins in a wheelbarrow down North Pearl, a few wagons on the street, not many since it's the Fourth, and Petey's sitting on two pillows, legs dangling over the front of the barrow, his smile as big as his straw hat. We get to State Street and I turn around and we're almost back to the barbershop, just a few steps from where we are right now, and Dummy Quain, one of the Lousy Dozen that hung around Dunn's Saloon, says, That ain't right, pushin' a nigger, and Dummy walks alongside me and says, This ain't right, George, and I say, Forget it Dummy, I lost a bet on Jeffries and I gotta pay the man. Dummy kept walking and then he grabbed the barrow and tipped Petey onto the cobbles of Pearl Street and said, Fuck you, nigger.

"I hit Dummy and he wobbled and fell against a horse and the horse bit him, but Gerber and Hosey from the Lousy Dozen were on Petey before he could get up, kicking him. Three young coloreds in front of Petey's barbershop—one of them was Petey's brother, Nigger Dick—were waiting to get their winnings out of Petey's safe and they come running. More whites poured out of Mahar's and two more coloreds walking down Pearl jumped into it. I helped Petey stand up and I said, We got a riot, and he hit Hosey. Gerber knocked me down and Dick Hawkins grabbed Gerber's arm with both hands and broke it. How's your arm? I asked Gerber and Dick give me a big smile. Then Petey saw more whites coming up Columbia Street and he says, Outa here, outa here, too many of 'em, and the six coloreds run up Pearl, Petey leadin' 'em toward the Third Precinct near Wilson Street with a dozen whites on their tail. I was running right with them and I saw Dick Hawkins coming last and then one of the whites yells, Pipe that big shine, and Dick turns around just as this heavy fella was swingin' at him with a piece of pipe, and Dick cut the man's arm and face so fast it's black lightning and a whole lot of blood, and the man's in a heap as Dick comes inside the Precinct. The Lousy Dozen was now a Lousy Two Dozen, and they were rattling the door. But the cop bolted it and waved his pistol at them. Lotta scenes like that all over the country that day—twenty-four coloreds killed and a couple of whites, and they burned stores and houses in the big cities, all because there wasn't no more white hope."

◈

Doc Fahey, in one of those detective cars that were coming up Pearl Street with the open siren, saw George sitting on the fender of a parked car in front of the Kenmore. Fahey and his partner, Warren Prior, put George and Vivian in their backseat and took them to Memorial Hospital up the block. Fahey called the *Times Union* to tell Quinn he'd found George, but Quinn was out, so Fahey left a message.

"How's the head, George?" Fahey asked.

"Which head?"

"Yours. The cut. Does it hurt?"

"Not a bit," said George.

"Did you see who threw the rock?"

"If I ever see him again I'll give him a swift kick in the candy."

"Don't get in any fights, George, back away. It's dangerous on the street tonight."

"No Quinn ever took a backstep for anybody. Jimmy Cagney said that to—Jimmy Cagney said . . ."

"You don't have to be as tough as Cagney, George. There's young black gangs out tonight and a lot of anger. Somebody already threw a couple of Molotov cocktails down by Dorsey's. You should take George someplace safe, Vivian. I'll call his son, Dan, and he'll come and get him."

"We're going to Cody Mason's concert over at the DeWitt," she said.

"That's good, Vivian. Call a cab to go over. Stay off the street tonight, all right?"

◈

When Roy arrived at the Brothers' storefront headquarters—two steps down from the sidewalk, three doors north of the Palace Theater's stage door, and directly across North Pearl from Memorial Hospital—the plate glass window was gone. Gordon Buford was nailing plywood over the opening but the plywood didn't cover it, more needed. The Malcolm X poster that had been in the window for two months lay curled over a table top in the office, a bullet hole in Malcolm's chin.

"Clarence was here when they shot out the window," Gordon said.

Clarence Gale, sweeping up shattered glass, said, "They missed me."

"You see who it was?"

"Three, four white guys maybe in a Buick station wagon. Couldn't see much."

"Whites cruisin' is bad news," Gordon said. "Lot of our kids out there too. Ben and I talked to some up on Ten Broeck Street, told 'em to stay cool tonight, cops are everywhere. But the kids didn't blink. Some of 'em'll be around the Four Spot for the dance."

"A dance?" Roy said. "Don't they know about the riot?"

"They just play some riot music," Gordon said. He hoisted a second piece of plywood into place to cover the broken window space.

Ben Jones was on the phone, sitting at a battered oak desk under a large hand-lettered sign that said: BROTHERS—WE NEED RENT AND PHONE MONEY. GET SOME! The phone company had cut service: the Brothers could receive but not make calls. A smaller sign advised, DON'T SELL YOUR SOUL FOR $5. PAY YOUR DUES, $5. The new edition of the Brothers' tabloid, *The Emancipator*, published every so often, was stacked on a table next to the desk and a large headline from an old front page was tacked to the wall above: FIVE BROTHERS WILL TESTIFY AT BEN JONES GUN TRIAL. At a back corner of the room was a refrigerator, a table with three chairs, a small stove, and a shelf with plates, glasses, knives, and forks. Here the Brothers fed a hot meal daily to eighteen children of parents who were in the hospital, or in jail.

"What happened today?" Roy asked Ben.

"Woman called, her son got robbed of eighty cents in front of the Palace. White woman. Four black kids, she says. She wants us to find out who they are so she can tell the police."

"That it?"

"Robert Gene called, he's hyper. Twenty kids hangin' out up on Swan

Street talkin' trouble. He wants somebody to go up and help cool 'em down. Can't do it alone."

"You send anybody?"

"Nobody to send. Everybody's out on the street."

Ben handed Roy two stapled, mimeographed pages. "The new Black John is out. Somebody pushed it under the door. That guy's cracked wheat."

Roy read the headline in typewritten caps: THE EYES OF ALBANY ARE ON YOU, BLACK MAN. This was a flyer, the third Roy had seen in recent weeks, always anonymous, always crude, race-baiting commentary: "Muslims are holding meetings down on Green Street. Albany doesn't need them. They don't vote, they don't smoke, they don't drink. But they *kill*! . . . Aunt Jemima of the South End loves her streets and sure does get her gabby self into the papers. But she can't get along without all those white folks hangin' on her apron strings. Pour a bucket of white pancake batter on your naps and be happy, Mammy, but watch out when it rains . . . Looks to Old Black John like the Mayor's being real nice these days—picking up trash in Arbor Hill, all honey and melon, but his political machine's thugs roam the city—kiss the black man in daylight, kick hell out of him at night . . . I see where Reverend Smathers got hit by a rock but didn't make a complaint. You know right away the good reverend is black. No white man would stand for that. White man would defend himself *to the death*!"

Roy looked up from Black John's screed to see somebody getting out of a car and coming across Pearl Street. Shades, muscles, white T-shirt, pressed pants—Zuki came through the door.

"Roy," Zuki said, "I finally got you."

"Got me?"

"You're hard to find. Just want to talk, pick your brain. I see you're reading Black John."

"You know John, do you?"

"No, but he's funny."

"Funny like cancer of the balls. He's out to make trouble."

"Who do you think he is? You think he's black?"

"He's black, but he's carryin' water for people who want to see us go down shooting one another. What's on your mind, Zuki?"

"This book I'm doing, I want to get at what's goin' on right this minute in Albany. History is happening here. And face it, man, the Brothers is where it's at and you're out front, you're a mover and shaker. I want to see you in action, listen in for as long as you can stand it, hang out for a week, a few days."

"A week?"

"Three days? Start with a couple of hours when something's taking shape, like tonight."

"You want to follow me around and take notes?"

"That's it."

"The Albany cops already do that," Ben said. "Probably tappin' this phone I'm talkin' on. They take pictures, too."

"I could talk myself back into jail," Roy said.

"Nobody will see my notes and I'll show you what I write before it's published."

"This is a book?"

"It's a long term paper, but I got somebody who'll publish it."

"What are you looking for?"

"See how a guy like you—guy looks ordinary but isn't—how people pay attention to you—your picket line against the Laborers Union, going to jail for poll watching, doing what you believe in, this is some new kind of gutsy behavior and young blacks look up to you. All the stuff the Brothers are doing—taking on the five-dollar vote, running for office, fighting landlords and police brutality, it's bigger than life, and kids find it heroic."

"Heroic my ass."

"I'm telling you what I hear."

"We been doing it for two years," Roy said. "They been doing it in the South a whole lot longer. You heard about Selma?"

"I know Selma. But the Panthers come to visit you, don't they? Eldridge Cleaver, Bobby Seale? And didn't Stokely come by, and Dick Gregory, and Ralph Abernathy? Not to mention Ramsey Clark and William Kunstler. Hey, Roy. You guys are a magnet."

"You're keeping track. I didn't like Cleaver. He was too tough on Baldwin. We liked Bobby Seale."

"See what I mean? You don't give a damn, you just do it and people know it."

"Gordon here, and Ben and Clarence, all the Brothers do it."

"Sure, but you did time."

"Ben did time, for nothin'. They busted fifteen Brothers in two years, a damn fortune just in bail money. They don't let up."

"I'll write about *all* the Brothers, write about tonight even if nothing happens. But heavy stuff could happen I hear."

"What do you hear?"

"Cops are out for blood, if there's a riot."

"Cops are always out for blood, our blood. That's no news."

"Cops are revved. Mayor told 'em don't take no shit tonight. Keep this town quiet."

"Who you talking to knows what the Mayor's saying?"

"It's all over town. Places closing, boarding up their windows."

"The Brothers been trying all day to put a lid on any riot."

"I wanna look over your shoulder."

"What about Baron Roland, what's he up to?"

"Teaching at City College, same as always, and still doing his thing at Holy Cross."

"Where is he tonight?"

"He'll be at the protest. He set it up."

"Are you working with him or what?"

"Part-time for the summer. I'll be full-time at the university in the fall. I was doing a couple of courses at Columbia till I come back up here."

"Back?"

"I lived in Troy as a kid. House where I roomed in Harlem got torched in the King riots so I come here."

Roy tried to figure out Zuki's face. Some white in him. Latin, maybe, but he's got no accent. Smart eyes, slick and savvy line. Students behave like this? Students got muscles like this? Follow you around like it's a documentary? Hey, Roy, don't trust anybody who parachutes in from outer space peddling hero shit. Lose this bird, take him outside. Why did Quinn ask about Zuki—a link to Tremont? Gotta see Tremont. Get outa this.

"Let's go outside," Roy said and he stepped up onto the sidewalk and Zuki stood with him. "I got some business, Zuki. I'll be at the Four Spot later. I'll think about what you said, see what it's like out there tonight."

"It's five-thirty now. When'll you get to the Four Spot?"

"Get there when I get there."

❖

Tremont woke up groggy, fuzzy, but with a lot less pain, and still on a stretcher after two hours of waiting to be admitted. Through the window beside him he saw Zuki and Roy coming out of the Brothers' headquarters across the street. They stood there and talked, the front window gone, boarded up. He saw them look toward the hospital as they talked and he decided they were talking about him. He moved one leg off the stretcher, felt pain, not that much.

An intern had examined him when he arrived, taken blood and medicated him; and from this, plus being horizontal, he sank into a fadeaway. Matt asked nurses twice about admitting him and was told we need a doctor's approval; we'll treat him here for now. So Tremont's a transient, a short-timer.

Matt pulled up a chair and watched Tremont sleep, he dozed a little himself. Then he went for coffee in the cafeteria and read the *Knickerbocker News* with the latest on riot potential in the city, and the protest against the silencing of himself by the bishop. The protest was set for seven-thirty in the basement of the First Church, Albany's old Dutch church, and a crowd of irate Catholics, students, and inner-city protesters was expected. It would also be a candlelight vigil for Bobby Kennedy, whose condition remained dire, but no one had yet said he would die. The assassin's weapon was an eight-shot .22 caliber revolver.

"Hey, Bish," Tremont said after he woke up, "I saw Zuki across the street. Talkin' to Roy."

Matt looked out the window. "Nobody there now."

"I think he's comin' in here to see me."

"How would he know you're here?"

"Zuki knows things."

"We'll have a little chat if he shows up," Matt said. And he saw George Quinn coming into the emergency room with a woman and an Albany detective Matt knew by sight, not by name. The detective delivered George to a nurse and left. When the nurse led George to a stretcher behind the screen next to Tremont, Matt went to him. "It's Father Matt, George, Martin Daugherty's son. I thought we dropped you at the Elks Club this afternoon."

George looked at Matt, he looks a little like Martin, and said he never got to the Elks. Vivian told Matt how George got his head wound and what she knew about his Elks detour. She recognized Matt from the news coverage and said that Father was courageous for speaking about the poor and politics, that she never heard a priest talk politics except Father Coughlin back in the '30s, a good speaker, but with a nasty tongue and I never liked him. Her brothers wouldn't even whisper against a politician or they'd lose their city jobs. I like your perspective, Vivian, Matt said, and he offered to call Dan Quinn and let him know his father was in the hospital. Vivian said Detective Fahey already did that and Matt went back to Tremont, who was awake.

"That guy over there, his name George?" Tremont asked.

"Right, George Quinn. Somebody threw a rock at a window and he got cut, down on Pearl Street."

"Ain't seen George in a whole lot of years. He wrote numbers."

"He wrote your father's hit in 1937, eleven thousand dollars, right?"

"Whoa! How you know that, Bish, how you know about my father's hit?"

"Quinn told me. George is *his* father."

"Yeah? I never put 'em together. Quinn, where'd he go to?"

"He'll be along. You're feeling better, Tremont?"

"Had to. Couldn't feel no worse. They got good drugs in this place."

A nurse came up to Matt with a note. "Father Matthew?" And Matt said yes. "We don't take messages but the caller said you're a priest. You're that priest in the papers."

"Guilty," Matt said.

Quinn's message to Matt: he was heading for the Fort Orange Club. The message came in a few minutes ago. "I have to make a phone call, Tremont, be right back."

Tremont propped himself up on one elbow. "Hey George," he said, and George turned to look. "You George Quinn."

"That's what they tell me." A nurse came to bandage George's cut and said he was lucky, the glass didn't penetrate, no stitches needed. She gave Vivian extra bandages for later.

"You remember me, George?" Tremont asked.

George took a good look. "Tremont? Big Jimmy's boy?"

"Yeah, George. That's me."

"You ran errands for Jimmy, and you set pins in Jimmy Smith's alleys on Green Street. They moved those alleys to State Street."

"What a memory. How you doin', George?"

"Getting something fixed up here. Had an accident. Your father owes me money."

"How much he owe you?"

"I don't remember. Two hundred, maybe. Jimmy'll remember."

"Jimmy won't remember. Jimmy died eleven years ago."

"Is that so? Sorry to hear that. You got old, Tremont."

"You too, George. Whole world got old since we saw each other."

Tremont looked out the window and saw Roy and Ben Jones come out of the Brothers, Zuki not in sight, but he could be outside waiting for me to come out. If he comes in here I'm a sittin' damn duck.

Vivian had gone to ask the nurse to call them a cab and now she came back and told George people were breaking windows in cabs, so no cabs are running downtown.

"We'll walk," George said. "It's a nice night out, isn't it?"

"It is," Vivian said. "It's a very lovely night, and we haven't even had dinner yet."

Tremont got off his stretcher. "Where you headed?"

"The DeWitt," said Vivian.

"Go down this hallway," Tremont said. "It's shorter. I'm goin' the same direction." He moved down the hall with them.

"What about your friend the priest," Vivian asked.

"Makin' a call. He'll be along."

Tremont lifted a towel off a small stack of laundry and put it under his arm, then led them out the hospital's south entrance, half a block away from Zuki already. He put the towel over his head and walked a step ahead of George and Vivian, blocking the rear vision of himself if Zuki was looking. They passed the Palace with a movie called *Up Against*, a black man's face on the poster. Tremont wanted a drink, needed a drink, found a few bills in his pocket, seven bucks left from the Zuki seventy-five. The Four Spot was right in the next block, ask George.

"Tell you what, George," Tremont said, "we go to the Four Spot over there. I'll buy a drink for you and your lady, pay off a little of what Big Jimmy owes you."

"We should get to the DeWitt, George," Vivian said. "They're probably serving dinner."

"Never stop a man from paying what he owes you," George said.

"I don't owe you, George. My daddy was who owed you."

"All contributions gratefully accepted."

George looked at the Four Spot, one of five buildings on Clinton Square. This was Johnny Palermo's place, steaks and chops, banquet hall in back, Johnny got a new sign. He ran it as a speakeasy in Prohibition with rooms upstairs in the building next door, you could bring a girl and if they raided it you could go up to the roof and jump onto Johnny's roof, then drop onto Chapel Street. George bowled with Johnny at the Rice Alleys on the corner, but the alleys are gone. Where did they go? Young Negroes going in. You don't often see them in Johnny's, once in a while maybe.

The bar in the Four Spot was half-full with twenty young black men and women, and more in the back room. All eyes went to George and Vivian as they stood at the bar.

"Double port, and what my friends want," Tremont said to the white bartender. He took the only barstool. "I don't sit down I'll fall down."

"A small lager, please," Vivian said.

"Make that two," George said. He looked at the hangings on the walls: Truman, Stalin, and Roosevelt on the cover of *Life*, World War Two victory headlines, troops marching through Fifth Avenue confetti. War, but not George's war. He looked carefully at all the young black men in the room, trying to remember the one who threw the rock. He didn't see anybody he recognized.

"You lookin' for somebody?" one older youth asked.

"He's with me," Tremont said.

"Yeah? Who *you* with?"

"We gettin' a little taste, that all right?" Tremont said. The talk stopped. *Chain, chain, chain,* Aretha sang.

"People come in here lookin' us over," the man said.

"What's wrong with lookin'?" Tremont said. "This man just come out of the hospital, got hit with a rock. We here gettin' away from rocks."

"Nobody here throwin' rocks."

"Then maybe we're safe," Tremont said.

"The cops were just in here lookin' around for somebody," the barman said. "They had a witness, somebody threw a rock through a liquor store window and looted it."

"They threw rocks in the trolley strike," George said to the young black who didn't like to be looked at. "The National Guard shot people throwing rocks and then they shot people who weren't throwing them. Nineteen-oh-one. They killed twenty-seven people. Frankie Pringle was standing next to me, got hit by a rock and then somebody shot him." George pointed at the door. "Down on Broadway, near the station, fella threw a rock and killed an old widow woman. He had to leave town. Thirty-seven people got killed, some with rocks, some shot."

George sipped his lager. "Beer is very good. Jimmy draws a good glass of beer. Thirty-seven people killed by rocks." *Chain, chain, chain,* Aretha sang and George asked the barman, "Johnny around tonight?"

"No Johnnys here, my friend."

The bartender, a burly man with slick black hair and wary eyes, doesn't seem to trust people. George asked, "You don't know Johnny?"

"No."

"You been here long?"

"About a year."

"What do they call you?"

"Howie. They call me Howie."

"I'm talking about Johnny Palermo," George said. "He owns this place. He used to make cigars. Had billboards all over town. Get behind a Palermo Cigar. He'd bring Jimmy Durante to town and raise thousands for St. Anthony's church. Johnny and I bowled together."

"The Marcello brothers own this place for ten years," Howie said. "Maybe they bought it from Johnny."

"Did you hear about anybody throwing Molotov cocktails?" Vivian asked.

"No Molotovs," Howie said, "but I make a great Manhattan. Have a few of those your head explodes, just like a Molotov."

"I don't think I want my head to explode tonight," Vivian said.

George turned back to the hostile youth, raising his finger as he spoke, as if the earlier conversation were still in progress. "I was born three blocks from here, on Columbia Street. You ever hear of my father? Daniel Quinn? Famous man in Albany. Did everything, went everywhere, saw everybody, shook hands with Lincoln, saw Lafayette when he came to Albany to be buried, wasn't anything he didn't know about this town and he was colored."

"Old honky's crazy," the youth said.

"What are you saying, George?" Vivian asked.

"You look at me and I'm white, right? I'm a white fella goes in and out of colored people's houses just like I was colored. When I was growing up they called me and my father paddyniggers. My father was a great man. He was all over the Civil War. I met Lincoln at the bar in the Delavan House, homeliest man I ever saw and I shook his hand before I was born. And he was Jewish. My father knew Grant and Sheridan. He was there when Sheridan took his twenty-mile ride and he wrote so much about it he made Sheridan famous. Sheridan was a little bit of a fella. Little Phil they called him. George Payne, he rode with Sheridan and he was a colored fella. Came home from the war and raised a family on Main Street up in the North End, first coloreds up there, only ones for years. My father wrote so much about George Payne that he made him famous. George Payne knew Sheridan better than the people down at West Point. My father didn't live long enough to meet Jimmy Walker. He died in a train wreck with my mother. She was a Cuban Creole."

"Your mother was a Creole?" Vivian said.

"That's right."

"Creoles in New Orleans," Tremont said. "I know Creoles."

"Creoles got mixed blood," Howie said.

"Paddyniggers and Creoles," Tremont said. "You're makin' this up, George. Why you tryna change your skin?"

"What Creole means is she didn't want slavery," George said. "She was a woman who knew the top people and she raised a ton of money for the Cuban war. My father always had to go to war. He was in the Civil War and when it ended he invaded Canada with the Fenians. Then he went to the Cuban war and came back and married my mother, who was a Cuban Creole."

"How was she a Creole?" Vivian asked.

"She was as white as those women ever get and my father knew the guys who started that damn war. They were all Cubans. But it was John Brown, that floo-doo—he was the one who got the slaves out. Quite a fella, John Brown." Then George sang:

"I got a white man workin' for me,
I'm going to keep him busy you see,
Don't care what it costs, I'll stand all the loss,
It's worth twice the money for to be a boss . . .

"I was born and raised in this town and I'll be here forever," he said, speaking to everybody now. "I don't know what you got against Tremont, best little kid on Dongan Avenue, smart, and he knows how you get where you're going and how you make money. You work for it, you set pins, you don't throw rocks at it. You go out like I go out, and like Tremont goes out, and you find out how it is and you ask for the money. And they give it to you. What the hell, they got no choice. They need you. You are there and you've got the goods. This is the next stop on the railway to heaven. Bless me father for I have sinned," and he blessed himself.

"Crazy old fucker," the black youth said.

Through the plate glass window George saw half a dozen people standing on the sidewalk, all coloreds. It was still light out, but North Pearl Street was empty, no cars moving. Two coloreds came in and joined those at the bar.

"Somebody threw a Molotov over on Sheridan Avenue," one said. "Hit a bus but it kept going."

"There's the cocktail you were looking for," Howie said to Vivian.

"Who threw it?" Vivian asked the youth, who looked at her but did not reply. The youth who didn't trust George shook his head and they both turned away from Vivian.

"Sheridan Avenue," George said. "They named that for General Sheridan. He was born there. Petey Hawkins had his barbershop on Sheridan Avenue."

"Petey Hawkins. I knew Petey Hawkins," Tremont said. "Lived up on Third Street. I knew the whole family. Petey's sister Seely was a good singer. She came to Albany in a musical and they hired my daddy for a part. He was seven feet two and he'd been singin' in sideshows as the Albany Giant, and when that musical come here they saw him and hired him and he was so funny they took him on the road with the show."

"Petey's brother Dick was a great friend of mine," George said.

"Don't talk about him, George," Vivian said. "Please don't say Petey's brother's name. Talk about Petey but not his brother. Do you hear me, George?"

"Don't say his brother's name?"

"Don't say it. Don't say it for me, all right, Georgie?"

"All right, I won't say it for you."

Matt Daugherty opened the front door and held it ajar, looked in. He saw Tremont and shook his head. He came in and let the door close.

"You ran out on me, Tremont," he said.

"Had to, Bish. Knew you'd find me, had to get outa there. You know why."

"No, I don't."

"I saw that guy we talked about, comin' right toward the hospital. I couldn't stay there like a damn sittin' duck."

"You're sitting here like a sitting duck. And you're drinking. They just treated you for the 'ritis and you're starting all over."

"They fixed me up, 'ritis ain't so bad now. I needed to settle down."

"They'll write you up, Tremont. You and your 'ritises'll go into the medical books. How are you, George?"

"Five or six flavors of excellent, and yourself?"

"I talked to Danny. He's worried about you."

"Danny worries too much. Worrying gives you hives. I got hives when Dewey closed down gambling in Albany. You get very itchy."

"Danny said you were going to a concert."

"We are if we ever get there," Vivian said. But she liked the newness of the Four Spot and she wouldn't really press George to leave.

"Danny wants to meet you at the concert," Matt said.

"Danny shouldn't worry so much," George said. "He'll break out in hives."

"I'll tell him," Matt said.

From his bar stool Tremont saw Zuki on the sidewalk, talking with Roy. No way you gonna lose him now, Tremont. No place to hide. But why hide? What can he do? Beat me up, I don't think so. Got the Bish and Roy with me. Maybe blow the whistle on me? But then he's in it as much as me. He wants to do something, I know that. All that badass talk comes outa someplace, like political. He a Panther comin' on like Joe College? Narc? And why he come to you, Tremont? Who'd you ever lick? Hey, Tremont's a good shot, he be the triggerman, he be the killer. Knock off the Mayor, then somebody knock off Tremont, everybody's happy.

James Brown was new in the smoky air of the bar, telling everybody, *I Got the Feelin*, and the mood of the room went into an upswing—heads going whichway, bodies revving, George nodding in time to James's feelin.

"Bish," Tremont said, "I got the feelin' myself, and you right about me bein' a sittin' duck in here. There's Zuki out there talkin' to Roy."

Matt looked out, saw Roy with the young blacks.

"Which one is Zuki?"

"Slick dude in the T-shirt and shades," Tremont said.

The two were standing with eight or nine youths in front of the bar. Roy was talking and the cluster was listening. Roy shakes his head, doesn't approve. Of what?

"What can Zuki do to me, Bish, throw me in the river?"

"He could do that," Matt said. "But not if you went public with your story, talk to Quinn's friend Doc, the cop, and you'd have a head start on him."

"You sayin' I should tell people Zuki wanted me to shoot a politician?"

Matt smiled at Tremont's volume, then saw that Howie the bartender, George, Vivian, and some blacks had all turned to look at Tremont.

"They just shot one of the Kennedys," George said. "I don't know which one. I was in Atlantic City when Czolgosz shot McKinley. They fried him at Sing Sing seven weeks later."

"You right again, Bish," Tremont said. "Goin' public's what I'm gonna do."

Howie came down the bar to Tremont. "What's that about shooting a politician? That some kind of joke?"

"No joke," Tremont said. "Guy wanted me to shoot somebody."

"In Albany?"

"Yeah."

"Who?"

"Didn't say who. Just had this idea."

"Who you talkin' about? What guy?"

"That guy out there on the sidewalk."

"Which one?"

"Guy with the T-shirt," and he pointed.

Howie looked out the window, then went down the bar and spoke to a waiter and went into the back room where the party was rocking with James Brown, getting bigger, and noisier.

"We better get you out of here," Matt said. "You didn't have to broadcast it."

"Let's have one for the road," Tremont said.

"Too late. George and Vivian, you should come with us."

"Give my regards to Broadway," George said.

Matt ushered the three of them out the door and went directly to Roy who was haranguing the sidewalk gang to get inside, the Four Spot's dangerous tonight if the town goes crazy. Cops been cruising with bullhorns telling people keep their kids indoors. Hanging out as a gang is asking them to bust your head, put you in jail. Nobody moved. Cops are all carrying shotguns tonight. You can't cope with shotguns. Nobody moved. They won't serve me inside, one said. We're waitin' for some guys, we ain't makin' trouble, what are you, a preacher?

"Roy," Matt said and pulled him aside, "Tremont just told half the bar Zuki wanted him to shoot an Albany politician. I think the bartender called the cops."

"Jesus, Tremont, is that true?"

"Wanted me to shoot the Mayor," Tremont said, not in a whisper.

"Oh, fuck me, this can't be real." Roy turned to Zuki who heard what Tremont said and was already walking toward Clinton Avenue. "Hey, Zuki," Roy said, "wait a minute."

Zuki kept walking and, as Roy went double-time toward him, Zuki ran, but Roy was closing the gap as they turned the corner out of sight.

Matt turned to Tremont and said, "Let's move on," but then Roy came around the corner with Zuki in a hammerlock.

"Tremont," Roy called out as he came, "is this the guy?"

"That's Zuki."

Two hefty white waiters and Howie the bartender, who was clutching a short baseball bat, came out of the bar. "Those two," Howie said, pointing at Zuki and Roy, "and this one," pointing at Tremont.

The black youths on the sidewalk backstepped away from the bar window. One waiter grabbed for Tremont but Matt moved his bulk between them and put his hand on the waiter's chest. "Don't touch him," he said to the waiter and Howie.

The two waiters moved on Roy and broke his hammerlock on Zuki. Roy pushed himself away, off balance, and as one of them grappled with Zuki the other hit Roy with a roundhouse and jumped him when he staggered.

"Hey, leave that fella alone," George yelled to the waiter struggling with Roy.

A black Chevy turned off Clinton Avenue onto Clinton Square, a one-block street. The driver slowed as two white men hanging out the front and back windows threw two Molotov cocktails into the crowd, the first smashing the Four Spot's window. Zuki broke the grip of the waiter grappling with him and ran toward Clinton Avenue. The bomb ignited Howie's apron and he dropped his bat, flailing at the flames. George picked up the bat and swung it against the skull of the waiter wrestling with Roy. The waiter fell to his knees and Roy backed into the street.

"I owe you for that," Roy said to George.

"You done the same for me more than once," George said.

The second Molotov had exploded against the stoop of the house next to the bar, splattering flame on the feet of the black youths and onto Vivian's yellow shawl. Matt lifted it off her shoulder and shook out the fire. The Chevy had turned onto Orange Street, sped up Pearl and was gone. The two waiters and Howie went in to fight the fire inside the bar's broken window.

With sirens screeching half a dozen police cars converged on the Palace Theater and Roy walked toward it, blotting his bleeding lip. He saw Ben Jones in front of the theater, hundreds of people coming out.

"We just got a call," Ben said to him. "White kid either fell down the balcony stairs or went over a railing, some kind of fight during the movie. Kid may be dead. They say black kids did it."

"Fuck," Roy said. "Fuck, fuck, fuck."

"That's what I was thinkin'," Ben said.

Tremont had crossed the street to watch the action, in no shape to fight tonight, Molotovs flyin', whites are crazy. Tremont wanted a drink, but can't go back to that place. Go to Dorsey's. Matt had George and Vivian by the arms and was crossing from the bar to where Tremont was standing.

"We're moving on, folks," Matt said, and he hustled the trio across Clinton Square Park and onto Pearl.

"Maybe we can get a drink down at Dorsey's on Broadway," Tremont said.

"Lead the way," Matt said, and they quickstepped down Orange Street toward Broadway as the wail of sirens grew louder.

"Too much goin' on in that bar," Tremont said.

"Too many loose wires in your machinery, Tremont," Matt said.

"Why did you hit that man with the bat, George?" Vivian asked.

"Dick Hawkins was getting the worst of it."

"That wasn't Dick Hawkins," Tremont said. "That was Roy Mason."

"That was Dick Hawkins. I've known him all my life."

"Whoever it was," Matt said, "you got him out of trouble."

"I thought it was exciting," Vivian said. "I loved every minute."

George sang:

"Just see the sweat poppin' out of his brow,
I've got him right where I want him now.

*Don't you dare to talk back, 'bout the white 'bove the black,
I've got a white man working for me."*

A steward at the Fort Orange Club told Quinn the Mayor was expecting him and led him to a carpeted second-floor room away from the main dining room and bar traffic, and from members reading the papers and sipping whiskies in the parlors. The room was one of a dozen in the club used for intimate private dinners, oak-paneled with a small chandelier and wall sconces offering a marginally brighter light than might have been cast in this room eighty years earlier when the Club was founded. Two W. Dendy Sadler prints with scenes in the artist's favorite nineteenth-century men's club—men toasting a vintage wine, and men polishing golf clubs—brought back a bit of the distant elite past that both clubs had in common. The Mayor had been president of this club not long ago, and his grandfather was one of its founders and pillars. He entered the room with a brisk gait, wearing one of his gray single-breasted suits with white shirt and rep tie, his uniform.

"Mr. Quinn," he said, and extended his hand.

"Mr. Mayor," said Quinn, and he shook the hand.

Quinn had been watching Alex Fitzgibbon behave for three decades. Supremely articulate, expensively educated, immensely charming, he epitomized the suave politician for whom no hostile question would ever pose a problem. The answer, whatever the question, was that there is no ready answer, the situation is too complex, quite ambiguous, a matter of opinion, not what we expected, in need of study, can't comment since it's under investigation, sorry but I don't have that answer, try again tomorrow. In the early 1940s his equivocal style was the understandable caution of a novice mayor, but he quickly shed the novitiate and raised vaporous improvisation to an elocutionary art form—graceful verbal effusion, devoid of specificity or meaning. I will tell you what I choose to tell you and nothing beyond.

Why, then, didn't Quinn talk to the police chief or the district attorney about the crisis in the city? Because *only* the Mayor was permitted to have a public thought. The evergreen memory in the Party was of the convention delegate who was allowed to make a speech and nominated the wrong man. Quinn was determined to draw the Mayor out by logic (unlikely) or trick or outrage or shame (impossible but worth a try), provoke him into uttering one consequential sentence, which would be a triumph.

"I hope we can keep this brief," the Mayor said.

"We can," said Quinn. "The city is on edge, blah blah, racial tension blah, and on top of this comes the shooting of Bobby Kennedy, which aggravates the situation, doesn't it? Your reaction?"

"National tragedy blah blah, might have been president blah, grieve for his family blah."

"The Albany Democratic organization didn't like Bobby. He didn't play the game, went his own way with his own people blah."

"We have nothing but admiration for Bobby blah. We would have backed him one hundred percent blah in November."

"You put out the word to cut Bobby when he ran for the Senate."

"You are misinformed."

"Patsy McCall said publicly that Bobby was a stiff and a louse. You have never reacted publicly to that remark."

"Is this an interview or an attack, Mr. Quinn?"

"How do you assess the public anger tonight blah blah, the downtown protest and vigil for Bobby, student anger over the silencing of Father Matt Daugherty, Catholics protesting blah blah, angry blacks fuming since Martin Luther King's death, other cities rioting."

"Yes, that's blah," said the Mayor, "doing all we can, police out in force blah, guns blah, won't abide terror on our streets, store windows broken blah, citizens hit with rocks blah."

"My father was one of those citizens," Quinn said.

"Yes, I heard, cut by flying glass," said the Mayor. "I met him this afternoon on Eagle Street. He was very cheerful."

"That's his nature. Have you been down to the scene?"

"Which scene?"

"North Pearl Street."

"You mean the Palace?"

"The Palace?" said Quinn.

"There was a killing there," the Mayor said.

Quinn waited. What was this?

"A young white boy is dead, attacked by Negro youths—that's our first report. You haven't heard?"

"No. When?"

"Five minutes ago."

"Anyone arrested?"

"Not yet."

"What does this do to your plans for controlling violence?"

"Our police force is equal to anything that happens blah."

"If there's a riot will you blah blah the State Police?"

"No. Our own police have tear blah gas, shotguns, and they won't tolerate any blah blah."

"Will they shoot to kill?"

"They will use their best blah."

"I talked to a black man today who was recruited to assassinate you."

The Mayor crinkled his eyes, leaned back in his chair.

"Really?" he said. "Who is he?"

"He's a friend of mine. Another black man named Zuki cajoled him into talking about it and took him for target practice with an AR-15. Have you heard of anyone named Zuki?"

"No. But your friend should tell our police chief about this."

"I'm telling you. You're better than the police. The man believes the police will throw him in jail, and he's probably right. Zuki is the obvious target here, a conspirator talking murder. He shouldn't be hard to find. He goes to the State University and has a part-time job at Holy Cross Institute."

"Was this why you wanted this interview—to sensationalize it?"

"I thought you should know people are talking about murdering you."

"I am grateful for your concern."

"But you don't believe it's real, do you?"

"I don't believe it? Off the record?"

"All right."

"Of course I believe it. Many people out there hate me."

"I know you have enemies."

"The Black Panthers talk openly about killing white police and they have counterparts in this city—and you write about them in your newspaper. Those fellows call me a racist but I'm no racist and never have been. *They* are the racists. They want me dead because I'm a white man with power over their lives and they're sending a message that white power is passé and Black Power is the new force to reckon with in this country. But their Black Power nonsense and their so-called creative conflict are just old-fashioned anarchism in new clothes, a national cancer that's destroying the blah blah bridges so painstakingly blah between the races. They're calling for blood and I think they'll get it. This country has to see this blah blah danger for what it is. Intelligent blacks don't want the cancer these barbarians are spreading. Your news is no surprise to me, Mr. Quinn. We know they have guns and will use them."

"This assassination talk is very like political theater."

"Target practice with an AR-15 is theater?"

"It seems far too stupid to be real. My man is a wino who's probably dying and I doubt he could shoot himself in the foot. But if he's set up as a would-be assassin, any group he's linked to is trashed."

"What groups is he linked to?"

"You know them and so do all the intelligence agencies, whose fingerprints seem to be all over this. Zuki looks very like a by-the-book provocateur. Did he ask your permission to assassinate you?"

"I think you should bring your man to see Police Chief Tobin."

"You know, Mr. Mayor, that people who give allegiance to City Hall have tried twice to entrap me over what I was writing about race and politics for the newspaper. And somebody offered me a job in Chicago to get me out of town. At one protest meeting I counted five undercover people, not provocateurs like Zuki, more like robotic stenographers, all out of place at such meetings, all reporting back to somebody's big brother."

"You have a conspiratorial flair."

The Club steward entered the room with a telephone saying the Mayor had a call and he plugged the cord into a wall jack. The Mayor spoke, listened, hung up.

"Some news that may interest you, Mr. Quinn. A black man named Tremont is at the Four Spot bar on Clinton Square talking about shooting a politician. They say he's wearing two-tone shoes. He's with an older man named George who's talking about shooting people for throwing rocks. The manager is trying to detain them both till the police get there."

"The anarchists have descended," Quinn said.

The Mayor smiled. "Ask them to stop by headquarters and talk to Chief Tobin." The phone rang and the Mayor answered. Then he said to Quinn, "Now a racial fight has broken out at the Four Spot and someone threw Molotov cocktails into it."

Quinn stood up. "So the revolution begins. Do you want to go down and make some notes?"

"I might be assassinated," the Mayor said.

"There's always that risk in a revolution, Mr. Mayor," Quinn said.

◈

When George stopped singing he walked a while in silence, then said, "What was all that back at Johnny's bar? That was some fuss."

"I'd say it was the hand of God that got us out of there," Matt said, "and God was especially handy with Tremont. Did you hear him talk about shooting a politician?"

"I didn't know what the hell he was saying," George said.

"The bartender did. He called the police and I'm sure they're looking for Tremont right now, don't you think, Tremont?"

"Cops been lookin' for me half my life."

"Those bartenders wanted to keep you there for the cops. We get to a phone I'll call somebody to come get us, figure the next move."

"Who do you want to shoot, Tremont?" George asked.

"Nobody, Georgie, don't wanna shoot nobody. Some guy talked to me about it, that's all."

"And he gave you a gun," Matt said.

Tremont considered that. "Gotta get that gun. It's sittin' down there in the bus station and somebody maybe gonna get at it before I do. Zuki, could be. He don't know where it's at, but I ain't sure he don't."

"What do you want to do with it?"

"Rub off my fingerprints. Put it someplace Zuki can't do nothin' to me about it. Shove it down a sewer."

Dorsey's Cafe was locked and its lights were out. A fire from another Molotov cocktail had left ashes on the wet sidewalk, and part of Dorsey's front wall was scorched. This was the last black bar on the urban devastation that was Broadway, a few vital blocks for nightlife that used to be called Little Harlem. The Black Elks Club was a couple of blocks up, but nothing started there till ten o'clock and then it went all night. The Taft Hotel's eight rooms were gone, and so were Martha's bar, a great spot for music, and the Carterer Mission, a haven for bums black and white. Union Station was boarded up, no more trains in this town. Most white saloons and restaurants had gone broke or been bought out by the city to build parking lots for stores that had also gone bust while they waited to park; and the horserooms, the pool crowd, the bowlers, the gamblers, and the hot mattress hotels had all abdicated to more fertile turf. Downtown was emptying into the suburbs. Broadway's streetlights were on but nobody was walking the street except these four pilgrims.

"Can't get no drink here," Tremont said.

"Whole street is closed," Matt said.

"Albany never closes," George said.

"You right, George," Tremont said. "Hapsy's on Bleecker Street, he's always open."

"We should get to the DeWitt for the concert," Vivian said.

"You'll get there," Matt said. "I don't want you alone on the street."

"What concert?" Tremont asked.

"Cody Mason," said Vivian. "It's his last concert. He's real sick."

"Cody is sick? Gotta go hear him. You need a ticket?"

"They're twenty dollars," Vivian said.

"I don't have twenty."

"You don't need it, Tremont," George said. "I'll go in with you. We'll back in and they'll think we're coming out."

"All right, Georgie boy, all right, you got the moves. What do you think, Bish, cops gonna come to the concert to get me? You see how that bartender at the Four Spot went after Roy? And one tried to get Zuki?"

"They'll round up everybody, including me, and ask questions tomorrow," Matt said.

"You think they'd arrest me, Father?"

"I think you're safe, Vivian."

"I don't feel safe."

"We should get off Broadway, walk the side streets."

They went up Columbia to James Street, then down James to State where Matt held everybody at the corner until he checked the street. Helmeted cops with shotguns were at State and Broadway, and also on two corners at State and Pearl. North Pearl was blocked to northbound traffic by two police cars and Matt could hear the blurts of squawk talk on the police radios. Three cars and a few people were moving up State. Matt hustled his charges across State to Green Street, which was as empty as Broadway but narrow, less traveled. When they were a block in on Green they heard a siren.

"Siren," Tremont said. "Probably goin' to the Four Spot."

"I know how you can get rid of that gun," Matt said. "Call Doc Fahey, turn it over to him, tell him how you got it."

"Fahey the cop?"

"A good cop. He knows you and he knows me a little, and he's good friends with Quinn. George knows him real well, don't you, George? Doc Fahey?"

"Vincent Fahey," said George. "They call him the Doc. He's one of the salts of the earth. When Peg dropped dead putting on her hat going to church, he's the one I called. Dan wasn't around, you can't keep track of his gallivantin' around the world, so I called Doc and up he came, in ten minutes. They don't make 'em any better. First water, first water."

"Surrendering that gun to Doc is just an idea, Tremont," Matt said. "But you gotta talk to somebody soon, and I mean the cops. Quinn can get you a lawyer."

"Every time I get a lawyer I end up in jail."

"The cops see you with that gun tonight you're a target."

"Long as I wipe off my prints so Zuki can't put it no place and say I shot somebody I didn't. Zuki's a bad ass."

"You said the gun's in a black bag. Cops know gun cases. Put it in something else."

"It folds up pretty good. Don't hafta look like a gun."

At the Greyhound station Tremont searched four trash barrels and found a burlap sack with oil stains. In the lavatory he soaped up a few paper towels and put them in the sack. He looked in the mirror, buttoned his collar, tucked in his shirt, pulled up his pants and tightened his belt. He stroked a kink out of the brim of his fedora and buttoned his double-breasted suitcoat. He went out to the locker and slid the gun case into the sack. Then he rejoined his drinking buddies. Spruced up. Armed.

They went south on Green Street toward Madison, the city moving into early darkness and who knows what else, and George felt a new urgency to get where they were going, wherever the hell it was. Vivian took his arm and George squeezed her with *his* arm and remembered that the way you grip a woman is a defining factor. Peg, or no, was it Vivian, whoever it was, was beautiful on his arm, and keeping a grip on her was the right thing. You had to squeeze her, let her know. Is Snyder's Lake part of it? Make the right moves and you'll be all right. The saints of history will praise your behavior, whatever the hell it is. George had a feeling it had something to do with love.

"He was so alive," Vivian would tell Quinn later. "He sang as we went and he walked me down that dark street with a bounce in his step. We seemed to dance along the sidewalk. When I met him near City Hall in the afternoon he didn't know my name or anybody's name, and now I just loved him because he knew so much and didn't care what he didn't know. Green Street was poorly lit and it looked truly dangerous to me, but he wasn't afraid of anything. I was on the lookout for police and crazy bigots with bombs but George was saying, 'Bing Crosby came down here and he sang "Shine." I got him a piano.'"

"Do you think we're all right, George?" Vivian asked.

"It's all very familiar," he said. "I worked down here. On this street."

"Why are we walking this way? It's away from the concert."

"We're taking the long way around, Vivian," Matt said. "We'll stay away from cops till I get us a ride. Also Tremont needs a drink."

"Now you talkin' Bish. Get us a drink and clean my gun."

"Where's that place you say is open?"

"Hapsy's on Bleecker, the bootlegger," Tremont said, "near Trixie's."

"Trixie's," Matt said. "I know that house. Hapsy got a phone?"

"Cost you half a dollar."

"I took a vow of poverty, but I got half a dollar."

"Big Jimmy's is just down there on Dongan," George said. "He owes me money. Let's go get him to buy us a drink."

"Big Jim's not around tonight, George," Tremont said.

"Too bad. Gayety Theater was right over there, a burlesque house, but they had stage shows, minstrel shows. Big Jim got his start there in *His Honor the Barber*. I used to be a barber. I saw that show twice in nineteen-eleven. That's where 'Shine' comes from. Jim went on the road with that show. The Hawkins girl was the star, Nigger Dick's sister."

"Don't call him that, George," Vivian said.

"That was his name," George said.

"We shouldn't use that word anymore," Vivian said.

"What word?" George asked.

"Nigger," Tremont said.

"No, we shouldn't say that," George said. "There's other words to use. Like 'Shine.'" And George sang:

" 'Cause my hair is curly,
'cause my teeth are pearly . . ."

"That old coon tune," Tremont said.

"Just because
I always wear a smile . . ."

"You're singing that because you're thinkin' about Big Jimmy," Tremont said.

"Big Jim sang that all the time," George said, and he sang:

"Just because my color's shady,
That's the reason maybe,
Why they call me 'Shine' . . ."

"Nobody calls you 'Shine,' George," Tremont said.

"You know that song, Tremont?"

"My daddy taught me. Why you like it so much?"

"It's got a lot of pep. Everybody oughta love it."

"You in a good mood, Georgie," Tremont said. "Big Jim used to say you brought luck and sunshine when you come into the club."

"Yeah, yeah, it's always wonderful down here," George said.

"Wonderful?" Tremont said. "You talkin' about Green Street, Georgie? This old street's fallin' apart, one of the lowest of the lowdown streets in this town. They're boardin' up houses, kickin' people out, pretty soon won't nobody be livin' here."

"I was on Green Street when I was young," Vivian said. "I heard it had houses of prostitution."

"That's a positive fact," said George, "but it didn't spoil the neighborhood. Madge Burns had the best house, and Davenport's was the most expensive. Big Bertha used to sit in her window and wave at you, French Emma's was the cheapest, and the Creole house on Bleecker was very popular. Very popular."

"You know all about it, George," Vivian said. "Did you go to those places?"

"Thank God I never had any need of them. But I took their play when I was writing numbers. There were some wonderful girls in those houses, lovely girls, not that I had any need of them."

"Those girls been down here forever, Miss Vivian," Tremont said. "My daddy said they had about a thousand when he was young, even more during World War One. Everybody knew Green Street. People came here from all over. Always been a good business."

"Still is, sort of," Matt said. "There's half a dozen houses right on Bleecker Street, busiest street down here. There—across the street, the one with the awning on the first-floor window—any house with an awning is doing business."

"How do you know all this, Father?"

"Claudia gave me a tour. Better Streets was trying to get the prostitutes to move off her block so the kids wouldn't have to grow up with all that, and Claudia asked me to help do it. But it's tough to close those places down, and if you move them their customers can't find them and you get a lot of rape. That's the argument, anyway. The madams pay off the police and the politicians, so they're well protected. I took a list of addresses up to the bishop's office—twenty-two houses of prostitution—and I showed it to the chancellor. He said Patsy McCall, the political boss of Albany, would never let such places exist and that I made it all up because I was a Republican agitator."

"He say that to you?" Tremont said, chuckling.

"I was never even a Democrat. Never belonged to anything organized, except the church, if you think that's organized. I do my thing. That's why they silenced me. I spoke to a few groups and I did criticize the Mayor in a couple of speeches. And that day you were poll watching, Tremont, my argument with those ward politicians got in the papers and the diocese didn't like it. I got a big mouth, no doubt about it, and they told me to keep it shut and stay off Green Street."

"But you couldn't."

"I didn't plan tonight, Tremont. You and your gun got us down here."

"My gun. Gotta clean it, can't wait no more, right here quick, sing us a song, Georgie, won't be a minute."

They were on Bleecker, a few doors from Trixie's and Hapsy's. Tremont went into an alley between two three-story brick houses, both dark. Matt watched him open his sack and gun case, remove the AR-15's magazine and put it in his coat pocket. He broke down the gun and with the soapy towels he scrubbed the stock, barrel, pistol grip, handguard, sling, and carrying handle, and then he held part of the gun with a towel and let it drip.

George took Vivian's arm and said, "I remember now that we did go dancing out to Snyder's Lake."

"I'm so glad, George. I remember it very well."

"You were good and honest and you never let anybody cut in," he said. "You danced every dance." Then he sang:

"I'm tying the leaves so they won't come down,
So the wind won't blow them away,
For the best little girl in the wide wide world,
Is lying so ill today.
Her young life must go when the last leaves fall.
I'm fixing them fast so they'll stay.

I'm tying the leaves so they won't come down,
So Nellie won't go away."

Vivian kissed George, which made him extremely happy. He felt like he'd hit the number. He had made the right moves. Was there anything more he should do? In the alley Tremont laid the cleansed AR-15 on the sack and scrubbed the gun case with a soapy towel. On the opposite side of Bleecker a white panel truck pulled up and parked. A white man and a black man got out and went up the stoop of a house with a first-floor awning. Vivian was holding George's arms and giving him short kisses. Matt was urging Tremont to hurry up with the gun. Tremont opened the sack and nudged the scrubbed gun case halfway into it with his elbow. He was holding part of the gun with a paper towel when a woman screamed and came out of the house that had the awning, running down the steps with something in her right hand. The black man from the truck was behind her, and then the white man, who was holding his ear and yelling, "Get that bitch." The black man closed on the woman who turned and lashed out at him with her right hand, without contact. She ran toward Green Street past the pilgrims who were watching from the other side of Bleecker.

Tremont came out of the alley and said, "That's Rosie." He put the AR-15 together, took the magazine from his coat and shoved it into the gun. He stepped off the curb to see Rosie punched by the black man who kicked her as she went down, then kicked her again. The second man, blood gushing from his right ear, said "Kill that bitch." Rosie rolled away from the black man and with a backhanded sweep cut his leg with what the pilgrims could now see was a linoleum knife.

"You cunt," the black man said. As he took a pistol from his back pocket Tremont shot him and he fell, his pistol clattering into the shadows of a housefront.

Matt pulled Vivian and George into a basement doorway under a porch. The second man looked to where the shot came from and with his bloody right hand took a pistol from his belt. Tremont shot him and the man fired his pistol once into the sidewalk and, as he fell, his pistol flew into the street. He got up and limped toward the panel truck as the first man crawled into a crouch and disappeared around the corner of Green Street.

Tremont crossed Bleecker and shot the panel truck's front tires, then shot out the windshield and fired shots into the engine. He kicked both pistols into a sewer and called to the fleeing white man as he vanished up the block, "Hey, buddy, you got a flat." He walked back to Rosie who was trying to stand up, blood all over her face and clothes.

"What they want from you, Rose?" Tremont asked.

"Oh, Tree. You're better, that's good. Gimme a hand."

Tremont tucked the AR-15 under his arm and lifted her up.

"I'm a mess," she said. "Take me to Trixie's."

"Pretty nice shooting, Tremont," Matt said.

"I been practicin'," Tremont said. He crossed Bleecker and picked up his gun case and sack from where he'd left them in the alley.

George and Vivian came up from the basement. "In all my life put together I have never seen this much violence," Vivian said. "Did they hurt you, dear?"

"Yeah, they did," Rosie said, "but I got a piece of one."

"Really? Are you bleeding? I've got bandages in my purse."

"I got this blood but I don't know if it's mine or whose. See what I look like in Trixie's."

Tremont took Rosie's arm and they walked up Bleecker.

"What's Trixie's?" Vivian asked.

"Trixie," George said. "I know her for years. Pretty girl. She used to work in the Creole house."

"Trixie's a madam, Vivian," Matt said. "And her place seems to be our next stop. Any port in a storm."

They followed Tremont and Rosie a block westward toward the oldest continuing whorehouse in Albany, a landmark, run at only two locations on the same block since 1937 by Trixie, no second name, never needed one, born Glenda Tilley, 1909, she of legend, business acumen, ambition, peerless sex, tan skin, a thrust of breasts and a stand of full hips—arcs and lineage that would send you or anybody like you around the bend—and of that bleached, golden, idolized pussy of legend that was neither given nor purchased easily, of mouth and smile that would have been iconic had

anybody been allowed to photograph it (her thirty police mug shots taken since 1931 were all unsmiling), who grew from adolescent dream girl into young beauty, came to understand that beauty meant money and so settled into keptness for a year, left that to join the Creole assembly on Division Street, the only one in town, saw the folly of being in the assembly when she could manage things herself, and so escalated to Madam.

In 1954, after Averell Harriman became governor, freeing Albany of twelve years of Thomas E. Dewey's foul Republican Puritanism, Trixie became Madam Impervious. In 1958 Nelson Rockefeller sent Harriman elsewhere and reinvigorated Republican hostility to everything Democratic, including Albany's prostitution. The public revelation that the sale of white puss was flourishing in Albany shocked the church, and so the political leadership that had allowed it to flourish for two centuries suddenly declared it taboo. The sale of black puss was deemed extremely wicked but not shocking, and so Trixie, in her three-and-a-half-story Bleecker Street protectorate, became Madam Queen of the Evening. And her reign continued on unto the dismantling of The Gut that was so egregiously in evidence on this brilliantly clear June evening in 1968.

Tremont went up the front steps of Trixie's place, a pair of town houses fused to double the size of her domain, and rang the bell. A second-floor window opened and a black girl thrust her head and one naked breast halfway out to inquire, "Y'all lookin' for somethin'?"

"Tell Trixie it's Tremont and Rosie, an emergency," Tremont said.

A light behind the front door went on and the black girl from the window, her nudity partially wrapped in a blue robe, held the door that opened into the front parlor where two white college-age boys were making decisions about four half-dressed, light-skinned black girls. Trixie, elegant in a long pink floral house gown and high heels, her hair in a lustrously two-toned upsweep, greeted the newcomers, but after one look at bloody Rosie and gun-toting Tremont she ushered them all into the back parlor where they settled into overstuffed armchairs and sofas, the Naked Maja staring down from one wall.

"Drink, Trix," Tremont said. "Lot of it." He sat on the large sofa and put the AR-15 beside him.

"Scotch if you got it," George said.

Trixie mumbled a drink order to the girl in the blue robe and then said, "Tremont, what's that gun and who you shootin' at?"

"Somebody give it to me," Tremont said.

"Two mothers beatin' on me, wanted to kill me," Rosie said, "but Tree shot 'em both. Saved my life."

"You killed two people, Tremont?"

"Just hurt 'em. I killed their truck."

"How come they on you, Rose? You got somethin' they want?"

"No, but they think I do."

"You cut or shot or what?"

"Got kicked and had to get off the street. I might be bleedin'." She raised her blouse. "I guess I'm bleedin'."

"I've got bandages," Vivian said, and she took George's emergency gauze and adhesive tape from her purse, and opened a small tube of ointment. "The nurse said this stops a lot of disease."

"Good," Rosie said. "I got a lot."

"You people want anything besides drinks?" Trixie asked. "Some beautiful people out there in the front parlor."

"We got places to go," Tremont said.

"Then why you here?" Trixie asked.

"Here because of Rosie," Tremont said.

"There was some sort of riot on Clinton Square," George said. "It was quite a good fight."

"Is that where you did your shootin', Tremont?" Trixie asked.

"What shooting?" George asked.

Trixie looked at George for the first time. "I know you," she said.

"Sure you do. You're holdin' up good, Trixie."

"George, that *is* you. You used to come 'round for the numbers."

"When you worked at the Creole place, and also at Big Jimmy's."

"That's too long ago. I can't remember that."

"Didn't you dance at Big Jim's?" George asked.

"I danced, I tended bar, did what people did for Jim."

"You look something like you used to, except your hair's got some white in it."

"It ain't white, George, it's frosted."

"George," Matt said, "do you know *everybody* in Albany?"

"I know the pretty ones," George said.

"George always had an eye," Trixie said.

Trixie's black bartender, a burly man in his thirties, useful also with the obstreperous, came into the parlor twice, with trays of glasses, ice, pitcher of water, four bottles of Stanwix beer and a fifth of Haig & Haig Pinch-Bottle. He poured whiskey into four glasses and added ice. Tremont took a glass and downed it in one swallow. They all took glasses and George took a Stanwix. Tremont held his glass out for a refill.

"You coverin' this check, Tremont?" Trixie asked.

"Put it on my bill."

"I've got cash," Vivian said. "How much is it?"

"You with George?"

"I've known George longer than you have," Vivian said. She opened her purse and put three twenties on the table.

"Drink up," Trixie said. She stared at Matt. "You're Claudia's friend. I see you with her down here."

"Matt Daugherty. I'm Tremont's friend too. Can I use your phone?"

Trixie took him down the hall to a phone in an empty bedroom. "You're that priest," she said.

"That's right," he said. "And I met you years ago down here when I was a kid."

"We get a few priests come by. They like to hit and run. Is Tremont flipped? He never used guns. I see him comin' up those stairs holdin' that machine gun like a baby and he look like one of those Black Panthers. Is that what he's doin'?"

"Tremont got himself into a crazy situation with that gun but we're working on it. He's in serious pain, just out of the hospital. I want to get him off the street, but no cabs are running. Too much violence out there."

"Yeah, Tremont shootin' people."

"Can you handle us till I get a car down here?"

"Do it fast. Get him and his gun on the road."

Trixie went to the parlor and sat next to the gun. "Tremont," she said, "how come you goin' around savin' women with a machine gun?"

"It's an AR-15, Trix, and I'd be doin' five to ten wasn't for Rosie."

He told her about the night he's walking on Quay Street, goin' here to there, and sees a woman facedown near the dock, looks close and it's Jolene. He goes to talk to her but she ain't much to talk to, dead drunk and wet. Then the cops turn up and take 'em both in and write up a charge says Tremont is Jolene's pimp and he strangled her, raped her, and threw her in the river. When Jolene comes to she agrees with the cop and swears yeah, that's how it was, Tremont did it. When Rosie hears Tremont's in jail she calls the Night Squad detective sergeant she snitches for and tells him Tremont's no pimp, he never went that direction. Jolene was bangin' sixteen guys on a freighter and got so drunk she fell outa the little boat goin' back to the dock and one of them sailors had to jump in and pull her out. Cop asks how Rosie knows this and Rose says I was with her. So the heavy steam woozled out of that rape charge against Tremont and he walked.

"Why they want to put you away, Tremont?" Trixie asked.

"That cop's been down on me since Election when a Democrat give me five to vote the right way and I took it. I was broke, Mary was sick as hell and five's five. I told Roy and he says you gotta give it back, but go public with a lawyer and tell 'em who gave it to you and the Brothers'll go with you for support."

Tremont did but they busted him, and his lawyer was useless. Patsy's D.A. had called a press conference about vote buying and said he'd prosecute anybody who gave a five, or took a five. So who's gonna admit taking one, and did you ever hear of anybody giving one back? The committeeman who slipped Tremont the fiver had a sudden heart attack, also a stroke, not to mention six or seven malignant brain tumors, so his family flew him someplace, nobody knew where, for emergency treatment; and unfortunately he couldn't be subpoenaed. Quinn wrote the story for the paper and it got a laugh, the Brothers advanced their crusade against election fraud, and the five-dollar vote was news for five minutes. Tremont walked again and now the cops were hovering, waiting for him to make a mistake. One cop decided Jolene was his mistake, but Rosie begged to differ. "Jolene was no good," Rosie said. "She didn't even know how to fuck right. She already dead, somebody got her, or maybe she fell in again."

"Buying votes, Big Jimmy used to buy votes," George said.

"That's right, he did," Tremont said.

"It's what got him in thick with the Democrats," George said. "There was a big run by coloreds coming up from Alabama and living in the South End and spending their money at Jimmy's club, seven-foot-two colored fella singing and you had jazz music day and night. Patsy McCall saw all those newcomers in Jim's place and got the idea to make Jim a ward leader. But you can't make a colored fella a real ward leader—those people are all Irish. So Patsy invented a ward that floated and he put Jim in charge. Jim rounded up coloreds no matter where they lived and fixed it so they voted in one of the wards down here. Jim saw the prostitutes weren't voting so he had the cops arrest them all and bring them to the polls in the paddy wagon."

"I voted twice that year," Trixie said.

"Jim paid four bucks a pop," George said, "and he'd do favors for anybody who asked. In the windup he got one hell of a bunch of voters for Patsy, who was so happy that he fixed it so Jim hit the numbers twice in one day. I wrote Jim's play that day, a Wednesday, but I didn't know it was fixed. Jim won thousands and poured free beer for a week. What a great fella. He'd give you the hat off his head and tell you what to do with it. I can see him at the bar in his brocade vest and pocket watch, and that size eight-and-a-half top hat he got from London. Remember his songs, Trixie?"

"A hundred of 'em."

And George sang:

"Just because my hair is curly,
Just because my teeth are pearly,"

"I hated that one," Trixie said.

"You can't hate that. It was Jimmy's tune. He'd get encores."

"I hated that shufflin' stuff."

"Coon songs," Tremont said.

And George sang:

"Just because my color's shady,
That's the reason maybe . . ."

"I used to wonder how could my daddy sing those tunes," Tremont said. "I told him people didn't want no more coon songs. He set me down right then and he talked like he never talked to me before:

"'Boy, you gotta know this,' he said. 'Wasn't for coon songs I wouldn'ta worked. Nobody hires giants, especially colored giants, but two summers the sideshow up at Al-Tro Park billed me as the Albany Giant—tap dances while he sings coon songs. Then *His Honor the Barber* come to town from Chicago and Seely Hawkins was singin' in it and she brought Mr. Dudley to see my act. He asked did I want to be in his show, and he put me in doin' a reprise of 'Shine.' That was Ada Walker's tune and she owns it, but I did it late in the show and some nights I got six encores. Show went to Harlem, two weeks on Broadway, then down to Virginia, Georgia, even Texas, and people loved that song and a whole lot of others, with Big Jimmy Van singin' 'em, and I got me a name in colored theater. I jumped into vaudeville when the show closed, played some theaters on Mr. Dudley's circuit, then came north and did the white circuits, and people all over this country got to know Big Jimmy Van. I made good money for years and come home and opened a club, got married and had a son I called Tremont. And he grew up to hate coon songs.'

"That stuff," Tremont said, "suckin' us into the lowdown—coon funny, coon foolish, wind him up and he smile, he shuffle. When I was a kid I said nothin' ever gonna make me do that. But it made Jim somebody. He always said the *Barber* was a new thing in colored theater. Mr. Dudley played the barber who dreams he wants to shave the president in the White House and then he gets to do it, even though it's just a dream. And Big Jim said to me, 'Havin' a story to go with the ragtime and the cakewalk, that was a different kind of show. We made a little bit of history and we got on Broadway and pretty soon a lot of colored shows had stories and they quit doin' the old minstrel stuff.'"

"I used to be a barber," George said. "I shaved the Mayor."

"The Mayor," Tremont said. "Big Jim knew all the Mayors, all the politicians. He was the most famous black man in this town, flush and connected, ask Jim and he'll fix it, if you're on his side. Hot time in the old town tonight, if Jim says so, and he never had no shame, other people had shame. Jim sang 'Shine' so much it got in my brain and now it don't matter what it means. Means Big Jim to me."

"Politics," Trixie said. "Tremont, why you foolin' with that five-dollar vote? If you needed money you shoulda voted twice and got two fives, not give it back. You ain't cut out for politics."

"Never could get into it like Big Jim," Tremont said. "He got me two, three city jobs but those paychecks wasn't enough to buy a pair of shoes."

So Tremont worked his own way, shoveling coal in a South End steam laundry, warehouse helper, short order cook in Chloe's diner. At night he dressed up, a dude like Big Jim, and played in the Skin game that Rabbit ran in the basement of his pool room on Madison Avenue, a lucky player, Tremont. After a while Rabbit hired him to play for the house and that was very fine until too many players lost too much too fast, fastest card game there is, and Patsy McCall sent the cops in—no more Skin in Albany. Small loss for Tremont. His hand and his eye, they were real quick, but he wasn't cut out to be a hustler any more than he was cut out for politics. Something direct about Tremont. He never understood it but it kept him straight. He got to be a broiler man in a new French restaurant, okay money.

Big Jim closed his club in the late '40s, gettin' old. Also nightclubs were dying from the cabaret tax and everybody was stayin' home to watch TV. Jim's wife, Cora, who taught in a colored grammar school, never liked The Gut, so Jim bought a house in the West End of the city, miles from The Gut, but two days before they were going to move in somebody torched it, and Cora went into a depression. Patsy came to see Jim after the arson and gave him a house on Arbor Hill for Cora. It was in tip-top shape and down the block from the Hawkins family, quite a few coloreds up there by now. Jim didn't own it but he never paid rent or taxes and he spent his last years there with Cora and he needed her. He went flooey at the end, told people he could fly and showed how he did it, wore a watch cap, arms tight to his side like doing a sailor dive. When it rained he took credit for moving the clouds because the flowers kept saying how dry they were.

When Tremont came home from Korea he moved into the Dongan

Avenue house and when he married Mary he moved her in too and they had a few good years until Big Jim passed and then Cora went away too, and one day Tremont got a tax bill in the mail. He went to the ward leader and told them who he was, and about Jim, and the ward leader said that's right, Big Jim had a free ride, but he's dead. Pay your taxes, Tremont, which he did for a while and then couldn't, so long, house. Things went like that, jobs, then no jobs, and he and Mary moved someplace else, two rooms. Tremont found Peanut and brought him home from the vacant lot and Mary sewed good for uptown women with money and Tremont drove a truck for a new laundry, so they both had an income and they hung in there and things weren't that bad. But it slid downhill and there was wine to cool the slide. Mary slid faster than Tremont, who lost his job driving the truck when the Teamsters organized the laundry and wouldn't let him into the union. He had to go on welfare when Mary got sick and he kept getting busted for drink and they were living in a rat hole and life started to piss Tremont off.

He couldn't steal and wouldn't hustle and he got so desperate in the shithouse they were living in that he said a prayer to Jesus, "Dear Jesus, please don't let me be found dead in this place, and don't let me ever be taken in by front men or front women." Those front men never took in Tremont's daddy, who was hip. So Tremont decided from now on he would be new: I'm gonna do somethin' that isn't what somebody says I'm supposed to do. I'm gonna do somethin' I want to do, or think I want to do, or don't know I want to do but I'm gonna do it. Nobody said I hadda walk on Roy's picket line or hang with the Brothers or go to Claudia's and be a poll watcher or take five and give it back. But sometimes you're ready for a little politics even if you don't know you're ready for it.

Nobody told Tremont to take that gun and go shoot target and then shoot those bums beatin' on Rosie. Zuki just give him the gun and says we're gonna have fun, scare a few people. But then he says to Tremont, we oughta shoot the Mayor.

We?

Yes, you.

Whoa, says Tremont, I don't do what somebody says I oughta do, and when he took a long look he saw clear that Zuki was a front man. And

Tremont had already took money and a gun from him. What the hell is wrong with you, Tremont? He started to drink again, nonstop, and when he got that pain he went down to Dongan Avenue and flopped on the stoop of his father's old house that he couldn't get into anymore and stayed there till Quinn and the Bish come by, and he told them about the gun and the Mayor.

Trixie tried to faint from shock but it wasn't in her repertoire.

"Shoot the Mayor, Tremont? Shoot the Mayor?"

Tremont poured himself a shot of Pinch and held up the bottle. "I know you like the Mayor, Trix. Don't you send him two cases of this stuff every Easter and Christmas? Seems I heard you say that."

"The Mayor?" George said, "Is that who you want to shoot, Tremont?"

"Don't wanna shoot the Mayor, George. Some fella said I should but I don't think so."

"Fella named Zangara shot Mayor Cermak of Chicago," George said. "He was aiming at FDR but he missed. He was an Italian with stomach trouble and he lost two hundred at the dog races. They gave him eighty years but when Mayor Cermak died they sizzled him in Old Sparky."

"Do the police know about the gun, Tremont?" Trixie asked.

"They might. It's gettin' around."

"Then you gotta get outa here right now. I don't want no part of this. No way I can explain you away if they come lookin'. And Rose, you gotta find your way home. What about that bleedin'? You bandage it up?"

"I can't go out there yet," Rosie said. "Gimme a little while."

Matt had come back and was listening. "All we need is twenty minutes, Trixie. The car is coming."

Trixie stood up. "Take ten and go down the back stairs and wait. Don't let Tremont out front with that gun."

"You got room for one more in that car?" Rosie asked.

"Sure," Matt said. "It'll be a squeeze."

"You leave them be, Rose," Trixie said. "You done enough. You just sit a while."

Vivian had been studying the parlor, the mauve drapes, the wallpaper with the Eiffel Tower and Arc de Triomphe, the Maja painting over the mantel, the soft, indirect lighting, the oriental rug; and Trixie herself with those green crescent earrings and six bracelets and the long gown Vivian now sees is silk, and her lovely cleavage that was there but not overly, and her legs so elegant in those tall, black heels. Over sixty, must be, but so classy, so sexy. Maybe Vivian could take lessons.

"Miss Trixie," Vivian said.

"Just Trixie," Trixie said.

"Trixie. I admire your furnishings and the way you dress. I've never been in a house like this and I wonder if I might see the rest. I don't want to intrude on anyone's privacy."

"Not much privacy here, honey. Most of it's out in the open."

They went out of the parlor and Trixie said, "That's a bedroom. We got nine of 'em . . . and the wallpaper, it's French, embossed . . ." and her voice trailed off as they walked down the hall.

"You're old friends with Trixie," Matt said to Tremont.

"Years. But I never sat in this room till right now. White dudes only down here. What the black man wants is to hug and kiss the girls, stay all night. The white man wants to get in and out and go home."

"Black man's always welcome in my parlor, you know all about that, Tremont," Rosie said.

"That's right I know it, Rose," Tremont said.

"You should put that gun away," Matt said, and Tremont broke down the AR-15 and counted the remaining rounds in the magazine, twelve gone out of thirty. He packed the gun in its case and dropped it into the sack.

"One for the road," Tremont said, and Matt poured him a shot, took a Stanwix for himself and passed a bottle to George. "Whose car's comin' to get us, Bish?"

"Priest from Siena, a buddy of mine. He borrowed a student's car."

"Where we goin'?"

"I thought I knew until you turned into the Lone Ranger. Someplace they won't shoot you on sight. I tried to reach Quinn to ask him about lawyers for you but he's on the street, probably going to the protest meeting."

"What size shoe you got, Bish?"

"Eleven, why?"

"I wanna borrow your shoes. They know I'm wearin' these two-tones. Everybody know my two-tones and they be lookin' for 'em."

"What size are your two-tones?"

"Ten, but they been ten for a whole lotta years."

Matt gave Tremont his loafers, tried on a two-tone and made it, but with laces loose.

"I be slippin' around in these," Tremont said, and he walked a few steps. "Holy boots. St. Francis, here come Tremont steppin' out."

"Now they're gonna shoot at me," Matt said, and he raised his right foot and shook it for display.

"I got shoes like that," George said. "Black and white, and brown and tan. And I got a pair of black and gray, dyed the toes black myself."

"You a dude, Georgie," Tremont said.

"Drink up, gents. We've got to move," Matt said. And he went to collect Vivian, who was talking with two light-skinned prostitutes in panties and transparent blouses. Vivian was asking how they liked their jobs and saying how difficult it must be to go with total strangers.

"We make friends pretty quick," one girl said.

Matt gave Trixie the exit gesture, gave Rosie a nod, and went with Vivian back to George and Tremont who were singing,

"I'm gonna dance off both of my shoes,
When they play those Jelly Roll Blues . . ."

Matt ushered them all down the back stairs to an alley that led to Franklin Street. Tremont picked up his gun and put a bottle of Stanwix in his coat pocket. Matt left the three of them standing in shadows on the corner and said he'd come back with the car. He walked on Franklin toward Bleecker and disappeared down the narrow, unlighted street.

"It's so dark," Vivian said. "Are you having a good time, George?"

"Life is just a bowl of cherries," George said, and he put his arm around her.

"I haven't had this much fun in years," she said, and she gave George a long, soft kiss. Then she remembered Tremont and turned to give him a smile of chagrin at being caught kissing, but Tremont wasn't there, and the alley was very dark.

◈

Nick Brady, the Siena priest Matt was closest to, taught Tacitus and Virgil and booked horses ($2 limit) in class for his students, borrowed a car from the student who had led the campus protest against Matt's silencing (of course take it, I'd do anything for Father Matt) and found Matt half a block from Trixie's. Martin Daugherty, Matt's father, was in the passenger seat, two canes between his knees. He looked like an old man but with young eyes. He squinted at his son.

"The sonsabitches kicked me out," Martin said. "I can't believe Patsy McCall would do this, but I know he could. But I can't believe it."

"I got the letter two days ago," Matt said. "I told them I'd get you tomorrow."

"They couldn't wait. They put me out in the hallway with my valise. I had no money for a taxi."

"A nurse called the friary twice looking for you," Nick Brady said to Matt. "They wanted you to pick him up this afternoon. I took the second call tonight but I couldn't reach you, so when I got the car I went out myself."

"The bastards," Matt said. "They did this to get back at me."

"I know," Martin said, "and I'm proud of you, son. You've done more for the church than Pope Paul. You've redeemed the goddamned priesthood."

"What about you? How've you been feeling?"

"I sleep a lot. I'm tired but I'm not sick. I'm just old."

"You're no older than you were five years ago."

"I'm older than most oak trees."

"How are you walking these days?"

"I walk like that actor with rubber legs. Leon Errol. But I'm all right with the canes."

"Did you have dinner? Did they feed you?"

"They gave me a cheese sandwich and an apple in a brown paper bag. I ate half the sandwich."

"We'll have to feed you. Do you need to lie down?"

"I'm all right. I slept in the chair in the hallway."

"Where do you want to stay? I'll set you up someplace tomorrow, but what about tonight?"

"Someplace that won't break the bank."

"We've still got some bucks in your account. I'll figure out someplace. But right now we've got three people to pick up in the next block. George Quinn and his lady friend."

"George. And a lady friend. He must be in good shape."

"He's a little spacey."

"It's going around," Martin said. "George and I were in France together during the first war. We were having a drink in Aix-les-Bains when we met Sergeant York in a hotel bar. He had just captured a hundred and thirty-two German soldiers and thirty-five machine guns single-handed, greatest hero of the war. We bought him a drink."

"George and his lady friend are going to the DeWitt for a jazz concert. We're also picking up Tremont Van Ort. You know him?"

"Big Jimmy's son?"

"That's him. He's in weird trouble. Somebody set him up to shoot Alex Fitzgibbon and they gave him an AR-15. He shot two thugs with it. They were beating up a woman he knew."

"Why in the hell are you picking up somebody like that?"

"To help him. He's a friend of mine."

"He's a trigger-happy felon with a gun."

"I know, and he's probably all over the police radio. Man with a gun. Dan Quinn and I want him to surrender himself, and the gun, to Doc Fahey, the Albany cop, before they kill him on the street. You know Doc Fahey?"

"Not as a cop. I knew him as a kid in North Albany."

"You don't get this kind of action out in the Ann Lee Home."

"We're all on the death watch out there. It's quite exciting when you hear that the fellow in the next room didn't wake up this morning. What do you mean they set Tremont up?"

"It's political. I don't think anybody wanted to shoot the Mayor. What they want is to bring down some local black radicals. Tremont's not really a radical but he can pass for one, and he mixes with the Brothers, who truly are radical for this town. You know the Brothers?"

"I read about them. I don't know their particulars."

"It's a good story. You'd be writing it if you were still working."

"Maybe so. This actually was my old territory. The *Times Union* was a few blocks up at Beaver and Green. All the papers were there—the *Knickerbocker Press*, the *Albany Evening News*, the *Argus*, and the *Journal* was down on the Plaza. I knew every inch of these streets, including this one we're on. This is Trixie's street. Are you in front of Trixie's for any priestly reason?"

"It's a long story, but yes, I'll tell you later. I like Trixie."

"She's the Queen Bee and has been for years."

They drove down the block and picked up George and Vivian but no Tremont.

"Hello, George," Martin said. "It's Martin Daugherty. How the hell are you?"

"Martin Daugherty," George said. "Wibble stu hobbleski, mox neex aus, I run with all mine shwiftness."

"You haven't forgotten your German," Martin said. "*Voulez vous promenade avec moi ce soir, mademoiselle?* Isn't that Vivian Sexton?"

"It is, hello, Martin. I haven't seen you in years."

"So George, I was just saying that we met Sergeant York in France. You remember?"

"We bought him a drink. Great fella. He captured five hundred Germans and seventy-five machine guns, all alone. A hell of a thing."

"You remember what he drank?"

"Coneyack."

"Right."

"He wanted a beer but they didn't have any. The French don't go for beer. All they get over there is grapes and watermelons."

"Where's Tremont?" Matt asked.

"I turned around and he was gone," Vivian said. "That was ten minutes ago. He never said a word to us."

"He's playing hide and go seek," Matt said. "Go around the block, Nick."

They circled the block and Matt went into Hapsy's, a small crowd out in front, a mecca tonight since so many legal downtown bars were closed by the tension. Hapsy had no bar in his place, more like a small grocery. He was a puffy black man wearing a skullcap cut from a fedora, said he hadn't seen Tremont. Among the crowd Matt saw Cole Travis sipping on a bottle in a paper bag. Claudia had taken Matt to see Travis and his wife, trying to get them help. They lived in a cellar across from Tremont, and over the winter Travis had chopped out his ceiling beams to feed the stove that took up half the cellar and was too hot to sit near even when it was below zero. Plumbing didn't work, no fridge, and Travis and his wife were deep into the wine; no job, no prospects, no friends, no money; how do they pay the rent, how do they get the wine? Two of the sorrowful mysteries. Matt talked to the city housing chief, brought students from Siena to clean, fix the beams, fix the toilet. But Travis kicked everybody out saying I'm movin' outa here.

Matt told the chancellor of the diocese about Travis (during the same visit when he presented his list of twenty-two whorehouses) and said we gotta help this man. The chancellor said the only thing that will save those people is religion, which Matt used without attribution in his next sermon—a discourse on Bonhoeffer's cheap grace and how it relates to the abstract, nebulous, gaseous blather that passes for morality in contemporary churches. Grace is a high-end item. You've got to work at it. Is it a healing church? Is the church the light on the mountain? Oh, yeah. Is the church the salt? Oh, yeah. What Bonhoeffer knew was the imperative to be extraordinary and Matt also threw in Augustine's take on God: higher than my highest. I'd work day and night down here if they'd let me—that was Matt's dream. Find a way to help the Travises. I beg for a floor to dance, a room to sing, a floor without walls, a room without ceiling, and when my prayer is outworn, there is no sap, no juice, no suckle. When each day is a dead mother, I remember when, and at that point the memory has sap, juice and suckle. Oh, yes it does.

For two years prayers had been coming to Matt and he wrote them down, direct from soul to page. He believed they were God's truths, also his own, and the prayers were fervent but querulous, for the God he was writing to was a muddle, no way around it. "Father, I walked down a street cobbled for pushcarts and hooves. Is this you?" . . . "Father, I seek soil, not dust . . . Soil is a full hand."

Quinn said he sounded like a dealer who liked the long odds, but Matt didn't expect his questions to make it to the big prayer book. "God shorted me," he told Quinn. "He knows I'm no poet. But the prayers keep coming.

I stick them in the sock drawer until I've got enough to send to an editor, and they do publish this stuff, not under my name, I'm not that egotistical, or that brave. I like to quote Paul on this—'What I do I do not understand, for I do not do what I want.' No way to do what I want." What's more, all prayer henceforth will be private. The political church and the pious polity have delivered their favored dictum on communion: Let there be silence.

Within the soul-hollow an abyss,
A dead child's bed, a widow's cell,
A Cain flushed of rage,
A voided snail shell.
My plea: I starve for the Great Fill.
You alone fill my God cave.

Father, bait and hook these predators.
Bags weigh heavy as I walk down an alley
Seeing my shadow thin on wet cobblestones.
To ease the burden I stop walking.
I cannot move.
This is a God tomb.

Do I hold onto this lie?
My joy, a morsel. My peace, a hovel.
A split-tongue never shields a traitor long.
The answer is surrender,
The price a shriveled soul.
But I am the dream of God.

If I drop the worry cloak,
If I cool the boil within,
If I cease dogging my will,
If I leave the carcass in your hands,
If I quit the God match, the God dare,
Then let them have their silence.

But I will not. No, I will not.

❖

Quinn made his case to Doc Fahey about Tremont—the faux assassin as a provocateur's dupe—standing in the lobby of the Palace Theater as police were closing it down after the death of the white youth. Doc was reasonably sympathetic; he'd known Tremont for years, one of the rocks on the street, not a mean bone in him, but you can't trust a wino, and with that AR-15 and the Mayor as his possible target, real or unreal, Tremont wasn't going to get the kid-glove treatment.

"Just so he's not shot on the street," Quinn said. "He did nothing illegal."

"If he keeps the gun in its case he'll be all right," Doc said. "The Chief gave orders today if anybody shoots, burns, loots or rapes, blast 'em. We all got twelve-gauge with twenty rounds of double-aught buck, and if one of the boys sees Tremont flashing that AR-15, he's one gone gosling. The Chief served five years in the Pacific and he's tough." Doc was wearing his 1956 narrow-brim gray straw hat with a black band, his equivalent of a riot helmet. He was natty, as usual: a two-button dark gray suit with slash pockets, black silk tie, cordovan wingtips.

"I'll have Tremont keep the gun under cover," Quinn said.

"Then maybe he won't have a problem. I'll be somewhere downtown. Page me through the switchboard, I'll be there in five minutes, unless Albany explodes. White guys in a car threw Molotovs at blacks over on Clinton Square and we hear whites are tooling around with shotguns. I already heard vengance talk for this thing here."

Quinn had called Jake Hess after his interview with the Mayor about some way of surrendering Tremont, and would Jake represent him if he did surrender?

"Savior of assassins, is this a new facet of your career?" Jake asked.

"My grandfather quoted Montesquieu that the people should be judged by laws, and the lives of the lowest subject should be safe, but that the Pasha's head should be always in danger."

"And you want me to represent the man who endangered the Pasha's head."

"The Pasha was in no danger from Tremont. I just want him safe and judged by the law. He qualifies as one of the lowest subjects in this republic, and he's a good guy."

"I never quarrel with Montesquieu," Jake said. "Tell me when to show up."

Quinn could feel the tension in the Palace lobby—it was in the air like pollen. A thirteen-year-old white boy had been hit on the head by a black teen, or maybe he was pushed or fell down some balcony stairs, and he died with his pockets inside out. Doc said this was the third incident in the last hour, in or outside the theater, of menacing black kids asking white kids for money. One white who didn't ante up was hit with a bottle. Police were looking for witnesses but Palace patrons only wanted their money back. Doc said six blacks had been arrested and one was a Brother, Roy Mason.

"On what charge?"

Doc didn't know.

Quinn had seen the film *Up Against* the first day it played the Palace, for he knew Julian Stewart, the film's star as well as its scriptwriter. Quinn had worked with Julian on the *Post* in Havana in 1957 when Max was editor. Julian was doing rewrite and copyediting when word came to Max from on high to fire Julian. He was a New York lefty playwright and actor and his Cuban wife, also black, was a communist. Max refused to fire the man for his color and his wife's politics and so Max was fired. Your shining hour, Max, no matter what else, you son of a bitch.

In the film Julian played a character named Blink, unreliable, a drinker, not bright, ousted from a radical Black Power organization. Angry over the rejection, Blink betrays his friend, the organization's leader, to the police for money—Judas in a black Chicago ghetto in 1967. Julian acted it well and his story reflected the deadly tension Black Power was now generating in America's big cities. Quinn saw the film with an audience of a thousand, mostly black. Every time a black revolutionary dissed or shot a white man a cheer went up, and a cry of "black power." When a black went down the call was "white power," but not so many voices. Quinn hadn't known Max was in the film, playing a detective. Obviously Max had kept his connection to Julian after Havana, but he'd been on the showbiz fringe since his Bing days. Max the spy, the editor, the actor, the criminal, the ongoing son of a bitch.

◈

Quinn sat on the aisle in the third row of chairs set up in the First Church's basement. He heard Claudia's voice and turned to greet her. She was enormous in a starched pink and white vertical-striped, short-sleeved cotton housedress to her ankles, her hair rolled in thick waves, and Quinn thought her flamboyantly lovely. She took his hand and shook her head at this mess, it never ends, then sat in a chair to the rear of the dais, staring into the crowd, her small smile missing, her lips moving in a silent whisper.

The protest had been conceived by Baron Roland to mount grievances against landlords and police—black youths beaten and jailed as gangs, the Brothers harassed, social agencies punished for helping groups like Claudia's, riots elsewhere bringing change from City Hall, but not here. Then Matt was silenced and Bobby shot, and Claudia marshaled her troops to raise hell—and here they came—three hundred in a room for two hundred. Three TV stations and both newspapers here to cover it.

Penny, who this afternoon predicted a disaster to Matt, was sitting with a young black man Quinn didn't know, both talking with Roland who looked roosterish with a forum this large. Quinn counted at least two spies from the Albany machine, plus half a dozen white and black clerics, two Franciscan priests and a cluster of students from Siena supporting Matt, the campus hero, and three College of Saint Rose nuns who supported everything Claudia did, and Father Howard Hubbard, just out of the seminary and grad school, working out of Holy Cross with the neighborhood groups, including Claudia's. Quinn saw a sizeable number of white first-timers he assumed were Catholics outraged over diocesan toadying to City Hall. Half the crowd was black, mostly women from seven neighborhood groups like Claudia's, for whom this was a major moment, and—can it be, just inside the door, Tremont, is that you?

Baron Roland spoke first, how great so many are here to stand for Father Matt. Tomorrow morning we picket both the diocese and City Hall, please join us. He gave the latest word on Bobby and said he believed he was shot because he had become a spokesman for the black race, just as Martin Luther King was killed because he had become the black messiah. Women were weeping in Rio de Janeiro, Ralph Abernathy was leading prayers at the Poor People's Campaign in Resurrection City, Willy Brandt had likened Bobby's shooting to Greek tragedy, and the president of Chile said it has caused all men in the world to tremble. Roland asked for a silent prayer, then introduced Claudia, the outstanding leader of Better Streets, the group Father Matthew worked with. Claudia stood up so quickly her chair fell backward; but with fervid purpose she moved her great weight to the microphone, made her hands into fists and shook them.

"I'm mad, I'm ashamed, and I'm sorry," she said.

"I'm sorry because when I asked the Mayor to come to the South End and see how bad things were he said he already knew, and I said I hope he chokes. I don't mean that. When I said that the devil had a hold of me. I also said I'm goin' up there and throw a brick through his window, but that was the devil again. I don't wish no bad things for the Mayor. I gotta die myself. S'pose I died with that statement on me. I'd bust hell wide open.

"I'm mad 'cause they're takin' Father Matt away from us. They say he can't come see us no more. When this man walk our streets it's like he's blessin' 'em, like he's blessin' us all. He been down here a year helpin' make those old houses somethin' we can live in, roofs leakin', rats runnin', so cold in winter the water pipes bust. Kids sleigh-ride in the hall and tell their teachers they sleep in a room with diamonds, which is ice. You go out in the mornin' and gangsters hustlin' our kids to buy their junk. Wineheads sleepin' on the street and you can't leave no clothes on the line 'cause they steal everything.

"So I go to this meetin' and they all talkin' about getting organized and we say what we want to do and some of 'em laugh and say landlords won't ever listen to you and you never gonna get no playground. But we knocked on doors and we got us some action and Father Matt was with us, chasin' those fools away, gettin' landlords to fix the pipes, tryna get a health clinic. He even walk into the Mayor's office with us to get the garbage off our streets, which the city won't do. But they don't want him speakin' up for us, the bishop don't. Bishop say he gotta keep quiet what's goin' on in the South End. Father Matt knows everybody and everybody loves him and we don't want him to go away. They took Martin Luther King and maybe they takin' Bobby Kennedy and now our Father Matt who ain't done nothin' but good. That's why I'm ashamed. But it's the bishop oughta be ashamed, good holy man playin' footsie with politicians. Father Matt bein' punished for what he say about vote buyin' and about the Mayor not doin' nothin', and they punishin' us 'cause we tryin' to make things better and they don't want that. You stay where you are is what they're tellin' us. You live there and die there just the way it is. This ain't any church talkin' I ever know about."

Father Thomas Tooher, a tall, fair-skinned man in his sixties, glasses, white hair, white collar, stood up from his seat in a middle row. Until two years ago he'd been pastor of a suburban parish with horseshows and celebrity parties if he needed money, but then he asked to be pastor of St. Joseph's on Albany's Arbor Hill, where he'd been raised when it was heavily Irish, but now was mostly black with a sparse congregation. "Mrs. Johnson," he said, "I'd like to say a word about the bishop."

Claudia nodded to him.

"The bishop didn't silence Father Matthew Daugherty," he said. "The bishop is a very sick man and hasn't been in touch with diocesan business for months. He doesn't know what happened on your streets that led to Father Matthew's silencing. That order came from the diocese in his name, but it didn't come from him. I say this now because I can't bear to hear one more attack on this very good, very sick man."

"If he didn't do it, who did?" Claudia asked.

"I have nothing to say on that," Father Tooher said, and he sat down.

A voice called out, "It was Callaghan," and Quinn remembered Matt's whorehouse list and Monsignor Callaghan, the diocesan chancellor, calling Matt a Republican troublemaker.

"It wasn't the bishop?" Claudia said. "Just one of his flackeys? I know that bozo Callaghan, and he be the one sayin' Father Matt gotta be punished for sassin' the politicians? He be the one lettin' politicians tell the church which is right and which is wrong?"

Claudia speeded up her words, volume rising.

"He tellin' this saint of a priest we can't see him no more? This little bozo, he be the one cut off Father's head so he can't see us no more?"

Then she screamed: "They cut off his head! They hate us. They hate us 'cause we black. THEY HATE US!" She jumped straight up with both feet, fists pumping, then jumped again, screaming, "We black and they hate us!" She jumped and jumped, her face streaming with tears. She jumped and no words now, just a long cry of rage and a long wail, and then she stood still, weeping. A nun came and gripped her huge left arm with both hands and led her to her chair. Claudia sat and could not stop weeping.

First Presbyterian pastor Bob Lamar stood and sang and the crowd joined him:

"Oh-o freedom, Oh-o freedom,
Oh freedom over me, over me.
And before I be a slave
I'll be buried in my grave,
And go home to my Lord and be free, and be free . . ."

When the song had run its course another voice rose from the back: Tremont's.

"Hey! Mighty powerful, Claudia," he said. "What you said about bein' black, I'm black, and my daddy was blacker than me. I love that song about bein' a slave. Slaves need them songs. My daddy was born and raised in Albany and he got slave ancestors back to the old timey Dutch who built this church we in. My daddy was a vaudeville singer and everybody knew him as Big Jimmy Van. He sang all over this country, made money, come home and went into politics. Wasn't no politician in this town he didn't call by his first name. He had power and he said a whole lot of what he wanted to say by singin', and I want to sing one of his songs, which he got a big kick out of 'cause hardly anybody liked it. But it was one of the biggest song hits in this country." And Tremont sang:

". . . My gal she took a notion against the colored race.
She said if I would win her I'd have to change my face.
She said if she should wed me that she'd regret it soon,
And now I'm shook, yes good and hard, because I am a coon.
Coon, coon, coon, I wish my color would fade,
Coon, coon, coon, I'd like a different shade.
Coon, coon, coon, mornin', night and noon,
I wish I was a white man 'stead of a coon, coon, coon.

"Hey, all you coons," Tremont said.

People were hissing and booing, standing up to get a look at this maniac, who the hell is he? But Tremont saw Claudia smiling, and then Quinn was pulling him by the arm, moving him through the crowd into the vestibule and up the stairs to the street.

"You gotta get out of here before they lynch you," Quinn said.

"Lynch me, lynch my daddy," Tremont said.

Quinn saw Tremont was drunk, again, but drunk now doing an encore for Big Jimmy, suicide by music, a new way to go.

At the DeWitt Clinton Matt went in with Vivian and George to make sure nobody got lost again. In the lobby George looked around at the marble walls and said, "This is the DeWitt. Jimmy Walker lived here. His wife was never with him. He'd say to her, let's go out and see a show, let's go to a nightclub, but she wouldn't go out of the house. That's what happened to him."

"What happened to him?" Vivian asked.

"He went out with somebody else," George said.

The ballroom was full of people eating dinner, but Quinn wasn't here and neither was Tremont. A six-piece band was playing the "Beale Street Blues." Vivian negotiated with somebody in charge of tickets.

"Thank you for a lovely evening, Father," Vivian said.

"You knew Martin in the old days," Matt said.

"For a few years. We went to the same places, dances, excursions on the boats. He was well known, famous, really, after the McCall kidnapping. He brought the kidnapped boy home to his father. I read his column all the time. Everybody did."

"You know he'd probably like this concert, if he's up for it. If he is will you keep an eye on him?"

"That would be lovely," Vivian said. "He'll be my second date."

Matt checked the front desk for room rates and availability, park him here for tonight, why not? All Matt needed was money. He'd borrow it from Quinn, or somebody. He liked all this—instant shelter, dinner, distraction, and Cody's great piano. He booked a double room, maybe he'd stay here himself. He told Martin the plan, which jazzed him.

"You live a hurly-burly life for a monk," Martin said.

Matt checked him in, sent his bags upstairs, gave his last twenty to the ticket-taker, and, penniless, walked his father into the ballroom for dinner, a concert, and a radical transformation of his evening.

Martin had been at the Ann Lee Home six months, a casualty of age, time, bad knees, retirement from the newspaper, inability to write anything else, and the death of his wife, friends, and ambition. He had never saved money, and retired on Social Security and periodic royalties from revivals of the plays of his father, Edward Daugherty, mostly *The Flaming Corsage*, his scandalous masterpiece. Martin's own books were all out of print. He gave up on living alone and cooking for himself and moved into the Ann Lee Home for the aged run by the Albany County Democratic machine, which took him in as a guest, one of their own, after a lifetime of association with the party's high and low, from machine boss Patsy McCall down to the exercise therapist who worked on his knees. As a guest he did not have to sign over his Social Security to the County as inmates did; he kept it in a savings account that Matt monitored. He viewed the Ann Lee as an inexpensive hostel. He could come and go if he could walk, and he still could, with difficulty. He went out for occasional dinners with Matt, who visited often and was on tap for emergencies, except today when he had an emergency of his own. When Martin moved in he knew a dozen or more guests and inmates, a few of them gone mindless, some still ready to talk politics and history, but he needed conversation less and less.

"This is probably Cody's last concert," Matt said as he walked Martin to George and Vivian's table. "He's dying."

"He doesn't have a corner on that market," said Martin.

"The concert's a fund-raiser for his medical bills."

"So this is 'So long, Cody,' a wake while he's still alive."

"I guess that's it."

"A work of mercy. Celebrate what's left of the man."

The band struck up a fast version of "Twelfth Street Rag."

"Are you really up for this action?" Matt asked.

"I didn't think I'd be in a scene like this again. I think it quickens my pulse."

"I'm glad you're out of that place."

"It was handy. Easy, and quiet. They make very tasty egg salad."

"You'll live to be a hundred. But you wouldn't have lasted there, I always thought it was wrong. We'll get you a new place. I've got some ideas, maybe we'll get a place together."

"In the friary?"

"No, an apartment. Downtown maybe."

"Downtown? You're moving to Downtown? Isn't that pretty radical for a priest who's supposed to be campused and silent?"

"Who said I was a priest?"

Martin stopped walking and stared at him. "You did. Since you were fourteen."

"That was yesterday," Matt said.

"Bless us and save us, said Mrs. O'Davis. I'm witnessing a miracle."

"More like a shipwreck," Matt said.

"*Dominus vobiscum*, boy, whoever he is. *Dominus vobiscum*."

When they left the church basement Quinn said, "Do you want to die, Tremont?"

"Not me. I want to go get a taste and then the world's gonna look just fine."

"The world's after you. You're a wanted man and sooner or later they'll find you. You have to surrender yourself. I talked to Lieutenant Fahey about you and your gun, and I also talked to a top lawyer who'll represent you. If you come in on your own they treat you differently than if they find you on the street with a machine gun."

"AR-15 ain't a machine gun."

"You want to die, Tremont?"

"I'm gonna live to be ninety-seven like John D. Rockefeller. Me and him got a lot in common."

"John D. didn't drink."

"Yeah, we didn't agree about that one."

"All right, we get the gun and meet Doc Fahey and you tell your story. Tremont, this is a way out; or else they'll be on you in packs. It'll be like a foxhunt."

"They shoot the fox?"

"The dogs get him."

They were walking on Chapel Street, half a block from the *Times Union*, and Quinn considered going up to the city room to brief Markson on his encounters. But another reporter was covering the Palace, and Quinn had time to write everything else for the final before deadline. If not, he'd call and dictate it. Except for Tremont's story. Now he had to put Tremont together with Doc. A car pulled to the curb alongside them and Matt leaned out the window.

"Hey," he said, and he got out of the car. "Tremont, you keep disappearing. Where'd you go after Trixie's? We looked all over."

"Came to the protest," Tremont said.

"He sang a song," Quinn said. "They would've lynched him if I didn't get him out of there."

Matt reported to Quinn on getting George and Vivian to the Cody concert, and the surprise arrival of his father, after being kicked out of the Ann Lee. "More payback by the machine," Quinn said.

"Where's your gun?" Matt asked Tremont.

"Down on Bleecker Street."

"You took it out of the locker?" Quinn said.

"He took it and he used it," Matt said. "Didn't you tell him, Tremont?"

"Never got a chance. I shot two fellas beatin' on Rosie. Didn't hurt 'em much."

"The police gotta be looking for him," Matt said.

"I was with the Mayor when he got a call about a political assassin at the Four Spot," Quinn said. "But they had you wearing two-tone shoes, Tremont."

"That ain't me," Tremont said. "I got me these holy priest shoes." He lifted his right foot toward Quinn.

"I got Tremont's two-tones," Matt said. "We swapped."

"The priest is a sport," Quinn said. "Listen, I set up a meeting with Doc Fahey. We need that gun."

"I'll come along," Matt said, and he told Nick Brady he was off duty as a chauffeur, and the three walked to Quinn's car and headed toward Bleecker Street. Downtown was as empty as four o'clock in the morning.

"I don't like this surrender business," Tremont said.

"You don't like dying either, am I right?"

"They ever get me inside they'll keep me there."

"You've got a sharp lawyer, Jake Hess. He's close to the Mayor, but he's a straight arrow, and he's taking you on. He knows your whole story."

"Nobody knows my story."

"We're trying."

"You talked to the Mayor about me?"

"I did. I told him you were being set up. It's out in the open."

"He know my name?"

"Only your shoes."

"I saw Zuki at the protest," Tremont said.

"You should've told me," Quinn said. "Roy is in jail."

"What happened?"

"They arrested him at the Palace after that kid died."

"What kid?"

"White kid. Hit on the head or pushed down balcony stairs by black kids."

"They ain't sayin' Roy pushed him."

"I don't know."

"Roy didn't do that."

"All I know is they busted him and five other black guys."

"Open season on the Brothers," Tremont said.

On Bleecker Street maybe ten men were drinking on the sidewalk in front of Hapsy's. Hapsy never let customers linger after they made a buy. He was a supply depot—booze, wine, and sneaky pete after hours, but tonight he was the emergency room, only place open down here. Quinn parked a block away. Chloe's Diner on the corner of Green was open, a pay phone.

"Where exactly is that gun, Tremont?" Quinn asked.

"I couldn't describe it. I gotta show you."

Quinn parked and slid the notebook he'd been scribbling in all day into his suitcoat pocket and the three walked to the corner. Quinn went into Chloe's and called Doc and told him where they were, then they walked up Bleecker, Tremont leading.

"This is where Tremont shot those thugs," Matt said. "That's their truck." He pointed to the corpse of the white panel truck—shattered windshield, three flat tires, holes in the hood. "Tremont left his mark."

"Impressive," Quinn said, trying to calculate what this freelance shooting might do to Tremont's surrender.

A black Chevy with four white men came up Bleecker from Green, moving slowly, the whites looking out at the black men on Hapsy's sidewalk through closed windows. People were sitting on the stoops of the old brick houses, some of the oldest in town, basking in tension. The light was almost gone, streetlights on now. The men at Hapsy's were in their twenties, a few teens (Hap didn't card people), some middle-aged, no women. Matt recognized three youths from the Four Spot. Music was blaring from a parked car and Stevie Wonder was uptight, everything's all right.

Tremont stopped at an alley three doors east of Hapsy's and greeted one of the drinkers, none of whom Quinn knew, and they were not smiling. What's whitey doin' on this block tonight is their question. Quinn saw another car parking behind his car, no one getting out of it. Tremont walked into the shadows of the alley toward a backyard piled with trash and a mountain of cardboard, Hapsy's bottle boxes? Quinn and Matt followed but Quinn turned back to wait on the sidewalk, and three young blacks moved toward him with querulous eyes, and now comes the game. Quinn has been walking this block for two years, writing about blacks, and who gives a goddamn? Well, a lot of blacks, some whites, a few editors, no politicians. Most people were antagonistic or skittish about what he wrote, knee-jerk racism, fear of the pols. But no amount of allegiance to black life could prevent Quinn from being a target of black rage here tonight, because he's just another white mother. Don't give me any progressive bullshit, shove your sympathy, get off my streets is the departure point for the future, the abiding revolutionary code, I love you, brother, but I'll meet you on the barricades. Nothing to be done. Quinn is as color-coded as they are.

One black youth said, "What's happenin'?"

"Where?"

"In the alley."

"They're investigating."

"What?"

"The situation."

"What situation?" The man tucked in his shirttail, streamlining.

"Nobody knows the situation."

"What situation you talkin' about?"

"There's a dead baby," Quinn said.

"White baby?"

"Nobody knows. My friend's looking for it."

"Which friend?"

"The black man."

"That's Tremont," another black said. "It's Tremont's baby?"

"I don't think so."

"Then why's he lookin' for it?"

"Ask him. The baby means nothing to me. It's dead. There's a good chance it isn't even there."

Quinn continues to resurrect the dead baby that doesn't exist: dead before a birth that never was, archetype of the meritocracy of the lost, who leave an unexpungeable stain on the imagination. Do the litany: the glass-jawed, the fallen away, the ignorant, the passive, the skeptics, the cocksure-never-sure—none of them know how to be otherwise—the color-coded, the suicidal rebels and the enraged have-nots, the martyrs and the clerics brainwashed by the mystery, the saints like King who always lose so grandly, the *santeros* who think they can ride out trouble on the backs of Changó and Oshun; also Bobby who might have been different for a few minutes, Hemingway at the end rediscovering how he used to lose, George and his ineluctable illusions, Gloria and Roy's clichéd racial duet, Cody and his dying music, Max and his hot money, Matt and his declension, Renata with her entropic rebellion, her seriality, and Tremont, the only man in town tonight who doesn't need a road map to get to the point: all members of the ad hoc collective that will not let Quinn sleep in peace.

Matt heard Quinn talking and came out of the darkness toward the street.

"Did you find the baby?" Quinn asked.

"He found something," Matt said. "Could be a baby."

"What you gonna do with that baby?"

"I don't know if it's a baby. Could be something else. Could be a pair of shoes. Could be a machine gun."

Tremont came out of the alley with the gun wrapped in the burlap sack. He heard the word "baby" and put his right hand inside the sack.

"These fellows wonder if you found the dead baby," Quinn said to him.

"I found a baby in a vacant lot ten years back," said Tremont. "He wasn't dead."

"Is that my gun, Tremont?" The voice was Zuki's.

"Any gun I find is mine," Tremont said.

Zuki and a young black stood behind the others. Zuki was the one with Penny at the protest.

"You're Zuki," Quinn said. "Who you working for?"

"I don't know you," Zuki said.

"I'm Tremont's biographer."

"And I'm his confessor," Matt said.

"I know who you are," Zuki said.

"Where did that gun come from?" Quinn asked. "Is that government issue?"

"I got no argument with you," Zuki said. "The man here borrowed my property. I want it back."

"Are you an Albany cop? BCI? FBI?"

"I need that gun, Tremont," Zuki said.

"Tremont needs it," Quinn said.

"Tremont, what game are you playing with me?" Zuki said.

"The dead baby game," Quinn said.

Zuki stepped toward Tremont and made a grab for the gun. Matt hit him with a right hand, a horizontal trajectory to the blow, 22 mph, and Zuki shuffled backward but didn't fall.

"Don't touch Tremont," Matt said. He eyed Zuki who drifted into the Hapsy crowd with his young buddy, casting glances Tremont's way.

The black Chevy that had passed them earlier came up Bleecker again, a second car behind it carrying five white men. The Chevy slowed as two white men hanging out the front and back windows flung Molotovs into the crowd, one exploding against the stoop over Hapsy's, the other hitting the front wall of the next house and splashing fire on two men on the stoop. "Keep rioting, niggers," one man yelled from the Chevy.

Quinn saw Doc's car turning off Green onto Bleecker and idling in the street, up from the corner near the dead delivery truck, and he grabbed Tremont's arm. "Now," he said, and the three quickstepped toward Doc's headlights, Tremont clutching the wrapped dead baby.

The Chevy driver peeled out wildly after the Molotovs, his tires screeching into a skid, his left tail sideswiping the car with Stevie Wonder. He swerved erratically, climbed the curb just past Hapsy's, ramming a porch with three more men on it, then tried to back out onto the street. But the blacks were all over the car and pulled him out and wrestled him and his passengers into a free-for-all with tire irons, pipes, and a sap wrapped around one white man's fist. Two women in silk kimonos came out of one house with brooms to fight a fire flaring on the porch, Trixie's porch. Quinn saw Trixie come onto the stoop in a long black kimono and stilettos, and with a brass fire extinguisher splash a stream on the fire that was getting so much attention, and it vanished. Two whites were down in the street, being kicked, and on the next stoop two men were in flames. Trixie's girls slapped at the blazing men with their brooms and half a dozen blacks were rocking the Chevy, trying to tip it.

The second car, a Buick station wagon with windows down—and men with more Molotovs, unlit but ready to fly, but the goddamn Chevy's a blockade—retreated backwards down Bleecker at rocket speed and past the dead panel truck, arriving at the corner seconds after Doc's car arrived, another goddamn blockade out of nowhere, and rammed Doc's left fender, twisting both cars sideways in the street. Doc and his partner, Warren Prior, leaped out of the car, billy clubs at the ready, not for the crazy whites but for a dozen black men coming at them.

"Jesus," Doc said, "it's downtown Nairobi."

Men had come streaming out of Bleecker Street houses as the invasion force was recognized, ready to unleash communal rage not only on the white bombers, whom they outnumbered two to one, but also on Doc and Prior, whom they saw as a third element of this Bleecker Street invasion force. Black youths leaped on Doc, pummeling him, trying to bring him down, but he was an immovable 230-pound hulk in his gray suit and straw hat, the club in his right hand a whirling appendage that never stopped moving. A black man punched Prior repeatedly in the back of the neck as he tried to cope with the attackers, and Prior swung his club a hundred and eighty degrees and the black man dropped. The whites in the second car had come out fighting and Doc clubbed his way out of an attack to deck a white man reaching into the backseat of the Buick for a shotgun. "Niggerlovin' cop," the man said as he crumpled under Doc's blow. Another black slapped open a straight razor in his palm and slashed Doc's front, cutting his suitcoat, then felt the slam of the club against his throat, and down.

Quinn, Matt (who had lost sight of Zuki) and Tremont stood out of the fray, near Chloe's corner, no one attacking them. Tremont pulled off the burlap sack to reveal the AR-15 all of a piece. He snapped in the loaded magazine, gave a Geronimo yell as he fired a shot into the sky, then showed the muzzle of his rifle to the blacks attacking Doc. The meaning of the yell, the weapon, the shot, did not get the full attention of all attackers, but they paused long enough for Prior to club one and for Doc to reach for his pistol.

"Way to go, bro," a black youth told Tremont. "Waste 'em."

"Let him be," Tremont said to the youth.

"He's a pig," the youth said.

"Let him be," said Tremont.

"Gimme that gun, I'll do it," the youth said.

Tremont fired two shots into the side of the Buick and the youth backed away and the fighting stopped. Blacks rocking the Chevy tipped it into the street, a few scrambling for cover at the sound of gunfire, which had elevated the battle to another level, and the wail of a siren was heard.

A black youth tossed a flaming book of matches into the backseat of the Buick, igniting spilled gasoline from the unused Molotovs, and everybody moved away from the car.

Quinn stepped in front of Tremont and snatched the rifle from him. "Goddamn it, man, I told you to keep this in its case. You want to get shot?"

Quinn handed the gun to Doc as three police cars arrived behind them and cops in riot gear fanned out over the block, the combatants black and white scattering into the deepening darkness.

"Hey, Tremont," Matt said, "these shoes are killing me."

❖

Quinn alerted Jake to Tremont and the AR-15 being in police custody and recapped Tremont's odyssey, plus his own role in the surrender to Doc Fahey and as a witness to Zuki saying the AR-15 was his. Jake would go to the detective office and find out if Tremont was being charged and get him bail if he was. But, Quinn said, they might think this is too serious for bail and hold him as a terrorist with half a dozen witnesses to his plot. It's possible, Jake said, but I doubt it.

Quinn went to the *Times Union* and alerted Markson at the city desk what he had in store for him. Then he draped his sport coat on the back of his chair and wrote his interview with Alex as fast as he could type, modifying the Mayor's hostility to the Brothers but reflecting the duel between them. He wrote a few paragraphs on the frenzy in the Palace lobby and what it added to the city's tension, as an insert for the story on the dead youth that another reporter was writing. He also wrote the protest/vigil story, leading with Tommy Tooher's revelation that the bishop was too ill to silence Matt for his politics, and he put in two calls to Monsignor Callaghan, the diocesan chancellor, until his housekeeper said the monsignor wasn't home and wouldn't be and he wouldn't talk to you if he was, so write whatever you want; a lovely touch that would further boil the pot on Matt's behalf.

Markson came over to Quinn's desk. "Tell me again about the riot. You don't have a riot story?"

"It's part of Tremont's story," Quinn said. "I can do a separate riot story if you want one, but Tremont's the main story—his biography as an activist with Better Streets and the Brothers, and the Zuki plot to destroy the Brothers—how all this related to the riot. I'll get the action of the riot up high, don't worry. But the riot isn't the story, it's Tremont. He's central to what's happening in this town tonight, and Matt Daugherty is his white counterpart, the pair of them on an odyssey of Franciscan politics and leftover jazz. If you can stand it I'll work in Trixie's stilettos and her fire extinguisher. I also want to underpin the political culture of the twenties with Big Jimmy the floating ward leader and his progressive coon anthem from 1911, and tie in the McCall-Fitzgibbon machine's bulldozer politics as manifested tonight by the faux assassination plot, with Tremont as its victim, a wild man with an AR-15 given to him by a provocateur who wanted him busted with it to prove the Brothers were urban terrorists, and that's the FBI at work and I know you won't print that, but that's what it has to be. But we don't need it. The victim foiled that plot, coming out of the alley where he'd hidden the gun and calming the riot with his shooting."

Markson nodded, obviously rattled by the complexity of the story; but he'd get it when he read it.

"I need the riot," he said, and he went back to the city desk.

Quinn considered whether he should include his own role in snatching the rifle from Tremont and handing it, along with Tremont, to Doc Fahey for safekeeping. But he decided it would intrude on Tremont's AR-15 salute that rescued Fahey and his partner from razors, knives, blackjacks, and shotguns in the hands of black and white rioters, who were all converging on the cops as primal enemies. This was not your ordinary race riot, but a spontaneous exercise in anarchy, the aim being not reciprocal death among racial antagonists but multicolored and miscegenational chaos. And the rescue would soon be seen by Tremont's peers as seriously ironic: Tremont suddenly the guardian angel of Albany cops, who are famous for brutalizing street demons like himself, and who knows how many other blacks who were caught up in the riot.

For Quinn it was the second time in his life he had taken a weapon from a shooter, the first being from Hemingway in the Cooney duel. But you are not the story, Mr. Quinn. And he decided there was no way to tell that tale, which would emerge somewhere in its own good time.

Quinn was on page three of Tremont's odyssey when Markson came back and peered over his shoulder, picked up the two finished pages, and said, I'll take this too, and pulled the third page out of Quinn's Underwood, went back to the city desk and sat and perused it all without a pencil, then came back to Quinn.

"This is great stuff," Markson said, "but don't write any more. We're not doing anything with your friendly assassin."

"He's not an assassin," Quinn said.

"Good for him, but whether he is or isn't it doesn't run tonight. Not one word about Tremont. Upstairs doesn't want it, doesn't think it's true."

"Every word I write will be true and provably true."

"Not tonight," and he dropped the three pages on Quinn's desk.

Quinn retreated, silent, and he pulled page four out of his typewriter. The back of his chair rocked and so he rocked himself. He folded the pages and put them and his notebook in his sport coat pocket. He went to the city desk and asked Markson, "Do you want a riot story?"

"I can take a few paragraphs. Eddie Fennell is writing about the roundup of blacks. They arrested eight or nine."

"No whites?"

"There's four in the hospital. Three blacks in there too."

Quinn went back to his desk and without notes wrote five paragraphs on the Molotovs and the white raiders, and the blacks tipping the car. He put the story in Markson's in-basket.

Markson looked up at him, an apology in his eyes. "If we don't write about the assassination plot," he said, "then it never existed and they have nothing to charge your man with. They'll let him go."

"Let him go?"

"That's what I said."

"Is the Mayor calling these shots?"

"Who else could?"

"But our publisher is going along with it."

"Take a guess."

"I'd guess that my day is done," he said. "And to fill the silence where my story was supposed to be I'm going to go listen to a little jazz."

"You'll find a way to put Tremont on the page one of these days."

Quinn decided he was again a failed witness to history, Tremont's story as lost as Fidel's, for history conspired against both stories. The medium—that so-called first draft of history—proved to be not the message but the anti-message. Quinn, always aware of these limitations, had finally decided he was furious with himself for believing he could work beneath the strictures, write what would not be countermanded, reveal history in language graceful but hip, simple but sly, exfoliating with the essential stories he had tracked down and wanted to tell to the world. Right.

How now to tell the story of becoming an obsolete white man, obsolete creole? Matt had the same story to tell, and Claudia's was similar. Black Power was confounding racial identity to the point that the FBI had become black, the media were in conspiracy against blacks and whites alike, and witnesses like Quinn were irrelevant. Markson was right about Quinn putting Tremont on the page, but it would take Quinn forty years to do it—in a novel, where he would also write Hemingway's duel and Renata's disappearance into a silence nobody could cut.

When she disappeared from the Holtz estate Quinn worked day and night in Santiago and Havana to find her, pursuing her trail to one dead end after another. No one in her family, none of the Directorio people Holtz put him in contact with, none of her friends at the museum, had heard a word from or about her. They found her car parked a block from the hotel in Santiago. Quinn drove it back to Havana but Esme told him to keep it until they found Renata. He researched her haunts, the Biltmore Yacht Club, the Country Club, the museum, which was closed and under repair from bullets and shelling, the cafés near the University (which Batista had closed, interrupting Renata's education). He went to the Ali Bar she said she loved and other of the night cafés where she grew up under Esme's eye, but he had no faith he'd find her in such places. She wouldn't have left him to cruise Havana's night world. He picked Max's brain, Esme's, her mother's, he found artists she'd talked about, but nothing. The police mocked him as a bridegroom left at the altar.

He awoke in his apartment in Havana on the fourth day after her disappearance and stopped his search, bereft of new ideas, and he began writing his interview with Fidel. He could not think clearly, and failed to convince his ex-editor at the *Miami Herald*, Henry McMullen, that a profile based on Fidel's intellectual views of revolution was the salient element of the story. Matthews already did that, McMullen said. Not the way I'm doing it, said Quinn. Then work it into the body of the story but we need a hard news dimension to justify it, said McMullen. You don't think the fact that he's alive is hard news, said Quinn, or that after we ended our talk he marched all day and half the night and captured El Uvero—how hard does it have to get? We did El Uvero yesterday in six paragraphs, McMullen said, what else have you got? I quit smoking last year but I smoked a cigar with Fidel, Quinn said. How great does it get? Very great, McMullen said. We'll put it on the comics page.

So Quinn wrote it the way he wanted to write it, giving a nod to the El Uvero raid, the bloodiest battle so far in the war, a great success for the rebels, and he used as his lead Fidel's farewell line that "I have an appointment with President Batista's armed forces." He drew a picture of a leader whose mother thinks he was born as a warrior god, his birth witnessed by Changó the Orisha. Nobody will know who Changó is. Let them find out. He wrote that Fidel had been born into the era where he belonged, a man who found his hour, as Faulkner put it. A hero is born, not made, right? Does Quinn really think that? Probably not. If McMullen doesn't use the story he'll give it to the AP or *The Washington Post*, somewhere there's an editor who values Fidel's personal take on his miraculous survival. Just write it.

While he was writing, Hemingway called.

"I got another letter from Cooney," Hemingway said. "Same stuff, a little more urgency. I decided I'd meet him. Pistols. Since you've been central in all this I want you to set it up and be the referee. Cooney trusts you. I'll also bring a second. We'll do it tomorrow, if he's not chicken. We'll meet at Colón Cemetery at dawn, that's how it's done down here. Six-thirty-two is sunrise. I'll pick you up at six. Meet at the main gate. I'll have to pay off one of the guards to let us in. The cemetery doesn't open till nine. Where do you live? And no press, not even you."

"What changed your mind?"

"I saw the whites of his eyes. Are you on?"

"I'm on. My wife disappeared but I'm on. Three days and I can't find her. I told Fidel about your duel. He thinks you have to do it, even though you're too valuable to take such a risk. If you can hold off till he wins the revolution he'll fix it so you win, but if not, then you should find a way not to lose because you're too valuable to die. He said he had *For Whom the Bell Tolls* with him in the Sierra and it taught him things about battle."

"Always glad to help a worthy cause. But I'll fight my own battles, without a fix."

"Is Cooney still at the Hotel Regis?"

"His letter was on their stationery."

"You'll need a doctor in case somebody gets shot. You think anybody will?"

"I'd bet against it," Hemingway said.

"You know a doctor who'll come?"

"Yes. What about your wife?"

"When I came back after Fidel she was gone. She must've been taken by the police or the SIM."

"What did she do?"

"She was close to one of the Palace attackers."

"Uh-oh."

"I know."

"Then you don't need this duel in your life."

"I have no direction to go in right now, nowhere to look. I'll do it."

"You married her. How did that happen so fast?"

"I was always told to get my story in the first paragraph."

◈

They would meet Cooney at the great Romanesque Arch that was the northern gate of Colón Cemetery, and then go to the southern section of the cemetery, which Hemingway had said was the least populated, with ample room for a bullet to fly toward the horizon and lose its momentum after a hundred or a few hundred yards without hitting anything but a tree. The place looked like a dwarf city, sidewalks and sculpted trees, a hundred and forty acres, so many mausoleums, family chapels, crypts, magnificent marble structures (the Firemen's Monument, which honors twenty-seven who died in 1890, looked about six stories tall), statues, domes, obelisks, an Egyptian pyramid, a Pietà, an hourglass with wings, a world of kitsch, a world of art.

"You know this cemetery?" Hemingway asked.

Quinn was alone in the backseat of the Chrysler station wagon, Hemingway in the passenger seat beside his driver, Juan, who came for him after the Cooney knockout. He would be Hemingway's second.

"All I know is that it's a spectacular place," Quinn said.

"It's where they put all the *famosos*," Hemingway said. "There's also thousands of Cubans the Spaniards starved to death back in '98, and your grandfather's pal Máximo Gómez is buried here."

"Why do Cubans fight their duels in a cemetery?"

"It gets you in the mood for death. And it's handy for the loser."

"Cooney's got two seconds that he flew in from Miami."

"He can have twenty. All I need is Juan to carry the pistols. I've got a pair of .38 revolvers I brought back from France. Cooney wanted .38s. He can use one of mine, either one."

"You think he'd use one of your pistols?"

"He can test it in advance if he doesn't trust me. Juan has extra cartridges."

"I didn't talk about that with Cooney. We assumed you'd each have your own."

"That's all right. I'm not fussy."

"You're pretty calm about this."

"If you get excited your aim goes bad. Cooney agreed on you being the referee, right?"

"He did. What does a referee do?"

"You'll have to imagine that for yourself, just like chapter six. By tradition we start back-to-back. Pace off to the count of ten, then turn and shoot. You do the counting, then duck behind the nearest tombstone."

"This is absurd," Quinn said, "absolutely nuts, you putting your life on the line. You're like goddamn Mount Rushmore and here you are diddling with some Baltimore salesman. I can't believe you're going through with it and I can't believe I'm part of it."

"It'll work out," Hemingway said.

"How?"

"You'll see."

"Bullets are bullets."

"You're right about that."

"If you kill him that's the end of you."

"I'll try not to kill him."

"He could kill you."

"He could, and some would say I deserved it, that I violated his honor."

"If he kills you you won't finish your book."

"That's the real tragedy. I've got four books to finish."

"You shouldn't do this. Why not apologize and get it over with?"

"Never apologize, never explain, John Wayne."

"Every duel Wayne ever fought they used blanks," Quinn said. "Juan, what do you think? *Qué piensa?*"

"*Papa sabe*," Juan said, not taking his eyes from the road. "He know."

"What does he know?"

"*Lo sabe todo.* Everyting."

"If you die my career is ruined," Quinn said. "I'll be the one who let you do this."

"You couldn't stop me."

"That won't matter. I'll be the goat, the man who let Papa die, the man who set up the duel. I'll be like Ralph Branca throwing that fastball to Bobby Thomson. How will it look on my résumé?"

"A writer doesn't need a résumé."

"Are you really ready to die?"

"Always."

When Hemingway blew off the top of his head with a shotgun Quinn felt he'd been cut off in the middle of a sentence that was going to explain an unknown that had obsessed him since he decided to become a writer. He hadn't seen the man in four years and his death was a shock that lasted for days. The key to the unknown might now be lost forever. Hemingway knew where it was. He had gone there and held it in his hand and came back to write and prove he had found it. If Quinn could find that place maybe he'd be able to figure out how to write what had to be written; but he wasn't anywhere near there yet, and with Hemingway gone the solution seemed very far off.

Wait a minute—only Hemingway had the key?

Others had it, but I knew him and could talk to him.

He couldn't have told you any secrets. He had four books going and couldn't finish any of them. He was fading. You met him too late.

He could still talk, even if his ambition outdistanced what was left of his talent. He found the answer early on and kept telling us what it was, but he never got it all out. It was his iceberg principle: only the tip revealed, the rest stuck in his throat.

On the street at the Romanesque Arch a new Chevrolet sedan was idling, the Cooney early birds, and a uniformed guard sat behind the wheel of another car. Juan got out and spoke with the guard and shook his hand, then went to the Cooney car and spoke to the driver. The guard opened the gate for the two vehicles and Juan got back into the car and led the way to the south section of the cemetery, a large open field of mown grass. The six participants got out of their cars. Hemingway wore a white guayabera and black trousers and black dress shoes, a dress-up occasion for him. In the new morning light Quinn could see an animation in his face akin to what it was like while Cooney was singing about slivers.

"Where's the doctor?" Quinn asked him.

"We won't need a doctor." ·

"There should be a doctor."

"It'll work out," Hemingway said.

Cooney had a small hat on, a modified Panama he'd cut into a tight brimless skullcap that covered his bandage. His lower lip quivered a bit, and why not? His friends wore pale orange Hawaiian shirts with muscles in them and they held guns in their hands, one each. They weren't ugly or grotesque, not American Gothic, but there was menace in their haircuts. Cooney was wearing a seersucker sport coat and made a point of taking it off and tossing it on the ground as he got out of the car. He walked toward Hemingway with an earned purpose that had brought about this moment, this confrontation of a little ol' Baltimore pissant with the greatest fucking writer of the century, and that's America for you, except this is Cuba. But Cooney knew time, God, fervency, and the pursuit of happiness were on his side. He was facing down the smile of a man of unknown dimension. His new knowledge of Hemingway could not really encompass what the writer stood for in American history or

273

the literary canon or even café society, and he couldn't possibly know what this endeavor of his would lead to—a fiasco, a disaster, a tragedy, a burlesque, a fantasy, a dream, a populist manifesto, a personification of democratic eventuation? Whatever it might be it certainly was like nothing he'd ever experienced, and he was still taking his second step toward Hemingway when he decided to spit—to the left—and Hemingway noted this without comment—and Cooney wondered if there would come a moment in which he would find a new lyric for a song that was apt for this instant—this confrontation between the nobody and the somebody who doesn't yet know I'm one hell of a shot, I can untie your shoes at fifty feet, old buddy. You're nobody till somebody shoots you. But get on with it Cooney, never mind this nonsense. Move ahead and spit in his eye. No, don't. He don't rate that. He showed up. He's some sumbitch, no doubt about it, to come and see this out with me. I'm gonna be all right. I got the best guns they are and he probably does too, but that don't matter. Go for it, bud, say what you gotta say.

"You punched me for no reason," he said.

"I had a reason," Hemingway said.

"What was it?"

"I don't remember."

"That ain't a reason."

"Wasn't much of a reason, whatever it was. Maybe that's why I don't remember it."

"I never done one damn thing to you."

"That's right, you didn't. Maybe something in you, or in that song you sang, rubbed me wrong. A lot of things in this world rub me wrong."

"And you punch 'em all out, do you?"

"I punch out some."

"Some of 'em punch back, I expect."

"You did."

"You can't say why you give me a sucker punch."

"I was pissed off. I don't know at what. You were a handy way of letting off steam."

"If that ain't crazy."

"Not the first time that's been said. You got all the gun you need? I got two .38s I got in France. You can have either one. Test 'em out if you want. Each one has a single bullet in the chamber now. But my man's got extra bullets."

"I don't need no French guns. I got a Smith and Wesson."

He motioned to the seconds and one of the men stepped forward with a paper bag and took out Cooney's weapon of choice, a .38 six-shooter with a four-inch barrel. The second cracked the gun and put one cartridge into a chamber of the cylinder. He snapped the barrel into place and handed the gun to Cooney. Juan opened the green velvet box with Hemingway's matching .38s, both with pearl handles and two-inch barrels, and offered them to the author, who took one, confirmed it had a single bullet in the chamber and showed it to Cooney.

Quinn stepped between the two men. "This doesn't have to go forward, you can solve this with words," he said. "Nobody needs to get shot here. The event that started it is long gone and you've both talked it out. I suggest you shake hands and get on with life."

"I didn't come here to shake hands," Cooney said.

"Well put," said Hemingway. "Start the count, Mr. Quinn."

Hemingway turned his back to Cooney and Cooney did the same.

"All right," Quinn said. "It's ten paces, then you turn and face each other. One shot is all that's allowed."

"Start the count," Hemingway said.

"One," said Quinn and the duelists stepped off and Hemingway turned and in an underhanded arc he tossed his pistol to Quinn.

"Two," said Quinn as he caught it, "hold it, you don't have a weapon."

"Three, don't need it," Hemingway said, stepping out, "carry on counting."

Four, and Cooney turned to see what had happened but kept moving forward, his gun in his right hand, his arm cocked.

"Five," said Hemingway.

"He don't have a weapon," Cooney's second said. "It's a trick."

"Six," said Hemingway. "No trick."

"Seven," said Quinn, looking to see if the pistol had a safety.

"Eight," said Quinn and Hemingway together.

"Nine," said Quinn. "Ten."

Hemingway turned to face Cooney and stood with his hands at his side, palms outward. Everybody had a gun in hand: Quinn holding Hemingway's .38, Juan with Hemingway's other .38, Cooney's second and his other friend each with pistols, and Cooney with his. Only Hemingway was unarmed.

"Shoot," said Hemingway.

"Shoot an unarmed man," Cooney said, his arm at his side.

"I've got arms. I choose not to use them."

"So you ain't got the guts to shoot at me."

"I got the guts. I would prefer not to."

"Don't shoot him, Cooney," his second said. "It's a trick."

"Trick is I shoot an unarmed man it's murder one," Cooney said.

"Maybe you'll miss," Hemingway said.

Cooney thought about that. He lifted his arm and pointed his pistol at a metal vase with a metal flower sitting atop a grave thirty feet away. He fired and the vase flew off the grave.

"Nice," Hemingway said.

"All right, a shot's been fired, it's over," Quinn said. He moved between Cooney and Hemingway and gave the pistol to Juan who was breathing heavily, and who kept his pistol in hand as he accepted Hemingway's discard. Cooney talked with his seconds and handed off his weapon. They all kept an eye on Juan. Cooney picked up his sport coat and put it on.

"So you have received satisfaction for your challenge," Quinn said to Cooney.

"Is that what you call it? I don't think so. He weaseled."

"You could have shot him. You had your chance. He told you to shoot. What else do you want?"

"He's a smart one."

"He is."

"Fuck you, Mr. Hemingway."

"Same to you, Mr. Cooney," Hemingway said.

Then they drove out of the cemetery, past the winged hourglass.

❖

When Quinn stepped out of the elevator on the first floor of the *Times Union*, destination Cody's concert, Renata and Max loomed. They'll be there, but then again she could be anyplace. She goes where she wants to go, and finds her way back home, oddly, and I never stop wondering why. But I'm there when she returns, and I never stop wondering why. Max is her comfort tonight, the old *cuñado* and savior. The blasé fugitive comes to Albany to see his old school chum, the Mayor, who has been plowing his daughter, and also to court his ex-sister-in-law, whom he once plowed, yes, just once, she insisted. But you can't believe her. Yet even if that once was true it was enough to bring him up here for seconds, dope entrepreneur on the run, a new career listing for him—Max the fugitive, if that's what he is. I should have checked Florida about him. So call somebody at the *Herald*.

He summoned the elevator, went back up to the third floor and to his desk. He called the *Herald*'s city room, identified himself to the night city editor, and asked for three old friends, none of them there. What about Charlie Sawyer? Yes, Charlie, a Quinn drinking buddy before the Cuban stint, was around. And yes, indeed, Charlie knew all about Alfie. Quinn told him, I knew Alfie in Cuba and when I heard his news I thought I might do a piece on him, and I'm looking for an update. Charlie said he'd get the clips and Quinn held the line and then Charlie read Quinn the *Herald*'s story on the bust. And there was Max, a key player who'd made a fateful career decision about showbiz that brought Alfie down.

A courier for a major dope importer, who was plea bargaining, gave up Max to the prosecutor, having seen him in *Up Against* two weeks back and remembered him from their meetings in the Drake Hotel in Chicago, and the Plaza in New York. The courier would arrive, call Max's number and Max would turn up with money—seventeen million delivered over four months in twelve installments, to pay for the thirteen or so tons of dope his bosses had sold to Alfie Rivero for Miami delivery. So Max carried a million plus in every briefcase he handed over to the courier. They talked about more than dope and money, listened to the Palm Court's harpist, drank dark Puerto Rican rum, which Max said was the closest to Cuban rum, which is the best, but you can't buy it in this stupid country. Max confessed he'd wanted to be an actor since high school, he knew some movie stars, Bing Crosby, and was trying, without success so far, to convince Bing to let him develop a documentary on Bing's career. Then last week, the courier said, I go to the movies and there's Max on the big screen playing a Chicago detective, first time I ever knew his name. Max wasn't hard to trace: apartment on Miami Beach, close to Alfie Rivero, a heavy duty dealer the Feds had been trying to bring down for a year. They raided Alfie's apartment and his loft, found a little dope, not much, also raided his town house in Brooklyn Heights. Alfie lived high, art works on his walls, tailored suits in the closet. But the Feds didn't find the man himself. What we hear, Charlie said, is that he got asylum in Havana, we're checking it out.

"Why did you do that movie?" Renata asked Max.

"Why not? What have I got to hide?"

"That you're a drug dealer."

"Never. This was economic opportunity, major wages for moving some money. I worried about being robbed, not arrested. Alfie liked my access to exclusive clubs in Washington, and in New York and Miami where he could do business with diplomats and see his customers from Sutton Place and Park Avenue. There was nobody on his payroll with my credentials. And the money I carried was always explainable. Alfie pays his taxes as a gambler and he makes heavy investments in real estate."

"The police would never believe that."

"He's been doing it for years and they never came after him till now."

"Alfie is not a drug dealer, and you're an innocent fugitive, so you can spend all afternoon at a bar."

"Hiding in plain sight."

"What did he gamble at," Gloria asked.

"Marijuana," Max said.

They were in the Dodge Coronet Renata had rented for Max in her name, with his cash. She had driven her car to the Avis lot at Albany Airport, with Gloria in the backseat, switched Max's suitcase to the trunk of the Coronet, and left her own car in the public parking lot. They then headed for the concert, which Gloria had not wanted to see until Renata persuaded her Roy might be there and she could talk to him.

Renata had not yet heard whether Max could enter Cuba, but she had begun the circuitous route of calls that would, perhaps, reach Moncho's ear in Havana. The question was, can Mr. X enter Cuba and if so, how? What her sources deemed likeliest was a Cubana Airlines flight from Gander, Newfoundland, to Havana. All Cubana flights to and from Europe refueled at Gander, and the reservation would be easy once Max had the okay. Next problem: enter Canada without confronting U.S. Customs; can't drive or fly, but the border is porous. You can walk across it, and many now do—peaceniks and draft dodgers avoiding the war, it's a migration. Max needed wheels to get near the border, hence the Coronet; then he needed contacts to help drop off the car and walk him into Canada to new wheels and a driver, and all that was in process. Money was no problem. It all depended on Moncho convincing Fidel that Max was a worthy visitor.

What would Max bring to the revolution? First, a lot of money. Also the frequent favorable coverage of Fidel's battle victories that Max had authorized as editor of the *Post*, despite pressure from Batista to ignore him. There would also be the revelation of his CIA history in Cuba and Miami, but would Fidel trust any of that? He will trust the money. Max is also a confederate of Alfie, one of Fidel's major gun suppliers, and he's a friend of the great Renata, and of Moncho, who is close to the Comandante. Outside of the money, Max, this doesn't add up to a whole lot. But Renata is on the case, even so, and just negotiating you into Canada is a giant step for any fugitive.

The aroma of the new Coronet's interior called up Renata's memory of the police car that they put her in when they took her out of the Casa Granda Hotel, flying her to Campo Columbia's airfield in Havana and shoving her into the backseat of another police car. Her guardian policeman kept the barrel of a Thompson against her neck, and now in the Coronet she could almost smell the oil on that gun again. She knows the Thompson, how to break one down and clean it, how to fire it, also she knows it fits unbroken under the front seat of a car. This she learned when she was driving Diego, two Thompsons between them on the seat and he said, hide that gun, and he slid one under his own seat. She did the same as two policemen ambled toward them, maybe ready to help, for the car had stalled and wouldn't start, wouldn't start, wouldn't start. Or were they coming to search the car, who knows why? Then the car started, and she waved them away with a smile, thanks but not necessary, and drove away from disaster, maybe death. Had the police searched and found the guns in the trunk, or the weapons under the seats, Diego would have shot them—both Thompsons were loaded—and Renata, God save us, might have done the same.

She was not then part of the Directorio, just a passionate friend of rebels, one in particular; and being such a friend means you help your friend unconditionally. It also means that such forceful allegiance has transformed you into a conditional cop killer, Renata, which suggests that you have lost your reason. But she shrugged that away, ascribing it to love and her passion for justice.

At the DeWitt Clinton Renata, Max, and Gloria sat with Matt and his father, Martin, he looks so old, and George and his new lady friend, *gordita pero* shapely, and quite stylish. George does look unusually happy, the poor man is starving for affection, living with us. The ballroom was nearly full, hundreds and hundreds of fans smiling to Cody's beat, some still eating, nobody dancing yet, and Cody beaming and playing and singing the tune he wrote, "Home in the Clouds." Yes, he's thin, but he looks fine, still handsome. Quinn was not here, but he will be, Matt said. He's over at the paper, writing his bombshells for tomorrow. And he gave them a brief summary of his and Quinn's odyssey through the assassination plot, the Four Spot fight, the riot, and Quinn arranging for Tremont to surrender himself and the AR-15.

"Roy Mason's also in custody," Matt said. "They may be charging him with inciting a riot and telling a group of black kids in front of the Four Spot they should have guns and he could get them for them. But those are both fake charges, they just wanted to bust him. His bail could be twenty-five or fifty thousand, which he doesn't have."

"Where is he?" Gloria asked.

"The Second Precinct lockup at headquarters. They may convene Police Court there tonight. They're holding forty people. If Roy doesn't make bail they'll put him in the county jail."

"Can I see him?" Gloria asked.

"I doubt it," Matt said.

"We should raise his bail money," Gloria said. "Can we put up anything, Aunt Ren? You only need ten percent of whatever the bail is. I've helped do that for a few people."

"That could be five thousand dollars," Renata said.

"I have some money, and there are people I can borrow from," Gloria said. "I'll go see how much it is. Headquarters is just down the block. I know some of the detectives."

"I don't want you out alone," Renata said.

"I'm all right."

"Of course you are."

"I am."

"You shouldn't be on the street by yourself, especially tonight."

"I can't stand that they put him in jail again."

"Let's find out what the bail is."

"I can do that," Matt said, and he got up from the table.

"I'll go with you," Gloria said.

As they left Renata said softly to Max, "I think she's seriously smitten with this young man. Would you consider putting up that money?"

"As a favor to you?"

"Yes."

"One good turn deserves another, and that was a good turn with you."

"Yes, it was. But I may not see you for a long time, and you keep rescuing me. You are a generous man."

"My generosity has only just begun. I'll put up his bail."

"Thank you, dear Max."

"Are you also smitten with this kid?"

"No, but I used to like his father."

"I remember," Max said.

When her guardian policeman pushed her out of the car she almost fell, and she knew then they really would hurt her. You are a coward, Renata, but you must not let them know. The one with the Thompson poked it into her back to hurry her along toward the grassy bank of El Laguito in the Country Club barrio. This is where they found Pelayo Cuervo Navarro after the Palace attack he had nothing to do with. But he was Batista's longtime enemy and they put three bullets in his back, five in his chest and dumped him here at the edge of the lake.

A second car pulled up behind them and a man in white stepped out and came toward her as she stumbled toward the lake: Pedro Robles Montoya, infamous, Batista's chief of naval intelligence, grown-up puffy boy bulging out of his white guayabera, white slacks, white shoes. Her guard pushed her to her knees, then into a sprawl, and dragged her to the lake. He ripped buttons off her blouse when he handled her and her skirt came up to her lap. She lay exposed, her face inches from the water. The guard grabbed her long black hair in his fist and twisted it once, then pushed her head into the water and held it under—forty, sixty seconds, then up.

"Who organized the attack on the president?" Robles asked.

She did not talk, spitting water, faking breathlessness. She was a serious swimmer, could hold her breath five minutes under water.

"I know nothing," she finally said. "I am a museum guide, I am a student, I know nothing of the Palace attack."

"You are in the Directorio."

"No."

"Who planned it?"

"I know none of those people."

"Your lover, Diego San Román, died in the attack."

"I hardly knew the man. I saw him in the museum, we talked of art. That's all there was, talk of art."

Robles nodded and the guard pushed her head under water, pulled her out, pushed her under again, out again, under yet again, confusing her breathing. He held her under more than a minute, turning her so she faced the sky. She came up truly gasping, they will drown me. Don't be a coward, you are a swimmer, you know how to drown.

"We found guns under your bed, a Luger, a .38 automatic, political literature for the Directorio, the Communists, the Socialists, the Twenty-sixth of July. Which do you belong to?"

"That was research, a paper I was writing when the president closed the university."

"The guns were research?"

"They were my cousin's guns. He lived with us and he gave them to me when he was dying. They've been in my family since the Machado era."

"Where are the survivors of the attack hiding?"

"I know none of them. I know nothing."

"We go to the Buro," Robles said.

The Buro was headquarters for the intelligence unit of the Cuban police force, a castlelike structure at Twenty-third Street and the Almendares River Bridge. Robles and the two guards drove her past the Buro's dock on the river where a small motor launch was tethered.

"You are a pretty child," Robles said, "and beauty sometimes protects its possessor. But not today. And you are a privileged child, but privilege has no meaning here, not today. No one of money or power or influence can deliver you out of my hands. You tell me what I want to know or you will feel pain. We will penetrate you, humiliate you, we will spoil your glories." He pointed to the motor launch. "And if you do not talk we will take you out in that boat and cut you, and when you are bleeding properly we will deliver you to the sharks."

They led her up many stairs into the castle, to a windowless room with rough concrete walls, a desk and a few chairs. The two guards hovered behind Robles.

"Who is in charge of the Directorio?"

"I know nothing of that," she said.

"You are a liar."

He punched her stomach and backhanded her face. She did not fall. Renata the martyr has the power to die for the revolution or live by talking to the fat fascist. It only takes a few names, you can name the dead.

"We know everything about your family, your work, your love affairs, your closeness to the rebels."

"I am not a political person," she said, and she moaned and covered her breasts with her arms. He shoved her against the concrete wall, damaging her back and her arm. She felt she was bleeding. He sat her on a chair and the guards held her arms and her head so she could not move. He took a leather tool pouch from a desk drawer and unfolded it. He lifted out a small, pointed iron rod with a wooden handle and he touched its tip to her left ear.

"Where are they hiding?"

"I don't know any of them," and she screamed this.

He inched the rod into her left ear, touching her eardrum.

"Who financed the attack?"

"I know nothing."

He shoved the rod through her eardrum, and she screamed herself voiceless. He moved to her right ear and inserted the rod. She screamed on but with fading sound.

"Who is left alive to lead the organization?"

She opened her mouth but could make only the smallest of sounds, and she shook her head. He pushed the iron through her right eardrum and she slumped in the grip of the guards, undone. She closed her eyes and wept her pain. The guards pulled her to her feet and Robles ripped her blouse off one shoulder, revealing the necklace Narciso had given her—Changó's tools and weapons.

"What is your religion?"

"Catholic." It was not even a whisper.

"Then why do you wear the necklace of Changó?"

"A gift."

"It is Santeria. You said you were a Catholic."

She was crawling toward Babalu Aye, half a cinder block tied to her ankle with rope, and she was pulling the block as she slid on her back toward the church. A shirt covered her but her back was already bleeding, and Babalu was very far away.

Blood was streaming from both her ears. Robles grabbed her skirt at the waist and swiveled, pulling her in a circle, steadily ripping the skirt as he hurled her against another wall. The side of her head hit the concrete and her pain was dizzying. She fell, her skirt around her ankles. One of the guards kicked her in the ribs, then stepped over her and kicked her ribs on the other side.

She flagellated herself with a switch as she moved toward the church of San Lázaro with the crowd. Her back, her thighs, her buttocks bled from the whipping. Babalu! Brother of Changó! Babalu!

Robles pulled her skirt off, grabbed her panties and tried to rip them but he could not. He pulled them off her legs. The guards lifted her to

her feet and held her against the wall. Robles poured water from a pitcher into a glass and put it to her lips. She swallowed, freshening the blood in her mouth. She was naked now, her bra askew. Robles put his hand between her legs. She looked into his face, blood coming from her nose, her head, her ears, her arms, her knees, her buttocks. She will have scars, a marked woman—she will gain status. While lying on the floor she had seen, under Robles' guayabera, his holstered pistol and a beaded belt of Ogun, brother and sometime enemy of Changó.

"Ogun," she said to Robles in a scratched voice, softly, very softly out of a broken throat. "You look to Ogun."

The words stopped him. He withdrew his fingers from her, his face inches from hers. She chanted through broken lips:

"Ogun lord of iron, who lives in the knife,
Ogun god of war who slaughtered a village,
Ogun outcast butcher, who eats the dog."

"You put Ogun's iron into me," she whispered to him. "You are killing me. But Changó will not let you do it. You will die before I do. My *babalawo* said when he gave me this necklace, show it to your enemy and if he hurts you, tell him Changó will plunge him into a long and thunderous death."

Robles waved the guards off and backstepped away from her. Leaning against the wall she swayed her head, moving in a slow rhythm, the beginning of a dance. She wanted to dance as Floreal had danced at the wedding but the pain everywhere in her body would not allow it. This was her honeymoon, without Quinn, courted by the butcher in his stead. She swayed only her head, using Floreal's cadence, and she chanted:

"Changó, who breathes fire at his enemy,
Changó, who owns all music,
Whose thunderstones burn down forests."

She could feel the oozing sores of Babalu Aye. She remembered Padre Pio channeling the stigmata into his body. Robles did not move, his arm hanging by his thigh, his pistol pointed at the floor. She saw the developing fear in his stare. He is a believer. She took a small step toward him, then another. Then, with strength in her right hand she did not know she had, she reached under his shirt and grabbed the belt of Ogun and jerked it. Robles backed off from her touch and the broken belt came away in her hand, its black and green beads rolling across the floor.

"Ogun is useless," she said. "Ogun is on the floor."

She dropped the belt and more beads rolled.

"Ogun has the iron sword but Changó has lightning. Can you fight lightning with a sword?"

"You have the diabolical in you," Robles said. She read his lips. She could not hear him.

"You are recognizing yourself," she said.

He had raped her as an unconsummated bride, but she had seduced him. He was killing her but she had prayed him into her vagina, where Changó often dwells, where he has been lying in wait since the wedding.

And in that place Changó's lightning had scorched the invader's will and silenced his soul.

"Robles," she said, "you will kill me no more."

◈

The music was cool, solid when Quinn entered the ballroom, the crowd poppin' and tappin', keeping together in time. Quinn counted at least five hundred people, at twenty a head that's ten thousand, fifty percent for the room, food, and wine, so five big ones for Cody, nice, a middle-aged bunch, maybe a third of them black, some in tuxes and dinner gowns to tone things up for Cody. Cody was wearing his tux, white lapel carnation, playing so fine, drum and bass backup, doing "Poor Butterfly" in up tempo, not wild, can't do those double-time breaks anymore, they punish his lungs; but his beat is there and why hasn't the rest of the world recognized the originality of this man's style the way Albany has? It certainly wasn't his fingers, you can get by with eight, he said, but ten is where it's at, and he always had ten, and some nights twelve. So what did he do wrong? Missed the subway and didn't show up in time for the recording session with John Hammond, the record producer, was that really it? A born loser? Can't stand prosperity? Doesn't believe he'll ever jump over the moon? He's humming, zum-zum-za-zum, those lungs not failing that part of him, and he looks all right, thinner, goes with the territory, all gray and almost militarily upright, as if he took West Point posture lessons, and there's that same tight mustache, same chin whiskers, same frowning down at the music he's making, always his own toughest critic.

Quinn saw Renata sitting between Max and Martin Daugherty, Vivian with Pop, Matt not here, or Gloria. Quinn inhaled like a pigeon, puffed up his chest, pissed-off husband. She has fucked Max, surely. She knows how to thank a guy. She looks so gorgeous, exquisite, can't blame Max for all that yearning. Now she'll tell Quinn it meant nothing. When he caught up with her in Miami after her disappearance from the Holtzes she apologized for fucking Max but what could she do? He'd saved her life. She and Quinn were still in the honeymoon stage then, two weeks after the marriage, which had never been consummated because Fidel intervened. "I loved our wedding, Daniel, and our dancing with Changó and Oshun, and then Changó saving me from Robles. I'm still your virgin bride and Max means nothing, he helped me, but I'll never be close to him again." Quinn was then fourth in line for her prize, after Changó, Robles, and Max. A new form of virginity: I can give it to you wholesale.

"Martin," Quinn said when he sat at the table, "where have you been, what brings you to the violent city?"

"I got bored out there in the deathbed city," Martin said. "It's nice to be comforted into the grave, but I'm not ready."

"Glad to hear it. Where's that big son of yours?"

"Over at police headquarters complaining about their methods, that's what he does. You two had a big day, I hear."

"We know how to have a good time," Quinn said. "You know Cody?"

"I remember when he played down in Big Jimmy's place, long time ago. Lot of talent. I didn't follow him. I went in other directions. But that was good jazz down there."

"I was only a kid. But I heard him. Never forgot him."

"How's your life at the newspaper?"

"They cut my throat tonight. I had a truly great story—a scam about assassinating the Mayor, which is really just a way of smearing the Brothers, and Roy in particular, and they wouldn't print it."

"I don't know Roy," Martin said.

"He'll be here. Pop, are you all right?"

"As well as can be complimented under the circumstances."

"Good. Vivian, I want to hear about your evening."

"It was thrilling," Vivian said. "Your father's doing fine."

"I can tell. I thank you for seeing him through a difficult day."

"It wasn't difficult. He got a little cut, that's all. We had a wonderful time. And it's not over, is it?"

"Not that I can see. Where's Gloria?" he asked Renata.

"She's with Matt finding out about bail for Roy."

"Bail for Roy? They weren't giving him bail."

"Somebody called Cody and said it was happening."

"I asked Jake Hess to represent Roy and Tremont. He must've changed their minds."

"Then you did a good thing," Renata said. "And Max says he'll put up Roy's bail."

"Ah, Max," Quinn said, looking at him for the first time, "very generous."

"I like that kid," Max said.

"How was your interview with Alex?" Renata asked.

"Predictable, but some things got aired."

"Did you talk to him about Gloria?"

"No. I didn't want to listen to him lie about something so important."

Quinn was bursting with the impulse to stand up and deliver a speech about the night they took away his story on Tremont. His publisher summarily declared history unpublishable, and the Mayor, who had orchestrated that history, affirmed that it had never happened. Tremont the assassin and Zuki the provocateur did not exist. It's odd how the Pashas reverse themselves, Tremont free, Roy bailed, Renata released from her torture cell (with divine intervention).

Quinn just listened as Renata updated him on the situation with Max: now waiting for the okay to enter Cuba, and when he gets it he'll leave for Canada, Gander. Complicated, but it's being arranged. The amazing Renata, who never lost her taste or her talent for intrigue.

Quinn leaned toward Max and whispered, "Alfie may be in Cuba."

"They let him in?" Max asked.

"That's the hot rumor in Miami. What does that do to your getting in?"

"I'll have to ask Renata's *babalawo*."

When Robles ended Renata's torture he had asked her what she wanted. I want my mother, she said. If they let my mother come to the Buro they won't kill me because she is a woman of means, of status, of influence. Robles had said influence doesn't matter here, but it matters. Robles had the guards wash the blood off her body, her face, her ears, her hair. He gave her a policeman's shirt out of the closet, small, it almost fit her, but nobody was her size on the police force. They put ice on her face where she had been cut and bruised to reduce the swelling, brushed her hair, then gave her a room with a cot to lie on until the morning. She feared they would kill her during the night. A woman came in and examined her and put drops in her ears and gave her water and pills and said, take three for your pain. Renata could not hear her voice. She accepted the pills but kept them in her hand. Pills might be poison, Diego had told her. I have no pain, she told the woman.

Robles was doing what Changó had told him to do. He ordered Renata's room locked and he kept the key and stayed all night in an office next to the torture room. At sunrise they brought her breakfast and more ice and at nine her mother was allowed to see her in the office and take her home on her arm, with Robles offering deferential bows to Celia who thanked Colonel Robles for his kindness and walked Renata to the car.

Diego had warned her that the police are liars, so do not trust anything they say or do. In the car her mother was saying her father had booked her on a flight to New York, she would stay with her cousin and have all the money she needs. She would be off the island tomorrow. But Renata had other plans. She told her mother to use her connections to get her into the Haitian embassy where she would seek asylum, also the Brazilian and Ecuadoran embassies, for her father knew the Brazilian military people and the Ecuadoran ambassador was in love with her; so she would have three safe places to go. Her mother insisted New York was safest and Renata said yes, but I will never get there, do what I ask, Mama, or they will kill me, not all the police are as afraid of me as Robles is. They will be coming for me very soon.

When they arrived home her mother drew a bath for her and examined her wounds and put Furacin salve on all of them, and wept when she saw what that devil did to her ears. He made her a deaf person. She said she would call a doctor but Renata insisted they call everybody they knew with clout to get her into one of the embassies. She went up to her room and packed five kinds of medicine, her passport, two blouses, two skirts, her makeup and sundries in an overnight case, tiptoed down the back stairs and heard her father talking on the phone about the Brazilian embassy.

She went out the French doors and through the garden, past the bougainvillea to the bus stop on Fifth Avenue, trying not to look like herself, and waited six months for the bus. Then she climbed its two steps feeling great pain in her ribs, god knows how many are broken, and why hadn't they pained her this way going up the stairs to her bedroom?

She shuffled toward the rear of the bus and put on a mantilla to hide her face and hair, and sat facing away from the window. She rode to Twenty-second Street and walked two blocks to the Haitian embassy, a two-story building at Twenty-second and Seventh Avenue where, she had heard two weeks ago, six rebels from Matanzas had found asylum. But now the corner was full of police cars and policemen were surrounding the embassy, something going on and she would not stay to find out what. She walked back to Fifth Avenue, every step a dagger in both her sides. She waited for a bus that would take her to the Brazilian embassy, which occupied suites in a nine-story office building on the corner of Infanta and Twenty-third at the Malecón. She told the guard she was the ambassador's niece but at the entrance to the embassy's suite she felt that she could not take another step. The door opened to her and she stared at a young man who looked like a diplomat in training. He welcomed her and gestured for her to enter. She tried to make the step across the threshhold but she could not move. She dropped her bag and swooned into the young man's arms.

Had she gone to the Haitian embassy forty minutes earlier she would have met two of her friends who had taken part in the Palace attack,

Carbó and Prieto, and Javier from the 26th, one of the killers of Quesada at the Montmartre. Two safe houses where the three might have gone had turned out to be under surveillance, pinpointed by captured rebels who had been tortured into revelation, and so the three went to where the six Matanzas revolutionaries had found a haven. The three had four pistols among them and refused to surrender any until they had received safe conduct. They sat in a first-floor room while the Haitian diplomats considered their future. Within less than an hour their arrival had reached the ears of the chief of the Cuban National Police, Rafael Salas Cañizares, who swiftly assembled a task force and alerted the news photographers who documented his front-page arrests, that he had found the gangsters who might have killed Quesada.

Salas marched his troops into the embassy, flouting the international convention that protects asylum seekers, slaughtered the Matanzas six and exchanged fire with the three newly arrived armed rebels, who all fell. One policeman was wounded. Salas, who could have served as a body double for Oliver Hardy, strode into the first-floor room and stood over the fallen trio, his lower belly and groin bulging under his trousers below the edge of his bullet-proof vest. Javier, dying on his back with a privileged vision of this exposure, slightly elevated his right hand, which still held a machine pistol and, with terminal energy, fired his last shot into the center of the puffcake. The police chief joined the fallen, lingered two days in a hospital, and died.

Within an hour of Renata's arrival at the Brazilian embassy the Cuban police knew she had found asylum, but the international outcry against Salas's contravention of protocol kept them from a second invasion. Renata announced to her soul that she would make a pilgrimage to Babalu Aye to thank him and his brother for their vigilance on her behalf.

❖

Quinn had just been served his reheated chicken dinner when he saw Gloria threading her way across the DeWitt ballroom to report that Roy's bail was the expected five thousand. Renata and Max left the table with her and walked toward the lobby where Quinn imagined Max in a shadowy corner counting off the five in cash and passing it to his daughter to liberate a young man whose intimacy with her helped liberate her into near suicide.

From a lobby phone Renata called her contact in New Jersey, Cuca, whom she'd known since childhood but never knew her politics, but who had worked for Fidel in Havana until she was marked, then fled to Miami where she raised money for Fidel; and after the revolution she stayed on with Fidel's extended intelligence family. Cuca said it was a go for Renata's unnamed friend. He drives to Plattsburgh and leaves his car where Avis can pick it up. He meets his driver and they go twenty miles to the ruins of Fort Montgomery in Rouses Point. Max walks north through a cattle pasture and thin woods, not half a mile, and he's in Canada. His driver crosses the border on 9-B which turns into Canadian route 223 and meets Max north of the Customs House. They drive two days to Gander and Max pays the driver one thousand dollars, then flies to Havana.

"I can't lug my suitcase through that," Max said.

"Travel light, leave it here," Renata said.

Max walked her out of lobby traffic, down an empty hallway.

"That bag is full of money," he said. "It was insane to carry it all, but when I heard they'd raided Alfie and were looking for me, I was gone in ten minutes. Your contact may be getting me on the road, but this money could get me into Cuba. Fidel doesn't do charity work."

"If you give it to Fidel how will you live?"

"I'll keep a few bucks. He wouldn't want an *americano* on the dole down there."

"Is this Alfie's money?"

"I made it through him. But it's mine."

"How much money are you talking about?"

"Nine hundred thousand, plus. I didn't have time to count it."

"You carried that much money on an airplane?"

"I chartered a plane from Miami."

"Max, what did you do to get such money?"

"I bought some weed with my own money and sold it to a few of Alfie's clients. Alfie didn't care. He deals in multiple millions."

Renata shook her head. Who can believe such talk?

"Can I trust this driver of yours not to mug me?" Max said.

"I'd trust my contact with anything."

"I don't trust anybody when it's money."

"She doesn't know you have money. Bury it, draw a map."

"I know a dealer who buried three million and can't remember where. Don't trust anybody, not even yourself. Your calls to your contact were probably tapped."

"We use pay phones. We know how to avoid the tap."

"They tap pay phones."

"The way we talk nobody knows what we mean. Put your money in a safe deposit box."

"That's about as safe as a mail box." Max touched her shoulder. "Renata, I need you to hold this money for me."

"You're not serious. I can't do that. I can't."

"Yes you can. You know how to protect it, where to hide it. I have no time, and it's too risky to carry it. I think I came to Albany to put the money in your hands, and I didn't know that until this minute. I'll pay you well. How does fifty thousand sound? Consider it yours, right now. When I need the rest I'll have someone pick it up. If anybody kills me all the money is yours, you're a millionaire overnight. I worship you, Renata. I don't trust anybody but I trust you with my life, and my fortune, if you think a million's a fortune. You're my primary beneficiary."

"What about Gloria?"

"I'll take good care of her. But she really doesn't need my money. She has Esme."

"You want to turn me into a drug dealer."

"Nobody will link this money to drugs."

"If they link it to you they will. How would I explain such cash? *Esto es ridículo,* Max, *ridículo.*"

"This is family. Your sister's rich and I'm your brother-in-law, and we've been pushing money at each other for years. Esme will swear to that. Worst-case scenario you have to pay some taxes. But keep it hidden. You are smart, my love, very smart. You can do it."

"I have to tell Quinn about this."

"I can trust Quinn."

"He doesn't trust you."

"That's about you, not money."

"He won't let me do it."

"Do it without him."

"I could never do it alone. I'm not as smart as you think I am."

"So you won't do it?"

They walked back to the lobby and she stared toward the ballroom. She could hear the music, faintly. Quinn will go crazy. "I will ask him," she told Max. I am a lunatic, yes? Yes. "Maybe we keep it until you are in Cuba, but then you send someone or I bury it and send you the map."

"Perfect," said Max.

"I'm not sure Quinn will think it is perfect."

She left Max in the lobby and walked into the ballroom and sat beside her husband to persuade him to become a felon. Quinn heard the urgency in her voice and went with her toward the lobby but stopped short of Max.

"You can get ten years for this," he said.

"It's saving his life. We keep it until he's in Cuba, then he sends for it. Fifty thousand dollars."

"It's piss money," Quinn said. "Shit money."

"But money. Much money, free money."

"If they trace it to him you'll look like the head of his syndicate. So will I."

"All we do is hide one suitcase. We could bury it in the woods."

"I buried a treasure when I was a kid. A week later I went to dig it up and it was gone."

"I'll divide it up, put it in different safe deposit boxes."

"All under your own name?"

"So put it behind one of our walls, make a new wall."

"I don't want it in the house."

"Are you saying no to Max? Are you saying no to me?"

"I'm saying he should find another patsy to mind his loot. It's a lousy thing to do to you. To us."

"He is a fugitive. You want him to go to jail? Do you hate Max so much?"

"Aiding a fugitive, another felony."

"So you are forbidding me to do this?"

Max came toward them.

"Where's your goddamn car?" Quinn said to him.

"Just outside," Max said. "Very close."

"I love you, Quinn," Renata said.

She led them out onto State Street where she had parked the Coronet.

"Do you have to take anything out of the suitcase?" Quinn asked Max.

"Shirts and socks, a shaving kit. I'll put them in my briefcase."

"How much is in the suitcase?"

"More than nine hundred thousand."

"What if it turns out to be six hundred?"

"We can count it. Most of it's wrapped and marked."

"We'll count it," Quinn said. But where? The town is crawling with police. Not even the dark side streets are safe. Inside someplace. How long does it take to count to a million? I'm hungry. I want to hear Cody play.

"We'll use the house of a friend of mine. He's probably home and his street's quiet. Renata will ride with me, you follow and park where I do and bring in the suitcase."

Quinn felt a warm loathing for Max the lech, the fugitive dilettante in solitude, the running man as victim of his appetites, hung with unwieldy riches, pursued as an outlaw for having his face on the big screen.

"Being in that movie was pretty stupid, Max."

"The lure of the Rialto, my boy, the lure of the Rialto."

"You really think you belong on the Rialto, Max?"

"No, but I've always been addicted to it."

"What'll you do in Cuba?"

"Try to stay out of jail. After that I'll think of something else."

"You do know how to get to Canada."

"I do."

"We don't want your fifty thousand."

"Now that's truly absurd. It means nothing to me and you're broke."

"I'm bent, not broke, and that's all right. We don't want it."

"Suit yourself."

Quinn's friend, Jesse Franklin, a regular at Claudia's Better Streets group, lived on Philip Street with Malinda, his bride of six months, who spoke in hoarse whispers. Quinn had been at their wedding. Jesse was ninety, the son of a slave, built like a fence post, did back work all his life, the only work an illiterate was fit for, man of a thousand ailments, none of which impeded his drive toward self-improvement and the big one-oh-oh. He had just earned a certificate for perfect attendance at a night class in reading and writing. Malinda was his fifth wife. Three he buried and one ran off, but he kept accumulating, didn't want to live alone, first wife got so big with the water dropsy she couldn't move. They took forty-five pounds of water out of her one time, thirty-five pounds another. When Jesse saw her in the hospital she'd lost so much weight he didn't know her. Malinda was sixty with a game leg, and was, like Jesse, a regular at Better Streets meetings. They matched up and now survived on two dollars a day from Social Security, his welfare and her disability checks, and congenial love. Jesse opened the door to welcome Quinn.

"You see any riots around here tonight, Jess?"

"I told 'em go over to the next block if they need to riot."

Quinn explained Max was passing through, needed someplace quiet to take some medicine and change clothes before he got back on the road. "And I thought of your kitchen," Quinn said.

"My kitchen's your kitchen," Jesse said.

Quinn left Renata in the front room to entertain Jesse and his bride, then he closed the kitchen door and toted up with Max, who was right: the cash was in hundreds, marked and counted: nine hundred and the loose seventy thousand, very little room for shirts. Max put a shirt, socks and shaving gear into his briefcase. Quinn crammed Max's leftover shirts and socks into one of Jesse's paper bags. Max picked up two packs of fifty thousand, put one in his briefcase, and marked the other with a Q and handed it to Quinn, who hefted it, decided it felt like a pound of coffee. He pulled a hundred out from under the Q wrapper and dropped the pack back into the suitcase.

"This is for our use of the kitchen," he said to Max, who closed and locked the suitcase and gave Quinn the key. Quinn lifted the bag, heavier than a bowling ball. He left it for Max to carry and went to the living room.

"Many thanks for the use of the room, Jess. My friend is very grateful." He handed Jesse the folded bill.

Quinn kissed Malinda's hand and said thank you. Jesse unfolded the hundred, held it up to the light and said to Quinn, "He want that kitchen for the whole month this'll cover it."

"He's got other plans. I'll see you for lunch one of these days, Jess."

Quinn checked the street, nobody walking, nobody in any windows. He opened the trunk of his '59 Mercedes 220S and gestured to Max to bring the bag. Max lifted it in and Quinn spread his blanket over the treasure, which immediately began to pulsate and exude gamma rays.

"Where will you park it?" Max asked.

"That no longer concerns you, does it?"

"I suppose not."

"It's my problem. You have other problems."

"I'm incredibly grateful to both of you for this, and I mean that with every bone in my head. The fifty is yours, all yours, period, end of argument."

"That's unbelievable generosity," Renata said.

"Thanks but no thanks, Max," Quinn said.

"Call me if anything goes wrong," Renata said.

Max kissed her on the forehead, nodded at Quinn, and they watched him drive away.

"Where will you park it?" she asked.

"The old Albany Garage, just down from the DeWitt. In the twenties it was a drop for the Albany machine's bootleggers bringing booze from Canada. That's a nice bit of symmetry, don't you think, parking Max's contraband there while he slinks off to Canada? It also reminds me of riding in Diego's car with you after the Palace attack. You were driving and the car had a trunkful of guns. I thought you were a crazy lady. And I was right."

"But you fell in love with me."

"I'd already done that at the Floridita."

"And so did I."

"But then what happened?"

"We ran away."

"We eloped and got married and didn't have a honeymoon."

"We had a honeymoon before we got married."

"There was somebody else in the bed that night."

"He was dead."

"And somebody had beaten me to the bed when I caught up with you in Miami."

"Max is nothing to me, nothing!" She raised her voice on this one. "He saved my life! What is one night with him? It's like having a drink at the bar. It's *nada, nada, nada!*"

"That's why you're saving his ass and minding his hot money."

"*Coño*, Quinn, *coño*. You are *un bobo.*"

"Plus he gives you fifty thousand for his latest excursion into your pants."

"Do you know what fifty thousand is? Do you know what it could mean to us? Do you know how much money we do not have?"

"You command a high fee. But I didn't marry you for your money."

"Stop the car."

He stopped, half a block from the Albany Garage on a dark one-way street.

"*Lléname,*" she said. "Right now." She raised her skirt and pulled off her panties. She backed against the car door, spread herself. "You are so worried about fucking. Fuck me now."

"I haven't had my dinner yet," Quinn said.

He drove up the ramp into the garage, up to the seventh floor and parked near the stairs. There were no other cars on this level. Renata was still in position.

"What does your gesture mean, and this language? Is this a gesticulation toward intimacy? If I make the move is that a decree of irrevocable possession? Is your offer made in good faith or is it meant to change the subject?"

"I said in the hotel that I loved you. Did you hear me say that?"

"I did."

"I have not said that in a long time."

"Neither have I."

"Do you no longer love me?"

"It's very hard to say."

"Try to say it."

"I find it very difficult to love you."

"But do you?"

"Well, somehow, somehow, yes, though I often think of it as my misfortune."

"But it is love. You still know what love is. It is still love."

"Such as it is, it still seems to be love."

"Then show me your misfortune. This is a night like we have never had. You don't understand that yet, but I do. I see you more clearly than ever. I know you. Put your misfortune into me."

Quinn shifted his weight toward her and stared her down. "All right," he said, "but I'm not paying for this."

They were nine at a table for eight, the chicken dinners of all but Roy in shreds and bones, and two new bottles of wine and another round for the Schlitz drinkers were on the table, ordered by Quinn. George and Vivian, Matt and Martin, then Tremont straggled in, Roy and Gloria arrived half an hour later, and Quinn and Renata finally returned after their disappearance, but without Max. Cody was at the piano, and he paused to say now he wanted to do a piece he'd written and recorded in memory of Fats Waller. He called it "Blues for Fats," who was a brilliant musician and funny and lived to play, too hard, played around the clock and kept going, dead at thirty-nine from an overdose of life. Cody had started this tune as an improvisation of what he'd felt about the man, then kept it going like Fats at a party, meditating on his early death and the depth of his talent, keeping it slow; but the piece got longer, eight choruses, right hand wailing melancholy arpeggios in the high register, Fats liked Bach, and then a last low chord and fade, the way Fats did. Cody stood up from the piano and the applause was wild, long, real, and it put a smile on his face that did not fade. He said he was going to cool out but he'd be back.

Mike Flanagan and his group moved back in, launched "If I Could Be with You" and people danced. Cody tried table-hopping to thank his roomful of friends but at the second table he felt weak and had to sit. Roy went to his table and touched his shoulder. Cody grabbed his hand and stood and gripped his arm. "You got out," Cody said, and his smile grew larger as they moved to a corner where Roy gave his father the news.

"I'm surprised you're here," Matt said when Roy came back to the table. "You had a rough night."

"This is Cody's night. I thought I'd miss him."

"What'd they charge you with?"

"Participating in a riot. The lawyer says they want me for inciting riot, that I told those guys at the Four Spot the cops had shotguns but I could get them guns to fight back."

"I was there. I didn't hear you say that."

"Albany cops do their thing. In the last eight months they busted all ten members of the Brothers' Council, me and Ben twice, and we both did time. Not one of the charges was worth a damn and most of them were thrown out, but they keep it up. Harass those mothers and maybe they'll go away."

"Maybe they confused you with Zuki. He could've come up with some guns."

"That son of a bitch has a lot to answer for."

"I gave him an act of penance down on Bleecker Street. I bloodied his nose. He was giving heat to Tremont."

"Best news I heard all day."

"Did you hear Tremont broke up a riot on Bleecker Street?" Quinn asked Roy.

"I heard he misbehaved," Roy said.

"Whites in cars came through with Molotovs and got trapped, people hacking, kicking one another, knives, wrecked cars, two or three houses on fire, and then Tremont walks out of the alley, unwraps his AR-15 and bang bangety bang—'Enough,' Tremont says, and the riot falls apart. People run off, cops arrive, not much left for them to do, but they arrest a dozen and carry off the wounded. I think Tremont saved lives. The AR-15 is his musical instrument of choice. You can't predict Tremont. At the First Church he serenaded the protesters with 'Coon, Coon, Coon, I Wish My Color Would Fade.'"

"I remember that," Martin said. "Nineteen-oh-one. A huge hit."

George sang the second line:

"Coon, coon, coon, I want a different shade . . ."

"We don't have to sing it, Pop," Quinn said. "I thought they'd strangle Tremont so I got him out quicktime."

"They wouldn'ta strangled me," Tremont said.

"You never know with liberals. I wasn't taking chances."

"Why'd you sing that, Tremont?" Roy asked.

"I'm sick of them songs about overcomin'. What we gotta do is change color. We'd fit in better. Wouldn't need no segregation."

"You're a clown, Tremont, but you can't do that old shit, tommin' the crowd, scratchin' your head."

"'Man in the Moon Is a Coon,'" Tremont said. "'Shine,' 'All Coons Look Alike to Me.'"

"Right," said Roy. "Deep trash."

"My daddy made a career singin' those tunes. That's the way it was."

"Long gone."

"You ever hear the Mills Brothers and Bing Crosby do 'Shine'?" Quinn asked.

"Doesn't matter. You can't shine shit."

Cody had been listening to the talk, standing behind Roy.

"I recorded 'Shine' with Count Basie," he said, pulling a chair next to Roy.

"I heard you do it with Crosby when I was a kid," Quinn said. "It was great."

"When Bing and the Mills Brothers sing it it's a joke. Always was. And the joke's on the guy who calls you shine."

"All right," Roy said, "all right. If Cody does it it's all right."

"Cody's all right," Tremont said, "but my daddy's shit you can't shine."

"Not your daddy, Tremont, the coon, the coon. Je-zus."

"Satchmo sang 'Shine,'" Tremont said.

"Satchmo," Roy said. "He smiles a whole lot for white people."

"Ella sang 'Shine,'" Cody said. "So did Django."

"Hey, Roy," Quinn said. "What happened to your sense of humor? Tremont was putting everybody on. That song is so far out it's anti-racist."

"Coons aren't funny," Roy said. "All that coon stuff is rat shit. Flush it all."

"How about shines?" Cody said.

"Oh, man, oh, man," Roy said, and he twisted in his chair to face Gloria.

"Don't get excited, Roy," she said. "Tonight's important, don't fight with your father."

"Damn," Roy said, "it's so nice you're here. But I don't want you here. I want you someplace else. We'll blow this joint."

"To go where?"

"Someplace quiet."

The father and son squabbling over the coon factor crystallized a musical lineage for Quinn—the slaves singing, dancing, cakewalking in their Pinkster revels, whites imitating them by blackening up as minstrels and turning it all into a theatrical phenomenon that would last more than a century, blacks then blackening their blackness and creating their own minstrel stage—mocking the white imitation of their cakewalk and the white-black argot, and filling theaters; Big Jim making the leap from sideshow minstrel to black theater and he's along for the ride when the slave song and dance (and the coon factor) arrive on Broadway, a long walk from slavery. Bert Williams is Broadway's black megastar as a singing blackface shuffler, Al Jolson is a white Broadway megastar in blackface, Satchmo, the ragtime genius trumpeter sings to the world in his arcane language of scat, and ragtime turns into jazz, a word Satchmo never liked. Bing Crosby and the Mills Brothers learn scat from Satchmo and rock the world with "Shine" and "Dinah." Fats, another smiling clown and musical wizard, discovers Cody Mason plays fine piano, and Cody emerges into jazz, formerly ragtime, first accompanist and early lover of Billie Holiday, the great-granddaughter of a slave: how those slaves do rise. Cody sees all these connections, understands where he came from, and how he got here, understands also that Roy now wants to obliterate this matrix that created his father and himself; and Cody quietly implodes.

But he changes the subject and says to Quinn, "It was great you got that lawyer. Roy called me about being busted, said he might get out on bail but didn't know how much. Next thing, he taps me on the shoulder. You and Max make things happen."

"Some things you can do so you do them. How are you and your lungs doing after all that exercise?"

"I'm holding. Didn't fall over."

"Bit of a generation gap here with Roy."

"He's in a hurry to forget things."

"You don't want to forget."

"It's so tough to get anyplace, you got to remember the moves. Big Jimmy, he was no coon. He owned that routine, turned it inside out, giant tapdancer, the singing shine, and he made it pay. He played coon like I play piano and he got someplace way beyond Coontown. He was big and he got bigger, he had clout. He opened that club and he took me in when I left New York. We blew a whole lot of jazz in his place and I turned a corner and down the road I got my own club."

"What happened that you lost that record date in New York missing a train?"

"Didn't miss any train. I cut a record with Brunswick, one session, eight tunes. I was going down to do eight more and then weed out the dogs, but the Brunswick big boys didn't like my first takes. John Hammond calls me leavin' the house, says you gotta know this, Sonny. They don't want a second session, I'm sorry. So I missed the train."

What they didn't like was Cody's timing—a little off on two cuts, speeded up, then fell back, but he'd been playing alone for months, no rhythm backup, could've been fixed, just give him a drummer. But he also blinked a few notes on two or three cuts, that won't do. You had to be Art Tatum to sell solo piano records. They put a label on Sonny because he's a little off one day, and it dogs him, and he's at the bar and meets these cats comin' through and they say, Here, Sonny, have a few, and they slip him some. He goes to his room and there's a knock on the door, what are you doin', man? I'm having a good time, he says, and they take him to the judge and somebody says he's a dope pusher. I'm no pusher, judge, I was just way down and I met these cats and they gave me a few. Three months. My old gal Billie died a junkie. Cops busted her for possession and all she had was eighty-seven cents. Forty-four-year-old queen of the damn world with eighty-seven cents.

"Your 'Blues for Fats' was very fine. You recorded it?"

"New record coming this month. Hank O'Neal put it together."

"I should write a piece on that. Anybody recording this concert?"

"I think Hank's got it covered."

Vivian reached across the table and touched Cody's arm. "Cody, George has a request. When you go back to play could you do a waltz? George was a prize waltzer. Do you play waltzes?"

"For Georgie, sure I do." And Cody went to the piano and welcomed all waltzers with "All Alone," "When I Lost You," and "Remember," Cody in a sentimental mood.

George walked Vivian onto the floor and said, after we leave here I want to go to Van Woert Street and show you the trophies I won for waltzing. We'll go tomorrow, Vivian said, and George guided her into his prize-winning moves, dancing on the balls of his feet, heels never touching the floor, because the judge puts straight pins in your heels and if you bend a pin you're out. He put the back of his hand on the lady's back (Vivian, is it?) so any sweat from his hand would not stain her dress, and he did his turns, the open strides, the reverses, which are always difficult and for some people impossible, but if you can't reverse you're out. He moved Vivian into the open rolls—toward her left, then her right—and holding her right hand with his left he circles backward, Vivian right with him, some things you do not forget, and after all she'd waltzed with George before, that night at Electric Park. George breaks, turns, recaptures and spins her, alone, then spins himself also to the rhythm of Cody's brisk pacing, and they reunite with graceful ease in each other's open arms; and on they glide across the floor, the stars of the evening.

At the table Renata put her hand on Quinn's. "Your father is a wonderful dancer," she said. "And Vivian reminds me of Ginger Rogers, with an extra twenty-five pounds."

"He always said he danced better than Fred Astaire. My grandmother would always say, 'You're a damn fool.'"

"Dance with me," Renata said.

"To a waltz?"

"I know the waltz. I didn't like dancing but I learned it. My mother was a prize waltzer."

"Ah, yes, so she was."

Cody segued into "Shine" in waltz tempo (Quinn had never heard it played this way) and did three choruses, then jumped to another beat, which Quinn's feet translated into a fox-trot. Cody stayed with "Shine" (making a statement are we?) and now Quinn realized this would be one of Cody's epiphanies, when he takes dominion over a song, enters it, owns it, transforms it. Quinn stopped dancing and moved with Renata nearer to the piano to watch Cody's hands, those long right middle fingers so straight, pointing the way into a serial revelation of what the song could become. Then Cody dropped in a new phrase, "I Ain't Got Nobody," not the tune, just the first four bars and he moved on, slowly, deep left-handed chords challenging the right, which rose to it with resonance, major to minor, very educated. There was beauty in his ease, his sureness, no clunked notes tonight, and he switches keys and ups the tempo, just a little, and ba-boom goes that left hand, the power of it, he's on a ride, six choruses and counting, feel that beat, beat, beat, that goddamn beat, this is stride on high, stride the way it's supposed to be, brilliant invention, the poor guy can't help himself, smothering the song with his gift, exploding it, and Quinn's pulse is up and cantering, those left-handed arpeggios, the glissando that surprises, and he notches the speed upward, I Ain't Got, eight choruses and the left takes over, the right playing catch-up, and they level at a gallop, Cody humming his zum-zums now and Quinn counts and discovers the man is using twelve fingers, the left six doing that resonant bounce and the right a syncopated strut—how that Cody Mason does strut. He's into his tenth chorus and running off limits into a double-and-a-half-time free-for-all, you can't stop him, a driving two-note beat and both hands racing, right foot on the pedal, left foot keeping time with the universe, zum-zum za-za-zum-zum he's a one-man band I Ain't Got it's a horserace between the hands and now Quinn counts fifteen fingers Cody kidnapped this piano and there's no more dancing, no feet can move this fast, the crowd is cheering, applauding every breakaway they could never have imagined and Cody is burning, a man on fire with maniacal speed, inhuman precision, colossal invention—oh, yes, I Ain't Got—and he coughs, he coughs, and he pauses, hits two chords with his left hand, one with his right, he stops.

The End.

He pulls his white silk handkerchief out of his lapel pocket and coughs into it, and everybody is standing, applauding, sending up screeches, cheers, hoots of joy and other eruptions that are rejoicings of what they can't utter, salutes to the ineffable. Cody gets it, and he plunges his hand into his coat pocket, gripping the handkerchief. Quinn glimpses blood on it. Cody holds on to the piano, smiles at everybody, shakes his head to tell them it's too much, he can't stand it, but on and on goes the applause and Cody still has that smile. He can't get rid of that smile. He always wears a smile. That's why they call him Shine.

❖

At the table Martin said, "That was a marvelous performance. He doesn't play like a dying man."

"No, but he's goin'," Tremont said. "Got a couple of months, what I hear."

Roy and Gloria left the table to talk to Cody, and Roy told him the playing was fantastic and the song was not bad, since it didn't have any words. Cody gave him a triumphal smile and they shook hands. Gloria said they were going to feed Roy since he didn't get any dinner. Quinn said he'd talk to the kitchen and get him dinner, but Gloria said he wants pizza, and Renata said, Daniel, *no quieren comer.* Renata told Gloria, "Don't you stay out all night, you're still convalescing." Gloria said of course and kissed her aunt and made a kiss mouth at Quinn.

At the table Matt asked Tremont where he was staying tonight. "You still have that place you had with Mary?"

"I got it but I don't go there anymore. Rats ate the bed."

"You have money?"

"Dollar and a quarter."

"That's not even enough for a flop. Last night you slept on that stoop."

"Won't do that again."

"I thought tonight you'd be in the hospital, or in jail."

"Missed out on both," Tremont said.

"So where can you stay?"

"I got friends. Mighta stayed with Rosie but they're knockin' down her house. Maybe the mission, if they got a bed, maybe the bus station. I'll be all right. It's warm, if it don't rain."

Quinn and Renata came back to the table on that line.

"What about the Corine Hotel, you stayed there," Quinn said.

"They make you pay."

"How much, ten, fifteen?"

"Like twenty."

"If you're in the Corine a few days, a week, can you get yourself together? Claudia wants you in rehab and that's a good idea."

"Oh, yeah. I'm good. Corine, rehab, I need that."

The concert crowd was thinning out, George and Vivian came back to the table and Quinn said quietly to Matt, "I can't take him, I've got a carful. Can you grab a cab and get him installed? I'll give you two hundred, get him a room for a week and give him maybe twenty for walking-around money. Hold on to the rest, or maybe you need it yourself."

"I need it. I have a dollar and a quarter less than Tremont. I can't pay for the room I rented here for tonight."

"All right I'll cover that and you keep the change of the cash. You're really not going back to campus tonight?"

"Really am not."

"Is this how you abdicate sainthood? Don't you have to turn in your robe?"

"I'll send it to the cleaners. I'll go through the tribunals, whatever is necessary. But I'm history."

"You're the life and death of the world in twenty-five words or less."

"Less. What's all this cash? Where did you get money to burn?"

"I hit the number, but I left the envelope in the car. I'll get it and meet you at the hotel's Eagle Street entrance in ten minutes."

Quinn told Renata about the money and where he was meeting Matt.

"You didn't want the money," she said, "but now you're Santa Claus with it."

"Consider it short-term borrowing. Max can take me as a tax deduction."

"It's not Max's money. It's mine, and yours."

"Not yet."

Quinn was now acutely conscious of the precise amount of money in his trunk. Corporations rise and fall on less. Max couldn't need that much to get into Cuba. He's got fifty-plus in his briefcase; send him another hundred and that's big money. Fidel will let him in for that. Won't he?

For a hundred, yes, Quinn decided. He would hold that much for pickup whenever by Max or his messenger. He'd stash it, safe deposit, maybe; that amount was finessable. Also he'd keep Renata's fifty. But the rest was too much—seven hundred and fifty thousand and change. Quinn needed to give that to somebody, someplace, where it would do some good.

This was precipitous, giving Max's cash away even before he's in Canada; but depriving him of three quarters of a million was a satisfying prospect. Would Max react like most humans, with rage and revenge against Quinn? No. He's dying, and too blasé. Money never meant much to him. It was only a means of moving with the high life on whose fringe he was always scrambling. All right, maybe a hundred isn't enough; give him back Renata's fifty. She doesn't need it. She only wants it. It was fast money as it came to Max; if it vanishes it's fast in the other direction.

Give the money to Matt and let him found a new order: the Church of the Benevolent Dollar. He'd give it all away in six months. And you're ready to give it away in three hours, Quinn.

Give it to Tremont? Instant disaster. The police would pull him in and do what they do so well with drug money: make it disappear.

Claudia and Better Streets? She'd spread it around, also buy a new house, new furniture, and everybody would see her sudden wealth as drug-related, which it would be.

Give it to the Brothers? That would really contaminate them—just what the machine wants. They'd sink forever as dealers.

Leave it on the street in front of Hapsy's and let it be a random find. If Trixie got to it first it would go into her bank vault and seduce her into early retirement, and Albany would never see a nickel.

Keep it yourself, Quinn, have a broker invest it, obliquely, even secretly; become, simultaneously, a philanthropist and a financial criminal. No. And no hiding it in walls, or banks, or underground, except for the hundred. Even that's a major risk. And, hey, your fingerprints are all over the cash and the suitcase; so are Max's, and who knows who else's? Face it: it's a goddamn worthless treasure.

"Daniel," Martin said, standing up from his chair, surveying the racially mixed stragglers, "what happened to this hotel? I'm surprised they booked this party. I've been coming here since they opened in 1926 and they always barred Negroes. They rejected Marian Anderson and Paul Robeson."

"Satchmo too," Quinn said. "I interviewed him in 1956 at the Kenmore when he was here to play the Palace. He was a world celebrity but no major hotel in this town would give him a room. Mixed parties here now? I suppose it's token time. But upstairs is still lily-white."

Quinn parked in front of Vivian's flat and put on his blinkers, turned off the car. George and Vivian were in the backseat and he said, "Pop, we're here."

"Where?"

"Vivian's house."

"Vivian? Vivian who?"

"Vivian me," Vivian said, and she grabbed George's face in her fingers and turned it close to her own. "Your date for the evening, one of your old girlfriends. It's time to go home, George."

"Then let's go."

"Yes, let's."

"Where do we go?"

"Here."

"Here? Where are we?"

"Columbia Street. The Court House is up a block, the Kenmore's down a block, and I live there, right up that stoop."

"God bless you. Columbia Street is a wonderful street. I was born on this street."

"Say good night to Vivian, Pop," Quinn said.

"Good night, Vivian."

"Good night, George. I had a lovely time."

"That's wonderful."

Quinn got out of the car and opened Vivian's door and took her hand. He walked behind her up the stairs. She found her keys.

"He was on his way to Beauman's dance hall when I met him near the Court House," she said. "Beauman's closed years ago. We both went there when we were young and dancing our way toward romance, maybe even marriage. I could see George was young again and a bit of the sheik, like the old days. But he had that cracked memory. Then at the Kenmore he was hit on the head by flying glass and you should've heard him talk."

"I've been hearing him all night," Quinn said. "It's a miracle. He resurrected memories that were gone forever, that he had no license to bring back. He got lost on State Street and was navigating among strangers, and then he bumped into you. Whatever you did, Vivian, it thrilled him. He doesn't know my name or his mother's name—'I'd have to go to the book for that's how he gets around it. But his mind cleared and there he was, walking the streets with a lovely woman, which indeed you are, Vivian, and he was again the old George Quinn out on the town."

"That's so nice, Daniel, but it wasn't me who did it."

"You had a great deal to do with it."

"He seems to be losing it again."

"He's had quite a bit to drink and that may be it. Or not. But what happened was spectacular—that singing and dancing George of yesterday was back, a resurrection, and nobody can tell me that it didn't nourish his soul, whether he remembers it or not. You can't write him off. If he can sing he's still up to snuff someplace in that threadbare brain of his. He'll have a new angle of vision on life tomorrow, whether he knows it or not, thanks to what he went through with you today."

"Oh, I hope so," Vivian said. "He was so alive. We were both very happy."

"We'll get you together again, Vivian, but however much he learned today, he might not know you next time."

"I'll make him remember," Vivian said.

"I'm sure he looks forward to that, even though he doesn't know what he's looking forward to."

George opened the car door and stepped onto Vivian's sidewalk. Renata opened her door. "Do you want something, George?"

"Look at that," he said, and he pointed at the Court House and traced a line across the night sky full of stars.

"What, George? The street? The sky? What?"

"What," George said, "what." He looked at Quinn and Vivian on the stoop, and he sang:

"What's that, who am I? Don'tcha know that I'm the guy,
I'm the guy that put the foam on lager beer."

He poked himself in the chest with his thumb:

"I'm the guy that put the salt in the ocean,
I'm the guy that put the leaves on trees.
What's that, who am I, don'tcha know that I'm the guy,
I'm the guy that bites the holes in Switzer cheese.
I'm the guy who put the hole in the donut,
I'm the guy who put the bones in fish.
What's that, who am I? Don'tcha know that I'm the guy,
In the wishbone I'm the guy who put the wish."

"Good night, Georgie, dear," Vivian said.

"Good night, young lady. The breath of me heart to you."

"Oh, my," Vivian said. "Oh, my."

❖

Quinn pulled the car into the garage and opened the side door to the house with his key and let George and Renata enter, up the stairs to the kitchen. He locked the door after them and padlocked the garage. He went to the front door to check the mailbox, tucked the letters between the pages of a magazine, picked up the *Knickerbocker News* inside the vestibule door, and opened the inner door with his key. George was standing in the living room with his hat on.

"Home the same day," George said.

"Actually it's the next day," Quinn said. "It's after one o'clock—already tomorrow. Take off your hat and stay awhile."

George took off his hat and set it atop the bridge lamp. Quinn lit the lamp and took the hat off it. He put the mail on the coffee table and hung his coat and George's hat on the coatrack in the dining room. He saw George's bandage and asked, "Does your head hurt?"

"Not at all. Should it?"

"Not if you don't think so. How are you feeling, are you ready for bed?"

George nodded. "Early to bed, early to rise, your girl goes out with two other guys."

"Wisdom on the hoof."

Renata came from the kitchen. "You want anything?" she asked.

"I'll have a nightcap, rum on the rocks with a splash," Quinn said. "Have one yourself."

"Did you enjoy your day on the town?" she asked George.

"There was a facsimile about it that was very comfortable."

"I'm glad you liked it. It was nice having Vivian as part of it."

"Vivian."

"You remember Vivian?"

"I'd have to go to the book."

"She was your dancing partner tonight."

"That was Paggy. Pog."

"You're thinking of Peg," Quinn said.

"Peg."

"Peg Phelan. Margaret. You married her. Your wife, Peg."

"Peg was a wonderful girl. She danced every dance. She was strong but not tough."

"What does that mean—not tough?"

"Good and honest. She wouldn't let anybody cut in."

"Do you remember how you asked her to marry you?"

"Why do you ask such a question?"

"I never heard you talk about marrying her. I always wondered how it happened."

"Don't you love your girl, for chrissake?"

"I do."

"I let her down, but she still comes around to love what's left of me. I have no room in my heart for the blues."

"That's a fine attitude. Do you remember that Peg was my mother?"

"Was she? God bless you." He stared at Quinn, a long silence.

"Do you remember?"

He nodded. He looked at Renata and back to Quinn. "You were the one and only one that come to us. You were my doll."

"I'm glad I got here."

George looked around the room. "You can't beat this hotel. Everything here is very katish."

"We do our best. We're pleased you're staying here. I think it's bedtime."

"Bedtime," George said. "There's always room for one more." He found his hat and went up the stairs. Renata went to the kitchen.

Quinn turned on the television and found a Bobby Kennedy retrospective, but no new news about his condition on any station. He went back to the retrospective—Bobby having his clothes ripped off like a rock star in the campaign for president. The crowd loved every inch of him. "We want Kennedy," they screamed. Quinn turned off the volume and let the images continue.

He sat on the sofa and looked at the mail: a letter from his publisher suggesting a schedule for publicizing his novel, signings at two local bookstores, a radio interview in New York, three local radio interviews, all of which add up to no push, no weight. So the book will develop momentum by itself, or it won't. Also, a letter from the Albany County Sheriff to George Quinn, dated yesterday. In terse sentences the sheriff notified George that as of May 15, 1968, he had been taken off the payroll and his service in the Sheriff's Office and the courts was terminated. George had not gone to work since his two cataract operations three months ago. He'd been in his slow fade for some months, who can count, but Quinn blamed the general anaesthesia the doctor gave him for its acceleration. The operation had begun with a milder sedative but it didn't sedate, and George kicked a nurse when someone touched his eye. The operations were a success but the patient went senile.

His weekly paycheck had arrived punctually until two weeks ago, a harbinger, and not really unreasonable after three months; but this belated letter had an edge to it: after the ejection of Martin Daugherty from the Ann Lee Home we have the ejection of George Quinn, both coinciding with the decision by the Democratic politicians to punish Matt and Quinn, a pair of pains in the ass, by punishing their fathers. The district attorney had smiled at Quinn yesterday in a corridor at the Court House and said cryptically but jovially, "You forgot your father." Quinn the reporter should have considered the fallout before publishing all that slum blather against the Mayor and the Party.

Renata came into the parlor bearing solace, two rums on the rocks, extra ice, and the bottle of Bacardi dark from Puerto Rico, where the distillery had relocated after Fidel won the war. Quinn watched her move and saw in her all the elements he had always loved; also saw another creature with no resemblance to the original: a chameleon, duplicitous, schizoid. But you bought into it, Quinn. Yes, but how could I have understood such shape-shifting when I was under the influence of the simple declarative sentence? The simple declarative sentence is an illusion.

"Did I put too much water?"

"Not at all," said Quinn, tasting.

"What's the mail?"

"I have a useless book tour ahead of me, and George has been fired."

"Why?"

"Why is the book tour useless or why George?"

"George."

"He's overdue at the office and he can't think or function or even find the Court House without a guide. It was inevitable. They've been kind to George even though they think they're punishing me by firing him. We lose his $34.50. How can we possibly live without it?"

"They did the same thing to Matt's father."

"You are perspicacious. We hurt them, they hurt us. I decided to write a novel about it."

"About George being fired?"

"About him, Matt and Martin, Tremont, Roy, Zuki, you, me, the Mayor, Gloria and Max, and on it goes. No end to the cast of characters."

"Do you want a refill?"

"The last time I refused a drink. Did you hear Martin and Pop talking about World War One tonight?"

"Bits."

"Pop always told World War stories, also his father's stories—from the Civil War, and riding with the ragtag Fenians, and with those ex-slaves fighting Spaniards in Cuba. But he was only eight when his father died, and he never sorted out the specifics of any of those wars."

"So your new novel is about George?"

"More about you than George."

"I'm not worth a novel."

"You're worth two or three novels. I have to put Tremont in it too. He's worth two or three novels. If I wrote your story would you be afraid of it?"

"You don't know my story."

"I know quite a lot."

"I'm not afraid of what you know."

"You should be."

"Your own imagination is all you know."

"It is a novel, after all. I'd have to write about our reunion at the Fontainebleau, that lovely mobbed-up luxury."

"That was Alfie. Max asked him about a hotel on the Beach and Alfie made a call to one of his friends."

"I knew that. Alfie also set up your flight out of Havana—your cousin Holtz again to the rescue. But back then I knew nothing about what was going on."

But when Quinn walked into the suite at the Fontainebleau, he knew everything. He called the front desk and asked for another suite; can't have your honeymoon on somebody else's hot mattress. Max had abdicated and Renata was now a bleached blonde (under that occasional blond wig), free of Batista and Robles, and reunited with this new arrival, the husband Quinn, but unable to hear anything he said. She stepped into her bridal lingerie, crotchless, and from the moment they touched in the new bed she delivered every element of passion in her repertoire, spoke to him in the language of love she had been learning since puberty, and convinced him that he was all there was in the world for her, that they'd be together forever, nothing could separate them, she would die before leaving him, and yes, he felt blessed in reclaiming her, possessing her in their new bed was a union beyond loving—it was consummation.

And, yes, they would continue forever, beginning here and into a second day, sixteen hours of love and food and sleep and rum and more love. He would repeat in memory every phone call to airlines, police, hospitals, friends, the investigation that failed. But Max hadn't failed. He'd found her through a Brazilian diplomat and launched the rescue without calling Quinn or Renata's family (who knew where she was and told no one—out of fear for her). Quinn had actually called the Brazilian embassy and two dozen others: My wife is lost, are you giving her asylum? No, *señor*, call the police. Max sent her an exit package: foofy blond wig, white dress, white heels, white sunglasses (did Max know how partial the adepts of Santeria were to white clothing?) and told her to wear them tomorrow. He arrived at the embassy with Alfie's friend Inez, who was wearing the same wig, white dress, heels, and shades, and ten minutes later Max left the embassy with Renata, the white simulacrum, while Inez changed into black for her departure.

"It may be I've been seducing Max since I met him, my dress too low with that young cleavage. I can't blame him for coming at me if I did that, but I don't love him, I repeat, *I do not love Max*. He's gone to Cuba forever and we have his money and I don't want his love. I'm sorry it wasn't you who rescued me from villains, Daniel. I'm sorry."

Quinn mixed a second nightcap for himself and Renata. She exuded calm, poise, a notable achievement in restoration after the Albany Garage, where they had gone at each other in a bout of brief, savage, self-vindicating sex and ended breathless, sweating, and temporarily purged.

"When did you first think about leaving me?"

"I got bored, Daniel."

"I asked you when not why."

"You were bored too. *El ladrón juzga por su condición.* Takes one to know one. We had never talked about ending it."

"Easy. You pack your lingerie and go. I keep the house, you take the nine hundred thousand."

"But that was yesterday. Today we have a second chance."

"What happened today?"

"I decided you were behaving like an Orisha."

"Changó?"

"Something like that. Subverting things. Throwing bombshells."

"Who, me? I'm a reporter."

"Matt said you were writing a bombshell tonight. And you wrote one about him yesterday."

"I was doing a serious, far-out story on Tremont, but they wouldn't print it."

"That was the assassination plot, no? Matt told us."

"The editors said they didn't believe it, but really they were afraid of it."

"Then that was a Changó story."

"If so then Tremont was Changó. He was the one with the thunderbolts. I watched it happen and took some notes I can't use. I'll have to put them in the new novel."

"Then it will be a Changó novel."

Quinn saw new activity on the television screen and he turned up the volume. Frank Mankiewicz, Bobby's press secretary, spoke into a microphone: "Senator Robert F. Kennedy died at 1:44 a.m. today, June 6, 1968. With Senator Kennedy at the time of his death were his wife, Ethel, his sisters Mrs. Stephen Smith and Mrs. Patricia Lawford, his brother-in-law Mr. Stephen Smith, and his sister-in-law Mrs. John F. Kennedy. He was forty-two years old."

Mankiewicz stepped away from the microphone.

The phone rang. Quinn looked at Renata who did not move. He answered in the dining room and Renata turned down the TV.

"Dan?"

"Doc."

"Your niece Gloria's in the burn unit at Albany Hospital, so is Roy Mason. Very bad fire."

"Wait a minute, Doc." Quinn gestured with the phone for Renata to listen. She stood beside him. "Go on, Doc. Gloria and Roy you were saying."

"They were in Roy's apartment on Van Woert Street. The whole house is gone. Man on the third floor died, firemen couldn't get inside to save him. His room didn't have any windows. Joe Crowley told me heavy flames were already going up the front and back stairs when they got there, and the Engine Two firehouse is only three and a half blocks away. Gloria and Roy went out a second-floor window with blankets, and the fall hurt them both. Dan?"

"I'm here."

"They're burned pretty good. Roy couldn't talk. And they got some smoke."

"Doc, the fire was set?"

"Too soon to say. And you know I can't say that out loud."

"But that's what you think. You."

"When you find fire in two separate places in one house . . ."

"Are you at the hospital?"

"I just got here."

"Wait for me if you can. I'm out the door right now with Renata."

"Listen, Dan, I saw them both. They're hurt and they're burned, but they're not dead. I'm telling you what I saw."

"Does Cody know about this?"

"No."

"You got his number?"

"I'll get somebody on it."

"Things have changed, Doc."

"Yes, they have. Look both ways at the crosswalk."

George came down the stairs wearing his navy blue gabardine suit with a gray felt fedora, a solid gray tie, and his gray shoes with the black cap toe: the full dude.

"I heard the bell ring," he said. "Are we ready?"

"That was a phone call, Pop. We've got to go out."

"We're going to the club?"

"Not tonight. Maybe tomorrow. I have to go somewhere, but I can't take you along."

"I'll stay with George," Renata said. "We can't leave him."

"You've got to see Gloria."

"I'll see her. I'll have Ursula take a cab and stay here tonight. She won't have to do any work, just take care of him. He does what she tells him. She can make a pot of tea with one arm. I'll pay her double. It's more important for you to be there if anything needs to be done, things I wouldn't know how to do. I'll join you as soon as she gets here."

"That's good on Ursula."

"You should do something with that money. You can't ride around with it."

"I'll do something."

❖

Quinn, using a flashlight in his dark garage, its door closed, opened Max's suitcase in the trunk of his car, separated a hundred and fifty thousand of wrapped cash, and put it in the cloth sack where he kept his road maps. He went down the garage's interior stairs to the cellar and put the sack on a low shelf beside his electric saw. He found two soft rags and went back up to the garage and rubbed all fingerprints off the exterior and interior of the suitcase. He then did the same to the two top layers of the bundled cash. He had never touched the bottom layers. Max had. He closed and locked the suitcase and the car's trunk, opened the sliding garage door, and backed the car out into the driveway. He got out and padlocked the garage, and then he got back behind the wheel and headed down Pearl Street toward the war zone.

He turned onto Van Woert Street to see the burned-out house. The once-Irish street was now mostly black. Two walls had partially collapsed into rubble and spilled into the street, which was wet and blocked by traffic cones. The ruin was three houses away from where George Quinn had been raised by the Galvins, cousins from Clonmel, after his parents died in the '95 train wreck. The Galvin house was a three-storied twin of the burned house, the Galvins long gone from Van Woert.

Quinn had met them as a child, making the rounds with George as he collected or delivered numbers money; but George fell out with them in the late '30s over an unpaid gambling debt. Quinn last visited the house in 1945 when he was a high school senior and went to pick up belongings George had left there in a steamer trunk thirty years earlier.

Quinn called Ben Galvin, who worked in the paint gang at the West Albany railroad shops, and was the only cousin left on Van Woert Street. Ben found the trunk in the attic, where George thought it might be, and there it sat in Ben's parlor, open and empty.

"What's he want with the trunk?" Ben asked Quinn.

"He doesn't want the trunk. He wants the trophies he won in dancing contests, six of them. We talked about them last night. He said his patent leather dancing shoes and a tuxedo were also here."

"None of them things were in it," said Ben. "Only this stuff," and he pointed to two books lying on top of a packet wrapped in brown paper and tied with cord, and a thick scrapbook jammed with folded newspapers. "Paper is all it is. Paper. That's the lot."

Quinn untied the cord and opened the packet: a manuscript written in ink on linen rag paper. He read the first line. "I, Daniel Quinn, neither the first nor the last of a line of such Quinns . . . " The scrapbook was fat with newspaper clippings about Civil War battles, about Fenian troops on horseback moving from Albany toward Canada in 1866, about Custer's defeat at Little Big Horn. The cloth bindings of both books had been slit and hung loose when Quinn picked them up: *The Personal Memoirs of General Philip H. Sheridan*, 1888, and *Going to See the Hero* by Daniel Quinn, 1872. Ben bent over to watch Quinn's hands closely as he handled the books.

"You knew about these?"

"Pop thought there were books here but he didn't remember what they were. My grandfather was a writer. This is his," and he held up the *Hero* book.

"Can't be worth much," Ben said. "Sixty, seventy years old."

The dance trophies couldn't have been worth much either and were probably pawned long ago, along with the tux and shoes. Quinn smoothed the cloth binding of the *Hero*'s spine. He could glue it.

"I heard of this book but I never knew we might have it," he said.

Quinn guessed Ben had cut the bindings, searching for hidden money. And he thinks it may still be in there someplace and that I know how to get at it.

"So that's it?" Quinn said.

"I should charge him rent for keepin' it here thirty years."

"How much rent would that be?"

"I'm not that kind of guy," Ben said.

Quinn, behind the wheel, stared at the Galvin house, measuring the odyssey that the *Hero* book had set in motion: a career in news and fiction that would deliver him into the Hemingway orbit, which would lead to the perpetual revolution and Renata, Max, Fidel, Tremont, Matt, others, and ultimately, now, back to George Quinn and the Galvin house. Next stop: the hospital burn unit, and the two latest casualties of this perpetual revolution.

❖

"George," said Renata after Quinn's departure and her call to Ursula, "take off your hat. We're not going out anymore. It's a handsome hat. Very stylish."

"I had a hat when I came in."

He set his hat on top of the bridge lamp. Renata lifted it off and hung it on the coatrack. They sat on opposite ends of the sofa.

"I loved what you said to Daniel when he asked you about Peg. You said, 'Don't you love your girl, for chrissake?'"

"I said that?"

"You did. It was a wonderful answer."

"All compliments gratefully accepted."

"I'll bet you had a lot of girls in the old days."

"There were a few in the shirt factory."

"You said Daniel was your only child. You said he was the only one who came to you."

"Daniel. Is he the one who owns this place?"

"That's the one."

"He's a very nice fella. He could lick his weight in gold."

"You said he was your doll."

George considered that.

"My doll." He paused. "The boy."

"Daniel Quinn. Your son."

"He was a wonder, smart as a cracker. Shot a hole in one when he was twelve with the driver I gave him."

"He's my husband."

"Is that so? I didn't know. He'll be a good husband."

"Yes, he will. But we haven't had any children. We've had no dolls of our own."

"Children come when they want to."

"Daniel wants to be a father, but we haven't been able to make that happen."

"If at first you don't give up."

"Yes. That's good advice. We tried again tonight. I did."

But Renata knows she doesn't have to be a mother of anybody. She was ordained to be a wife, or a lover, and the life she leads is opportune. She goes with what she intuits. She had a chaperone until she was nineteen and three lovers before twenty.

"I do have a niece who is like a daughter. My sister's child, Gloria. You know Gloria."

"Gloria?"

"The lovely young blond girl who lives here. You see her every day."

"Yes. I think I've met her."

"She's in the hospital. She was in a fire on Van Woert Street."

Renata's girl is now scarred because she has Renata in her. The two are alike, out of Margarita, born to ride the wave of willful and passionate change, that wave that was about to separate her and Quinn. But now it throws them together on the shore with Gloria and they will enfold her, and she will be reborn to them in the oddest way. If she doesn't die.

"I used to live on Van Woert Street," George said. "I lived there with my cousins after my parents died."

"I know you did. That's why I mentioned it."

"I remember the Fitzgeralds had a fire several doors down from us. The firemen saved the cellar."

"Gloria was seriously burned tonight. So was Roy."

"Roy who?"

"Roy Mason. The son of Cody Mason. Cody played the piano tonight."

"Cody Mason's a good fella."

"So is Roy. The fire was deliberately set in Roy's house. Somebody wanted to hurt him. Or kill him. They didn't kill him but the fire killed a man upstairs."

"Who would do a thing like that?"

"People who fear Roy because he's angry about what happens to black people. He talks about it publicly, gives people a voice."

"Black people have problems," George said. "They try to do their stuff and those fossie-fossies pick them right up and take them around."

"Fossie-fossies," Renata said. "You mean forces? Bosses? Falsies? Fossils? What does that mean?"

"Fossie fossils, that's it, the boys with the money," George said. "People who don't have any money don't have any luck. They hit the number once in a while but it's stacked against them. Sometimes they don't even collect when they do get a hit. The boys refuse to pay them off. They've got to change their luck. When you're lucky you can strike oil in the attic."

"Very true, George. You know we've got money now."

"We do?"

"Much more than we've ever had in this family. I don't know why I'm telling you this, but it could be almost a million dollars."

"If you've got a million dollars you could be my best friend."

"I'll keep that in mind. Would you like a cold beer?"

"After the dog a cold beer is man's best friend."

"Good. Ursula will be here in fifteen minutes. Drink your beer and when Ursula comes you can go up to bed. She'll stay over and take good care of you."

She brought him an Irish Cream Ale and a glass and then opened the phonograph and put on a Mitch Miller sing-along, because it had some waltzes, "You Tell Me Your Dream" and "Let Me Call You Sweetheart." Daniel had bought half a dozen Mitch Millers for George and played them randomly and often to ease his anxiety—the music of his day, lyrical suggestion to soothe the ravaged memory. Sometimes George sat and listened, or hummed along. Sometimes he left the room. Renata had the impulse to give him some of their new money, let him buy what he wanted; but he wouldn't know what to buy, or where to buy it. He was off the money standard. He'd leave torn bits of newspaper or maybe a folded tie on the kitchen table after breakfast as a tip for Renata, the waitress. Mitch and his chorus were singing "If You Were the Only Girl in the World."

"That's a waltz," George said,

"Yes, and you're a prize waltzer."

"I do waltz. Yes, I do." He put down his beer and stood up. "Would you do me the honor?"

"Certainly," she said, "but I'm not in your league."

"As long as you can move your feet."

He buttoned his suit coat, embraced her, and moved her forward into a pivot in the open space between the parlor and dining room. She followed him, a very strong leader, with ease, and she felt she was moving in her mother's footsteps. She really should be at the hospital with her Gloria but here she was dancing with her father-in-law. Was this at the edge of some sort of primal scene? She drew back slightly from the embrace so she could look at his face. He was smiling, not at her but reveling in his own artistry as he moved her with astonishing control. He is dancing me back in time, she decided, he's dead to this day but alive in history: you are dancing with a ghost, Renata.

Mitch sang:

"A garden of Eden, just made for two,
With nothing to mar our joy . . . "

She tried to picture what Matt told her about George with the bat, hitting the man who was beating up Roy, because Roy looked like George's black friend of sixty years gone, another ghost. George had moved with speed and purpose as he whacked the man's head just once, which crumpled him, and his grip on Roy fell away. George dropped the bat and crossed the street, then off he went into the ridiculously dangerous night.

"You had a big day today, George," she said.

"Did I? Maybe I did."

"You certainly did. You got lost in the city, you got cut and went to the hospital, you had a romance, you were in a fight, a race riot, and a shooting, you went to a house of prostitution and a concert, you danced a waltz, and you serenaded a very lovely woman who seems to be in love with you."

"I wouldn't go into those places."

"Of course not, only in emergencies."

"I don't fancy romance. Romance isn't qualified."

"But it does happen. We all know that romance is wonderful, George, and it's a great adventure."

"It has some inferences."

On they danced, George holding her in a way that some might consider ardent, his traditional style, obviously absurd, yet there it was—the music, the nostalgic lyrics, the movement itself arousing in her what was unseemly and must not even be contemplated. But it was in her as it had been after the shooting in the Montmartre, as it had been when she relieved her grief over Diego in the arms of the stranger Quinn. What was also rising was her intense hatred of the would-be assassins of Roy and Gloria, the racist killers, the politicians, the provocateurs, whoever they are, the faceless enemy. She thought of Oshun and of going to Gloria's apartment to find the Oshun necklace Gloria had left behind when she fled. Renata had given her that necklace for her twenty-first birthday, affinities of beauty. Beauty save beauty now—and she conjured Oshun to join her and George in this peculiar dance. When she closed her eyes she could see the beautiful Orisha and the dance became a ritual: keeping together in time—life, love, and death moving to a three-quarter beat.

The invoked presence of Oshun truly moved her and she clutched George tightly. He reacted by whirling her into a dizzying cycle of turns, the movement generating an excitement in her that she had felt driving into danger with Diego; and such angry defiance she had not known since after the Selma March; she would do anything to neutralize the haters. But her unconditional embrace of the movement had been rejected in the following months in the name of black power, whites no longer welcome. Conditioning worthiness to serve the cause on skin color was not her kind of revolution. In Cuba revolution had always been racial. Diego looked white but he believed he had black blood. She felt new pressure now to do something against the enemy. She and Quinn could find some way to send the message. Maybe they could do it with the new money. You can do anything with money. As the song ended she saw Ursula step out of a taxi and walk toward the front stoop. She broke from George, kissed him on the cheek, then kissed him again, almost on the mouth. She went to the phone to call a cab. In the hospital she would find a corner, or an empty room, and make love with Quinn.

The doorbell rang.

◈

Quinn entered the hall, his very black hair thick in a torsion to the right, giving him the air of a casual savant with warrior tendencies. He smiled at the group, mostly men, a few women among them. The audience seemed to be diminishing, but so imperceptibly that he wasn't sure it was happening. He had his text in hand but did not look at it as he spoke.

"All wars are similar," he said. "We have just witnessed the battle intensifying from matriarchal complaint to anarchic threat. With four unfinished, unfinishable books the warrior Hemingway hung the sign 'Former Writer' on the door of his room at the Mayo Clinic, where he was receiving shock treatments."

No one seemed to understand the connection Quinn was making.

"Money is the evil the poor cannot do without. La buena vida es cara. The good life is expensive. There are other ways of life that are not expensive, but that's not life." Then he added, rhythmically, "Doosaday sosadah spokety spone."

The audience erupted with raucous laughter and Quinn grew confident, even though only a handful remained in the hall. He spoke about political duplicity and how we need it to survive, which was a gaffe, for everyone in the audience was dead.

"We treat our political divinities like pets," he said. "Without the resolute will to enter into significance, there can be no access to the heroic."

He expected major applause from this remark but the two remaining women in the room silently left their chairs.

"Ours is a cosmos in motion," he said, "moving relentlessly in an arc of justice." He smiled, fully aware his remarks were menacing. The room was now empty.

"In an arc of justice," he said.

What a line.

"In an arc of justice," he said again.

Always leave 'em laughing.

❖ ACKNOWLEDGMENTS ❖

This novel is full of true stories of both revolutions it addresses, and of the people in them. I have changed dates and names, and telescoped time and events to control the story; any real people have been reimagined.

I am indebted to many Cubans for providing me with personal or historical memories of the revolution, most notably Natalia Bolívar Aróstegui, who gave me abundant access to her remarkable life story; I have drawn on it, but she should not be held accountable for the behavior of any Cuban women in this novel, unless she wants to be. I am also profoundly grateful to Norberto Fuentes, a longtime friend and chronicler of the revolution in fiction and nonfiction. His counsel on Cuban political and cultural history has been invaluable to this book.

Among the many witnesses to the revolution who told me stories I must mention Manuel Penebaz, the late Amadeo Lopez Castro, the artists Aldo Menéndez and Ivonne Ferrer, Rafael Del Pino, Patricia Gutiérrez, Eloy Gutiérrez Menoyo, the late filmmaker Tomas Gutiérrez Alea, Helmo Hernández, Pablo Armando Fernández, Gabriel García Márquez, Richard Burton of Miami, William Irizarry, Max Lesnick; also Joanne Dearcopp, the late artist Peter Taylor of Troy, who knew Hemingway; also Omar Gonzalez, Alfredo Guevara, and Fidel Castro.

There are too many books to list but I must note an important few: *El Asalto al Palacio Presidencial* by Faure Chomón; *Asalto*, edited by Míriam Zito; *The Mambi-Land* by James J. O'Kelly; *Diary of the Cuban Revolution* by Carlos Franqui; *Cuba* by Hugh Thomas; *Episodes of the Revolutionary War* by Ernesto Che Guevara; *Salida 19, Operación Comando* by William Gálvez Rodriguez; *Fidel Castro: My Life* with Ignacio Ramonet; *The Autobiography of Fidel Castro* by Norberto Fuentes; *Fidel* by Tad Szulc; *Behind the Burnt Cork Mask* by William J. Mahar; *Ragged but Right: Black Traveling*

Shows, "Coon Songs," and the Dark Pathway to Blues and Jazz by Lynn Abbott and Doug Seroff. Writings of Daryl Pinckney, Julian Mayfield, and Caryl Phillips were of particular importance, as was a Florida State University master's thesis by Scott Freeland, *Kinking the Stereotype: Barbers and Hairstyles as Signifiers of Authentic American Racial Performance.*

In Albany I am indebted to Leon Van Dyke of the Brothers, whom I have known for forty-six years; also Brothers Earl Thorpe and the late Sam McDowell; also my old friend Peter O'Brien; the late Olivia Rorie; the late George Bunch; the late jazz pianist Jody Bolden (a.k.a. Bobby Henderson); Hank O'Neal, who salvaged Jody's work; my legal counselor, David Duncan; Father Nellis Tremblay; the late Reverend James U. Smythe; Larry Burwell; the late Dottie Ann Kite; Jane Schneider; Michael Nardolillo; Richard Collins; my splendid researcher, Suzanne Roberson; my editor, Paul Slovak; my agent, Andrew Wylie; my perennial translator, Betsy Lopez Viglucci; and my early readers: the poet Peg Boyers, my son Brendan, and my gorgeous wife, Dana.

ALSO AVAILABLE FROM PENGUIN

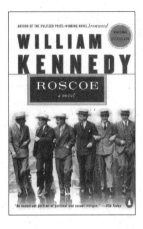

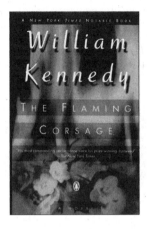

Roscoe
ISBN 978-0-14-200173-8

An Albany Trio
ISBN 978-0-14-025786-1

The Flaming Corsage
ISBN 978-0-14-024270-6

*Riding the Yellow
Trolley Car*
ISBN 978-0-14-015992-9

PENGUIN BOOKS

ALSO AVAILABLE FROM PENGUIN

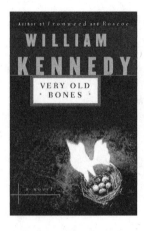

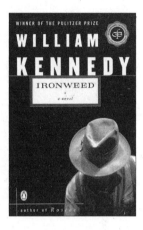

Very Old Bones
ISBN 978-0-14-013898-6

Ironweed
ISBN 978-0-14-007020-0

Quinn's Book
ISBN 978-0-14-007737-7

Legs
ISBN 978-0-14-006484-1

O Albany!
ISBN 978-0-14-007416-1

*Billy Phelan's
Greatest Game*
ISBN 978-0-14-006340-0

PENGUIN BOOKS